ANARCHY OF THE MICE

JEFF BOND

ISBN: 978-1-7322552-7-2

www.thirdchancestories.com

PROLOGUE

Piper Jackson didn't like the look that passed between her brother and the plant foreman, Mr. Sampson. She stood by them at a floor-to-ceiling window in the foreman's office. Twelve stories down, a pair of police cruisers and a municipal van had entered the circle drive.

"Marcus." Mr. Sampson backed away from the glass. "Can you get to the stuff?"

"Yeah, yeah, I'm on it." Her brother pivoted for the door. "Dumpster?"

"Right." Mr. Sampson ran to his computer, fingers jittery on the keys. "No! No, they'll check the dumpster—use the cellar."

Piper eyed the pair of men. Well, one man. Her brother was almost a man, nineteen.

She was seventeen. "What're you typing? Why is he running off to the cellar?"

Mr. Sampson stayed focused on the screen. He pecked the keyboard standing up, tall like Marcus but stocky, with a handyman mustache.

Marcus said from the threshold, "You didn't do *a thing*, sis, remember," then bolted.

Piper checked the window. Below, the cruisers had parked

1

crookedly end to end. A woman burst from the van with a clipboard. She tossed hairnets to each of four officers and pulled one on herself, all of them hurrying for the entrance.

"I asked a question," Piper said.

Mr. Sampson finished typing something. Whatever it was, it didn't work. "Stupid thing won't let me in. Can you get this file deleted while I go deal with this?"

"With what

"This! These...ah, inspectors. Dang it. I gotta go. Can you try to delete the file?"

Piper said she would. He stabbed out one last command, got beeped at again, and rushed off.

She walked to the computer. The file Mr. Sampson had been clicking was named *Q3productionCosts_true*.

Why exactly would a person stick "_true" at the end of a file name?

Piper felt scared, mad, and vindicated—all at once. She'd known it. From the second Marcus had gotten promoted out of the mail room to manufacturing trainee, four lousy months into the job. The leading producer of organic food in North America was going to trust her brother, a kid with no college and a rap sheet?

Mom had told her to quit being negative. *They're investing in this city. They want to keep jobs in America. Why not Marcus?*

Then they'd made him full-time. Then two months later, he'd become deputy production manager. *Manager?* And that was supposed to be legit?

Now Piper tried opening *Q3productionCosts_true* and got the same error Mr. Sampson must have.

FILE IN USE BY ANOTHER USER.

She logged in with the credentials they'd granted her for the summer. Piper was unpaid. Mr. Sampson had needed somebody to de-crud his departmental computers but had no budget, so Marcus had suggested Piper. She had computer skills to burn, but not the school kind, meaning this "internship" was about the best gig she could get.

A simple scan showed which other workstation was using the file. Piper remote-desktopped in and closed it. Then she switched back to Mr. Sampson's machine and tried deleting it again.

As *Q3productionCosts_true* vanished from the screen, Piper felt a hiccup of doubt.

Was that smart?

Before she could worry much, her phone buzzed. A text from Marcus.

need 10 minutes, keep cops away from factory!

Piper sprinted for the stairs. Secretaries and salesmen leaned out of cubicles to see. Her elbow nicked a bowl of green apples, and two tumbled to the carpet.

She raced down eight flights before reaching a stairwell that overlooked the factory floor. Below, Marcus was struggling with a giant bag labeled *Franklin Food Services*, carrying it away from the grinder with backward-chopping steps.

The other factory worker, Russ Doan, watched him with hard eyes.

Piper kept bounding down, three stairs per stride, near free fall. She eased up into the last flight, hearing Mr. Sampson's voice in the lobby.

"...heads-up would've been nice," he was saying, "but of course we'll cooperate. Can I take another look at that paperwork?"

The woman from the van handed over her clipboard peevishly. As Piper came to stand beside Mr. Sampson, the policemen raised their chins.

She raised hers back.

Mr. Sampson took a while reading. He moved the document closer and farther like it was written in a foreign language.

"As you know," he began, "ingredients are our top priority at Harvest Earth. We could've outsourced to China like the competition and saved ourselves—"

"We need to see the factory," the woman interrupted. "Now."

"Right, yes...the factory. We can certainly *show you the factory*," Mr. Sampson said, almost shouting in the direction of Marcus and Russ Doan.

How many of those Franklin Food bags had to get moved?

Piper said, "No. You can't."

The inspector looked at Piper. An aquiline nose and deep-sunk eyes pinched together menacingly. One cop smirked like he'd heard this hustle before.

Piper shuffled close to Mr. Sampson until there was no space sepa-rating them. With one hand, keeping that side of her body perfectly still, she unclipped the key ring from his belt. So the metal wouldn't make noise disengaging, she pinned the key ring hard against the small of his back. Then she slid the keys behind her own back.

The keys were too big to hide in a fist, so she dropped them into her pants. Over the underwear would've been better, but she misjudged fabrics and they ended up against her bare butt.

"Keys are up in the office," she said. "I saw them hanging off the coatrack."

Through their touching sides, Piper felt Mr. Sampson stop breathing.

"Shoot, that's right," he managed. "I forgot to bring them down. We'll have to go upstairs."

The woman grimaced, but when Mr. Sampson gestured to join him at the elevator banks, she did. The cops followed. Mr. Sampson flashed Piper a relieved look, then he snapped his fingers in the direction of the factory.

The second the outsiders had rounded the corner, Piper booked for the south entrance. Supply closets, printers, a water cooler—all whizzed by in her periphery. Approaching the door, she dug into her pants for the key ring, metal raking her crotch.

Marcus was carrying two Franklin Food bags backward through the door.

"Dude," Piper said. "What's in there?"

"Cereal," said Marcus's voice from behind the bags.

"*Cereal?* Like Frosted Flakes?"

"No, like the cheapest crap there is by volume!" Marcus said, stag-gering to a nearby stairwell. "It's filler, now help me get the rest downstairs."

Piper puzzled a moment. "Where you even get that much cerea—"

"Who cares, grab a bag!" Marcus disappeared down the stairs.

Four more bags were stacked in an industrial locker. Piper looked to Russ Doan. *Why isn't he helping?*

She hoisted a bag of cereal that must've weighed sixty pounds, squatting and wrapping her arms around the base. The top teetered and slammed into her face—she both heard and felt crunching through the burlap. She lurched to the door, knocking hard hats off hooks, crushing a sleeve of plastic packaging underfoot.

Marcus met her at the threshold. Without a word, he accepted the load and carried it the rest of the way to the cellar.

Piper caught her breath and hoisted another bag. She and her brother moved the next two without trouble.

Working together, her arms and thighs burning, Piper flashed back to the long days they used to put in helping Mom at the nursery—before the box stores drove it out of business. Toting around mulch, sprinkling handfuls in each other's hair. Sweaty all summer. Before Marcus's arrests.

Piper was struggling with the last bag when a hand gripped her sleeve.

"Time to face the music, you two."

She turned to find Russ Doan with his lip pushed up, looking dumb and righteous.

Marcus was back from the cellar. "She's got nothing to do with this." He stepped up to Doan. "Take your hands off."

Doan tightened his grip.

"*Ow!*" Piper said. "Why don't you help? They find this stuff, it's your job too."

Russ Doan said nothing. She knew from Mr. Sampson, who dished gossip to her on slow days, that Doan had been with Harvest Earth eighteen years. The sole survivor from an original union workforce of three hundred. The production line, almost fully automated now, required only a certified machinist (Doan) and operator-manager (Marcus) to run.

That the operator-manager didn't have to be union was a sore spot for Doan. Piper figured he had other beefs with Marcus.

Marcus took another step, bringing their faces an inch apart.

"I said hands off."

Russ Doan sneered, all nose hair. "Figured it. Too good for honest work."

There was a gloat at the corner of his mouth.

Piper said, "Shut the hell up," and flinched away.

The bag broke. Cereal cascaded to the floor, covering all their shoes and Piper's pants to the cuff in gray-yellow flakes. Dust filled her nose, dry, corn-sweet stink. She retreated a step and trampled some, the sound like a million bugs festering.

Doan smiled.

From the side, Marcus decked him. Right fist to the ear. Doan fell in a heap, slumping into the cereal—more crackling bugs—then didn't move.

"There's cops here!" Piper said. "*Stupid*, man. You already got two strikes."

They dragged Doan behind the thermoforming machine, making a trail of flakes. Marcus got brooms and they pushed the cereal out of sight. He got some down the drain and underneath the sink station. Piper made a pile in the recessed area behind a spinning whiteboard.

"There's still a lot of dust," she said. "You guys keep a Shop-Vac or something around?"

"In the supply closet." Marcus wiped his brow and went for it.

Piper wondered how this would shake out, assuming they lucked out and got past today's inspection. Would Doan keep quiet? Would Mr. Sampson have to pay him off or something? Maybe she and Marcus deserved hush money too.

How much cash was this cereal-filler scam worth to Harvest Earth? The company had bilked the city for millions in tax breaks to keep the plant here. A city that was already bankrupt. Money that should've gone for roads and school lunches.

Returning to the grinder, Piper heard footsteps. She looked to the door, expecting Marcus.

It was Mr. Sampson.

"Right this way, please," he said, pulling his spare key from the lock. "Our wholesome-frank process is just over here."

The inspector and her police escorts entered the factory floor warily. Marcus pulled up the rear—they must have bumped into him.

His face was ice.

The woman said, "Marcus here runs the whole show? Single operator?"

Mr. Sampson said they did have a second worker, but yes, the level of automation was impressive.

He looked from Piper to Marcus. "Where is, uh...Russ?"

All four cops swiveled to Marcus.

Piper said, "Russ stepped out. Had to pick up flowers for his wife."

Mr. Sampson barely kept a straight face. Russ Doan didn't say much, but when he did, it was usually to complain about his wife. *Sheila the Spender*.

The inspector paced the floor, jotting notes on her clipboard. The cops poked after her like ducks.

"And every ingredient," the woman said, "is organic. Non-GMO. Gluten-free. As declared in the certification?"

Mr. Sampson coughed. "Y-yes. Correct."

The inspector capped her pen with clear disappointment. "Everything seems in order. We had an anonymous tip about some impure inputs. Must've been a prank."

Piper and Marcus locked eyes, then looked without looking to the thermoformer.

Doan.

One cop said, "Smells over here."

He was standing near the whiteboard.

Mr. Sampson volunteered, "Soy gets a little funky, very common." He placed a hand on the inspector's shoulder. "We should get y'on your way, that Friday traffic is murder—"

"Dust." The inspector frowned. "There's dust all over. Where did it come from?"

She shook off Mr. Sampson's touch and started that way. The cop gripped the whiteboard between his thumb and forefinger and spun it parallel with the floor, revealing the mountain of cereal behind.

Piper felt her insides shrinking to a cold, brittle dot.

A different cop said, "What color is gluten?"

The inspector stabbed a cereal flake with her pen. As she raised it to eye level, a lot was going on with Mr. Sampson. His hands were rubbing in front of his shirt. His mustache twitched, and the ingratiating smile below began to fade.

"Obviously, there's been a mistake," he said.

"So it seems." The inspector scooped a few flakes into a baggie, and on her command, two officers donned gloves and began gathering samples.

The remaining officers produced handcuffs from their belts.

Mr. Sampson said, "We—er, that is, I pride myself on giving my team free reign, but I never imagined..."

Again, all eyes found Marcus. Piper expected her brother to shout, or run, or grab the steel pitchfork leaning against the mixer.

Marcus didn't do any of this. He just dropped his head.

The whole deal was rigged. Mr. Sampson had planned for this possibility, Piper saw now. He'd always given Marcus instructions privately, huddled in his office or some stairwell. He'd made Marcus the sole driver of the Harvest Earth van.

Marcus had been proud.

Piper didn't need to check Mr. Sampson's computer to know he wouldn't have referenced the cereal-filler scheme in email—that the only electronic trace he'd left behind was that file.

The one Piper had just zapped.

"This is junk!" she said. "My brother didn't do it, it wasn't his idea."

But Marcus was already cuffed. One of the baggie-filling cops had spotted Russ Doan, and Doan had revived enough to confirm everything Mr. Sampson was saying about Marcus: that he alone had managed the input stocks, that he sometimes acted shifty.

Piper ran at Mr. Sampson, driving her forehead into his side.

Marcus, wrists joined, managed to pull her off. "I'll be okay."

"No, this is bullsh—"

"It's how it is. How it is right now."

The cops were jerking Marcus away, tugging his collar, kicking the backs of his knees.

"But *hey*." Marcus resisted to face Piper, to look at her square. "You get them back, sis. You hear me? You get them back."

Tears streamed down Piper's face. "Get who back?"

Marcus's expression darkened, a hint of that rage she had wanted him to show. His gaze traveled the factory walls and ceiling, seeming to penetrate studs and plaster and glass.

"Everybody," he told her. "Get 'em all back. Every last cheat."

PART ONE

CHAPTER ONE

New Jersey - Six Months Later

The first I ever heard of the Blind Mice was from my fourteen-year-old son, Zach. I was scrambling to get him and his sister ready for school, stepping over dolls and skater magazines, thinking ahead to the temp job I was starting in about an hour, when Zach came slumping downstairs in a suspiciously plain T-shirt.

"Turn around," I said. "Let's see the back."

He scowled but did comply. The clothing check was mandatory after that vomiting-skull sweatshirt he'd slipped out the door in last month.

Okay. No drugs, profanity, or bodily fluids being expelled.

But there was something. An abstract computer-ish symbol. A mouse? Possibly the nose, eyes, and whiskers of a mouse?

Printed underneath was, *Nibble, nibble. Until the whole sick scam rots through.*

I checked the clock: 7:38. Seven minutes before we absolutely had to be out the door, and I still hadn't cleaned up the grape juice spill, dealt with my Frizz City hair, or checked the furnace. For twenty minutes, I'd been hearing *ker-klacks*, which my heart said was construction outside but my head worried could be the failing heater.

How bad did I want to let Zach's shirt slide?

Bad.

"Is that supposed to be a mouse?" I said. "Like an angry mouse?"

"The Blind Mice," my son replied. "Maybe you've heard, they're overthrowing the corporatocracy?"

His eyes bulged teen sarcasm underneath those bangs he refuses to get cut.

"Wait," I said, "that group that's attacking big companies' websites and factories?"

"Government too." He drew his face back ominously. "Anyone who's part of the scam."

"And you're *wearing their shirt*?"

He shrugged.

I would've dearly loved to engage Zach in a serious discussion of socioeconomic justice—I did my master's thesis on the psychology of labor devaluation in communities—except we needed to go. In five minutes.

"What if Principal Broadhead sees that?" I said. "Go change."

"No."

"Zach McGill, that shirt promotes domestic terrorism. You'll get kicked out of school."

"Like half my friends wear it, *Mom*." He thrust his hands into his pockets.

Ugh. I had stepped in parenting quicksand. I'd issued a rash order and Zach had refused, and now I could either make him change, starting a blow-out fight and virtually guaranteeing I'd be late my first day on the job at First Mutual, or back down and erode my authority.

"Wear a jacket," I said—a poor attempt to limit the erosion, but the best I could do. "And don't let your great-grandmother see that shirt."

Speaking of, I could hear Granny's slippers padding around upstairs. She was into her morning routine, and would shortly—at the denture-rinsing phase—be shouting down that her sink was draining slow again; *why hadn't the damn plumber come yet?*

Because I hadn't paid one. McGill Investigators, the PI business of which I was the founder and sole employee (yes, I realized the plural name was misleading), had just gone belly-up. Hence the temp job.

Karen, my six-year-old, was seated cheerily beside her doll in front of orange juice and an Eggo Waffle.

"Mommy!" she announced. "I get to ride to school with you today!"

The doll's lips looked sticky—OJ?—and the cat was eyeing Karen's waffle across the table.

"Honey, weren't you going to ride the bus today?" I asked, shooing the cat, wiping the doll with a dishrag.

Karen shook her head. "Bus isn't running. I get to ride in the Prius, in Mommy's Prius!"

I felt simultaneous joy that Karen loved our new car—well, new to us: 120K miles as a rental, but it was a hybrid—and despair because I really couldn't take her. School was in the complete opposite direction of New Jersey Transit. Even if I took the turnpike, which I loathed, I would miss my train.

Fighting to address Karen calmly in a time crunch, I said, "Are you sure the bus isn't running?"

She nodded.

I asked how she knew.

"Bus driver said, 'If the stoplights are blinking again in the morning, I ain't taking you.'" She walked to the window and pointed. "See?"

I joined her at the window, ignoring the driver's grammatical example for the moment. Up and down my street, traffic lights flashed yellow.

"Blind Mice, playa!" Zach puffed his chest. *"Nibble, nibble."*

The lights had gone out every morning this week at rush hour. On Monday, the news had reported a bald eagle flew into a substation. On Tuesday, they'd said the outages were lingering for unknown reasons. I hadn't seen the news yesterday.

Did Zach *know* the Blind Mice were involved? Or was he just being obnoxious?

"Great," I muttered. "Bus won't run because stoplights are out, but I'm free to risk our lives driving to school."

Karen gazed up at me, her eyes green like mine and trembling. A mirror of my stress.

Pull it together, Molly.

"Don't worry," I corrected myself. "I'll take you. I will. Let me just figure a few things out."

Trying not to visualize myself walking into First Mutual forty-five minutes late, I took a breath. I patted through my purse for keys, sifting through rumpled Kleenex and receipts and granola-bar halves. Granny had made her way downstairs and was reading aloud from a bill-collection notice. Zach was texting, undoubtedly to friends about his lame mom. I felt air on my toes and looked down: a hole in my hose.

Fantastic.

I'd picked out my cutest work sandals, but somehow I doubted the look would hold up with toes poking out like mini-wieners.

I wished I could shut my eyes, whisper some spell, and wake up in a different universe.

Then the doorbell rang.

CHAPTER TWO

Q uaid Rafferty waited on the McGills' front porch with a
winning smile. It had been ten months since he'd seen Molly,
and he was eager to reconnect.

Inside, there sounded a crash (pulled-over coatrack?), a smack
(skateboard hitting wall?), and muffled cross-voices.

Quaid fixed the lay of his sport coat lapels and kept waiting. His
partner, Durwood Oak Jones, stood two paces back with his dog.
Durwood wasn't saying anything, but Quaid could feel the West
Virginian's disapproval—it pulsed from his blue jeans and cowboy hat.

Quaid twisted from the door. "School morning, right? I'm sure
she'll be out shortly."

Durwood remained silent. He was on record saying they'd be
better off with a more accomplished operative like Kitty Ravensdale or
Sigrada the Serpent, but Quaid believed in Molly. He'd argued that
McGill, a relative amateur, was just what they needed: a fresh-faced
idealist.

Now he focused on the door—and was pleased to hear the dead
bolt turn within. He was less pleased when he saw the face that
appeared in the door glass.

The grandmother.

"Why, color me damned!" began the septuagenarian, yanking open the screen door. "The louse returns. Whorehouses all kick you out?"

Quaid strained to keep smiling. "How are you this fine morning, Eunice?"

Her face stormed over. "What're you here for?"

"We're hoping for a word with Molly if she's around." He opened his shoulders to give her a full view of his party, which included Durwood and Sue-Ann, his aged bluetick coonhound.

They made for an admittedly odd sight. Quaid and Durwood shared the same vital stats, six one and 180-something pounds, but God himself couldn't have created two more different molds. Quaid in a sport coat with suntanned wrists and mussed-just-so blond hair. Durwood removing his hat and casting steel-colored eyes humbly about, jeans pulled down over his boots' piping. And Sue with her mottled coat, rasping like any breath could be her last.

Eunice stabbed a finger toward Durwood. "He can come in—him I respect. But you need to turn right around. My granddaughter wants nothing to do with cads like you."

Behind her, a voice called, *"Granny, I can handle this."*

Eunice ignored this. "You're a no-good man. I know it, my grand-daughter knows it." Veins showed through the chicken-y skin of her neck. "Go on, hop a flight back to Vegas and all your whores!"

Before Quaid could counter these aspersions, Molly appeared.

His heart chirped in his chest. Molly was a little discombobulated, bending to put on a sandal, a kid's jacket tucked under one elbow—but those dimples, that curvy body...even in the worst domestic throes, she could've charmed slime off a senator.

He said, "Can't you beat a seventy-four-year-old woman to the door?"

Molly slipped on the second sandal. "Can we please just not? It's been a crazy morning."

"I know the type." Quaid smacked his hands together. "So hey, we have a job for you."

"You're a little late—McGill Investigators went out of business. I have a real job starting in less than an hour."

"What kind?"

"Reception," she said. "Three months with First Mutual."

"Temp work?" Quaid asked.

"I was supposed to start with the board of psychological examiners, but the position fell through."

"How come?"

"Funding ran out. The governor disbanded the board."

"So First Mutual...?"

Molly's eyes, big and leprechaun green, fell. "It's temp work, yeah."

"You're criminally overqualified for that, McGill," Quaid said. "Hear us out. Please."

She snapped her arms over her chest but didn't stop Quaid as he breezed into the living room followed by Durwood and Sue-Ann, who wore no leash but kept a perfect twenty-inch heel by her master.

Two kids poked their heads around the kitchen doorframe. Quaid waggled his fingers playfully at the girl.

Molly said, "Zach, Karen—please wait upstairs. I'm speaking with these men."

The boy argued he should be able to stay; upstairs sucked; *wasn't she the one who said they had to leave, like, immedia—*

"This is not a negotiation," Molly said in a new tone.

They went upstairs.

She sighed. "Now they'll be late for school. I'm officially the worst mother ever."

Quaid glanced around the living room. The floor was clutter free, but toys jammed the shelves of the coffee table. Stray fibers stuck up from the carpet, which had faded beige from its original yellow or ivory.

"No, you're an excellent mother," Quaid said. "You do what you believe is best for your children, which is why you're going to accept our proposition."

The most effective means of winning a person over, Quaid had learned as governor of Massachusetts and in prior political capacities, was to identify their objective and articulate how your proposal brought it closer. Part two was always trickier.

He continued, "American Dynamics is the client, and they have deep pockets. If you help us pull this off, all your money troubles go *poof.*"

A glint pierced Molly's skepticism. "Okay. I'm listening."

"You've heard of the Blind Mice, these anarchist hackers?"

"I—well, yes, a little. Zach has their T-shirt."

Quaid, having met the boy on a few occasions, wasn't shocked by the information. "Here's the deal. We need someone to infiltrate them."

Molly blinked twice.

Durwood spoke up, "You'd be great, Moll. You're young. Personable. People trust you."

Molly's eyes were grapefruits. "What did you call them, 'anarchist hackers'? How would I infiltrate them? I just started paying bills online."

"No tech knowledge required," Quaid said. "We have a plan."

He gave her the nickel summary. The Blind Mice had singled out twelve corporate targets, "the Despicable Dozen," and American Dynamics topped the list. In recent months, AmDye had seen its websites crashed, its factories slowed by computer glitches, internal documents leaked, the CEO's home egged repeatedly. Government agencies from the FBI to NYPD were pursuing the Mice, but the company was troubled by the lack of progress and so had hired Third Chance Enterprises to take them down.

"Now if I accept," Molly said, narrowing her eyes, "does that mean I'm officially part of Third Chance Enterprises?"

Quaid exhaled at length. Durwood shook his head with an irked air —he hated the name, and considered Quaid's branding efforts foolish.

"Oh, Durwood and I have been at this freelance operative thing awhile." Quaid smoothed his sport coat lapels. "Most cases we can handle between the two of us."

"But not this one."

"Right. Durwood's a whiz with prosthetics, but even he can't bring this"—Quaid indicated his own ruggedly handsome but undeniably middle-aged face—"back to twenty-five."

Molly's eyes turned inward. Quaid's instincts told him she was thinking of her children.

She said, "Sounds dangerous."

"Nah." He spread his arms, wide and forthright. "You're working with the best here: the top small-force, private-arms outfit in the Western world. Very minimal danger."

Like the politician he'd once been, Quaid delivered this line of questionable veracity with full sincerity.

Then he turned to his partner. "Right, Wood? She won't have a thing to worry about. We'd limit her involvement to safe situations."

Durwood thinned his lips. "Do the best we could."

This response, typical of the soldier he'd once been, was unhelpful.

Molly said, "Who takes care of my kids if something happens, if the Blind Mice sniff me out? Would I have to commit actual crimes?"

"Unlikely."

"*Unlikely?* I'll tell you what's unlikely, getting hired someplace, anyplace, with a felony conviction on your application..."

As she thundered away, Quaid wondered if Durwood might not have been right in preferring a pro. The few times they'd used Molly McGill before had been secondary: posing as a gate agent during the foiled Delta hijacking, later as an archivist for the American embassy in Rome. They'd only pulled her into Rome because of her language skills —she spoke six fluently.

"...also, I have to say," she continued, and from the edge in her voice, Quaid knew just where they were headed, "I find it curious that I don't hear from you for ten months, and then you need my help, and all of a sudden, I matter. All of a sudden, you're on my doorstep."

"I apologize," Quaid said. "The Dubai job ran long, then that Guadeloupean resort got hit by a second hurricane. We got busy. I should've called."

Molly's face cooled a shade, and Quaid saw that he hadn't lost her. Yet.

Before either could say more, a heavy *ker-klack* sounded outside.

"What's the racket?" Quaid asked. He peeked out the window at his and Durwood's Vanagon, which looked no more beat-up than usual.

"It's been going on all morning," Molly said. "I figured it was construction."

Quaid said, "Construction in *this* economy?"

He looked to Durwood.

"I'll check 'er out." The ex-soldier turned for the door. Sue-Ann, heaving herself laboriously off the carpet, scuffled after.

Alone now with Molly, Quaid walked several paces in. He doubled his sport coat over his forearm and passed a hand through his hair, using a foyer mirror to confirm the curlicues that graced his temples on his best days.

This was where it had to happen. Quaid's behavior toward Molly had been less than gallant, and that was an issue. Still, there were sound arguments at his disposal. He could play the money angle. He could talk about making the world safer for Molly's children. He could point out that she was meant for greater things, appealing to her sense of adventure, framing the job as an escape from the hamster wheel and entrée to a bright world of heroes and villains.

He believed in the job. Now he just needed her to believe too.

CHAPTER THREE

D urwood walked north. Sue-Ann gimped along after, favoring her bum hip. Paws echoed bootheels like sparrows answering blackbirds. They found their noise at the sixth house on the left.

A crew of three men was working outside a small home. Two-story like Molly's. The owner had tacked an addition onto one side, prefab sunroom. The men were working where the sunroom met the main structure. Dislodging nails, jackhammering between fiberglass and brick.

Tossing panels onto a stack.

"Pardon," Durwood called. "Who you boys working for?"

One man pointed to his earmuffs. The others paid Durwood no mind whatsoever. Heavyset men. Big stomachs and muscles.

Durwood walked closer. "Those corner boards're getting beat up. Y'all got a permit I could see?"

The three continued to ignore him.

The addition was poorly done to begin with, the cornice already sagging. Shoddy craftsmanship. That didn't mean the owners deserved to have it stolen for scrap.

The jackhammer was plugged into an outside GFI. Durwood caught its cord with his bootheel.

"The hell?" said the operator as his juice cut.

Durwood said, "You're thieves. You're stealing fiberglass."

The men denied nothing.

One said, "Call the cops. See if they come."

Sue-Ann bared her gums.

Durwood said, "I don't believe we need to involve law enforcement," and turned back south for the Vanagon.

Crime like this—callous, brash—was a sign of the times. People were sore about this "new economy," how well the rich were making out. Groups like the Blind Mice thought it gave them a right to practice lawlessness.

Lawlessness, Durwood knew, was like a plague. Left unchecked, it spread. Even now, besides this sunroom dismantling, Durwood saw a half dozen offenses in plain sight. Low-stakes gambling on a porch. Coaxials looped across half the neighborhood roofs: cable splicing. A Rottweiler roaming off leash.

Each stuck in Durwood's craw.

He walked a half block to the Vanagon. He hunted around inside, boots clattering the bare metal floor. Pushed aside Stinger missiles in titanium casings. Squinted past crates of frag grenades in the bulkhead he'd jiggered himself from ponderosa pine.

Here she was—a pressurized tin of black ops epoxy. Set quick enough to repel a flash air strike, strong enough to hold a bridge. Durwood had purchased it for the Dubai job. According to his supplier, Yakov, the stuff smelled like cinnamon when it dried. Something to do with chemistry.

Durwood removed the tin from its box and brushed off the pink Styrofoam packing Yakov favored. Then allowed Sue a moment to ease herself down to the curb before they started back north.

Passing Molly's house, Durwood glimpsed her through the living room window. She was listening to Quaid, fingers pressed to her forehead.

Quaid was lying. Which was nothing new, Quaid stretching the truth to a woman. But these lies involved Molly's safety. Fact was, they knew very little of the Blind Mice. Their capabilities, their willingness to harm innocents. The leader, Josiah, was a reckless troublemaker. He spewed his nonsense on Twitter, announcing targets ahead of time, talking about his own penis.

The heavyset men were back at it. One on the roof. The other two around back of the sunroom, digging up the slab.

Durwood set down the epoxy. The men glanced over but kept jackhammering. They would not be the first, nor last, to underestimate this son of an Appalachian coal miner.

The air compressor was set up on the lawn. Durwood found the main pressure valve and cranked its throat full open.

The man on the roof had his ratchet come roaring out of his hands. He slid down the grade, nose rubbing vinyl shingles, and landed in petunias.

Back on his feet, the man swore.

"Mind your language," Durwood said. "There's families in the neighborhood."

The other two hustled over, shovels at their shoulders. The widest of the three circled to Durwood's backside.

Sue-Ann coiled her old bones to strike. Ugliness roiled Durwood's gut.

Big Man punched first. Durwood caught his fist, torqued his arm behind his back. The next man swung his shovel. Durwood charged underneath and speared his chest. The man wheezed sharply, his lung likely punctured.

The third man got hold of Durwood's bootheel, smashed his elbow into the hollow of Durwood's knee. Durwood scissored the opposite leg across the man's throat. He gritted his teeth and clenched. He felt the man's Adam's apple wriggling between his legs. A black core in Durwood yearned to squeeze.

He resisted.

The hostiles came again, and Durwood whipped them again. Automatically, in a series of beats as natural to him as chirping to a katydid. The men's faces changed from angry to scared to incredulous. Finally, they stayed down.

"Now y'all are helping fix that sunroom." Durwood nodded to the epoxy tin. "Mix six to one, then paste 'er on quick."

Luckily, he'd caught the thieves early, and the repair was uncomplicated. Clamp, glue, drill. The epoxy should increase the R-value on the sunroom ten, fifteen, units. Good for a few bucks off the gas bill in winter, anyhow.

Durwood did much of the work himself. He enjoyed the panels' weight, the strength of a well-formed joint. His muscles felt free and easy as if he were home ridding the sorghum fields of johnsongrass.

Done, he let the thieves go.

He turned back south toward Molly's house. Sue-Ann scrabbled alongside.

"Well, ole girl?" he said. "Let's see how Quaid made out."

CHAPTER FOUR

I stood on my front porch watching the Vanagon rumble down Sycamore. My toes tingled, my heart was tossing itself against the walls of my chest, and I was pretty sure my nose had gone berserk. How else could I be smelling *cinnamon*?

Quaid Rafferty's last words played over and over in my head: *We need you.*

For twenty minutes, after Durwood had taken his dog to investigate *ker-klacks*, Quaid had given me the hard sell. The money would be big-time. I had the perfect skills for the assignment: guts, grace under fire, that youthful je ne sais quoi. Wasn't I always saying I ought to be putting my psychology skills to better use? Well, here it was: understanding these young people's outrage would be a major component of the job.

Some people will anticipate your words and mumble along. Quaid did something similar but with feelings, cringing at my credit issues, brightening with whole-face joy at Karen's reading progress—which I was afraid would suffer if I got busy and didn't keep up her nightly practice.

He was pitching me, yes. But he genuinely cared what was happening in my life.

I didn't know how to think about Quaid, how to even fix him in my brain. He and Durwood were so far outside any normal frame of reference. *Were they even real? Did I imagine them?*

Their biographies were epic. Quaid the twice-elected (once-impeached) governor of Massachusetts who now battled villains across the globe and lived at Caesars Palace. Durwood a legend of the Marine Corps, discharged after defying his commanding officer and wiping out an entire Qaeda cell to avenge the death of his wife.

I'd met them during my own unreal adventure—the end of my second marriage, which had unraveled in tragedy in the backwoods of West Virginia.

They'd recruited me for three missions since. Each was like a huge, brilliant dream—the kind that's so vital and packed with life that you hang on after you wake up, clutching backward into sleep to stay inside.

Granny said, "That man's trouble. If you have any sense in that stubborn head of yours, you'll steer clear."

I stepped back into the living room, the Vanagon long gone, and allowed my eyes to close. Granny didn't know the half of it. She had huffed off to watch her judge shows on TV before the guys had even mentioned the Blind Mice.

No, she meant a more conventional trouble.

"I've learned," I said. "If I take this job, it won't be for romance. I'd be doing it for me. For the family."

As if cued by the word "family," a peal of laughter sounded upstairs.

Children!

My eyes zoomed to the clock. It was 8:20. Zach would be lucky to make first hour, let alone homeroom. In a single swipe, I scooped up the Prius keys and both jackets. My purse whorled off my shoulder like some supermom prop.

"Leaving now!" I called up the stairwell. "Here we go, kids—laces tied, backpacks zipped."

Zach trudged down, leaning his weight into the rail. Karen followed with sunny-careful steps. I sped through the last items on my list—tossed a towel over the grape juice, sloshed water onto the roast, considered my appearance in the microwave door, and just frowned, beyond caring.

Halfway across the porch, Granny's fingers closed around my wrist.

"Promise me," she said, "that you will not associate with Quaid Rafferty. Promise me you won't have one single thing to do with that lowlife."

I looked past her to the kitchen, where the cat was kinking herself to retch Eggo Waffle onto the linoleum.

"I'm sorry, Granny." I patted her hand, freeing myself. "It's something I have to do."

CHAPTER FIVE

M y liaison at Rainey Personnel took the news peevishly. The First Mutual contract specifically called for thirty-six-hour cancellation notice. Reliability and professionalism were what made Rainey the crème de la crème of Eastern New Jersey temp agencies. He was taking me off their list. He hoped I enjoyed slumming it with lesser agencies. Next time I needed work, he expected they'd have some collating jobs for me.

The call left a bad taste in my mouth—I hated disappointing people. I was tempted to phone the guys right away with the good news I'd take their job, but I stopped myself.

Don't make it so easy.

If I acted all tickled pink about Quaid's offer, he would be right back in the driver's seat, where he'd been the last ten months while McGill Investigators went bankrupt.

I did call Quaid, but I led with a demand: "Four thousand a week."

A gasping chuckle sounded over the line. "I feel like I'm back in office negotiating with the pipe-fitters union."

"It's dangerous work," I said, "and the mortgage company just tripled my interest rate."

Which was true—the financial markets had been fluctuating wildly since the Blind Mice started their attacks.

Quaid eventually accepted my terms. He said he needed to catch up with some people in the city today, but that I could get started by familiarizing myself with the Mice. He and Durwood would swing by later to see how I was doing.

I plunked down at my computer with coffee and a banana, and got going.

Mainstream news outlets provided the basic facts. The Mice ranged in age from their tweens to midtwenties. Motivated by financial disparity, they had concentrated their attacks on their "Despicable Dozen" multinationals. The nose-eyes-whiskers symbol had become ubiquitous, graffitied across bank billboards and insurance company vans.

Public reaction had been mild. Corporations pulling down billions annually in profits didn't engender much sympathy, and most people seemed to view the Mice as high-tech Robin Hoods. (Minus the part about giving to the poor, it seemed to me.)

As I expanded my research to the dark web—installing something called Tor and probably flagging my computer with Homeland Security—a gauzy picture of the group emerged. Only a few names surfaced, and who knew if those were real. Piper Jackson, the über-hacker embittered by the incarceration of her brother. Hatch, no last name given, Libertarian blogger at DetonateTheWorldOrder.org.

The most renowned was Josiah, the Mice's supposed leader. Some said he was autistic. Some said albino. He was rumored to have studied one year at Brown before becoming disillusioned and crossing Asia on foot, eventually joining a hacktivist faction of Anonymous.

Nearly every account mentioned his temper. *He chawed this business-man's iPhone,* said one commenter. *Literally, teeth marks in Gorilla Glass.*

I happened to be eating lunch as I read this, pickle-and-tuna-salad sandwich. I didn't eat the second half.

In the afternoon, I dug up more of Josiah's story. Tweeting as josiah-TheAvenger, he'd begun proselytizing on greed and revolution. Ten months ago, he held an open invitation at the Brooklyn cafe Lewd Brew, and a mob of eight hundred jammed the entrance. By the end of the night, all eight hundred had been inked with the nose-eyes-whiskers symbol, and the Mice had settled on a motto: *Nibble, nibble. Until the whole sick scam rots through.*

Today, with the FBI issuing statements on the Mice's possible whereabouts, there were no such open calls. So how was I, mother of two and a decade past my midtwenties, supposed to join up?

"Unfortunately, they've gone invite only," Quaid explained when I posed the question.

He and Durwood sat on either side of me at the computer. Zach was out skating with a friend. Karen was playing dolls in her room.

I asked, "How do you get invited?"

"You have to impress them somehow." Quaid passed a hand through his wavy hair. "Supposedly, they recruited this kid who posted YouTube videos of himself dropping water balloons on Goldman Sachs traders as they left their offices."

I rolled my wrist, sore from using the mouse. "I'm not...real active on YouTube. And I hate filling water balloons."

"We anticipated as much," Quaid said. "That's why Durwood took the liberty of setting up your bait ahead of time."

"My *bait?*"

I knew Durwood fished a lot on his farm in West Virginia, but I couldn't even guess what sort of bait—real or metaphorical—Quaid meant now.

Durwood leaned across me to type in my browser, *www.Molly-WantsChange.org.*

A mostly blank webpage appeared. The site's title spanned the top of the screen in large, strident letters. Along the left side was a picture of me.

"That's me!" I said. "How—er, where did you get a real picture of me?"

Durwood said, "Your Facebook."

Now that I looked closer, I recognized the image. It was a few years old, and I wasn't smiling—I'd just gotten the wrong drink order at this dive bar my girlfriends used to drag me to.

"So I'm a blogger?" I said.

Quaid nodded. "Molly Wixom"—he pointed to the caption—"is a

blogger. And if the Blind Mice run the name through a records check, which we anticipate they will, they'll find you're a twenty-three-year-old card-carrying member of Greenpeace."

I stared at my picture. I definitely looked dissatisfied with the status quo: I hated fruity drinks, and I'd just been handed an amaretto sour.

Quaid explained, "Nowadays most of the Mice's recruits come from the blogosphere. *HuffPost,* Daily Kos. We need to establish your left-wing bona fides."

I had trouble imagining anything I wrote on huge websites like that —most of my social media activity consisted of "Happy birthday, hope it's a great one!" posts—but Quaid assured me his contacts would be able to get my posts exposure.

I asked what I should write about.

He shrugged. "Whatever pisses you off."

I'd just read an article about hedge funds that manipulated the municipal debt of struggling cities for profit, which the guys agreed was a good enough place to start.

I typed up my first post on the spot. I was surprised how quickly the paragraphs flowed once I started typing—once I started thinking about those powerful Wall Street firms taking advantage of small towns that couldn't afford to pay their retirees.

As I clicked *Publish,* Quaid already had his phone out.

I asked, "Who are you calling?"

"The *New York Times,*" he said. "The Opinion page doesn't run many bloggers, but the managing editor owes me a favor."

CHAPTER SIX

That was the beginning of my run as an internet firebrand.
I pushed myself to write at least two stories per day, every day, no matter what. This forced me beyond easy topics into territory I had no credentials whatsoever writing about. Drone strikes. Prescription drugs. Cannabis policy. I opined away, *tap-tap-tap*, on a mission to get noticed by the Blind Mice.

At first, I was skeptical about my chances of sticking out in the vast sea of online mouthing off. I had once taken a McGill Investigators case for a food blogger whose recipes were getting mysteriously scooped, and she said it'd taken *three years* to build a decent following. But Quaid's network of influencers proved deep and powerful—quickly, I was being linked and retweeted all over the web.

Having readers was amazing. I loved the affirmation of that first comment, how people got into intercoastal fights over this thing I created every morning in my kitchen, magically out of coffee and my own snap reactions to current events. I loved it when Jake from Baton Rouge said my post on usurious college loans *rocked his world!*

Of course, this was a double-edged sword. I loved it significantly less when BoneDaddy from Mendocino, California, said I should loosen up about sex tourism to Thailand. *Don't knock it till you've tried it, wink emoticon.*

The schedule was great. I wrote and responded to comments while the kids were at school, then I had afternoons free with them.

At dinner one night, Zach asked, "What're you doing with those two...characters?"

I paused a bite of chicken marsala at my mouth. "Well, I'm collaborating with Quaid and Durwood. We're doing a project together."

Karen said brightly, "What kinda project?"

"It's a case," I said. "A bit like the ones I had with McGill Investigators."

"So, like, lying husbands!"

I'd given the kids many examples of cases my PI business took, but for some reason, Karen had latched on to "lying husbands" as most representative.

"No husbands yet in this one," I said. "But if I find one, and he lies? I'll tell you all about it."

Karen shivered with pleasure. I nodded toward her salad, and she took a bite.

Zach was looking at me crookedly. "You know, that cowboy one carries a gun."

I bulged my eyes in Karen's direction.

"What?" Zach said. "She knows the shape guns are, and that bulge around his waist is definitely—"

"Durwood is a former marine," I interrupted before Karen caught on, "and I'm sure whatever is or isn't on his waist, he handles it responsibly."

"Does he have a permit?"

I felt my lips going white.

Zach continued, "Because New Jersey's not a concealed-carry state, and—"

"Where are you learning about New Jersey's gun laws?"

He puffed his cheeks.

"New topic," I said. "Halloween's coming up, time to start thinking about costumes..."

I sweated out the occasional close call like this, but mostly the kids were indifferent about my work.

Things were going well, I felt. The first four-thousand-dollar check had gotten me closer to current on the mortgage. My online persona was growing. In addition to blog posts, I was in the mix on other sites, commenting, finding kindred spirits in the mass of overheated rhetoric. The fact that we all interacted through screen names made connections strangely easy—like confession at church, the curtain's reassuring anonymity.

Then, two weeks in, Quaid and Durwood showed up to our daily briefing with bad news.

"Just had a discussion with Jim Steed," Quaid said. Steed was CEO of American Dynamics. "The Mice crashed another AmDye server last night, which sets their steel and lumber production back six weeks. He wants to start seeing results."

I pulled up my blog stats, which showed MollyWantsChange.org with nearly a million followers.

"Look, we're doing awesome," I said. "If the Blind Mice are paying attention at all, they—"

"You've done everything we asked," Quaid said, "but it's too slow. I once courted an Italian duchess for three months in the Baron of Saluzzo's salon, and all I got from it was a deep-seated hatred for poetry."

I looked to Durwood, whose leathery face showed the same confusion I felt.

Quaid said, "We need to engage the Mice directly. No more footsie. No more flowery verse. It's time to declare our intentions."

"How do we do that?"

"Ever heard *Blogger Royale* on NPR?"

"Sure," I said. *Royale* was produced by the Seattle NPR affiliate, the highest-rated political program on the dial.

"Their roundtable is discussing the Blind Mice tonight," Quaid said. "Six of the biggest bloggers in the country are going to rail about how destructive the Mice's criminal acts are. How counterproductive they are to the liberal movement in America."

As he talked, a tiny dread started in my gut. I sat up straight and hugged my elbows.

"The last time I listened to *Blogger Royale*," I said, the tiny dread growing, "their roundtable didn't have six bloggers. It had seven."

A grin broke across Quaid's lips. At my shocked expression, he draped a bracing arm over my shoulder. Every nerve in my body tingled at the touch.

"Bingo," he said.

CHAPTER SEVEN

I was going on the radio.

As the microwave clock turned four thirty, the time *Blogger Royale* had instructed me to dial in, different modes competed in my brain. Excitement. Calculation. Fear. Thousands, millions of people were going to be hearing my voice—which my high-school choir director had once described as "full of heart, but with certain chipmunk undertones we should modulate."

What would they think?

Would I come off as a fierce advocate for the disenfranchised, or nuts? What if ballet practice ended early and Karen got dropped off in the middle of the call?

Would anybody like me? Respect me?

Probably not, given what I needed to say.

After sliding the beef stroganoff into the oven to thaw, I sat clutching the phone in both hands. The afternoon had been a whirlwind. The guys thought I should tease my position ahead of the show, so I'd written a new blog post explicitly defending the Mice—a thing we'd avoided so as not to seem obvious.

Some readers were confused by the harsh turn. Baton Rouge Jake commented, *is everything cool-ish with u?*

Other readers loved it. My page traffic spiked 5,000 percent, and Quaid got his Politico friend to link me under the headline: "Blogger Says the Unsayable, and Readers Cheer."

Now I dialed the eight-hundred number. A long blip-*bleeeeep* answered.

"Hello?" I said. "Molly Wixom for the roundtable?"

An intern came on the line and asked a few preliminaries. Preferred pronouns? Secondary number in case of disconnection? With shocking speed, I was live on air.

"We're pleased to welcome," said the moderator's silk-studious voice, "a relatively new voice in the blogosphere who's electrified the discourse of late with her writings on factory farming, wage inequity, and today's primary topic, the Blind Mice. We'll have more to say of the Mice, but let us begin now with Sri Lanka."

I had to stop myself from groaning into the phone. The Mice showed no interest in foreign policy so I hadn't posted a thing about Sri Lanka, nor had I researched it during my afternoon cram session.

While other panelists gave vivid anecdotes of abuse, I scrambled for my laptop.

"The situation is...grave...quite grave, certainly," I hedged when my turn came, phone pinned at my shoulder. "We must curb casualties, even if—and, you know, I'm sure the UN is doing all it can, but the juntas should be held accountable."

So much for electrifying the discourse.

My next tries were better. As the subjects moved closer to home, I stalked around the kitchen island and railed against insurance companies, decried a "quote, 'tax-reform' bill" moving through Congress, and even corrected another blogger who misrepresented the NAACP's stance regarding the death penalty.

It was 4:50—Karen's ballet finished at five—before the moderator came to the Mice. "Molly, let's start with you. Just today you posted a stark defense of—"

"If I may," interrupted the blogger I had corrected—a Portland environmentalist. "I believe it's important to call a spade a spade here: the Blind Mice are terrorists."

The sentence had barely finished before others began piling on.

The Progressive Movement had no room for violence... In actuality, the disadvantaged bore the brunt of these pranks...

The response reminded me of a psych experiment I'd assisted with in grad school where subjects watching a speaker getting berated for her opinion were 300 percent more likely to criticize her than those hearing the same words spoken to a neutral audience.

For two minutes, I held the phone away from my ear.

"Well," I said once the arrows had stopped zinging. "I see things differently."

I closed my eyes a moment, then opened them to slits.

"I understand the panelists' concerns. I don't relish padlocking windows or worrying every time my children board their school bus. At the same time"—my teeth gritted—"what is it going to take? Round and round we go, and nothing changes. Executive pay continues to skyrocket. Local governments continue to be held hostage by companies threatening to outsource jobs without sweetheart tax deals—deals that decimate the social safety net. The Blind Mice target data networks, websites, corporate supply chains. Never people. Not one individual has been killed in their attacks."

"What do you call eight motorists dying in a pileup caused by dark stoplights?" asked the Portland guy.

I was opening my mouth to answer when the doorbell rang.

"I—er, obviously, downstream effects are something every change agent grapples with," I said, hustling through the living room. "The Mice, uh, at least I imagine, are cognizant of what..."

I reached the door before my thought could finish or become remotely coherent. Norm Beale, the father of Karen's friend Makayla, smiled at me from the porch. I opened the door and beckoned Karen inside, rolling my eyes apologetically at the phone.

Norm whispered, *"Girls did great. The tulip dance is just too cute."*

I nodded thanks, my neck muscles throbbing from keeping the phone in place. I reached for Karen, but she and Makayla were giggling and pirouetting on the doormat.

Dimly, I heard another panelist condemning me.

"Sorry, one sec," I said into the phone, catching Karen by the tutu and pulling her inside.

Infuriatingly, Norm Beale remained on my porch, smiling, dopey. He had a mild married-man crush on me ("My wife just doesn't have your body type") that was usually easy to ignore.

I placed my hand over the receiver now. "Thanks, Norm, I appreciate your bailing me out."

"Not a problem," he said. "And if you need help Mondays—"

"Right, I'll call."

"Or text!"

I closed the door and resumed into the phone, "As I was saying, whether you agree with their methods or not, these young"—I groped for a nonjudgmental term—"*activists* have shaken corporations out of their comfort zone. Monsanto just raised salaries for line workers. Panhandle Oil & Gas Consortium agreed to publish its members' particulate counts online. These are real reforms."

Karen had taken off her dance slippers and wore them on her hands like puppets. "Mommy, what are 'preforms'? Like TV shows?"

I guided her to the art table, gathering crayons and a *Frozen* coloring page. *Yes, honey, like TV shows*, I mouthed.

Back in the kitchen, I laid out the rationales Quaid and I had rehearsed. From the Industrial Revolution on, had anything interrupted the will of big business? Truly slowed its abuses? Provocateurs had always faced resistance. The unanimous condemnation by mainstream interests only confirmed the Mice's thesis that the status quo was worth a lot of money to a lot of people.

As my fervor grew, the interruptions stopped. By the time I'd finished, the panel was silent.

"That...wow," the moderator finally said, as though he might be dialing 911 on some emergency red phone. "Quite an impassioned defense."

The roundtable ended soon afterward. Quaid and Durwood both texted that I'd done great, but I worried I'd come off sounding too extreme. A helicopter passed over the house—a noise that seemed to become more frequent every day—and when its thunderous *whop-whop* paused, I was sure the FBI was descending upon me.

Luckily, household demands soon overtook my nerves. Zach got back from skateboarding with friends. I spooned stroganoff onto plates and threw together a salad. Karen scraped her knee; Granny helped me apply Neosporin and a Band-Aid.

That night, I lay awake in bed a long while. I thought about Good and Evil. I thought about the Bible, on which I was raised—how my conception of it had grown in adulthood. I no longer believed God had created the world in six days, but I did believe in the Book's examples, in the accumulated wisdom of Christian society.

Or did I?

Sleep refused to come. I burrowed into the comforter, hoping its plush folds might cool my thoughts. I wrapped both arms around the breastfeeding pillow I'd used with Karen and still kept in my bed.

I stared at my laptop on the night table until it seemed like a living being—a being with ideas and opinions and eyes and ears and a mouth that could talk to me.

At three thirty a.m., it did.

The high, metallic chirp of new email. I dropped one leg out of bed and groped through the darkness to the computer. I clicked my inbox.

The message had come from an unfamiliar address: #%&*@___._23__. The subject line read: *for the fledgling pup.*

At first, I figured it was spam. Every morning, I had five or six new porn-Viagra-refinance messages and no idea when or how they'd gotten there. Now I knew.

I dragged my finger along the trackpad intending to shut down— yawning, finally feeling tired—when the body of the message appeared on-screen.

My eyes blazed at the words. Adrenaline erased any trace of sleep.

Nibble, nibble. Until the whole sick scam rots through.

MOLLY WIXOM: dOeS YOUr HeaRt RAGE TRuLY?

CHAPTER EIGHT

New York City

Sergio Diaz had certainly made the mayor's office his own. A mahogany sideboard dwarfed the famed desk of Fiorello La Guardia, its columns wrought of ornate mythical animals, smoky-glass liquor bottles arrayed like chessmen across its surface. A Don Juan portrait hung over the fireplace—a nod to the slur his opponent had used in the final desperate days of the campaign.

The man himself matched his furnishings' scale. Six foot six and barrel-chested. Jet-black hair without a speck of gray tamed to a bullet atop his head. He charged from his chair to embrace Quaid.

"Señor Diaz," Quaid said, using the salutation favored by the Sheikh—their frequent host in Ibiza, where they'd jaunted as rising stars in the Democratic party. "I come bearing bonhomie and wishes of favorable demographic trends in the outer boroughs."

"Nonsense." Sergio grinned. "Like everyone who visits me, you come for money."

Quaid's tongue lodged in the side of his mouth. "I couldn't help noticing, on my way in, that your crosstown shuttle's running right on time."

The mayor grunted acknowledgment. Last spring, Quaid and

Durwood had foiled an extortion plot that'd shut down the subway for a week.

"True enough," he said. "But I can't pay you. The city is broke. These stoplight pranks are sending NYPD overtime through the roof."

"Slip us in as a discretionary item," Quaid said. "Who'd quibble over a measly fifty-thou credit to Third Chance Enterprises?"

"Nothing is above quibbling when your approval's in single digits like mine." Sergio fished three pills from a Tylenol bottle and dry-swallowed.

Quaid was desperate. Outside of a modest monthly stipend, the American Dynamics job was pay-on-completion. The guys' previous engagement in Guadeloupe had been pro bono and drained Quaid's personal funds.

All fiduciary responsibilities for Third Chance Enterprises fell to Quaid. Durwood refused to take an ownership stake, preferring "an honest wage" for his time. Fortunately, Durwood was a grinder and could be stiffed more or less indefinitely, so long as he believed in the moral underpinnings of a job.

Molly was proving tougher to satisfy. Quaid owed her another eight grand, and she was threatening to shutter MollyWants-Change.org until payment was received.

Quaid told the mayor, "Your PR people need to turn this story around. The frame is all wrong. The city's inability to stop the Mice isn't incompetence; it's *a failure of civic infrastructure.*" He dropped his voice an octave. "Our reliance on technology has grown, but our technology budgets haven't kept pace. We brought it on ourselves by scrimping."

Sergio agreed, "There's millions in pork to be had. Unfortunately, I'll be jobless by the time any of it passes Albany."

Quaid pulled two tumblers from the sideboard. "Actually, I may be able to help. Part of the reason I'm here is those pesky Mice."

"Oh?"

"We're running a mission against them, and I'm curious where law enforcement stands."

The mayor, his tongue loosened by frequent scotch pours, gave Quaid the lowdown. The FBI had told Sergio its traps were set and it was only a matter of time before the Mice were captured, but they'd given similar assurances in March. Meanwhile, city engineers had been seeing deeper database intrusions. Property deeds, legal writs, DMV files. Somebody was probing for weak points.

Quaid said, "You're certain it's the Mice?"

"We are certain of nothing," Sergio said. "I can't say what time the Yankees play tonight." Apparently, the stadium jumbotron had been hacked. "But I'm told these things have identifiable patterns, and the intrusions fit the pattern of the Mice."

As they talked, an aide brought knishes from Schimmel's. Quaid bit through golden crust to potato and gloriously unctuous sauerkraut. He missed this about politics. The perks. The pleasurable in-between moments. You couldn't ask for a more capable partner than Durwood Oak Jones, but the man was a lousy conversationalist whose gastronomic interests plateaued at venison jerky.

He was just about to reengage on the issue of payment, hoping the scotch might loosen Sergio's purse strings too, when the door burst open. A sharp-faced man plowed inside, all briefcase and thrusting handshakes.

"Todd Finley, Forceworthy Services. Frigging pleased to meet you."

From the hall, Sergio's assistant apologized: "I said he needed to make an appointment and return later, I tried to stop him."

"It's alright, Ingrid," Sergio said, then to Todd Finley: "As you see, I'm in the middle of other city business. Perhaps later in the week, we can find—"

"Security can't wait for later in the week," Todd Finley cut in.

Slick as any blackjack dealer Quaid knew back home in Vegas, the man fanned an array of brochures across Sergio's sideboard. The top was titled, *Go Mean: Forceworthy's New K-series Attack ATVs*, and featured a glossy photo of soldiers in riot gear against a backdrop of smoking buildings.

Sergio said, "New York has a substantial security force, sir. I'll ask again that you—"

"I'm not talking rent-a-cops and rubber bullets." Finley raised one urgent finger. "What I offer is serious border enforcement."

"I have no border to enforce. Canada lies four hundred miles—"

"Sure y'do! Or you will soon, the further this unrest goes. It's cancer and it's just about to hit the lymph nodes." Finley felt around his neck with a queasy expression.

"With respect," Sergio said, "the city has relationships with suppliers of armored vehicles. The contracts are negotiated years in advance—"

"Good 'cause I'm not offering vehicles, I'm offering comprehensive solutions." The man licked his thumb, paging ahead in a brochure. "We fully staff your checkpoints. The premium packages include lifetime failover support in case of overruns. We don't dump a shipment of steel on your doormat and cut. We stick with you, keeping you and your city safe."

Todd Finley glanced darkly about the mayor's office. "Plus the Blind Mice, and all these copycat gangs? Our security professionals may be on...oh, let's say *familiar terms* with them."

The mayor passed a hand over his chin. "How so?"

"They're tough guys—and tough guys run in similar circles. Turns out in lotta places, Forceworthy has a built-in back channel."

Now Quaid was getting interested himself. "You're saying you can reach the Mice?"

"I shouldn't overpromise," Finley said. "What I will say is this: You buy from Forceworthy, you're buying more than guns and ammo. You're buying relationships."

He punctuated the point with a pregnant look, that wink salesmen give without actually winking.

The mayor checked his watch. "That's all well and good, but I have a constituent meeting." He rose, taking a last knish. "Why don't you talk to Ingrid about coming back another time?"

Sergio strode for the door, but the salesman blocked him.

Quaid set down his drink. "Cool it, pal. Mayor Diaz has been more than generous with his time."

Todd Finley—broad, maybe a former wrestler—didn't budge. "Where's your body detail, Mayor? Surely you're aware kidnappings are up five hundred percent year to date."

Sergio straightened to his full six foot six. "I will give you the benefit of the doubt and assume that was not a threat."

"Oh no, no no no no," Finley blubbered like a lawn mower. "Just trying to make sure everybody understands this new world we're living in. Lemme put you down for a dozen fence-line drones. Stop the bleeding at those shipyards?"

Quaid felt a cold tickle on his neck. Sergio had mentioned the shipyard thefts earlier in passing and said the city was keeping it out of the press. How did this guy know?

Also, when had Forceworthy started manufacturing fence-line drones and attack ATVs? Quaid found it disturbing that the Mice's unrest was already being product-ized like some fitness craze or new Disney princess.

Sergio said, "Another time."

He lowered his head and bulled forward. Finally, the salesman did stand aside. Quaid had a feeling, though, that they'd be seeing more of Todd Finley—and his type—soon.

CHAPTER NINE

Durwood sat with his back against the train station tile. An olive surplus jacket hung loose over his shoulders. Sue-Ann lay curled beside him. Commuters streamed by, an ant-trail of clomping shoes. Occasionally one dropped a nickel in his cup, which said *Vet* on the Styrofoam. Which he was.

"Sight."

At the command, Sue-Ann's milky eyes ticked up. She looked and made no sound. Meaning the target was clean.

The Mice had chosen their drop shrewdly. *Find Fran's poisoned kale, NOT BEFORE 6:00,* had been their message to Molly. News of Franny in Penn Station was the logical spot—busy, a million things going on to hide their man.

Or woman.

Durwood had been here since two thirty. At four o'clock, they'd had Quaid enter News of Franny and browse the cool case. He'd found the organic ginger-kale smoothies on the top shelf and examined them. None had been marked.

It was five thirty now. Different stockers had come to replenish the pinned chips, the pop. Take away stale donuts. Durwood had laced his shoes when the pop vendor had reached through the cooler curtain around five, but the man had kept to the low shelves.

Molly's "initiation," as the Mice had been calling it for two weeks, had been cloak-and-dagger all the way. Notes pinned under subway seats. A postcard with glued-on newsprint. Texts from burner phones, never the same number twice. They'd asked for Molly's date of birth, social security number, voting history.

Kooky stuff too. If she were to sketch a cartoon of the ExxonMobil CEO, how would it look? Then stick it in an envelope and leave it between the third and fourth boxes of Cheez-Its at some gas station.

The drops seemed to be a test. No reason the messages couldn't all be texts. The Blind Mice wanted to check Molly's commitment. Her mettle.

Durwood pulled himself tighter against the tile. More shoes clomped by now, it being rush hour. Enough cover that he dared to check News of Franny himself instead of using Sue.

Several customers were browsing the case. Durwood watched their hands. The Mice's operative would be working on the top shelf, in the kale smoothies.

Durwood looked hard. His head throbbed.

Sue-Ann mewed, pointing up the terminal toward Amtrak. Her eyes tracked a kid pulling a hand truck. Caucasian. Hat, blue uniform. Midtwenties. Certain squirrelly way about him that Durwood associated with tattoos or drug use.

The hand truck carried four levels of drinks. The bottles were right-sized. The ones in the third level from the bottom were green like the kale smoothies.

Durwood stood and collected his cup. Sue-Ann hurried up too, slipping on the tile.

"Easy, girl," he told her.

The kid steered through the crowd to News of Franny. His head moved quick, on a swivel.

Too quick?

The kid waited out a jam-up at the entrance before wheeling back to the cool case. He removed three sleeves of drinks and disappeared through a back-room door.

Durwood put Sue-Ann in a stay, and pursued.

"Hey," a businessman said. "You can't just leave your dog in the middle of Penn Station."

Durwood's gaze didn't leave the cool case. "Be fine."

Over chatter and loudspeaker announcements of track changes, Durwood heard the *plink* of glass bottles knocking together. The kid, unseen in back, had restocked a chute of fancy waters and teas. Now he was doing smoothies.

Durwood passed the register. Walked by the hot bar, smells of teriyaki and baked beans.

Six paces out, he saw the front ginger-kale smoothie rock forward, then rattle upright.

He walked faster. The kid emerged from the backroom, hand truck empty, but Durwood couldn't follow yet. He needed confirmation. He grabbed the first two smoothies and twirled them in his palms like a picker checking for wormholes.

Nothing.

He grabbed the next two, and the two after. He shook each bottle vigorously to dislodge any interior notes.

Nothing.

Seven bottles deep, he found something. A frayed label.

Durwood's gut revved. With dull fingernails, he peeled back the paper. The adhesive gave too easily. Tampered with. The label's underside had a message scrawled across it.

6:66 tOMoRRoW. tHe MArK.

Shoving the label in his jeans, Durwood ran. The kid was gone. Durwood cut between a husband and wife and knocked over a display of candy bars. He froze in the middle of the terminal.

Sue-Ann spotted him. Her black-and-tan face was keen.

He called, "*Git.*"

The dog crouched, and after a rusty moment, sprang up the corridor. She ducked briefcases and slipped gaps—a series of short, graceful flights with paws clicking tile in between.

Durwood followed quickly as he could. He saw the hand truck career up a handicap ramp in the distance, then vanish.

But Sue-Ann had the scent. She bounded up stairs and knifed

through commuters, unrecognizable from the sack of fur and bones she usually was.

Aboveground, Durwood scanned right to left. Marquees, pigeons, a line of taxis. The city noise—harsh, blaring—made his headache worse.

At the corner of Thirty-Seventh and First, he spotted them. Sue-Ann had the kid by the pants.

"This crazy dog yours?" the kid said. "He's savage, almost bit me!"

Durwood clucked, and Sue-Ann released.

"Hardly scuffed you," Durwood said. "Now tell me about the Blind Mice."

"What? Screw you, cowboy, I dunno what your deal is—"

"Those kale ones you dropped off." Durwood gripped him by the shoulders. "Where'd they come from?"

The kid squinted around as though looking for a camera, Durwood part of some gag.

He said, "Same place they always come from. LDS, Gramercy Park distribution center."

Durwood peered into the kid's eyes. Was there a fox inside? Or a rabbit?

He thought back on the pattern of behavior. The kid's pace. His mannerisms. Had he done the kale smoothies first or last? Either would've been suspicious.

He'd done them in the middle.

Still, the last two weeks' hunt for the Mice weighed on Durwood. Feeling compressed now—by the riddles and tweets, by all these dang people—Durwood yanked the kid's sleeves up his arm. One sleeve tore. He checked the kid's wrists and forearms for ink.

"You *freak*, what's wrong with you? I got nothing!"

Durwood ignored this, kept scanning skin. When the kid whimpered, he gripped tighter.

"Where? Where'd they put it?"

"What are you talking about?" the kid said.

"The tattoo. I know it's here."

The kid's face changed. He bit his lip and breathed in sharply. "Okay, okay—you don't have to kill me. I got it on my back."

Muttering that he didn't see what the big deal was, the kid

untucked and raised his uniform shirt. Durwood felt a red surge within.

Sue-Ann's muzzle twitched.

The tattoo was in the middle of his spine. Some Chinese symbol.

The kid explained its meaning, a swear. "I figured what's the harm, who's gonna know?"

Durwood gave his heart a moment to settle. Then he picked the hand truck off the sidewalk and offered the handle to the kid.

The Mice had planted the note upstream, most likely at the distribution center.

"I apologize," Durwood said, slipping two twenties from his money clip. "For the shirt."

CHAPTER TEN

New Jersey

W e interpreted "6:66" to mean 7:06, carrying the one from the minutes digit, but just to be safe, Durwood and I started waiting at six. If form followed, the Mice's next instructions would come by text.

"The mark," from what we could determine online (not all sources agreed) referred to the nose-eyes-whiskers tattoo.

Were they finally ready to take me? Was I going to interact with a real live member of the Blind Mice?

"Ideally," Durwood said.

I was divvying out pasta portions ahead of dinner, the kids busy upstairs.

Crinkling my nose, I said, "I suppose there isn't any good way to, maybe, opt out of the tattoo?"

Durwood didn't answer.

I continued, "I've just never gotten one, is the thing."

"Folks redo 'em," he said. "Change them into flowers and such."

"Right." I placed handfuls of bagged salad onto plates and dribbled over ranch dressing. "But with Zach, I have this strict no-body-art policy."

"He wants body art?"

"No. Well, I don't know. Not yet. I just hate to be hypocritical."

Durwood paused in setting the table with a thoughtful air. I knew he'd raised two sons. One had died in the military like his wife, and the other—according to Quaid—was "estranged."

He said, "Be a risk to refuse."

I also knew Durwood kept all sorts of gadgets in the Vanagon—cheekbone enhancers, colored contacts. "You don't have any, I don't know, fake skin? Something we could paint over my ankle and peel off after the job?"

He shook his head. "Nothing that'd feel real to the touch."

I sighed and called Granny and the kids to dinner. Granny came down first in her best calico dress.

She smiled at Durwood. "Wonderful, you left the louse at home."

Durwood ducked his head respectfully. "Quaid had work with the mayor."

"Mayor Diaz? Mayor of New York City?"

"Yes'm."

Granny whistled, fixing her napkin in her lap. "Boy, that makes a pair."

Durwood didn't answer. From earlier remarks, I knew he wasn't sold on Quaid's mission tonight. Quaid and the mayor were meeting a security-equipment salesman at some exclusive Manhattan party. Quaid said the salesman was linked to the Blind Mice and believed "cultivating the relationship" might "bear fruit."

Fruit? Durwood had asked, hearing about the party.

Quaid had said, *Yeah, fruit.* He hoped to make it back in time for my engagement with the Mice.

Now Granny said, "Anyone ever tell you you resemble Harry Truman?"

Durwood choked on his water.

"In the bridge of the nose," Granny said. "It's subtle."

Sue-Ann, sprawled out below, cocked an eye up at her master. Behind Granny's back, I mouthed, *Sorry.* Durwood shrugged.

In another minute, Zach smelled sustenance and came to the table. Karen followed, and we enjoyed a pleasant family meal despite Durwood and I being on high alert.

The kids, who'd gotten used to the guys' presence, were talkative. It seemed the Mice's antics were filtering down to the schools—Zach told about eighth graders grabbing extra pie with impunity from beneath the cafeteria sneeze guards, and Karen said her field trip to the planetarium had been canceled after the sponsor—a member of the Despicable Dozen reeling from lost sales—had pulled funding.

It steeled me up to think my mission tonight could impact my children. So often they felt unreachable, Zach especially. Here was a bona fide opportunity to make their world safer.

My phone buzzed at 6:57 as I was loading the dishwasher. I fumbled a fork, and it fell through the bottom rack.

Relax, I told myself. *You're ready for this.*

I replaced the fork in the silverware caddy and checked my phone. As I read the message, my anxiety deflated.

"False alarm." I turned the phone around for Durwood to read.

Forceworthy angle looks promising, need to stick here at the party. Sorry to miss. Knock 'em dead. Q

I knew Durwood was more than capable of supporting tonight's mission himself—listening in by secret microphone, intervening if (when?) things turned dangerous.

Still, it was a letdown Quaid hadn't found a way to be here. Maybe he and the mayor had a great lead. Maybe this salesman had introduced them to someone in the Mice leadership and Quaid was on the verge of a breakthrough.

Or maybe he was doing body shots with models.

When it came to Quaid Rafferty, I was containing my expectations. It was hard because when we were together, it was so good. He was a natural with the kids—"Karen, I've seen all seven wonders of the world, and that should be number eight," he'd said of her shoebox dollhouse creation yesterday—and exhilaratingly fun to be around, dancing me around the kitchen with every success, chatting about the news, generous in discussing my mood or his own.

He was generous with massage too.

In those moments, as his fingers would stray from my neck forward to my collarbone, or down toward the small of my back, I kept my head. *This is how he passes the time*, I thought. Flirting was automatic for

Quaid, a tool he'd honed as a politician and now relied upon as an operative. *Don't read too much into it.*

I finished loading the dishwasher, an effective anger-mitigation task, as Durwood wiped down the surfaces. Granny left to watch her cable news. Zach headed upstairs, texting. Karen chose a Popsicle for dessert.

At 7:06, my phone buzzed again.

Bzzzt. Bzzzt.

Durwood set down a dishrag and moved to my side. We read the message—from *NUMBER UNAVAILABLE*—together.

BE nOWHeRE iN 14M.

Those mixed upper- and lowercase letters crawled into the pit of my stomach. I felt my knees go jelly—but in the next moment, I found resolve. My jacket and purse were ready on the coat-tree. I grabbed them, confirming with Granny that she'd be okay watching Zach and Karen by herself.

Durwood and I huddled out of earshot.

"Fourteen minutes?" I said. "How do you go nowhere?"

Durwood removed a paper from his jeans pocket. It contained a list, in his spare handwriting, of tattoo parlors. I followed his finger halfway down the page.

Nowhere Tattoo Parlor.

He'd already copied out the address and pushed it into my palm.

"Remember, I'll be listening." He pointed to my left earring, a microphone transmitter disguised as a turquoise stud.

I plunged through my purse for the Prius keys, checked my bob in the hall mirror—angled and dyed jet black in anticipation of a possible Mice meeting—and found Karen for a goodbye peck.

Then I left.

My phone gave an estimated drive time to the tattoo parlor of eleven minutes. I had twelve minutes to make the Mice's deadline.

As I whipped the Prius's blocky back end out of the drive, my pulse beat in my throat. I sped toward Washington Street and had to slam on the brakes for a red light.

What if I was late? Would the Mice take back their invitation? (If this even *was* an invitation.) Would the last two weeks be a total waste?

I accelerated through the intersection and drove fast, following my phone's prompts.

Nowhere Tattoo Parlor occupied the end store of a dingy strip mall. The mall's anchor had been a big-box electronics store; its windows were dark like the other tenants'. I zoomed through the lot and parked any which way across three spots, dizzy with stress.

The time was 7:20—exactly fourteen minutes after the Mice's text.

NOWHERE was painted across the front windows in telescoping blood-red print. A metal grate covered the door. A cardboard doorknob sign had been flipped to CLOSED.

I cupped my eyes and peered into the interior—which resembled a grungy, indifferently sanitized beauty shop. The vinyl of the stations' seats was cracked. X Games posters covered the walls. Needles criss-crossed on trays. A bare neon tube gleamed down on one station, fuzz white.

I checked my phone.

7:22.

Was I late now? Was I required to actually *make contact* with the Mice in fourteen minutes? It didn't seem fair to penalize me for their vague instructions—but the Mice had shown, in all sorts of ways, that they had their own ideas about fairness.

A sudden *clang* broke into my worries. The metal grate screamed up—*kak, kak, kak*—and just about clipped my nose.

The door opened, and inside stood the largest, most abrasive man I had ever seen.

CHAPTER ELEVEN

"I'm Hatch," he said. "Welcome to nowhere."

Instinctively, I pinned my purse tight to my side, which was dumb. If this giant wanted my stuff, my elbow wasn't stopping him.

I couldn't speak. The man occupied the entire doorframe. Was he seven feet tall? Maybe. Tattoos covered his skin from head to toe, looking like teaming snakes over his canvas of bulging muscle.

I could barely make out individual designs in the poor light, but a few stood out—a bald eagle flaring up out of his shirt, a pair of classic hot rods breathing fire down either forearm, the Declaration of Independence in loopy script across his shaved skull.

Distributed over his broad knuckles was the URL I already knew: *DetonateTheWorldOrder.org.*

He gestured to my car. "Good mileage?"

It took my tongue a couple tries, but finally I managed words.

"Yeah," I said. "Sixty if I'm lucky."

He nodded—up, not down.

I felt like I needed to say more, so I pointed to the only other vehicle in the lot, a rusty pickup with tires the size of boulders. "And the truck's yours?"

He confirmed it was.

I said, "Do you own this place?"

His eyes were active, impenetrable. A wind howled through the shop behind him—he stood in the doorway, his bulbous calf propping the door—and I thought I heard something like a dental hygienist's scraping.

"Did you come alone."

This wasn't inflected like a question, but Hatch's twitching biceps seemed to demand an answer.

I gulped. "Yes. Like you said."

"Are you attempting to join the Blind Mice in concert with law enforcement."

"No."

"Are you attempting to join the Blind Mice for journalistic reasons, or in concert with a third party of any other sort."

My thumb and forefinger started for the lobe of my ear, the one with Durwood's microphone, but I stopped them. "N-no." Hearing the crack in my voice, I repeated, "No."

Hatch inhaled, which made the beak of his bald-eagle tattoo stretch across his Adam's apple. "Are you angry?"

"Yes."

"Why?"

I thought. *Long or short answer?* "I'm angry about what this country's become."

The trace of a grin appeared. Quickly, he was serious again. "Do you believe it can be fixed?"

A bright part of my brain almost answered, *Of course it can!* But I stopped in time.

"No." I shook my head grimly.

Hatch folded his arms over his chest.

I continued, "It needs to get blown up first. We have to start from rubble."

The giant considered me for several seconds. I kept my eyes on his and hiked one hand up my hip, forcing a defiant pose even though I felt like shrinking into the pavement.

Durwood had said tonight would be "the key moment." I had completed their questionnaires, solved their riddles, but now came the hard part. The sniff test. No keyboards. No screen names or avatars. No unlimited time to compose answers.

Face-to-face, could I pass for a Blind Mouse?

Hatch asked if I knew what a pup was.

"Like a puppy? A juvenile dog?"

"No. The generalized form of the word, which also applies to rodents." As Hatch's diction rose, I got a whiff of the philosophical tint his blog sometimes displayed. "Ninety-five percent of individuals that reach this point in the process become Blind Pups."

"What's a Blind Pup?"

"A lesser tier," Hatch said. "Pups may post to our website and propagate mayhem under our rubric, but they cannot participate in— or receive information pertaining to—official missions."

"Basically a fan club?" I said.

Without answering, Hatch turned and walked into the tattoo parlor. The clap of boots on tile boomed about the deserted strip mall.

I followed.

Inside, Hatch led me to the station with the bare neon tube and spun the chair around. When he tried lowering the vinyl seat, its kick pedal stuck. He banged with the flat edge of his fist, and it yielded with a deafening *oof.*

He picked a large pen-like needle off a tray, poised his massive fingers around its shaft, and raised his eyes to me.

I said, "That gets sterilized?"

He tapped the base of the needle. "Autoclave cooks at two hundred fifty degrees. Sterile enough for you?"

I gave a small, gulping nod.

Hatch shuffled on his stool, squaring me up. "Wrist, ankle, or back?"

Determinedly, I avoided watching the ink climb to the tip of the needle. I thought of Karen's smile. Of zinnias in my garden, pink, symmetrical. "This means I'm becoming a Mouse, right?"

"Not necessarily," he said. "Pups get the mark too. Judgment comes after."

I reared back. "That sucks."

The word just popped out. Generally, I don't use it, Zach and his friends having ruined it for me with overuse long ago.

But Hatch didn't seem upset. "Nobody said life was fair. So what'll it be?"

I glanced at each of the three candidate body parts. Wrist was out unless I wanted to wear sleeves for the rest of my working life. Ankle would jeopardize sandal wearing, and I love sandals.

I asked how big it was.

He unbuckled his belt and started wresting up his shirt. For a moment, I hooded my eyes, thinking he'd misunderstood, but he kept his pants on. His mark was beside his belly button.

I had seen the nose-eyes-whiskers before, online and on Zach's shirt, but now, staring out from this huge man's stomach, the symbol shocked me with its raw, insistent rage. The slant-fill eyes. The missing ear.

I asked, "How come yours isn't wrist, ankle, or back?"

Hatch tucked his shirt back in. "Because it's anarchy."

Fair enough.

I chose the small of the back. Hatch worked professionally, never exposing more skin than necessary, his hand steady through sirens and dog barks and a car backfiring outside.

You hear different things from different people about whether getting a tattoo hurts. The word I would use to describe it—and I've given birth to two children—is "excruciating."

Steady or not, Hatch was essentially gouging a steel hook through my skin. The eyes and whiskers parts burned, a kind of slow, unrelenting beesting, but it was the mouse's nose that truly killed. The pain peaked over my spine, the needle's vibration reaching into my bone and traveling all the way to my teeth.

Hatch stroked out the final whisker, then swabbed antiseptic across the whole design and kick-lowered my chair. I popped out feeling like we should shake on it, or admire his handiwork in some mirror—but neither seemed to be in the cards.

He held the grate as we headed back outside, powerlifting it clear of my head.

"I respect your blog," I said. "You take risks. You say tough stuff."

We stood under the shop's awning. Had I made a mistake acknowledging his identity? He'd said his name, and the URL *was* right there across his knuckles. So far, Hatch had treated me decently, but could I really expect consistent behavior from a man with a pentagram on each earlobe?

Hatch reached into his fatigue-style pants and produced a scrap of paper.

I thought I glimpsed numbers. "Is that the address for Lewd Brew?"

He muttered something about not believing the crap you read on the internet. Then he propped a foot on his truck's running board. Rust flaked to the asphalt.

From his back pocket, he produced a larger scrap.

"This," he said, indicating the second scrap, "contains a list of dates. Rallies, flash mobs. Occupy marches. Also private email addresses for every CEO in the Despicable Dozen. It's what we give Blind Pups."

I swallowed.

"And this"—twiddling the smaller scrap—"is good for one night only. Tonight. For full-fledged Mice."

Hatch raised the smaller just off-center of our shared sight line, seeming to gauge it beside my face. Then he performed the same comparison with the other scrap.

I clutched the cuffs of my jacket so tightly, a button bit into my wrist.

I was on the verge of joining, or not joining, a band of outlaw revolutionaries. People a full decade younger than me who wanted to bump the world off its axis. I understood there was heavy psychology at play—a goal I'd been working toward, vindication in the eyes of Quaid and Durwood—but this fact remained: I wanted it worse than anything.

What happened if I only made Pup? Could I keep blogging, rant my way back into consideration? Somehow I doubted it. Maybe I should get the truck's license plate—that would at least give Quaid and Durwood a place to start in case my part of the job was ending.

After a full minute of contemplation, Hatch reached through his driver-side window and felt above the visor. His hand came back with a book of matches. He picked one out with his teeth and grinned tightly around the wooden stem.

"Nibble forth," he said.

And struck the match, and held its flame against the smaller scrap. The scrap's edges began curling into red-black ash.

My heart sank. I was starting to console myself with the memory of that 95 percent figure when two strange things happened.

Hatch wadded the larger Pup scrap and tossed it back into the truck's cab. With the opposite hand, he flicked the burning scrap toward me.

I danced back and crossed my arms over my face. Dimly, I heard an engine rumble to life and tires squeal. When I dared to peek, the truck was gone.

My eyes dropped to the asphalt. Inches from my feet, the scrap was smoldering. Heat licked at my toes. The flaming paper threw just enough light for me to read its contents.

Z7976. 16M.

I said each number three times in my head before the scrap crumpled to cinders.

CHAPTER TWELVE

New York City

The rendezvous with Todd Finley was to occur at the Dakota, the famed hotel where John Lennon was assassinated in 1980. Quaid and Mayor Diaz arrived by limo, the mayor instructing the driver and trail car to wait at street level. His security chief objected, but cursorily. He was practiced in looking away during the mayor's dalliances.

"I'll text Finley and tell him we're here," Quaid said in the lobby. "Drink order?"

Sergio, scarcely recognizable with his jet-black hair down and wearing a shimmery shirt, said he'd take a caipirinha.

Quaid tapped out his message. The operation had been his brainchild, floating the possibility of the city doing a Forceworthy trial in exchange for introductions to the company's supposed heavies, who might lead them to the Blind Mice. The mayor had loved the idea. How better to resuscitate his approval rating than by nabbing the Mice? Since he couldn't risk direct communication with unsavory types, Quaid had served as go-between.

Was it a high-probability operation? Not *high* high. Finley could've been blowing smoke, saying whatever it took to get the trail. Still, Quaid believed. And over the seven-year history of Third Chance Enterprises, his belief had pulled the gang through more than once.

Finley took a while answering the text. Quaid and Sergio decided to head up to the party, figuring it must be too loud to hear a phone chime. A gold-plated elevator ferried them to the seventh floor. The suite hosting the party featured a three-story balcony overlooking Central Park.

Quaid secured a prairie fire, his signature drink, and the mayor's caipirinha, then they squeezed through the crush of bodies to the balcony.

The view was sublime. Joggers and bikers weaved beneath park foliage, horses pulled carriages, vendors handed foil-wrapped goods out of steamy carts—all framed against skyscrapers at twilight.

"Outlaws are living well," Quaid observed, checking his sport coat in the balcony door—a sine wave of rippling glass.

"Too well," the mayor agreed.

The fact that Finley's heavies would be seen here, mixing with star-lets, being served by an Oslo-trained mixologist, was troubling. The Blind Mice had become a cause célèbre among the glitterati, who seemed to be following a sort of chic nihilism down, believing the society had so deteriorated so fully that we all deserved this.

Quaid and the mayor mingled substantially before bumping into Todd Finley.

"Gentleman!" The salesman broke off speaking to a petite redhead. "I knew we'd meet again. *Knew it*—never a doubt in my mind."

The handshakes he'd given at city hall turned into bro-worthy embraces here. Finley introduced the redhead, along with her two friends.

Quaid got paired up with one named Contessa. As they chatted, her slender fingers finding his elbow at every quip, he felt a twinge of guilt.

Molly hadn't answered his text saying the Dakota operation was a go. No doubt she and Durwood were sore at him.

Well, what could he do? In the operative business, sometimes socializing went hand in hand with the mission. Powerful people liked to enjoy themselves.

While Finley and his companions disappeared after more drinks,

Quaid and the mayor stayed on the balcony. A conversation above them got loud.

"Time Warner, let's do it!" a voice gushed through the deck boards. "They're at Ten Columbus Circle, straight shot south. Six people, six guns."

"Why them?" said another voice. "How about Fox?"

"We'll hit 'em both!"

The exchange veered from fake news to ingrained patriarchy to where guns could be gotten. Quaid heard at least four distinct voices.

He asked the mayor, "Should you be cluing your people in about this?"

Sergio rubbed a hand down his face. "It's only talk. Fashion. NYPD is swamped with false leads—they don't need more to chase."

Quaid supposed he was right. Still, hearing such revolutionspeak tossed off not ten feet overhead was chilling. The younger generation was always bolder, more recklessly confident in their ability to affect change, but this felt different. The vibe was charged, tinged with some social-media gasoline that seemed to put any sort of upheaval in play.

At eleven o'clock, Todd Finley handed them drinks (their seventh? eighth?) with a new sparkle in his eye. "You boys ready to talk turkey, get serious?"

Sergio excused himself from a discussion of shelter reforms. "Your friends have arrived?"

"If I'm being honest," Finley said, "they aren't friends. They aren't paid to be friends. Not mine, not yours."

The salesman skidded straight into his Forceworthy pitch, laying out the value proposition of his premium ATV-helicopter-Humvee package, suggesting Boston and Philly were on the verge of signing up too.

Quaid shared a weary look with the mayor. All they cared about was Finley's in with the Blind Mice, but they couldn't show outright disdain for the security trial.

The mayor asked, "How long has Forceworthy been around?"

"Nine years," Finley said. "Founded by a four-star general named Dane Packer who recognized the dearth of high-end security options in the private sector."

Quaid made a mental note to ask Durwood if he'd heard of Packer. "Seems it's grown well beyond private security."

"Different times. Nine years ago, all anyone had to worry about was Islamic terrorism."

Then Finley, a dog with a bone, wrested the discussion back to the trial—asking the mayor about turnaround times on city contracts, whether he'd like to go for the new Platinum tier, which incorporated real-time satellite surveillance.

Quaid hiccupped. *Satellites?*

Sergio said, "I'm intrigued. Before we go further down this path, though, I would like to meet these associates of yours."

Finley held a drink at his lips. "I can trust you guys?"

"Of course."

"You're not gonna scan my boys' faces and shoot 'em over to the FBI?"

"Certainly not."

Finley's fingers tightened around the balcony rail. He peered up and down Central Park West as though looking for SWAT teams.

Quaid saw the man needed a push. "Look, the mayor wants to start a back channel with this new element of the city—these troublemakers. It can be through you and Forceworthy, or it can be through somebody else."

Todd Finley kept scanning Central Park West.

Quaid knocked back the dregs of his prairie fire. To the mayor, he said, "Forget it, let's roll. It was worth a shot but—"

"No!" the salesman said. "You're right—I'm in, I'm in. In it to win it. Give me one sec, go touch base with my crew."

He suggested the powwow happen on the balcony's lower level—discreet, fewer people—then darted inside. Contessa and the other two women, who'd been busy with their own conversation, slinked off after Finley.

Quaid joined the mayor in descending a flight of winding spiral stairs, watching the tassels of his own loafers swing to and fro. He felt pleasantly drunk, his face warm, the periphery seeming to roll gently left. The mayor, too, wore a glassy expression.

JEFF BOND

The lower level was indeed discreet. More like deserted—the whole party seemed to have migrated to the top floors.

They waited a full minute. Quaid had a stray notion or two on how to deal with the Forceworthy heavies but didn't trouble much. He'd dealt with rough-and-tumble characters before. Nubian master stick fighters. Azerbaijani separatists. The basic principles of negotiation varied little. When the time came to dance, he'd dance.

Shhh-pop.

The sound of the door seal startled Quaid—the interior of this level had been off-limits. They turned away from Central Park. The sine-wave doors receded to the wings. From the dark within, the trio of women emerged.

"Did you miss us?" asked the redhead.

Quaid perceived a faint accent he hadn't noticed before. French? The three women strode forward, their elbows crooked.

The mayor said, "Terribly," but with none of his usual cool.

Quaid hesitantly took Contessa's arm and allowed himself to be led into the interior. *So these three were with the heavies? Advance spies?*

She was tugging toward the suite too insistently, and there was a tension in her body that put Quaid on alert. His instincts, though, were swimming upstream against the fog of intoxication and arousal.

Lights blared on inside. A dozen commandos in ski masks jabbed rifles at him and Sergio. On the ground before them, bound and gagged in a fetal position, lay Todd Finley.

CHAPTER THIRTEEN

New Jersey

Z *7976?*
16M!

The second line I thought I understood: sixteen minutes. But sixteen minutes to do what?

Could "Z7976" be part of a phone number? A coded location, maybe GPS coordinates? Latitude-longitude?

Was I officially *in* the Blind Mice now, or did I still have this one last puzzle to solve?

I was standing in the weedy strip-mall parking lot, wracking my brain, woozy from the whirlwind of the last hour—and possibly the exhaust fumes from Hatch's truck.

It took me thirty seconds to realize Hatch couldn't see me anymore, and I was free to call Durwood. I dug my phone out of my purse.

Durwood answered, "What's it say?"

Apparently, he'd intuited the scene from my earring audio.

"It has two lines," I said, and recited them from memory. "I assume the second part means sixteen minutes. What do you think about the Z number?"

The line was silent. I was shivering—the sun had set while I'd been inside getting inked.

"The way those sevens repeat," I said, "and with the six being an upside-down nine, I thought it could be in code. Should I try Google? Do you have anything in the Vanagon for—"

"Zip code," he said.

"Huh?"

"Z for zero," Durwood said. "Oh-seven-nine-seven-six, northern New Jersey."

My mouth hung open, but there was no time to wonder at the ex-marine's photographic recall of geography. I sprinted to the Prius, punching the digits into my navigation. Durwood said to call if I needed him—he was heading that way himself and wouldn't be far off if things turned hairy.

I zoomed from the parking lot, racing north by my phone's stiffly enunciated directions. With the kids in tow, I'm cautious as they come, but now I honked and gunned yellows and changed lanes without signaling. My stomach bottomed out as I caught air over a speed bump.

I accelerated up the entry ramp to the turnpike. My electric motor *vre-eee-ed* as I slipstreamed past a Mercedes. Nearing my exit, I could see larger homes over the soundproofing banks—boats, three- and four-car garages.

Where were the Mice leading me? Was I going to be blindfolded, or forced to do some initiatory computer hack?

I reached the correct zip code just in time. An upscale mall consti-tuted its western border. Frantically, I looked around the massive Bloomingdale's sign for some arrow or button or ambassador I could register my arrival with.

My phone buzzed. I checked the message.

mAYHeM @ 23rd & Pinecrest

Fingers trembling, I updated my navigation with the intersection and put the car back in gear. En route, I called Durwood and gave him the location.

Block by block, the neighborhoods were becoming richer. Pavement yielded to cobblestone roads. Chain-link fences became cross-hatched wood.

I thought of that scrap Hatch had thrown back into his cab, the one for Pups. *Private email addresses for every CEO in the Despicable Dozen.* Maybe they had physical addresses too.

At Twenty-First Street, I passed through an imposing wrought-iron gate that set off an even more exclusive subdivision—an enclave within an enclave. At Twenty-Second, a bicycle stood crookedly in the street.

Bicycle?

In my neighborhood, people left rakes against tree trunks or basketballs in driveways overnight—but not here.

I peered down a cul-de-sac and saw three more bikes, plus a ratty Toyota Corolla slathered in bumper stickers.

I slowed and tried to guess something about the assortment of vehicles. Teenagers having a party? Or the Blind Mice?

Now I was coming up to a property with ascending boulders leading up to its driveway. Behind the lowest boulders, tucked between azalea bushes, two pairs of jeans and sneakers were poking out. Closer to the drive, I saw—thought I saw—more body parts. A stocking cap. The tail of a flannel shirt.

I let the Prius drift to a stop, peering through the dark at letters chiseled into the tallest, broadest boulder.

BLACKSTONE.

I palmed the back of my neck, which felt unnaturally bare with my new bob cut. *Blackstone... Blackstone...* Where did I know that name from?

"Too close!" a voice hissed through my passenger-side window. *"Park around the corner."*

My toes spasmed against the accelerator. The Prius revved—I jammed the brake. Catching my breath, I eased forward in electric mode and glided noiselessly around a dark bend.

Here I found two other cars parked, wheels jutting away from the curb. I nosed in behind the last.

A blue blip across my hood spooked me. I looked up and saw, rising above the canopy, a utility pole topped by a circular light. In another few seconds, it blipped again.

I tucked my cell into my pocket, leaving behind my purse, and stepped carefully over cobblestone tiles back toward the Blackstone residence. My ears tuned to every rustle of the aspens overhead. The streetlights, a nouveau-antique burnished brass, gave almost zero light —on foot, I noticed several bicycles and a Vespa scooter I'd missed from the car.

I'd almost reached the boulders when a hooded figure stepped from the shadows. A penlight flashed in my face.

"Show your mark."

All I could make out was the sinewy fist around the penlight's shaft. I twisted and raised my shirt. Night air whistled over my back. The tattoo still tingled.

It occurred to me that if this thing was going to be used like a badge, wrist would've been the better choice.

"Yup," the sentry said.

I tucked my shirt in. The sentry produced a wand of some kind.

"Arms up," he said.

"You're checking me for weapons?"

"Nope." He flicked a switch. The wand warbled briefly. "Frequencies."

He dropped to one knee and guided his wand around my shoes, up my ankles. A meter flickered in the green range.

The earring!

I was toast if they detected Durwood's earring mic.

The sentry was scanning my pockets now. His wand fuzzed around my phone, which he said was allowed. With painstaking care, I moved my hand to my left earlobe, flicked off the earring back with my thumb, then in a single motion, palmed the turquoise stud and flung it to the street. It clattered away off cobblestone.

The sentry glanced at the noise—but only for an instant.

Finishing his scan, he flicked off the wand and stowed his penlight. "Walk inside the curb to the intercom box. Then crawl. The security cam sees you otherwise."

I nodded. Saliva was flooding the back of my mouth.

The sentry made way. "Nibble forth."

"Nibble forth," I said back, because it felt like I should.

From the intercom box, I inched toward the *BLACKSTONE* boulder on all fours. I saw, through a crevice, a group of eighteen or twenty people on the lawn. Their faces were faintly illuminated by phone screens. They had messenger bags, ripped jeans, shoes like Zach's. They sat in a kind of wedge formation, and was that...electrical tape on the lawn?

The unmistakable obelisk-like form of Hatch stood near the head of the group.

I crawled between the boulders to join a group of four. A girl to my left looked sixteen. A guy to my right with amazing hair could've been twenty-four. He up-nodded. I up-nodded back, going for aloof but not unfriendly.

Nobody in my group spoke. Every last person had one eye on the mansion beyond and one on their phone, many thumbing the screen. I took mine out to fit in.

There were six new messages, all from Durwood. The latest, one minute ago: *Check in when possible. At bloomingdales awaiting your location.*

I tapped off a quick reply, describing the neighborhood. A moment later, he asked whether I had received any operational details.

None, I typed.

He answered that I should hold position and "keep gathering intel." He was two minutes away "in case extraction is needed."

I closed messaging—I didn't need anyone seeing those—and scanned the lawn. Exactly what "intel" was I looking for? Not a lot was happening in my circle. I thought Amazing Hair Guy stole a glance at my chest or lower, but that could've been projection.

The action seemed to be in the lead group, where Hatch and two others were talking in stern whispers, gesturing sharply at the mansion.

An attack?

It seemed bizarre that the Blind Mice would risk assembling, exposing themselves, for a simple theft—cash, cars, jewelry. Every mission I'd ever read about had involved technology.

Could there be some ultrasecret safe inside with router passwords or network keys or...whatever else you needed to wreak havoc online?

I spotted an African American girl working on a laptop next to Hatch. She was short and wore a knit beanie.

The legendary Piper Jackson?

She typed furiously, lips curled tight against her teeth. Hatch and the third member of the circle kept turning to check her screen.

I was just considering sneaking closer when Hatch saw me.

His inked head—which rose above the scene like some wildly decorated periscope—froze. The others in my circle noticed him noticing me, and shuffled a step away. The Libertarian grinned, but there was a tautness in his face I didn't love.

Did I mess up somehow? Had he meant for the scrap of paper in the parking lot to burn through without my reading it?

What if they'd intercepted my texts with Durwood? Maybe that's what Piper Jackson was doing, clicking through Verizon's database and reading all my messages.

Would they kidnap me? Torture me for information on my collaborators? I told myself that no matter how overheated their rhetoric, no matter how extreme their appearances, the Mice cared about social justice. Surely, people who campaigned for a living wage weren't capable of pulling out fingernails with pliers.

At the height of my fears, Hatch stepped aside, and I was able to make out the third member of the lead group: a pale, gangly figure in cargo shorts. His bones didn't seem quite to fit, elbows and knees jangling liquidly. Ghost-white hair flowed back from a high forehead like exotic Asian noodles.

His eyes, small and pink tinged, pulsed with a heady, unhinged intensity—and they pulsed straight at me.

Josiah.

He began walking toward me. I started to stash my phone. Then I thought, no, that would look guilty. Then I clutched it, remembering the stories about teeth marks and Gorilla Glass.

Every eye was on Josiah. He was impossible to look away from, his gait hypnotic, his kaleidoscopic limbs slashing the space between us.

I felt my head swirling up, out of this wealthy New Jersey suburb. Two hours ago, I had been boiling pasta water. Now I was facing the most wanted criminal in the United States.

With a last erratic stride, he brought his face close to mine. He smelled of mint—not any familiar kind like spear or peppermint, but aggressive, like I imagined a street drug would.

"Now, Molly Wixom," he said in a reedy voice, "you shall be baptized in mayhem."

CHAPTER FOURTEEN

I prayed six times over the next hour. For strength. For more trees, then for fewer trees. For better shoes. For a redo of that first morning Quaid and Durwood had showed up on my front porch so I could've gotten us out the door just *five minutes earlier* and missed them altogether. And finally, for my children to live full, happy lives if I never saw them again.

The "mayhem"—that was the perfect word for it—didn't start immediately. After his ominous welcome, Josiah left to rejoin the head group. He continued debating with Hatch and Piper, whispering heatedly over the hacker's laptop, flailing at the mansion like some mad wizard casting spells.

When a black sedan approached, the leaders rushed us all behind the azaleas. I hunched in the grass and waited, tensed, knees and elbows bumping. The sedan's headlights swiveled and swelled as the car turned the bend—then disappeared.

I was holding a fistful of sod.

I eavesdropped as much as possible on the leaders. The guy with amazing hair was too—we exchanged a look as their argument got heated. Josiah was making swoopy gestures around one side of the house. Piper Jackson shook her head vehemently. Hatch stepped between them, clapping his bear-claw hands over their shoulders.

"Keep it simple," I caught Piper saying. "This is bad enough, what I just did."

Josiah urged up on his stringy calves. "Insufficient, P. We're redressing atrocities. Atrocities must be answered in kind."

Before the hacker could respond, Josiah bounded off as though unable to stop his own legs—up the drive, around the side of the mansion, gone into the night.

The group waited. A bat flitted past overhead. I squinted around at the rest of the Mice. Besides Hatch, I recognized a few other bloggers with impressive followings—a contributor to Daily Kos, a section editor for *HuffPost*.

As Josiah's absence stretched on, I started hearing murmurs. One kid stepped outside the taped-off wedge to glimpse around the mansion—Hatch yanked him back.

I whispered to Amazing Hair Guy, "What's with the electric tape?"

He pointed to an oblong camera mounted on a pike above. "Security. They can't see us if we stay inside the wedge."

I thanked him. He smiled.

Ten minutes later, and Josiah still hadn't returned. I heard the spring of a kickstand and somebody pedaling off. It was eleven o'clock.

Suddenly, a cacophony of phone chimes broke the quiet. The others looked down at their screens, then back up with cryptic expressions.

My own phone hadn't buzzed. What had I missed? Had I already been taken off some list?

Amazing Hair Guy, noticing my consternation, said, "Twitter."

I leaned against his shoulder to see his phone's screen.

josiahTheAvenger had tweeted: *THE TIME OF ATONEMENT HAS ARRIVED. THEY SHALL PAY EXQUISITELY.*

Reading the words, I felt a bone-deep chill. A subscript showed more than eight million followers for Josiah's feed. I realized that his message was being read in bars, in suburban teens' bedrooms, in Singapore, in Arizona—and that whatever "ATONEMENT" he had in mind was going to involve me.

The rest of the Mice seemed to be having similar thoughts.

"Does anyone know the plan?" someone said.

"I don't think he *wants* a plan."

"They know what they're doing. No sweat."

"But what if—"

Piper Jackson's voice cut through, "Y'all shut up!"

The chatter stopped.

"You're nervous, right?" she said. "So am I. We're all nervous. Suck it up."

Piper was no taller than five three, but she projected a towering authority. Underneath tight cornrows, her eyes darted from one face to the next. She held her laptop overhand like a crowbar.

Finally, a dark figure appeared moving away from the mansion. Josiah. He picked his way along the grass, prancing like some half-frog supervillain on speed.

Breathless, he joined us behind the cover of the azaleas.

"The pig's in his study. On his computer. Probably denying claims for kicks." Josiah spat every consonant. "Check it out, P—let's see what filth he's up to."

Piper opened her laptop and tapped a few keystrokes. "Unsecured Wi-Fi. I got the bitstream." Her eyes bore into the screen. "URLs look like money. Bank of America. Vanguard."

Josiah's whole face squeezed as though his skin could barely contain the energy boiling within. He took out his phone and tweeted.

PAYMENT IS DUE. PAST DUE. WE ARE OWED BY OUR CORPO-RATE MASTERS. THE MICE SHALL COLLECT.

Again, phones buzzed through the group. I read from Amazing Hair Guy's phone again, our sides touching. I considered sending Durwood an update—since he'd be deaf without my earring mic—but decided not to risk it.

Josiah turned to Piper. "Miss Jackson, would you please relieve this Viagra-pushing douchebag of his spoils?"

Piper didn't argue with this.

As she did something on her laptop, it occurred to me where I knew the name Blackstone. Blackstone Health Management. Of course!

I remembered from the forms—the temp agency had used them for medical coverage.

But Blackstone Health Management wasn't a member of the Despicable Dozen. Could they be owned by one of the Dozen?

Now Piper started a flat, blow-by-blow account as she typed. "401(k), gone... Long-term bond fund, gone... Emerging Markets Challenger fund, let's take your balance down to about zero..."

Josiah's mouth stretched in a sick-bright grin. He glared at the mansion.

In another minute, Piper clapped shut her laptop. "That's it. We're good."

As she stood to go, the Mice let out a collective breath. I checked the time. Eleven thirty.

Perfect. All I needed to do was separate from the group long enough to get Durwood a text. He would swoop in and nab Josiah while I slipped away in the Prius. With luck, I would be home and kissing Karen's and Zach's warm foreheads before midnight.

"No," Josiah said. "We're not good. We're nowhere remotely close to good."

He stared ahead at the mansion. Every few seconds, his elbow spasmed as though some live current ran loose inside.

Piper seemed to speak for everyone in saying, "What're you thinking, a break-in? You know his security's gonna be crazy tough."

Josiah said nothing.

She tapped a knuckle against her laptop. "We nailed him. Let's roll back to the joint, I'll hack the website too. Blackstone'll be serving up 404 errors for days."

Josiah shook his head. "Same old tune we've been playing for eight months."

"That's because it's a sweet tune."

Josiah's head continued to shake, eyes on the mansion. "Not sweet enough."

Voice rising, he continued, "Tonight we raise the stakes. Tonight we graduate from netroots pranks. These corporations don't change unless they have an *incentive*"—he growled the word—"to change. You have to change their equation, and do you know where you change it? At the top."

He tweeted: *YOU CHANGE THE EQUATION AT THE TOP.*

As he spoke, I felt the group's jitters harden to resolve. The sheer force of Josiah's outrage was spreading like locusts over a crop field. Jaws set. Backpack straps were cinched. Despite my fear, despite not really being one of them, I felt it too. We followed Josiah's words around the showy wealth, the burnished brass streetlights, the tennis courts, the inground pools with black-shimmer surfaces and lane buoys.

"...*how perfectly comfortable here,*" he hissed, "never mind the sick in India—or Indiana—who can't pay his ransom for drugs they need. You know what they should do with the bodies? People who die because they can't afford treatment? They should mulch 'em. Use them to fertilize these chem-perfect lawns. Brighten up these petunia beds."

Josiah ripped out a swath of these very flowers, his pupils dancing. "Our next phase demands pure hearts. If yours isn't, if you don't believe in this, then go. We will bear you no ill will."

The neighborhood remained silent apart from the rustling aspens.

Blood beat in my eardrums. It occurred to me to beg off, retreat to the Prius and text Durwood from there. Maybe he could capture Josiah before this—whatever it was—happened.

Surveying the faces around me, though, I didn't think so. I didn't think Josiah's pledge of "no ill will" truly reflected the group mood. *They were in.* Anything less than total solidarity would be unacceptable. I'd never make it off the grounds.

When Josiah started around the side of the house again, everyone followed.

Me included.

CHAPTER FIFTEEN

Durwood sat in the Vanagon cabin watching the blurry action on a monitor.

"Unbelievable," he muttered.

Sue-Ann, sprawled against a crate of frag grenades, snuffled in her sleep.

Tonight had differed from Durwood's expectation in just about every way an event could differ. For weeks, the Mice had been cautious. Their drops were textbook. Their electronic trails vanished. The identity of each and every go-between had been guarded.

Now they were letting Molly, a fresh recruit, see a great chunk of the group's membership? Allowing her to participate in an on-site attack—itself a reckless escalation of tactics?

So it seemed. The action was hard to decipher—with Molly's earring dark, he'd had to scramble to position long-range video. Even Yakov's light-enhancing lenses had their limits.

It was the sort of opportunity you don't plan for, but must capitalize upon. There was no telling when or whether it would come again.

Durwood climbed forward to the steering wheel. He drove without headlights through the ritzy subdivision.

Two hundred yards out.

One fifty.

Coming to a gentle rise, Durwood cruised to a stop.

He felt confident he'd made out Hatch's large form on the feed, but whether other leadership—like Josiah—were present, he couldn't say. He would apprehend who he found. The rest could scatter like chaff.

If he did get Josiah, the contract with American Dynamics would be fulfilled. In all likelihood, the Blind Mice would be done as a functional unit.

Would the broader unrest stop?

No telling. Cutting off the head of the snake sure couldn't hurt, though.

Durwood chambered his M9 semiautomatic and opened the door.

Before his boot had struck cobblestone, his phone rang. He expected Molly, calling with news of the Mice's operation.

The caller ID read, QUAID2: the backup phone his partner kept in an inner sport coat pocket.

Durwood answered.

Quaid said, "Wood, hey! We need you—they grabbed us. They tossed us in the back of a semi."

The connection was awful—grinding, staticky. Quaid's voice had the familiar warble of drink.

Durwood asked, "Who?"

"Dunno. I would say Finley sold us out, but he was tied up himself."

"What's around you?"

"I'm blindfolded so it's *hard*"—he hiccupped—"er, hard to say. Maybe boxes? Crates?"

"Any guards?"

"Up in the cab, yeah," Quaid said. "Not back here."

Durwood gritted his teeth. He considered the two events taking place simultaneously. The Mice's escalation of tactics and a kidnapping involving the mayor of New York City.

Interesting.

He said, "Where are you?"

"I, well, they've got us next to some of these crate-things, and Sergio thinks—"

"The semi. Whereabouts is the truck?"

"Uuuuhhh...lemme think, they snatched us from the Dakota...then it felt like we were heading toward the Avenues." He asked Sergio, garbled, "We've been driving, what, ten minutes?"

Durwood waited out a conversation between Quaid and the mayor. On the monitor, the Blind Mice had left cover and were approaching the residence.

"...conned us with girls," Quaid was saying, "and Sergio thinks the accents were Brazilian, but to my ear, Portuguese makes more—"

"Stop talking." Mouth tight, Durwood listened. "The horns sound like Doppler. They take you in a tunnel?"

Quaid's answer was unclear.

"Holland Tunnel," Durwood said. "Ventilation system whooshes like that."

Over the line, Quaid and the mayor sounded like they were arguing.

Durwood hung up and started the Vanagon's motor. He checked the video feed, which showed no trace of the Mice now. They might have penetrated the residence.

Might have left too.

Durwood hated the idea of leaving Molly. She'd managed fine all night, though. It was true he'd doubted her at the start of the job, but she had proved herself capable. Running the blog. Saying what needed saying in the roundtable. Keeping her cool at the tattoo parlor.

She could handle it—whatever the Mice were up to.

If the mayor of New York City met a poor end, the unrest would accelerate. Thugs and hooligans would be emboldened. For all Durwood knew, the Mice leadership was behind the kidnapping anyhow—driving Quaid and Sergio's semi.

The drive to Manhattan took twenty-eight minutes, fast as Durwood dared. When traffic did not require his full attention, he thought. Pain grew in his forehead.

He wondered how drunk his partner had gotten, whether impairment had led to the capture. Quaid's role required a certain amount of fraternization. Not as much as he did.

Quaid Rafferty was the promoter of the pair. Durwood never could've landed the jobs he did, possessing neither charisma nor the gift of gab. Before Quaid had come along, Durwood had been a lone contractor. He'd done security and surveillance in the Middle East. Private tech retrieval. A bit of contract combat when he believed in the cause. Honest, unexciting work.

With Quaid had come involvement in coups, intrigues in the oil-gas and aerospace sectors, space lasers and phantom subs and other doomsday weapons—as if cooked up by the force of the ex-politician's imagination. Durwood enjoyed the challenge. And the money was nothing to sneeze at. It was nice being able to buy a seventeen-thousand-dollar radar-sighted rifle if you liked.

But Quaid could be infuriating. He'd nearly ruined the Guadeloupe job romancing a bartender. The man had a self-destructive streak. He was distractible and easily bored. Never happy with taking a plain task and doing it well.

The Holland Tunnel was jammed as usual. Durwood swung the Vanagon wide of the far toll lane, past a hog line of cars. He parked in a cluster of Port Authority vehicles. Found a hard hat in the cabin and walked with purpose to the narrow ladder leading to the maintenance crawl space. Nobody stopped him.

Tracking Quaid by his phone's GPS, Durwood covered a quarter mile of tunnel before reaching the signal. He descended by the closest porthole, hurrying. If he overshot and missed the semi, it was unlikely he'd catch up on foot.

Fumes and horns and whipped-hot air struck his face. Quickly Durwood saw an eighteen-wheeler moving toward him in lane three. He couldn't make out whether the driver looked Brazilian. Or Portuguese.

Durwood checked the GPS beacon again. He appeared to be on top of Quaid—though, this close, interference could be distorting the signal.

Durwood climbed down the access ladder. His boots fought for purchase on rungs slick with condensation. Bricks in front of his nose smelled sour. He lowered himself to a three-foot shoulder.

Traffic slowed now—a blessing. Durwood walked to the rear of the semi. A taxi driver shouted. Durwood ignored him. He climbed the bumper and laid his ear to the door.

Quaid had called just once. His phone could've been taken. There might be guards on him and the mayor.

They might've been shot dead.

Durwood could hear little over the tunnel racket. He lay down flat across the bumper—about nine inches wide. Then reached up and tapped the cross latch loose, pressuring just enough to start the door rolling up.

Durwood's body tensed. He gripped the underside of the truck with one hand. With the other, he gripped his M9.

The door accelerated, slamming into its ceiling tracks. Durwood felt footsteps pounding closer.

A squat, muscular man appeared. A weapon stuck out of his belt. He leaned past the bumper, glancing left and right into traffic.

"Freeze," Durwood said.

Aiming the muzzle of his gun at the man's chest, he pulled himself up into the semi. The guard backed away, eyes wide, spooked at Durwood's materializing out of nowhere.

Quaid and Sergio sat side by side on a wheel well, bound.

"See?" Quaid said to his drinking buddy. "I told ya, an hour tops."

A roll of twine was sitting out. Durwood secured the guard. Then he freed Quaid and the mayor with irked thrusts of his switchblade.

Sergio said, "Please accept my heartfelt thanks. On behalf of the entire city, I am in your debt."

Durwood said, "What happened to your security detail? How come they didn't follow?"

The mayor explained he'd ordered them to wait at street level. "We were taken underground. The semi was waiting three blocks away. They planned shrewdly."

Durwood thinned his lips. "See any tattoos?"

Quaid looked at the mayor, and they both shrugged. "Nothing out of the ordinary. The redhead had that, what was it, an owl across her shoulder blades?"

Sergio said, "Phoenix."

As they discussed what type bird, Durwood led the guard behind some boxes. Out of the man's view, he planted a transponder in the spare-tire hold. Next, he used a handheld scanner to check the cargo for radioactive/WMD-signature materials. Finding none, he packed up and gripped the rear latch.

"Train's leaving, you two," he said.

The mayor broke off explaining the shape of phoenix wings. "We are letting them drive off? Aren't you going to subdue them?"

Like Durwood was Captain America, capable of corralling hostiles of unknown number and armament by snapping his fingers.

"I got someplace else to be. Give this to your police chief." Durwood wrote out the transponder's serial number. "Lead right to 'em."

With that, the three men dismounted the semi and weaved their way back to the access ladder. The taxi driver shouted again. Durwood saw a gap in the traffic and kept moving.

Quaid—who'd yet to ask about Molly—yelled at the cabbie. *"Show some gratitude to your mayor—he's the only thing stopping Uber from putting you on the dole!"*

Cars kept zipping by. An SUV screeched to a halt just in time.

Again, Durwood's head tightened around a core of pain—and pressure.

They made the ladder. Quaid was still yapping at the cabbie.

"You talked enough," Durwood said.

Quaid allowed the mayor to climb up first. Then he hitched his loafer onto the first rung and glanced back at Durwood. "Lighten up. Fine, I should've been more vigilant tonight. Not my best performance. But it worked out. How's, uh, how's McGill? She do okay?"

Durwood looked past him to the crawl space above. It was a quarter mile back. Even if he left these two, it would be twenty minutes to the Vanagon. Then another half hour driving to the Blackstone residence, best case.

"Did fine," he said. "No thanks to you."

CHAPTER SIXTEEN

I wished I hadn't seen the pictures.

Rushing from the shattered conservatory—Josiah and Hatch had busted in with tools from the Olympic-size swimming pool—and through the hall to the Blackstones' study, I was physically incapable of missing a series of framed photographs. The Blackstones had twin girls. Seven or eight years old. Barely older than Karen.

Here they were in blazers and ponytails on the steps of the Pennington School. There they sat on a porch glider. Each portrait twisted my heart. Trick-or-treating. Chasing a soccer ball. Those perfect, blameless eyes.

My strides slowed. The few Mice behind me clambered past.

Karen hadn't liked soccer. *The ball's so hard, Mommy.* Maybe if I could've afforded high-end cleats like the Blackstone girls wore. Maybe if I gave it another year, hauling her to practice, setting up cones in the backyard.

Will I ever get the chance?

Now I was bringing up the rear. Glass had gotten into one of my arches, and I moved with a kind of limping gallop to minimize rubbing. Still, I kept up. I never lost sight of the others.

The group reached the study and began pooling outside open

French doors. I'd almost caught up when heavy footfalls sounded behind.

The police? Should I split off and try to escape? If the Mice were about to be captured anyway, wasn't my mission moot?

But it wasn't the police. It was Hatch—tromping ahead, stashing a Bowie knife in his messenger bag.

At my puzzling expression, he said, "Bye-bye landline."

I joined the rear of the group as Josiah, flashing back a fanatic's grin, stepped through the French doors into the study.

It was several seconds before I could make sense of the scene, straining on tiptoes, looking over shoulders and around ears.

Somebody growled. Somebody else muttered, "Gross."

Piece by piece, the décor of the health-care executive's study came into view. Floor-to-ceiling bookcases with sliding mahogany ladders. An antique globe perched on a claw-foot stand. An array of plaques and awards on the walls, portraits of Grace Kelly and Jayne Mansfield, mixed among an assortment of arcane weapons on pegs: spiky morningstars, glinting daggers, a crossbow whose stock was carved in the elaborate form of a scorpion.

In the middle of all this, a man held a lance. He was wearing silk pajamas, the sleeve's red-velvet fabric billowing about the lance's domed grip.

"It's real, and I know what to do with the business end," the man said. "I have fifty hours of period-correct training under my belt."

Josiah approached him without regard for the sharp, quavering tip. "Ah, the corporate warrior act. Pillage the customer, then blow ungodly amounts on Renaissance fair trinkets and pretend you're Sun Tzu." His pink-tinged eyes narrowed. "Weren't you an EE major at Rutgers, *Ted*?"

Blackstone shuddered hearing his own name. "Who are you? What're you doing here?"

Josiah kept coming until mere inches separated his chest from the lance. "Who we are is the Blind Mice. Why we're here?" He smiled devilishly. "You know, Ted. Deep down, deep in the marrow of your bones, you know."

Blackstone scanned our ranks while at the same time covering Josiah, who was stuttering and jerking the lance.

"What—but—but Blackstone Health isn't on that list," the executive said. "That list of yours, the Despicable Dozen, right?"

The corners of Josiah's lips stretched grotesquely toward his ears. "You're in a special category. You get special justice."

He punctuated these words with a primal attack, a simultaneous kick-shove-scream that sent Ted Blackstone's lance clattering to the floor. The antique globe was knocked off its stand. Josiah, seeming energized by the disorder, hopped up onto a massive partner's desk and began hurling documents, staplers, some trophy with a golden golf ball.

"Let's rearrange your corporate bric-a-brac," he said. "It's feeling hella stale."

Josiah flung himself at the man's books, ranting about "banker's biographies" and "soft-science manifestos." He pulled down section after section of books. Other Mice joined in. The *HuffPost* blogger smashed the girlie posters with Blackstone's morningstar. Josiah urinated on an exquisite mohair rug.

I took a step toward the hall.

Ted Blackstone backed away, circling behind his desk. "You have no idea the magnitude of this mistake."

Josiah, zipping his fly, sauntered to the desk and nodded to Blackstone's computer. "How's your rate of return looking?"

"That was you?" the executive said. "I—I thought it was a bank glitch."

With a grandiose sweep of the arm, Josiah indicated Piper Jackson. "It was. A permanent glitch."

The hacker sniffed. She hadn't participated in the destruction, but she wasn't shrinking from Blackstone's gaze either.

"But why worry?" Josiah went on. "With your stupendous take-home pay, the funds will replenish in no time. About three million a month, isn't it?"

"The stockholders approve my compensation every year in a nonbinding vote."

"*Nonbinding*," Josiah said. "Sorta like if I asked my compatriots here, 'Shall I sever Ted Blackstone's ear and puree it in his stainless-steel food processor?' and even if they voted twenty-two to zero against, I could ignore them. I could start slicing away."

His loose limbs seemed to ripple in place as he spoke. I wondered what sort of brutality he was capable of. Surely, he was just spooking Blackstone. We'd already trashed his house and put the fear of God into him. Probably, Josiah would come right up to the edge of violence and be done.

I reminded myself again that the Blind Mice were progressives. They'd never targeted people.

"Let's talk this out," Blackstone said, mastering his voice. "What do you hope to accomplish? What're your goals?"

"Accountability," Josiah said. "When you blow eighty thousand taking the corporate jet to a golf tournament in Florida, where does that cash come from?"

Blackstone's throat made an indeterminate noise.

"Your customers' *cells*," Josiah said. "You insure bodies and brains. Every dollar you waste comes out of their organs, the puss-filled tissues you deny treatment for. *That's* where."

"I—well, it's rare that I take the jet, only when absolutely necessary for a meeting or—"

"A hundred thirty-seven times in the last fiscal year," Josiah said, "which translates to twelve million dollars. How many valid claims did your adjusters have to deny to make up that expense?"

"Our adjusters are impartial, our controls are best in breed—"

"Spare us your buzzwords." Josiah started around the desk, his steps slow and full of fury. "Tell me about your policy on lifetime caps."

Blackstone kept inching back. "We have them—the whole industry has them, otherwise you're bankrupt."

"What is it? The cap on your standard policy?"

"I'd have to look it up," Blackstone said. "I know it gets adjusted regularly to account for—"

"One-point-three million dollars," Josiah said. "Lasts about fifteen months when you have pancreatic cancer. Runs out right about the time you cross eighty pounds, when your eyes turn yellow from liver failure and your toes are blue from lack of circulation."

The room was silent as a tomb. A down feather from a destroyed couch cushion floated past my face.

I understood, hearing the crack in Josiah's voice, that he wasn't speaking in abstracts. He wasn't debating public policy.

But Blackstone didn't.

"Diseases are cruel, that's a fact of life," he said. "But my shareholders expect what they expect."

Josiah dove at the man's face. They caromed to the ground, toppling a chair, struggling, grappling, clawing.

"*My mother,*" Josiah spat. "Doctors wanted to try high-intensity ultrasound, but it was 'experimental.' By the time the mediator decided in Dad's favor, she'd hit the lifetime cap."

Blackstone was bleeding from his nose and a gash in his silver hair. "It's tragic, but you can't possibly hold me to account."

"Then Dad hung himself. Two months later, in shame. For what he didn't do for her."

Looking around at the other Mice, I saw I wasn't the only one getting this information fresh. Eyes dropped. Faces darkened. There were different rumors about Josiah's parents online—that they'd died in a car crash, that Josiah had disavowed them over his materialistic upbringing.

Never a whiff of this.

Ted Blackstone, stunningly, pressed his case. "I'm an executive. I don't deal in individual outcomes."

The word left my lips before I could stop it.

"*Bastard.*"

Amazing Hair Guy, standing right beside me, gave me a fist tap.

Someone said, "Let's educate him about individual outcomes!"

The whole group was buzzing, crowding closer. Josiah seemed to be feeding off the accumulating energy. His grin tightened and stretched more—seeming ready to fly off his face. His eyes shone with ghoulish intensity.

Frigid air poured in from the hall—those shattered conservatory windows. Lampshades wobbled. The fringe of a lace doily bubbled off its table. The antique globe had settled against the arced legs of a Queen Anne chair, South Pole facing up.

I glanced outside. *How great would it be if Durwood busted in right about now?*

Blackstone tried, "You're just kids, you don't realize what you're doing." Eyes frantic, looking for takers. "It's not too late! Don't follow this weirdo, he's a fraud, he's mixing you up in a bunch of nonsense..."

As the man spluttered out, Josiah found his phone in his cargo shorts. He tapped for thirty seconds.

Our phones all chimed.

I checked Twitter.

"I'm an executive. I don't deal in individual outcomes." LAST WORDS OF TED BLACKSTONE.

Josiah pocketed the phone again and faced us. Tendons bulged in his neck. He eyed several of us in turn, then approached Hatch. From the tattooed giant's messenger bag, he pulled the Bowie knife.

He walked back to Blackstone. Before the executive could respond, he'd sliced the top button of Blackstone's silk pajama top.

Plink, it landed on the floor.

I heard gasps. Now I took a step forward and opened my mouth. "Maybe we shou—"

Amazing Hair Guy jerked me back. His foreboding eyes seemed to say, *Are you crazy?*

Ted Blackstone stood perfectly still. His Adam's apple shifted and bobbed under the point of the blade.

He was completely stone-faced, as though he were facing down a labor union or hostile regulatory body. Classic psych profile of a chief executive. Even if you're terrified inside, on the outside, you're a sphinx.

I wished he would crack. Whimper, beg for mercy, something— because every second he didn't, Josiah's grin was stretching wider.

I shrugged off Amazing Hair Guy and stepped forward again. I didn't care if I got kicked out of the Mice. This had to stop. "Let's step back one sec—"

Before my words could register, Josiah raked the blade across

Blackstone's throat. The pajamas' silk collar immediately began changing from red to black.

"Oh God, *what*?" I heard.

Hatch lunged forward like a bouncer stopping a bar brawl, but this fight was over. Blackstone's face looked like old dough.

"You...killed him," Hatch said.

Josiah was passing the knife frenetically between his hands, right to left, left to right. "Inevitably, there was a first."

Hatch looked between Josiah and the body. "We should have talked about this."

Josiah ignored this, opening his rawboned shoulders to the rest of us.

"Nothing changes until the people at the top are compelled to change," he said. "Until *their* equation changes. And we just started changing it."

CHAPTER SEVENTEEN

People scattered. I felt a strong urge to join them, but at the sight of Hatch hoisting Blackstone's corpse over his shoulder, I stayed. I moved into the room against the wild foot traffic and, not knowing what else to do, supported the executive's limp torso.

"Leave him!" Josiah ordered.

Hatch met my eye. Then he did lower the body to the carpet.

"Yeah," he said. "No point."

The two leaders joined the stomping avalanche out of the study. I took a last look at Blackstone, my insides crunching. *What did we do to this man? To this family?*

Then I thought about my own family and ran too, away, through the study doors, past Blackstone's soccer-ball-chasing daughters. More glass got stuck in my shoes. Noise crisscrossed in my brain—siren *bloops*, yelled instructions, shrieks. I kept my head down and my legs moving.

Outside felt twenty degrees colder than before. People were running all directions, trampling flower beds, tripping over garden hoses.

Where's the Prius? To the left, to the right?

Beyond the Blackstone's tennis court rose a majestic willow tree.

Curtains of leaves whipped my face as I passed underneath. Rumors swirled around me—that somebody had fallen off a balcony and broken his leg, that Blackstone's wife was chasing us, that the cops were out front.

A biker whizzed by, breathing hard and pumping her pedals.

There was obviously no escape plan. There was no plan at all—Josiah had decided to kill Blackstone on the spot.

We were all going to end up in jail.

I took a second to pick the glass out of my shoes. Then I ran. I was aware dimly of crossing a property line, the grass taller or maybe just mowed at a different angle.

Amazing Hair Guy was running next to me. *"Did you hear which rendezvous point?"*

I blinked. Maybe there was a plan. "No. I—tonight's my first night."

"Oh. Cool." He grimaced, seemingly at the stupidity of this comment given our situation. "I'm Garrison."

"Molly." I raised my hand, like a wave.

He ducked his head, diverting mellow hazel eyes. I'd guessed twenty-four earlier, and looking at him up close now, that seemed about right.

A decade younger than me.

"I can't believe that happened," he said. "This is so borked."

I started to nod along, but the lingo stopped me.

"Sorry," he said. "I'm a coder. You probably blog, huh?"

"Right." I squinted along the road for the Prius—small talk could wait. "You said something about rendezvous points?"

"It was supposed to be a gas station or this one IHOP, but that was before we, you know."

My stomach turned at his use of "we."

"Do you have a car?"

"Not here. I caught a ride with a guy." He fluttered his fingers toward the mansion. "Whatever. No, no car."

I described where I'd parked, and together we figured out which direction to move. A piked privacy fence ruled out behind us, but both left and right were clear.

"I vote we get as far away from there"—I gestured to the Blackstone property—"as possible."

Garrison was gathering his hair behind his neck. "For sure."

We took each other's hands and sprinted for the road. A car engine started nearby, then another. Headlights swept across the chimney of the Tudor whose yard we'd been crossing, throwing yellow zigzags all around.

Garrison asked, "What color's your car?"

"Blizzard pearl," I said automatically—that's what the want ad had said.

He quirked his brow only a second before pointing questioningly through a copse of juniper bushes.

"That's it!" I said.

As we darted between a garden shed and the chains of a swing set, I whipped out my phone. I swiped it alive expecting missed texts from Durwood, but there was nothing.

Why? He'd lost audio from my earring, but still—wouldn't he have detected the break-in some other way? Had he been detained by security?

What sort of security could miss the Blind Mice but catch Durwood Oak Jones?

Lights came on inside the Tudor. Across the street too. A dog barked. The neighborhood seemed to be realizing it'd been violated.

Police would be here soon.

Finally, we got to my car. I clicked my key fob and took the wheel. Garrison scampered into the passenger seat, his shoes crunching Target receipts and kids' worksheets.

"My apartment's in Highland Park," Garrison said.

I twisted to check behind me and pulled away from the curb. "Gotcha. If we don't get arrested, I'll walk you to your door."

He smiled and said that sounded like a plan.

Reversing us out of a cul-de-sac, I fought off gruesome, guilty memories and focused on tactics. What had happened to Durwood? Quaid Rafferty might let you down—given enough time, he almost certainly would. But Durwood? Never. Had he peeled off after Josiah?

Or rushed in and tried to revive Blackstone? Why hadn't he come to meet me yet?

I told myself it didn't matter.

Durwood isn't here. It's all you.

An elderly couple had emerged from their house. The woman pointed as I drove past, and her robed husband craned his neck. *Did they get my license plate?* I couldn't worry about it. I gunned it through a stop sign, the Prius leaving electric mode and beginning to guzzle gas.

Moments later, we were zipping underneath the subdivision's wrought-iron gate when trilling sounds reached our ears.

"Is that...a vehicle?" Garrison said.

I slowed down, going right at a fork in the road. The trilling became louder, coming from behind.

"Maybe a vehicle moving fast."

Suddenly, lights shone in both my side mirrors. They weren't blue like police sirens, though—and when I turned around, the car coming at me didn't have dome lights like a cruiser.

It came careening, rocking, using the entire road. The car's grill seemed to be laughing raucously.

I eased us toward the curb. "Let's just give them room."

Garrison and I watched through our headrests as the car barreled on. It bucked through a stop and sped right at the fork—I had a flash memory of Karen's favorite board book, *Sheep in a Jeep*, those flighty sheep always forgetting to steer.

The headlights swelled. The trilling intensified. Twenty feet out, the car went into a power skid that I thought would carry it safely past us.

At the last moment, the front end fishtailed and slammed the side of the Prius.

We spun a quarter turn from the impact. Garrison pitched into the dashboard. I held on to my headrest, but my legs whipped out from underneath and landed in Garrison's lap.

"Are you okay?" he asked, supporting my calves.

"I'm good," I said, untangling us. "We need to keep moving."

Though it'd felt like an iceberg hitting the *Titanic*, the Prius was still running. The other car had spun too, such that its driver's side was aligned with mine. Through panes of spider-cracked glass, I saw who was behind the wheel.

Josiah.

"To the turnpike!" he yelled. "We're golden! Don't sweat the cops, Piper's got the cops."

"O-okay," I said. "But shouldn't we..."

What, exchange insurance information?

Before I could finish the thought, Josiah said, "Just go, *roll!*" and blazed off, one mirror dangling by its wires, knocking against the door like a tin-can wedding streamer.

His car's trilling—which had a hiccup to it now—receded, and for one confused moment, I wondered if I'd dreamed the last thirty seconds.

Then I tried turning to say something to Garrison and my neck seized to stone.

Nope: the wreck had been real. Just like the murder of Ted Blackstone.

I followed Josiah to the turnpike, driving swiftly but obeying traffic laws. Congestion wasn't bad on New Jersey 10. Neither Garrison nor I spoke, deep in our private dreads.

I-95 was within sight, its cloverleaf ramps curling high into the night sky ahead, when the sirens began.

Bloo-bloop, bloo-bloop.

Nausea jolted my midsection. I gagged over the steering column and peeked in the rearview.

Here were the blue lights. Several hundred feet back, but coming.

Garrison sat with wrists pinched together, like he was trying to hide his Mice tattoo. "They told us it was just data, zeroes and ones."

I looked back to the road. "For tonight?"

"For always," he said. "We were just supposed to zap data, start everything back at zero."

Ahead, Josiah whirred through a traffic circle and started up the turnpike ramp. I pegged the accelerator to keep up.

You're officially running from the police.

I was going to jail. Shortly. In my head, the kids were already in foster care. Karen would go to a kindly childless couple who'd buy her princess Barbies and never challenge her. Zach would bounce from one overcrowded group home to the next, learning the worst from each pack of lost boys.

The sirens wailed louder. Garrison looked at me across the dash, and our shared regret was palpable.

Why couldn't I have stuck with First Mutual? Or backed out at the tattoo parlor? Or scrammed at the azalea bushes, or when I saw the portraits of the Blackstone daughters?

This was my mess. It had started with Quaid and Durwood's assignment, but I was the one who'd given MollyWantsChange.org its voice. I'd done more than play along—I'd adopted the Mice's grievances. Otherwise, I never would've pulled it off with *Blogger Royale* or at Nowhere Tattoo.

I whispered a silent prayer that He deliver me to safety, and grant me a chance at redemption.

Then, at the stroke of midnight, all the sirens stopped.

PART TWO

CHAPTER EIGHTEEN

Three Weeks Later

J im Steed insisted on meeting at the American Dynamics factory in Pittsburgh. A big man with a lunchpail jaw, he pumped Quaid's and Durwood's fists, scratched Sue-Ann under the ear, and led them up the rickety catwalk.

"Git 'er done, Tommy!" he called down to a man working the stamper.

Quaid rolled his eyes as Steed yucked it up with his men, asking around whether Roethlisberger would play this week or if the—insert female anatomy here—would sit again with a sore shoulder.

He explained, "Walking the line—it's the only way to get your head around morale. Do it every Thursday. Corporate security wants me to stop. I'm supposed to restrict myself to 'secure sites,' long as the Blind Mice are at large. Screw that."

Quaid rubbed his nose. "You drive five hours both ways to check morale?"

"More like three forty. State police got too much on their plates to mess with speed traps—I floor it on I-76."

Quaid glanced at the copper lines running beside the catwalk, caked with white-green gunk at the joints. The grease and solvent smells were noxious despite a thunderously sucking hood every twenty yards.

"Yeah," Steed continued expansively, "being CEO is no different from commanding a unit. In 'Nam, I always took patrol duty with the men. They see you muddied up, bamboo stalks poking through your socks? It matters."

He looked back to Durwood for affirmation, but the ex-marine had stopped to free Sue-Ann's paw from the grate.

"These fumes are brutal," Quaid said. "Sue's gonna keel over and die if we hang out here much longer. So what's up? What's so important we had to schlep out to the Rust Belt?"

Steed ambled to a stop, draping an arm over the catwalk railing. He filled his cheeks, pausing for drama.

"Gotta terminate your contract," he said.

Quaid squinted. "You're firing us?"

The AmDye CEO set his jaw. "Not seeing the results. It's been two months."

"Maybe *you* need to get away from these fumes. Are you bonkers? We have our man—well, our woman—planted inside their organization."

"Lotta good that does me."

"Half the law enforcement agencies in the country are after the Blind Mice. Nobody's laid a finger on them—and we missed by a fluke. A break or two goes our way, and they're in the slammer."

Quaid didn't need to see his partner to know those steel-colored eyes were boring into his back.

Steed said, "That was three weeks ago. Since then, the pissants have scrambled our supply chain, put porn all over the websites—we're still finding it. And you got nothing."

"It's tough," Quaid said. "They went to ground after Blackstone—we spooked 'em."

"You're saying the scent's gone cold?"

Quaid passed a hand through his wavy hair. "We still have our asset in play. She's in the fold, right there among the Mice leadership. As soon as Josiah surfaces, we take him down."

He was painting a somewhat rosy picture. Molly hadn't seen

anyone in the Mice leadership—not Josiah, not Hatch, not Piper—since the Blackstone mission. Her sole link to the group at this point was Garrison, the wimpy longhair she'd fled with. (Quaid didn't know if he was actually wimpy, but assumed so based on McGill's description.)

In fact, Molly had been making noise about quitting.

"I'm a *single parent*," she kept saying. "If I die, my kids become wards of the state."

"Nobody's dying."

"Ted Blackstone died!"

Quaid had assured her Blackstone was a thrill kill. Josiah had gotten carried away. Never happen again.

Durwood had grunted from the wings.

Yesterday, when a text had arrived from a burner number inviting "Mice of all tenures" to a mission at a Lower Manhattan office park, Molly had balked.

"Garrison says it could be a trap," she said. "There's a rumor they're flushing out traitors."

"Nah," Quaid said. "That punk's too busy coiffing his hair to have the first clue. This is our shot. We've got a good, firm location—Wood and I can set up way in advance. We'll bag 'em."

But Molly had refused to commit. It was too dangerous. She'd lucked out the night of the murder, escaping after the police mysteriously pulled up. She wasn't about to chance it and risk squandering that minor miracle.

Okay, Quaid had said. *So that was it? They could keep their four grand a week? Great.* Durwood kept saying the Vanagon needed repairs, and he personally intended to catch one of these bargain fares the cruise lines were offering to entice travelers during the unrest.

Good luck with that mortgage.

For all that, the best he'd gotten from her was, "I'll think about it."

Now Steed's administrative assistant, a woman with a blond uptwist who traveled everywhere with him, ascended the catwalk to deliver a stack of mail.

"Thank you, Cindy," Steed said.

Leaving, the woman tossed her hair and a wink at Quaid. She and

Quaid had enjoyed a low-simmer flirtation for years, banter over coffee in the break room, handsy farewells at the ends of jobs.

Steed held up an envelope with *Exclusive Offer: 50% off Forceworthy ExecutiveShield!* in red cursive.

"These guys." He shook his head. "Like I'd pay somebody to protect me."

Quaid fished out the pamphlet, whose cover showed a businessman addressing a crowd from a sort of glass-enclosed truck bed. "Does look pretty slick."

"I got no budget for slick, and besides..." Steed leaned close to the guys, scowling. "I hope this Josiah punk comes for me. I honestly do. I'll gut him like a fish."

Again, he looked to Durwood after the macho claim.

Durwood said nothing.

Quaid picked up the previous thread. "I didn't wanna get into this —but you try to fire us, I guess I have to." He filled his lungs, deciding how far to embellish. "Tomorrow afternoon, we have this thing...and we'll probably, oh, eighty percent chance, catch Josiah."

As Durwood ground his teeth audibly, Quaid sketched the broad outlines of the Lower Manhattan mission—leaving out the precise time and location.

"And this happens tomorrow?" Steed said.

Durwood did a farmer's blow off the catwalk.

"Tomorrow," Quaid confirmed.

Steed sighed and launched into a familiar refrain about the various fronts on which American Dynamics was besieged. Regulation. Asian tariffs. A-hole activist investors.

"...and all this instability, capital markets are tighter'n the queen of England's cooch." He shifted his lunchpail jaw. "No idea how I'm gonna pay back that federal bailout money in February."

Quaid's back was getting stiff. "Makes you feel any better, I have contacts in all three branches of government—and nobody expects AmDye to pay back one red cent of that."

"Damn it, I do!" Steed's words boomed throughout the factory. "I make a commitment, I honor it. But I'll never get us back into the black with these hacker kids shooting at us from the reeds."

Quaid allowed his vigor to dissipate. "Tomorrow."

"Tomorrow," Steed repeated.

Both their heads were bobbing.

Quaid said, "Day after today."

As they continued to eye one another manfully, Quaid considered the worst-case scenario. If they crapped out tomorrow and got fired, Third Chance Enterprises would be back on the market—which wouldn't be the worst thing in the world.

Chaos made for fertile ground in the small-force private-arms space. Quaid had been receiving calls lately from various prospective clients. The Brazilian opposition leader, Vitor Gonçalves, wanted help suppressing the ruling party's media machine. Fabienne Rivard, CEO of the French conglomerate Rivard LLC, had promised "extraordinary compensation" for a matter she would only discuss in person.

Neither of these jobs would rise to Durwood's moral standard— Quaid would have to do them as sidehustles.

But sidehustles could be fun.

CHAPTER NINETEEN

Lower Manhattan

The guys drove me as far as Battery Park. From there, I caught a northbound subway and rode two stops to the rendezvous point. Climbing out of the station, I peeked around to see if anyone was paying special attention to me.

The coast seemed clear. A man wearing a suit looked away abruptly when I caught him staring, but he was fortysomething—not a Mouse. A girl wearing sparkle-seamed tights, sixteen or seventeen, followed me for a block on Barclay, but then split off to an Apple store.

As I approached the office park, I undid the top button of a knit sweater. The instructions had been to dress "corporate-ish," which I could manage.

How would the other Mice do? What could Hatch, with his head-to-toe tattoos, do to fit into Lower Manhattan?

Skyscrapers rose in every direction, sheer facades of steel and black glass piercing the cloud cover. Wing tips clipped by. Cart vendors waved tongs and took cash for paper-wrapped souvlaki.

Between buildings, I caught a glance at the Freedom Tower. I thought about 9/11, those nineteen men who'd wanted to make a statement so badly they'd sacrificed their own lives—and thousands of innocent ones too.

What statement does Josiah want to make today?

I descended a half flight of stairs to a recessed plaza. In the windows above, floor after floor of office workers were engaged in their daily routines. Commodities traders. Bonds salesmen. Secretaries. Florists.

I hadn't expected to come today, even though Durwood had promised he could protect me, and Quaid was applying his typical pressure. I was in no mood to listen to Quaid, especially after he'd bailed on me for the mayor's party.

But then the mortgage company raised my rate. *Again.* And Garrison, pinching his mellow eyes over video chat, said the mission sounded more legit now—he was going.

"Fine," I told the guys. "I'll do this for my last four thousand. Then I'm done."

To replace that weekly money, I was thinking of reviving McGill Investigators. I'd focused on domestic cases before, but with the unrest like it was, there should be all kinds of cases now. Yesterday the news had reported locking mailboxes were out of stock across New Jersey.

Now I scanned the recessed plaza for faces I knew. I saw none at first, just masses of humanity streaming in and out of the skyscrapers' revolving doors. Then a few dots began to resolve themselves in the crowd—a shock of purple hair, a young man's lazy gait as he went no place through the plaza.

The Mice were here.

I saw them one after another after another, like the first ant outbreak of spring. My pulse began to pound. There was Piper Jackson wearing a brown delivery uniform, leaning against a pillar and looking at her laptop—which any outsider would assume was a confirmation tablet.

Wasn't it incredibly risky for all of us to be hanging out here? In public, with probably dozens of cameras watching? Surely, the FBI or NYPD was using facial-recognition software—what if they had our faces from Blackstone's security system?

This attack, whatever it was, needed to happen soon.

A hoarse voice behind me said, "You came."

I turned to find Garrison in a shiny dress shirt that bunched around his pecs.

"I said I would," I told him, a slight tease in my voice. "Where are we supposed to go, have you heard?"

He moved close and spoke into my ear, *"Somebody saw a package."*

"Like a...so like a big package?" I said. "Big enough to be..."

I didn't finish. Garrison's face was still.

Now a college girl in a baggy blazer that probably belonged to her mom rushed up to us. "Okay, d'you guys know the plan?"

Garrison started to answer, but I tugged them both out of the plaza, into a travel store.

"We need to blend," I said. "Let's browse. When you work in an office, after lunch, you browse. It's what you do with extra time."

I demonstrated by fingering neck pillows and trying out massage knobs, all the while watching through the window.

The Mice I recognized from the Blackstone mission were milling about, tugging at clothes they weren't used to. Businessmen and - women streamed past from sidewalks or subterranean wells, but fewer with each passing minute. It was nearly one thirty: cart vendors were closing up, scraping griddles and gathering up condiments and napkins.

This nearest one sold brats and hot dogs. I did a double take at the cook's size—he kept ducking to miss the skillets overhead. He wore a hat and sleeves, and his collar fastened at the neck.

His face almost looked—it was hard to tell at this distance—green?

Hatch.

I told Garrison and the college girl to wait and hustled out of the store.

A man in a puffy Yankees coat was gazing at Hatch's menu board. I waited for him to move away—he never ordered—then walked swiftly to the order window.

"Hey, it's me," I whispered.

Hatch kept wiping off the nozzle of a mustard bottle.

I continued, "I think most of us are here. We probably ought to—"

"I'm sold out," he interrupted.

His eyes roamed past me. In his off hand, the hand not wiping nozzles, he held a small silver device.

"People are, uh..." I felt like I should code my words. "*The onions are starting to get soggy,*" I said, bulging my eyes. "We should get them out of sight."

He clenched his teeth, glancing behind him. I thought his thumb clicked the silver device.

Was it a counter? Stopwatch?

"Yeah, I know," he muttered, then gestured for me to clear out.

As I headed back to the travel store, I wondered why Hatch had disguised himself as a sausage vendor. Why risk interacting with all those customers? The cart was large—maybe he had something inside, something he was smuggling. The package Garrison mentioned?

My phone chimed. It was a text from Durwood.

any sign of Wack?

"Wack" was the guys' code name for Josiah.

I tapped back, *None.*

been told the target?

Nothing yet.

correspond when you have it.

Each of Durwood's responses came instantaneously. It was hard to imagine his calloused, work-worn fingers navigating a phone as deftly as a teenager's, but they did.

I sent, *Will do.*

He responded, *what was in his hand? metal or plastic?*

I swiveled my head around the plaza and didn't see the Vanagon. How had Durwood seen into Hatch's cart? Had he placed cameras around the plaza ahead of time?

I wrote, *Metal I think.*

Durwood didn't answer.

In the travel store, Garrison was surrounded by a trio of female Mice now—he glanced at me but couldn't seem to get away. I watched the plaza from the window.

Piper Jackson was still hunched intently over her laptop, though she was leaning against a different pillar.

A security guard seemed interested. He was drifting her way, fingers pressed to an earpiece.

Were his lips moving?

What would happen if he caught her? The guys' contract with American Dynamics, as I understood it, called for Josiah's capture. What if Piper gave Josiah up under interrogation? If the police tracked down Josiah, was the job over? Was I off the hook?

What if Piper gave us all up?

Garrison was at my shoulder. "Maybe we should go find an Algernon."

Algernons, I'd learned, were a kind of upper tier of Mice. (Garrison had joked it was like high school all over again, the popular kids—and I'd joked back that there was *no way* he wasn't popular in high school.)

"I just talked to Hatch," I said.

"And?"

I shook my head. "He sent me away. It seemed like he was waiting for something."

Then I nodded to the plaza, positioning him with my hand on his back, and showed him Piper. The security guard was almost on top of her.

I urged up on my tiptoes, stomach clenched. Garrison squeezed my hand as we watched. Feeling the heat of his palm, it occurred to me that we'd gotten pretty comfortable with physical contact—for people who'd known each other three weeks.

I told myself it was just the situations we'd found ourselves in—extreme, dangerous. That was all.

The security guard said something to Piper. She looked up sharply and, seeming wary at the uniform, swiped her tablet. She showed him something on the screen.

The guard squinted. I was sure he'd reach for his handcuffs, but instead, his eyes rose and he pointed to one of the skyscrapers at the opposite end of the plaza.

Then the guard left.

Garrison said, "She faked him out!"

I found myself smiling with relief too—even though Piper's capture might've sent me home, back to my children.

Meanwhile, Hatch had finished closing up shop. He cinched a tarp snugly over his cart and crossed the plaza to join Piper. He handed her a wrapped hot dog. She gave him cash.

The mismatched pair—Hatch towered over the hacker—spoke for a minute or two with closed postures. Hatch kept peeking back at the cart.

Why?

What was inside?

A sourness was spreading through my body. The movement started by the Blind Mice had gotten darker since the murder of Ted Blackstone. While some supporters had been repulsed, others were emerging—a more vicious element.

Copycats had broken into the home of a Big Tech CEO in Silicon Valley and executed him with a machete. Quaid's friend Sergio had been tackled brazenly on the steps of city hall.

The violence kept escalating.

Considering all this, and contemplating what Hatch was hiding in his cart, my heart felt sick.

Then things got much, much worse.

I glanced past the cart and saw, striding through the plaza in a suit that almost—*almost*—prevented me from recognizing him, Zach.

CHAPTER TWENTY

Durwood monitored the action from the Vanagon cabin. They were parked halfway down a ramp, in the loading dock of a ninety-story building. Two blocks from the plaza.

"Moll's spooked," he reported.

Quaid was sitting on the titanium tube of a Stinger missile, ready in the NYPD blues they'd chosen for a disguise.

"What happened?" he asked. "She was doing fine."

Durwood said he didn't know. Using a joystick control, he panned off Molly and across the plaza. Saw taxis. Steam curling up from vents. All four skyscrapers intact—no fires or evacuations or suspicious activity. Yet.

He spread out a plat map of the plaza and read through the tenants. Citibank was the most prominent. There was a satellite office of Daimler-Benz. One outfit called InfoBlast. Another called eDeed.

None of these companies were among the Despicable Dozen. None, so far as they knew, had wronged Josiah or Josiah's family.

Quaid was fussing with the collar of his uniform. "What's our giant Libertarian friend up to? Did he go back to the sausage cart?"

Durwood used the stick to shift the camera. "Negative. Cart's all by itself."

Sue-Ann, sleeping against his boot, kicked out her foreleg.

Quaid suggested they text Molly again. Durwood took out his phone and tapped out, *problem?*

As he sent, he zoomed tight on her face. Molly kept staring out into the plaza. Either she hadn't heard the chimes or she was ignoring them.

Quaid said, "Maybe they gave her the target. Maybe it's bad."

Durwood considered this. Last night, he'd infiltrated two of the skyscrapers and wired the fire alarms. One push of a button now would set them all blaring.

Everybody'd run. Whatever the Mice had up their sleeves, it'd be off.

Durwood cycled through security feeds from each skyscraper lobby. Leaning over his blue jeans, he scanned for anomalies. A briefcase that looked wrong. Air that had an off color. A visitor smiling too wide at reception.

He saw nothing.

Still, Durwood's head hurt. *I'm missing something.*

Not just now, today. He had a keen sense they were blind to a large piece of the puzzle. More than one piece. Maybe half the board.

The Mice should not be succeeding, given their training (none) and experience (limited). The escape after Blackstone's murder—police sirens cutting out at midnight—was strange, but even the hacks didn't make sense.

Folks had been trying to penetrate public infrastructure for years. Anonymous. Cult of the Dead Cow. State-funded hackers from Iran or North Korea.

Some had squirmed in and caused a blip. Nobody'd been as consistent and elusive as the Mice.

It didn't figure. A squirrel might clean out your bird feeder. But when he gets into your refrigerator for cold cuts, it's time to wonder.

His next camera sweep, Durwood saw what had spooked Molly. The son. Wearing a suit and flicking hair out of his eyes. He walked up to Hatch and Piper Jackson and seemed to ask a question. The big'un sent him away to a group of Mice huddled at the east end of the plaza.

When Durwood panned back to where Molly had been, in the travel store, there was nothing.

She'd gone.

A moment later, Durwood's phone rang.

"Do it—trip the fire alarms!" Molly said. "Zach's here, I dunno how he's here but he is, we have to stop this."

"I see," Durwood said. "Relax, we have eyes on him."

"How did he get here? How did he get invited? Has he already done *missions* with them?"

Durwood told her no, this had the look of first contact.

"We'll extract him," he said. "Best thing is for you to keep your cover. Just sit tight, and—"

"Sit tight? No, I won't *sit tight*. My son is out there trying to join up with terrorists!"

Durwood held the phone back from his ear. He understood Molly's concern. He could still remember the call from Miramar informing him his son Joel had died at TOPGUN.

It was a vice admiral that called, three star. He started going into how Joel died—last day of the competition, dipping below the hard deck to finish a kill.

Durwood barely heard. His son was gone. His son he'd taught to throw a curveball, and read to when the fish weren't biting.

When he didn't answer at once, Molly said, "If you won't trip the alarms, I will. I'll run into one of the buildings and yank—"

"Hold up now. We have—"

"Zach can't be a part of this." Her voice over the line was a brick wall. "Nothing else matters."

Quaid motioned to the phone. "Give it here. This situation exceeds your powers of persuasion."

Durwood didn't argue.

Quaid put on a hundred-watt grin as he accepted the phone. He had a theory that positivity could influence reality, could bump quarter-truths up to a half, or halves up to near facts. "If you believe it," he liked to say, "they'll believe it too."

"McGill," he said now. "I know it looks bad. I know you're worried. But we're going to take this lemon and make lemonade."

CHAPTER TWENTY-ONE

H unched in the travel store bathroom, I listened to Quaid's plan. It was daring and brilliantly simple. It required finesse on my part, quick reactions from the guys, and a little luck from the universe. It had two parts—if both succeeded, everybody got their problem solved in a single stroke.

And if not?

Quaid wheezed over the line. "Durwood has guns."

I knew I had to try. Sitting here on the cover of a toilet seat, getting knocked at by some pushy man ("Is someone *still* in there?") wouldn't save my son.

I smoothed my slacks, undid the bathroom dead bolt, and walked out. Mr. Pushy had had his knuckles ready, about to knock again.

"All yours," I said. "Hope you managed to hold it."

Garrison, trailed by his girl posse, had moved to the store's Sharper Image section. I avoided them on my way back to the front window.

Outside, Piper Jackson was working on her laptop again. She looked even more intense now—even thirty yards away, I could see tendons in her forearm as she vigorously swiped and tapped.

Beyond her, by the east skyscraper, Zach was shuffling in place with a group of Mice.

I left the store and started toward Piper, choosing my route such that Zach couldn't see me. I stopped a few feet away from the hacker and didn't directly face her.

"I need a favor," I said.

Piper kept swiping and tapping. Without looking at me, she muttered, "Bad time for favors."

"I know, but this is about my family." I gulped, remembering the advice Quaid had just given me. *Focus on relationships. Let her feel you caring.* "It's my little brother. He's here."

Piper's finger froze in the middle of a keystroke.

I said, "I just saw him, he's behind me—over by that black building."

The hacker's eyes twitched that direction. "Which one."

"He's wearing a suit. Bangs on the long side?"

Piper kept working on her laptop, screwing up her eyes and mouth. I wished I could see the screen, what she was up to. The guys thought Citibank might be the target, some massive balance wipeout.

I'd almost decided Piper had forgotten about me when she said, "Cool for you to be in the Blind Mice, but not him?"

For one fierce moment, her eyes flicked to me, then away.

"He's fourteen. And I'm..." I took a moment remembering Molly Wixom's age. "Twenty-three. I understand the risks. I made an informed judgment that joining the Mice was worth it."

Piper said, "And is it?"

Her flat tone made me wonder if she'd been asking herself the same question.

"I think so," I said. "It feels like change is coming."

Piper blew out a sideways breath. "Got that right."

As I waited to see what she'd do about Zach, I thought about Piper's own brother. Marcus Jackson, according to the internet, had been convicted of industrial fraud while working for Harvest Earth. She'd testified that the plant manager had ordered her to delete a file that would've exonerated him—but the jury hadn't cared.

Now I said, "Could you just, maybe, run my brother off? Tell him there was a mistake processing his application?"

"We don't do applications."

"Right. But just...something. Do something to chase him off. So he'll go home."

Piper considered this, her mouth firm. "He wanted big numbers today. *More soldiers.* Already got too many."

I assumed "he" meant Josiah.

Even though she seemed to be talking to herself, I said, "My brother's no soldier. He's just a kid."

Piper rubbed her skull at the base of her cornrows.

Then she marched across the plaza to Zach.

With a mixture of relief and sympathy, I watched Piper single my son out of the group, say a few words to him, and point to the street.

Zach left right away.

Whether he'd recognized the famous hacker, or been given a reason for his dismissal, I had no idea. He slinked off down the sidewalk, chin bumping his chest.

I was so used to battling Zach, to his being this loud, sarcastic obstacle. Seeing him among the Mice—looking small and so, *so* young —reminded me how quickly his world was growing.

Girls were becoming girlfriends. College would be on the horizon soon. His friends were getting into drugs and petty crime, against this new societal backdrop where drugs and petty crime didn't seem like much.

Here and now, I resolved to keep this bigger picture in mind. I wasn't going to let Zach shout at Karen or me (Granny he never dared speak disrespectfully to), but I would keep fighting to engage him. I would correct his mistakes with compassion.

Piper was back at her pillar.

"Done," she said.

I nodded. "Thank you."

Her eyes looked softer than before—and I realized the moment had come for part two of Quaid's plan.

Here goes nothing.

"Uh, I'm so glad he's safe," I said with a breathy flutter. "I feel like I owe you—is there anything I can do to help?"

A hard line appeared in Piper's forehead. My own words, and that breathy flutter, had sounded so fake coming out. Part of me wanted to run back to the travel-store bathroom.

"Maybe," she said. "I was gonna use Amber...looks like she raided her mom's closet."

She glanced at a girl in a pantsuit that didn't square with orange-tinted hair.

I stood tall before her, feeling good about my knit sweater and tailored slacks.

Piper chewed her lip and said, "Yeah. Yeah, you'd be better."

By "better," of course she meant older. But I'd take it.

"Better for what?" I asked.

"For a nonthreatening bureaucrat."

"I can do nonthreatening," I said, hoping she'd elaborate.

She didn't.

Hatch returned in another minute. He and Piper, after a quick conference, summoned the various pockets of Mice to a subterranean tunnel connecting two of the skyscrapers. The passageway was well hidden, dank and concrete.

Garrison rushed up to me. *"Hey, I was looking for y—"*

He broke off when he saw Piper with me.

Hatch was circulating with an oversized ziplock bag, punching out its corners.

"Phones," he said.

One by one, the Mice dropped their cell phones into the bag.

My heart roared in my chest. *Were they going to check everybody's messages?* Even if not, the bag was clear—Durwood's texts would flash on my screen for anyone to see.

I whipped out my phone and held down the side power button.

Come on, come on, shut down.

Hatch was two Mice away. The dialogue box asking if I was sure I wanted to shut down appeared. I tapped *Yes*, but nothing happened. I ground my finger into the screen. The screen turned off, then came back the same.

Turn off already!

Hatch reached me just as the message, *Your phone will now shut down*, finally appeared.

I explained, "I just thought—you know, I didn't want my notifications to annoy."

"Unnecessary," Hatch said. "The bag's RF-blocking. Nothing goes through. No tweets, emails. Nada."

As I dropped my phone in, and Piper and Hatch did the same, I wondered why the Mice were taking this step. Were they still worried about traitors? What about this RF-blocking; did they think somebody's phone was compromised?

Hatch slung the bag over his shoulder and said, "Follow me, gang. Time to make the mayhem."

As everyone fell in behind the tattooed leader, Piper caught my elbow.

"Hang back," she said. "We gotta work on our disguises."

As Garrison and the others clomped off down the tunnel, I touched my sweater. "I thought I was disguised."

Piper, who'd traded her delivery uniform for slacks and pants, pulled two pairs of glasses from her bag.

"Not enough. The lobby we're hitting has facial recognition. These'll throw off the 3D mapping. Slow it down at least."

She slipped on a chunky-framed pair and handed me one with silver rims.

As I put the glasses on, Hatch's group—along with my phone full of Durwood texts—was pulling away down the tunnel.

"Aren't we going with them?" I asked.

Piper shook her head. "They're going to tag a subway station— Hatch brought spray paint." Was that all he had in the sausage cart? "One of those newbs could be a plant, trying to feed our position to somebody outside."

I tried focusing on my fake glasses, adjusting them on my ears. "So what...er, I guess they'd get kicked out, then?"

Piper smirked. "I guess."

From her pocket, she removed a cellophane sheet of browns nubs. They reminded me of those candy buttons I'd eaten off paper growing up. She peeled one off and stuck it high on her cheek.

"Take two," she said, passing me the sheet. "You got freckles— that's good. But the moles should mess with it even more."

Tentatively, I unstuck a pair of squishy fake moles. I placed one on my cheek like Piper's and the other at the left corner of my mouth.

Next, Piper gave me a short stack of business cards. "In case they ask for proof."

The top card read, OFFICER OF THE INFORMATION SECURITY TASK FORCE, NEW YORK STATE, above an Albany address.

The embossed letters seemed to dance on their creamy cardstock.

We're impersonating government officials? I went back and forth between figuring what this might mean and worrying about Hatch and his bag of cell phones.

Was he going to inspect all the phones while the others were busy tagging the subway station, try to flush out the traitor? What if he checked the messages?

I couldn't let him check mine.

I asked Piper, "Shouldn't we have phones?"

She looked up from her tablet.

"For the disguises," I said. "If we have cards, and we're bureaucrats —wouldn't we have phones too?"

She glanced back the way Hatch and the others had gone, looking conflicted.

"I'll go," I offered. "I can grab them. Yours had the red case, right?"

She didn't say yes, but she didn't say no—so I took out jogging through the tunnel, aboveground now. I caught up with Hatch two blocks from the plaza and explained Piper and I needed our phones back. "For the disguises, you know?"

His expression stayed stern for a second, but he did open his bag for me.

I stopped myself from gushing, Thank you, thank you, thank you!, fishing around until I found our phones. Then I rushed back underground and through the tunnel.

Piper was off her tablet, holding it overhand, waiting. I gave her her phone, and she gave me a business card with something scribbled on the back.

"My number," she said, "in case we get split up. Which we might." She nodded to the phones. "That was smart."

We checked each other's appearance—Piper moved my moles

farther apart—then emerged from the tunnel, heading for the south skyscraper. Outside the revolving doors, I glanced up. A window washer's cart hugged the building's upper third, impossibly high, its cables disappearing into cloud.

Piper saw me looking.

"All that glass," she said. "All that shiny steel."

"Yeah." I felt like I should say more. "All those executives looking out their corner offices."

Piper set her jaw and led the way inside.

As I followed, I was thinking not about executives but about administrative assistants, and HR reps, all the businesses here that weren't in "greedy" industries.

The lobby was a cathedral of marble and brass. A chandelier of gleaming crystal rectangles spiraled down from the ceiling. Receptionists with Nordic features manned a luxurious desk.

Piper approached the one below a *Visitors* sign.

A statuesque blond receptionist nodded to Piper's tablet. "All devices must go through screening."

"Naturally," Piper said.

"Any other electronics on your person?"

We both took out our phones and placed them in a tray. Piper also reached inside her uniform and pulled out a silver oval-shaped object. For just an instant, she seemed reluctant handing it over.

Was she worried? Worried it would be tested for residue, something like that?

Regaining her cool, Piper pulled the oval apart to show a USB plug.

"Thumb drive," she said in a bored tone.

The receptionist took the (supposed) thumb drive, Piper's tablet, and both our phones to a screening table. A uniformed woman wearing baggies over her shoes swabbed a cloth over all sides of the items and placed the cloth in a machine.

She pressed a button. A red plane of light blipped left to right over the cloth, then back right to left.

I don't think I was breathing. If Piper and I were caught with explosives in the lobby of a skyscraper...

The machine made a faint *beep-bloo-beep*.

Five seconds later, an indicator turned green.

The receptionist returned our items. "Now who are you here for?"

Piper tucked the silver oval securely back into her pocket. "eDeed Global Solutions."

The receptionist tapped his keyboard and read from the screen. "eDeed Global Solutions, eighty-eighth floor. Take elevator C in the middle."

We boarded a packed elevator car, riding up with several office workers and one food delivery driver. Drawing on my temp experience, I kept my eyes on the infotainment screen above, but Piper was shuffling uneasily in place. It reminded me just how young she was—and how reckless it was, putting my fate in her hands.

We disembarked at eighty-eight. eDeed occupied the entire floor. The woman working the switchboard held up one finger for us to wait.

Again, Piper didn't know what to do with herself—pacing, her face tense.

I forced a grin and asked, "Did you catch *The Bachelor* last night?"

Piper looked at me like I'd grown a third eyeball.

"It's down to Tara and Stephanie," I said. "I'm so glad he didn't give Bree a rose."

Again, Piper didn't answer, but the switchboard operator overheard and gave me a long, knowing nod. When she finished her call, she turned to us with a sweet smile.

"Thank you for your patience, ladies," she said. "How can I help you today?"

Piper cleared her throat. "We're here for James Keiter."

"You have an appointment?"

"Yes. Should be in his calendar."

"One moment please."

As the woman raised her headset and tapped a four-digit extension, I shimmied closer to Piper.

"*Do* we have an appointment?" I whispered.

She touched her tablet. "What do you think I've been doing?"

I stood tall, hands joined behind my back. A slogan on the wall read, *Ditch the survey pins and crumpled maps. Let eDeed revolutionize your records,* alongside testimonials from the mayors of Trenton and New Brunswick.

Now the switchboard operator replaced her headset and announced, "Mr. Keiter is ready for you."

She pointed the way to the man's office. I kept my eyes forward, trying not to see all the regular office workers here—the mother and fathers, the uncles, the grandmothers.

What are we about to do to this company? To these people?

I wished the guys would swoop in to stop it, but I knew they wouldn't. Not until Josiah showed himself.

According to James Keiter's nameplate, he was vice president of information technology. He greeted us with a quizzical look. "Now you two're from some information security task force?"

"Correct," Piper said. "State of New York requires us to run some diagnostics on your systems."

Keiter, a nervy man with cauliflower-shaped ears, cocked his brow at Piper. "You work for New York State?"

"Occasionally, they do hire black people."

Keiter stuttered, "N-no, I'm sorry, of course they do. I didn't mean..."

What he meant, I realized, was that Piper looked awfully young to be conducting state business.

I jumped in: "I've managed Ms. Robinson"—the name on Piper's card—"for two years, and I can assure you she is more than qualified."

Piper glanced back sharply. If she was upset about me pretending to be her boss, it passed when James Keiter insisted she use his workstation to run the diagnostics, typing in his password, pulling out his chair for her.

Piper plugged her silver device into the man's computer.

As it began its work, she said, "Phase two is a visual inspection of your servers. Be sure they're secure. Perhaps you can show my supervisor, Mrs. Horace"—the name on my card—"the server room while I do the scan."

Keiter hesitated. "I—I'd like to be around in case any problems arise."

Piper didn't seem to hear, hunched over the mouse. *Is her device not working?*

I said, "Oh, the scan's a cinch. The visual inspection's more exciting —my part." I smiled. "Trust me."

The man's eyes moved down my sweater.

"I can do that," he said. "I'll show you the servers."

We left to the hall, Piper still zoned in on the screen.

I could hardly believe what I'd just done, vaguely flirting with this older (and married—he wore a ring) man to pave the way for the Mice's sabotage. James Keiter was chatty now, talking about how cold the server room could be, describing eDeed's rapid growth as he got doors for me.

I held up my end of the conversation with fake questions. *How many employees had access? What were the procedures for locking up after hours?*

Keiter used his fingerprint and a seven-digit pass code to enter the service room. "Did you need to have a look at the SSL certificates?"

I struck a thoughtful pose. "Sure. I always like to be sure the paperwork's in order."

He looked at me funny. "SSL certificates are digital."

It took my brain's hamster wheel a few seconds.

"Digital, right." I smacked my head with an open palm. "I misheard—yes, of course the SSLs would be digital."

I followed along with his guided tour, asking occasional questions but mostly thinking about what Piper was doing in Keiter's office.

Was she zapping all this property boundary data? Surely, eDeed had backups.

Keiter asked, "How long do your colleague's diagnostics usually take?"

We were in a dim part of the windowless room. He leaned his elbow casually into a rack of blipping machines.

"It varies," I said. "Maybe fifteen, twenty minutes."

Keiter nodded slowly. Suspiciously?

Suggestively?

He asked, "Are you inspecting other companies in the area today?"

"I believe so. Piper—er, that is, my colleague Ms. Robinson has the full list."

"Probably doing Tyrell—they do a lot of state work."

"Yes," I said. "I think Tyrell is on our list."

"Their CIO and I graduated Carnegie together ninety-four. Leslie's good. They should be all buttoned up."

"I look forward to talking to her."

"Him. Leslie is a man."

I blushed hard—even though there was no earthly reason I would know the Tyrell CIO's gender.

"I think you've satisfied my concerns," I said, deciding to stop this inspection before any more gaps in my knowledge emerged. "Shall we head back, see the results of the scan?"

With a trace of letdown, Keiter said he supposed we should. We walked back to his office.

Piper was just unplugging her silver device.

"Just finished up," she said.

Keiter hitched both thumbs into his waist. "How'd we do?"

"Perfect score," Piper said with a crooked smile. "No malicious code, no vulnerable ports. New York State's happy."

And then, with surprising abruptness, we left. Past the switchboard operator, down the high-speed elevator, around the Nordic receptionists. Piper kept her gaze straight ahead and so did I. My spine was a cold, stiff rod.

Did the mission succeed?

What did Piper think of my performance? Was it possible they'd make me Algernon?

There was no sign of the other Mice in the plaza. Piper walked without pause past Hatch's closed-up cart, past the travel store, and entered the stream of sidewalk traffic heading north. I felt a blister on my heel.

After three blocks, Piper zipped into an alley behind a drugstore. I recognized her bike leaning against a dumpster.

She said, "You did good."

I was breathing hard. "Thanks."

She swept her kickstand up and made sure of her tablet in her bag.

As she leaned into one pedal to go, I said, "Did it work? Your thingy?"

Piper leaned into her handlebars, staring down at her front wheel—or at the ground. Or at nothing. Her eyes were tired.

"Yeah," she said. "It worked."

CHAPTER TWENTY-TWO

The guys caught up with me shortly after Piper left—they'd been holding their position, waiting for Josiah. They wanted to do an immediate postmortem, but I said no. I was riding a train back to New Jersey: back to my children.

At home, it took every iota of restraint not to march straight upstairs and confront Zach. There was no way to explain what I had witnessed—and, more importantly, blowing up at him would only close him off.

I started baked potatoes in the microwave and heated a skillet for pork chops.

Karen was busy in the living room grouping her dolls according to their interests. Zach breezed downstairs and plucked an arc of bell pepper off my cutting board.

"How'd your day go?" I asked. "Big happenings in the world of Zach McGill?"

He rolled his eyes as expected. "Same boring stuff."

"Did you have that quiz in European history?"

He shook his head. "Ms. Jebson had a sub. Quiz tomorrow."

European history was seventh hour, the exact time he was in Lower

Manhattan. But it was possible he'd texted his friends and this was true.

I asked, "Are your friends planning to go to the carnival Friday night?"

He popped another bell pepper into his mouth. "Carnival's canceled."

"Why? I was going to make my German chocolate cupcakes for the cakewalk."

Zach rubbed his stomach rapturously. "Oh, do make those. But no carnival. Principal said the school doesn't have money for extra security. They can't 'guarantee our safety.'" He made exaggerated air quotes.

Granny's slippers came sliding into the kitchen now.

"Guarantee *whose* safety?" She took her customary spot at the head of the table. "It's awful out there. News is saying New York can't tell anybody where their property line is."

I stopped in the middle of making carrot matchsticks. "Property lines?"

"Aw, it's a mess!" Granny said. "Hannity's right—the liberals wanted to put everything on computers, now look what we got..."

I let her burn off her gas without comment—the best way to handle it—but my head was spinning.

eDeed *didn't* have backups? How was that possible?

I noticed Zach, who was sneaking sour cream from the tub, smiling to himself.

I began, "It really is a mess. Without property lines...and that school carnival—you know, people look forward to that. Students, parents. It's a shame."

Ostensibly, I was talking to the whole room, but my eyes were fixed on Zach. When he looked up from the sour cream, our eyes met through a tuft of his bangs—and his didn't blink.

I guess I'd have to adjust to the fact that from now on, I would never—no matter how extensive my psychology training—know with full confidence what my son was thinking.

I hadn't been hard enough on Zach. I'd been too guilty—that his father wasn't around, that our home was as far from Norman Rockwell as it got. I could still remember picking him up from the third grade after a fight. I'd showed up livid, but after Miss Hansen took me aside and explained the other boy had been teasing Zach about his father, asking why he never helped coach or watched any of the games, I'd lost my resolve.

I told Zach it was never okay to hit another human being. But the tears crumpling my eyes sapped my words of their force.

The rest of our evening was pleasant. The broadband was out again so nobody could watch TV. Granny threw a fit, but Karen happily marched her dolls through Gym, Library, Spanish, and "Lockdown"—which entailed cramming all their plastic forms in Tupperware, wrapping the Tupperwares in towels, and stashing them in a deep, dark corner of her room.

I loved that Karen could entertain herself, but I worried sometimes she was withdrawing from reality *too* much. Could all this playacting be a reaction to her uncertain world?

You couldn't blame her if it was.

Eventually, Karen drew us all into her game. Granny reprised her frequent role as the doll's garrulous school district superintendent. I was a carpet salesperson. (Don't ask.) Zach—after much prodding from me—stood in for a fifth grader trying to foil the villains' plot, which involved both booby-trapping electronic pencil sharpeners in the teachers' lounge and slipping ghost peppers into the sloppy joe sauce.

He actually got into it. By the end, his evil cackle had Karen rolling around on the ground in hysterics.

After the kids' bedtime, I texted the guys an all clear. The Vanagon rolled up ten minutes later.

Quaid was bursting with questions. *How and when had they zapped the eDeed data? Was Josiah involved?* Durwood wanted to know how we'd beaten eDeed's security measures.

When I explained about the silver device, Quaid asked, "Where'd it come from? Did the Jackson girl make it?"

"I assume," I said. "She knew just how to use it."

"What exactly did it do? It must've done more than erase data—because they would've had backups."

"I don't know," I said.

"Does it—is it some virus that stays in their systems?"

"I don't know."

"Is there a mechanism to reverse it? Some antidote where they hold the data hostage until certain conditions are met?"

I turned my palms up, rather than repeat myself again.

Durwood's expression had grown dark. "Let's bring Jackson in. Try to turn her."

"Right," Quaid said. "We have McGill schedule a meeting"—I'd told them about getting her number—"and then we nab her. She gets her pick: jail or giving up Josiah."

Durwood nodded.

"Excuse me," I said. "But Piper Jackson is not going to give up Josiah."

Quaid asked how I knew that.

"Because she isn't motivated by self-preservation," I said. "And after what happened to her brother, betrayal is her one unpardonable sin."

Quaid pulled a flask from his sport coat, took a pull. "Look, we aren't sitting on good cards. I told Jim Steed tonight was it—we'd deliver."

"Why'd you tell him that?"

"Because he wanted to fire us!" Quaid took another, longer pull. "We have to start making our own luck."

I folded my arms. "If you want Piper, you're going to have to get her without me."

Quaid picked one loafer up and set it across his knee. He and Durwood shared a look.

"Moll," the ex-marine said. "Piper Jackson is a terrorist."

I didn't like being under the glare of Durwood's steel-gray eyes, but I was not going to bend. "She kept Zach out of the Blind Mice for me."

Quaid said, "I don't see how that's relevant to the AmDye job."

"It's relevant to me," I said.

Quaid took a third drink from his flask.

"You've got that big heart, McGill," he said, "and it pains me to say this, but it makes you blind. This thumb drive, whatever it is? If it's capable of wiping out data like how it did today, the situation could go downhill in a hurry."

I started to answer, but Quaid kept going. "If you wanna play it soft and lose this chance because you think you're friends with Piper Jackson, that's your choice. But know this: The dominoes that fall afterward? They're on you. All the lives. All the destruction. When Zach's running drugs on the street? When Karen gets mowed down by stray machine-gun fire, playing with dolls? Remember this, the chance you had to stop it."

Durwood took his partner's upper arm. "Let's get some air, step outsi—"

"I don't need air." Quaid jerked away, eyes boring into me. "I need somebody with guts."

I stared right back. In different parts of my head, I wanted to punch Quaid, to cry, to run upstairs and be near my children—and get away from these comic book superheroes.

All along, it'd been my life on the line. Me writing the blog posts. Me facing scorn on *Blogger Royale*. Me enduring Hatch's scrutiny and needle at the Nowhere Tattoo Parlor. I'd risked arrest at Ted Blackstone's mansion, and again today at eDeed.

Maybe my resume didn't match Quaid's or Durwood's. Maybe I did care too much about people and let that cloud my judgment.

But so what? Durwood's worldview was harsh, black and white. Quaid saw whatever shades of gray he needed to suit his agenda. My way was different—and I liked it different.

I crossed the living room to the screen door. The corners of my eyes were wet, but I didn't wipe.

"It's time for you to go," I said. "Please."

CHAPTER TWENTY-THREE

Quaid harassed Durwood into stopping by the shishi sandwich place on the way back to the hotel. He got a number seven, duck confit with wasabi mayo. Durwood got nothing. He'd eaten almonds and a hard-boiled egg earlier.

Back in the Vanagon, Sue-Ann perked up at the scent of Quaid's sandwich.

Quaid felt his partner's hard gaze across the center console.

"If you're worrying about Molly," he said, "don't. She'll come around."

Durwood breathed through his nose.

Quaid continued, "And if you're mad at me, tough. I know people. I don't tell you how to clean a gun or fire missiles."

The hotel was another ten minutes from the sandwich shop. Quaid chewed and thought, thought and chewed. When a shred of Napa cabbage dropped, he nudged it back to Sue-Ann with a tasseled loafer. Durwood gripped the wheel tight.

Whatever Piper Jackson had on that doohickey of hers, Quaid believed, was the key. It raised the stakes, elevating the Blind Mice from the realm of pranksters. Quaid felt both frightened and exhilarated by the development. Piper might be more important than Josiah, even—which was why it was imperative they bring her in.

Durwood parked in a shadowy corner of the hotel lot. He took a few minutes activating countermeasures. Especially in these times, you couldn't leave an arsenal like his unsecured.

He turned knobs and flipped switches with quick, firm fingers, anger pouring off him like steam.

Finally, he helped Sue-Ann down and they walked to the rooms.

At the door to his, Quaid said, "You think I was harsh with McGill."

Durwood's lips pinched.

"If you keep saying nothing," Quaid said, "I'm going to assume we're fine."

Durwood's hat sat askew. His leathery face reddened—likely, he was getting another one of his headaches.

"Alright, then." Quaid, holding the crusts of his sandwich, pushed through his door and into his room.

The door didn't close.

"We're not fine," Durwood said. His boot was planted inside the jamb. "Nowhere near."

At his side, Sue-Ann mewed.

Quaid said, "You don't think that device Jackson used is dangerous?"

"I do."

"You disagree we should take her in? You see a different play?"

Durwood shook his head.

Quaid asked, "Then what the hell's the problem?"

"The *problem*"—he gnashed the word—"is it's not right, forcing people into what they're not capable of. Moll won't betray Jackson. We'll find another way."

"She's capable. She's just reluctant," Quaid said. "We're the pros— it's our job to bring her along, find the correct motivation."

"Like the safety of her family."

"Sometimes people need rattling. They need their deepest, darkest insecurities dredged up and held against their noses. As of this afternoon, the state of New York *has no official record of who owns what.* This is breakdown-of-basic-society level stuff."

Durwood said, "Moll's a civilian. The fate of society isn't hers to worry over."

"I'm civilian!" Quaid thumped his chest grandly. "So are you—the marines kicked you out years go."

Durwood dropped his eyes.

Quaid continued, "You know your problem? You think you're in some dime-store Western. Molly's no damsel in distress. She's tough. She's proved herself."

"She's been rearing children half her life."

"So?"

"So have some honor."

They'd drifted into the room. Now Quaid took the first thing he saw from the minibar and downed it.

"With respect," he said once the burn subsided in his throat, "you know nothing about women. They're done with honor. They've been done with it for a while."

"That right?"

"It is right. Women don't need Bubble Wrap. They don't break when handled—and I've had my hands on enough to know."

Durwood gave an irked chuckle. "Hog rolls around all day in mud, don't make him a landscaper."

This nugget of hillbilly wisdom escaped Quaid completely. He stood dumbstruck for a moment. Then he noticed Sue-Ann licking her chops.

"All yours, Sue," he said, tossing his crusts to the carpet.

The dog flinched half out of her fur going after the scraps.

"*Leave it,*" Durwood snapped.

But the command was too late. Sue-Ann's jaws were already working. Her legs spasmed at Durwood's words—particularly the bad left side—and she looked up shamefaced. She kept chewing, though.

Durwood turned to Quaid. "Guess you're not happy till you ruin everything."

"Nothing's ruined," Quaid said. "How many years does that dog have left? The poor animal can't enjoy a few crumbs that smell of duck confit?"

"She shouldn't have scraps from the table."

"Why? Look at those nostrils go. She'd be smiling ear to ear if you'd just back off the guilt trip."

"A dog finds true happiness by pleasing its master."

"Who do you suppose decided that?" Quaid said. "The masters, I'll bet. If dogs could talk, I'll bet they'd say, 'We're tired of sitting up and fetching slippers for you jerks. Give us our duck confit."

Durwood removed his hat and passed a hand back through the part of his hair.

"Too many words," he said.

Quaid was depleting the minibar at a brisk pace. "We Homo sapiens use words to communicate. You should try it."

Durwood put his hat back on and turned to go, muttering.

"*What's that?*" Quaid called.

Durwood stopped at the threshold. "I said you and the mayor, folks like you two. Real good talkers."

"What's that supposed to mean?"

"Means that's what you're good at. Talk."

Quaid looked incredulously at the ceiling. "Well hey, Mr. Action, I hate to break it to you, but we're zero for two. Blackstone and eDeed."

"Whose fault's that?"

"You're the tactician, right? You made up the plans."

Durwood's eyes boiled.

Quaid said, "Don't take this personally, but it's gonna be hard to keep advertising ourselves as the premier small-force private-arms operators in the Western world on a track record like this."

"Good," Durwood said. "Never cared much for your advertising."

They fought another ten minutes. Durwood wondered if Quaid's haste to finish the job had to do with wanting to hit the town with the mayor. Quaid accused Durwood of self-sacrificing to the point of indulgence. Maybe he should try joining him and Sergio one night. How long had it been since he'd been kissed by an actual female, not counting Sue-Ann's slobbers?

They were poking sore spots, dredging up topics they'd success-fully ignored for years like an old married couple in a blow-out fight.

At last, Quaid said, "I don't know what to say. Maybe this thing's run its course."

Durwood looked out the window, not disagreeing.

CHAPTER TWENTY-FOUR

New Jersey

The guys didn't call to pressure me the next day like I thought they might. Quaid was only saying what he thought he needed to to make me betray Piper Jackson—with time to reflect, I saw that.

I wasn't going to be harassed into it. But I wasn't sticking my head in the sand either.

"Who's this?" Piper answered on the second ring.

"It's me, Molly," I said. "Are you free?"

Clacking keys sounded, then: "Free enough."

I was out in the backyard where the kids couldn't hear, pacing with my cell phone. It was Saturday. I'd divided the morning between Chutes and Ladders with Karen and agonizing over this call.

"I've been thinking about yesterday," I began. "What we did at eDeed. The property deeds."

Piper said, "Yep."

"So the data that you, I guess, zapped? Will that come back? Is it temporary?"

There was a long pause. I pressed a finger to my non-phone ear— sometimes reception was bad back here. I was deciding whether to repeat my question or backpedal when Piper answered.

"Wrong kinda conversation for the phone," she said.

"Right, right," I agreed. "Should I...is there anyplace we could meet?"

I braced myself to hear, *No, I'm busy,* or, *What are you, crazy, wanting to meet out in public?* I felt Piper's skepticism over the line, and tried to think what I could say to draw down her guard.

I tried, "I just wanna be in the loop. I deserve to know where this is all heading. I was there yesterday, participating. And I was at Ted Blackstone's too, which—"

"You hear what I said about bad phone conversations?"

"Sorry, I know," I said. "I just want to talk. Okay?"

Piper wasn't enthusiastic about it, but she agreed. "You know Montvale rest stop on the turnpike?"

"Sure."

"There. Forty minutes."

Montvale was a trek from where I lived, Morristown. "Can we do an hour?"

"An hour, yeah," she said. "I'm not hanging around if you're late."

I hurried inside for my keys, told Granny and the kids I needed to check in with the guys about "the case" (I'd managed to keep things vague), and hit the road.

The turnpike had only gotten scarier with the unrest. I saw two guns waved out windows, a motorcycle gang enforcing an ad hoc toll —on southbound traffic, thankfully—and disabled cars on the shoulder, picked over to their rusty skeletons.

Navigating all this, I made it to Montvale with two minutes to spare. Piper was sitting at a picnic table, no laptop.

"My bus leaves in ten minutes," she said.

I told her ten minutes should be plenty, settling onto a weathered bench seat.

She looked to either side, confirming we were alone.

"You want to know about the kernel," she started.

The kernel...the kernel...

"Y-yes," I said. "I definitely want to understand the kernel."

People say my eyes are big—"marbles of pure emerald," Quaid calls them—but Piper's looked humongous just now, deep brown, probing.

"Thing we used yesterday," she said.

"Oh," I said. "It's called a kernel? Like popcorn?"

"Not like popcorn."

"It is sort of like a computer virus?"

She stared into the slats of the picnic table. I couldn't tell if she was chewing gum, or if her jaws were just working against each other.

"Worse," she said. "It wriggles into the core software. Wipes out any datastores, takes all the zeroes and ones and makes 'em all zero."

"What about backups?"

"That's the worst part. The second a datastore hits the system, it's infected. Goes instantly to zero. Backup all you want..." She trailed off with a fizzing noise.

"Is it reversible? Is there some kind of antidote?"

Piper sat back from the table, those big eyes turning squinty. "Already told you more than I should. This is Algernon stuff, all of it."

I matched her posture, backing off the edge of my bench seat.

The guys would want me to press further. I hadn't told them about contacting Piper today—not the call, and definitely not this. I didn't want them following and trying to pick Piper up.

Something told me probing was the wrong move here.

"Why did you agree to meet?" I asked.

Piper shrugged. "Said you wanted to talk."

"I did. But you didn't have to tell me all this about the kernel."

She tugged at the collar of a thermal shirt. "You have doubts. I respect that."

"Because you have doubts of your own?" I asked.

"Everyone has doubts."

"Even Josiah?"

A lopsided grin came to Piper's lips. "Josiah, he's...I don't know."

"*Crazy?*" I suggested.

She nodded. "A little. But what all's going on, maybe it takes a little crazy to fix."

I felt like I needed to tread carefully now. She had misgivings, but too much griping behind Josiah's back—like sniping about the queen bee in high school—would only make me look bad.

I asked, "How come Josiah wasn't there for eDeed?"

"He's lying low after Blackstone," Piper said. "Only Algernons can see him now. I've only seen him once myself."

This Algernon thing again.

"How do you become an Algernon?" I asked. "Is it based on tenure?"

Piper shook her head. "Nah. You just have to step up."

"Step up?"

"You have to make an offering," she said. "Prove your worthiness, your commitment."

Offering had all sorts of connotations I didn't like. "What exactly counts as an offering?"

My face must've been ghostly, because she said, "You don't have to sacrifice your brother or anything."

I took a second remembering yesterday—when Zach had been my brother. "Oh. Yeah, of course."

She explained, "You have to deliver us a high-value target. Preferably one of the Despicable Dozen."

"What do you mean, 'deliver'?"

"Info," she said. "You gotta get inside, give us details we can use."

"Use..."

"To hit 'em. To attack."

I tried to think what sort of offering I could make. With Durwood's help, I could probably identify a target and pass along the information. How "high value" would it need to be?

I asked for an example.

Piper said, "Did you notice Blackstone's wife and kids were gone?"

"Yes."

"Somebody hacked his travel agent," she said. "Gave us a date and time he'd be home solo."

As I considered this, Piper checked the time on her phone and stood.

"My bus is boarding," she said. "I gotta head."

I stood, too, and walked behind, heading for the bridge leading to New Jersey Transit.

As we got closer to the terminal, a wild notion swirled in my brain. I knew the guys would've wanted to vet it, or tweak it, or scrap it for their own plan. I didn't care. I didn't want to strategize or listen to their lectures.

I had an idea, and I thought it was a good one.

"I'm ready to be an Algernon," I said.

Piper stopped with a confused look. "I just told you, you have to make—"

"An offering, yes." I smiled, hoping this would cover my pounding heart. "I've got one."

CHAPTER TWENTY-FIVE
Pittsburgh

Durwood arrived in Pittsburgh on Monday. This gave him three days to prep the mission site. To test sight lines on video surveillance, to coordinate microphone frequencies. To look at blueprints.

For each prep he did, Durwood started a fresh notepad. He carried the pad around with a pencil, tucked into his blue jeans. By job's end, it was generally filled.

Monday evening, Durwood took the lay of the land. He mapped access and egress points for the entire American Dynamics facility—nine buildings, twelve factory lines, three hundred acres altogether.

He took extra notes on the old steel plant. Jim Steed's office.

Molly's instinctive decision to dangle Steed—whose schedule and security detail the guys knew—in front of the Mice had been brilliant. Firstly, it gave them a chance to apprehend the Mice in the attack itself. Second, it elevated Molly within the group. There was no question it advanced the mission.

So long as they kept Jim Steed alive.

Quaid wasn't showing up until Thursday, the day of the Mice's attack. So it was just Durwood and Sue-Ann now. He got dinner from Hardee's and they slept in the van, in the AmDye lot.

Tuesday before dawn, he placed motion-activated microcams throughout the facilities. He spent the rest of the morning adjusting thresholds and shutter speeds, making sure of angles and low-light scenarios.

The cameras were fresh out of their packaging, a few pink Styrofoam shreds hanging around. The devices were excellent quality. Tiny but solid. USA steel. Yakov had outdone himself.

Wednesday, Durwood narrowed his focus to Steed's office. He installed a remote-triggered diffuser and loaded it with blinding powder. The diffuser was bulkier than he would've liked, 240-volt motor inside, but a fishing plaque of Steed's camouflaged it well enough.

"Boy, that was a doozy," a voice boomed from behind. "Won the tournament on a forty-pound channel cat, no lie."

Durwood took the bit off his dress press. "That right?"

Jim Steed nodded, hanging his coat. "The bastard broke my line, but I managed to get a gaff into him. Took three of us to drag 'im aboard."

Sue-Ann was lying at Durwood's feet.

Steed juked at her—*Whaddaya know, girl?*—then glanced about the office. "How're we looking? All buttoned up now?"

"Getting there," Durwood said.

Steed clapped him on the back. He believed the guys were simply adding extra security this week. Durwood hated misleading the man, but Quaid had insisted.

If he finds out the Mice are coming for him, Quaid had argued, *it'll get mucked up. He'll tip them off, or wanna go all Marlon Brando in* Apocalypse Now, *something.*

This was likely true. And Quaid deserved to make the call. He was the one who'd smoothed things over with Steed, explaining Molly's role in eDeed and how close she now was to Piper Jackson. He'd kept the job alive—for all his faults.

That night, the eve of the mission, Durwood completed his prep. Afterward, he walked Sue through downtown Pittsburgh, covering a wide swath. You couldn't go two blocks without seeing crime—drugs, auto theft, gun fighting. The world had truly lost its way.

Toward the end of his route, Durwood entered a blighted area bordering the AmDye complex. A kid wearing a sideways ball cap was nosing around a rusty Dodge, gesturing to some buddies in the shadows.

Pain flared in Durwood's head.

He called ahead, "Not tonight."

The kid was confused. He twitched at Durwood's voice. When he found its speaker, he drew up tall. Rangy, loose-limbed kid in his twenties.

"You want some of this?" The kid opened his coat to show a piece. "Huh? *Huh?*"

Durwood tipped his brow toward the coat. "Got yourself a .22. Steal it?"

With unhurried strides, Durwood approached. The kid snatched his piece and aimed, unsteady, stepping in place.

"I'll put you down, old man," he said. "I'm not afraid."

"Oh, you're afraid." Durwood laid his forearm into the Dodge.

"No, I'm not! You take *one more step* and I'm firing."

Durwood took half a step. Sue-Ann trotted up to sniff the kid's shoes.

"I'm about to shoot—I'm *about* to!"

"Do," Durwood said. "Shoot. Me and Sue are about as slow'a targets as you'll find."

The kid squinted down at Sue, who licked his shoe. He made a distasteful face and stood there mush-mouthed, peeking over at his buddies.

Durwood's hand shot forward. The gun clattered away. In the next moment, the aspiring car thief's collar was closed at the neck by Durwood's fist.

"Now *listen*," Durwood said, lifting the kid an inch off the ground. "This you live through. Next one, maybe not."

"I wasn't doing anything!" the kid spluttered. "You can't prove it, you can't prove I did anything."

Durwood released his collar and moved his hand slowly—firmly—onto the kid's skull.

"Proof's in here." Durwood's hand squeezed. He didn't want to stop it. "You know what you were fixing to do."

The kid muttered some excuses. Durwood found his skull's hardness intoxicating. His thumb pressed the dent of the kid's temple.

The kid clenched his eyes shut. "Okay, okay, it's true. We were thinking of stealing it."

"Thinking?"

"No, we were gonna—we were gonna," the kid said, answering either the question or the pressure of Durwood's thumb.

Durwood had a bright urge to punish, to take this small drop of mischief and crush.

Then, by the moon's light, Durwood caught sight of a smokestack. It came from an American Dynamics factory opening for third shift.

The sight lifted Durwood out of himself. He thought of the workers inside and why he'd come to Pittsburgh—to restore order, to end this devilry once and for all.

He took his hand off the kid's head.

"This time, you live," he said.

CHAPTER TWENTY-SIX

The day of the attack, Piper texted me a street address in Mott Haven, a rough neighborhood of the Bronx, with instructions to meet there before caravaning to Pittsburgh. I kissed the kids off to school and confirmed Granny could handle bedtime if necessary.

She said, "Do I look dead yet?"

"No. You look comfortable," I said with a nod to her slippers. "Please remind Zach he has an algebra quiz tomorrow."

She said she would, and I hopped in the Prius. The turnpike was less crazy than the other day—it was earlier; maybe bikers slept in—and I made the George Washington Bridge in decent time.

My phone's navigation took me over the Harlem River at 145th, then down to Mott Haven, dropping me on a draggy dead-end road. Spray-painted across a store's boarded-up windows was the message, *EVERYTHING WAS TAKEN.*

I parked next to an overturned oil drum.

Durwood had insisted I bring a gun. I'd resisted at first, but when Quaid pointed out Mott Haven had been dicey *before* the unrest, I agreed. I was glad to feel the Ruger's weight in my purse now as I walked the scarred sidewalks looking for signs of the Mice.

I saw plenty of the nose-eyes-whiskers symbol: sprawled across the awning of a smoke shop, inside an abandoned pet supply store. The pet store's graffiti must've been old—mold spores almost totally covered the whiskers.

A lopsided truck turned onto the street from several blocks up. It only had half a front grill, and the bumper was sparking against asphalt.

Instinctively, I ducked into the alley next to the pet store. I'd just drawn my weapon when an egg rolled to a stop beside me.

An egg.

Carefully, with my fingertips, I picked it up. It felt hard-boiled. Somebody had written across the white shell in shaky ballpoint, *Nibble around back.*

I turned on my haunches. The back alley looked scarier than the road, loose trash spilling out of overflowing dumpsters, the ground covered with green-glass shards like flower petals across a wedding aisle.

Still, I'd come this far. Holding the Ruger out in front like Durwood had taught me, I hugged the building's bricks on the way to the back.

Razor wire separated the alley from a row of dilapidated homes behind. Tight-skinned dogs barked from behind the fence. I ignored them, focusing on good breaths.

Along the rear of the building were three unmarked doors. The middle was propped by a folded square of cardboard. I heard faint noise inside.

Voices?

Music?

Peeking back to be sure I hadn't been followed by the driver of the wrecked truck, I slipped inside.

I found myself at the top of a stark, narrow stairwell. As I started down, the sleeves of my jacket brushed the walls. Another door awaited me at the bottom. There was a sign nailed over its frame: *LEWD BREW.*

The original Lewd Brew, the Brooklyn cafe where the first Mice had picked a slogan and gotten inked, had been shut down long ago. They must've smuggled out the sign.

Putting my gun back in my purse—but leaving a hand on the grip

—I walked in. The place was buzzing. A guy in ripped jeans offered me a stack. Two baristas stood behind an espresso machine, but instead of making coffee, they were flicking the tips of hypodermic needles. The lighting was harsh from yellow fluorescent tubes. The air felt busy on my skin, metallic.

I looked around for Piper, but Garrison found me first.

"*Something's up,*" he said, placing his body between me and the rest of the cafe.

"You think?" I said.

He nodded vigorously and led me by the arm to a corner. We'd only talked once since I'd fed Piper the AmDye information—I had said I was waiting for our next instructions, same as everybody.

"I heard Otis and London saying there's another attack today— another *big one,*" he said. "I don't know, man. I don't know."

He dug a hand into his perfect hair. When he pulled it out, hair fell into his eyes.

He didn't move it, so I did. "Does anybody know the target?"

Garrison shook his head. He seemed calmer after my touch. "I thought they were playing it safe. I thought they were being conservative now."

I chuckled. "Have you *met* Josiah?"

After my joke and my touch, he was definitely calmer.

"Heh, I guess." A crooked smile poked out. In this tight space, it felt like we were alone. "Are you gonna go, if there is a mission?"

I looked up at him. I wasn't sure what to say. I didn't think I should tell him about my offering. Piper had accepted my story that I knew about Jim Steed's Thursday trips to Pittsburgh from my Merry Maids job in town—but Garrison might dig deeper. *Really, they let a temp know the CEO's travel schedule?* He was curious like that, at least with me.

I said, "Are...you gonna go?"

Garrison's crooked smile spread to his whole mouth. "Maybe if you go."

His face was moving toward mine, and mine was moving toward his. I felt my eyelids close and mouth open.

What is this? What am I doing?

"Ehem."

My eyelids snapped open, and there was Piper Jackson.

She said, "I can come back."

"No, no," I said as Garrison pulled his hand off my hip. "I was looking for you."

Piper gave Garrison a look—like she was at a club and skeptical of the guy her girlfriend was dancing with.

"We're getting the Algernons together, meeting." She gestured to a door. "You in?"

I felt Garrison's surprise like a shield between us. But what could I say?

"Definitely," I said. "Now?"

She nodded.

With a backward look at Garrison, who'd stuck both hands in his pockets, I followed Piper to a back room.

My thoughts were scrambled from what'd just happened—or almost happened. *Would I have kissed Garrison?* Pretty clearly, yes, that is exactly what would have happened.

We'd been in extreme situations together, and our texting—I'll admit—had gotten flirty. But kissing? I think I felt insulated by the difference in ages, but of course as far as Garrison knew, we were both in our midtwenties. Obviously, the chemistry was there.

I drifted after Piper, preoccupied, barely registering my surroundings as we entered a back room. Seated at the head of a long table was a figure I hadn't seen for a while—or expected to see today.

Josiah.

"Our newest Algernon," he said. "Helping us make the world a little less despicable."

His voice seemed even reedier than at Ted Blackstone's—terrible, on the verge of falling apart.

I said, "Just, you know, contributing to the cause."

He pointed to a laptop on the table, which looked like Piper's. "Come, join the fun."

I noticed Piper's mouth tense, but she let Josiah take the laptop's keyboard. I came up behind him—noting his dangerously thin legs in shrink-wrap jeans. The screen showed New York City divided into sections by bright-green outlines.

"What're we doing?" I said.

"Treating darkness with darkness," Josiah answered.

It wasn't just his voice that seemed starker today. Josiah's stringy ghost-white hair looked so unnatural—but not in a dyed way. As he moved Piper's mouse, the bones of his wrist looked sharp. That aggressive mint smell accompanied his cryptic words.

"Is that the power grid?" I asked. "Can the kernel—"

I stopped, wondering if I should hide my knowledge of the kernel. *You are an Algernon, right? Own it.*

I asked, "How did you get access?"

Josiah deferred to Piper.

"Relay tables," she explained. "The kernel's installed to where it can scramble the relay tables. Takes 'em about thirty minutes to figure out an override."

"Thirty minutes without power?" Examining the map, I confirmed it didn't go far south enough to cover Morristown. "That's hospitals. And schools. And fire stations. That could really..."

"*Be bad?*" Josiah said, expelling a fresh blast of mint. "Wreak havoc? Force corporations to address our demands?"

Again, Piper's expression—I thought—showed less than 100 percent agreement. Josiah was spiraling out of control, constructing this messianic rhetoric on the fly. I considered excusing myself and texting the guys Josiah was here, they could come grab him. But they were both in Pittsburgh.

Piper had retaken the keyboard. "Let's go—I'm in the relay tables now. The longer I hang out, the more risk we're exposed. Which county?"

Josiah's pink-tinged eyes fixed on me. "Why don't we let our newest member pick?"

I glanced at the map. "Oh, I'm good."

His pupils spiraled in place. "Albany Electric services ninety-five percent of the New York metropolitan area. They turned out the lights on eighteen hundred disadvantaged households who'd fallen behind on payments last year—while pulling in fifty-two-point-two million dollars in profits."

There was no point debating. I reminded myself that if our plan worked tonight, this would all be over. Then Josiah could try his grand arguments on a judge.

"Fine," I said. "I can pick."

I leaned close to Piper's screen. My first thought was to pick a tiny zip code, but it occurred to me that tiny zip codes were tiny because they contained large concentrations of people—likely poor, at-risk people. I pointed to a medium-size zip code in Staten Island.

Piper jabbed a few keystrokes and waited. The borders of my chosen section blinked, then dimmed—her laptop made a tinny *fzzzz*— then went black.

Josiah's bony fingers closed around my arm. "Do you feel that? It's five thousand seniors hyperventilating because *The Price Is Right* is gone, writing their congressmen about Albany Electric. It's businessmen panicking. It's justice reversing, gerbils eating their own tails."

He took out his phone and tweeted the part about justice and gerbils.

Josiah stood and stretched his arms high overhead like he'd just woken from a nap. He walked to the door, which led to the rest of the cafe.

Piper said, "Where you going?"

"To address my righteous army," he said.

Piper glanced at Hatch, who'd been quiet through the power grid episode.

She said, "What happened to keeping out of sight? It's all kinds out there, not just the Algernons."

Josiah was staring at a clock over the door. The clock was weird, trippy. Its face was comprised of counter-spinning circles of red, purple, and green. The hands seemed to move in opposite directions.

"Factory-farmed meat is putrefying in warm refrigerators..." he resumed, trancelike. "Wallpaper is bubbling up in great blisters...black holes are forming to other universes...and it's all happening in triple speed, blooming, replicating..."

I glanced sideways to Piper, to the rest of the Algernons. Was everybody hearing this? Were we still on board?

Before any voice of dissent emerged, Josiah's phone buzzed. He broke off intoning and checked it—then became suddenly focused, all otherworldly dreaminess gone.

"Hello?" he said, hunching away from the table.

All the Algernons watched. Josiah spoke quietly, his lips near the phone, but his arm gestures were big, intense.

When the call ended, nobody asked who it was.

Josiah returned to the door and pulled it open wide. I heard gasps from the rest of the cafe as the non-Algernons caught sight of him.

"And now," Josiah said, stashing his phone away, "we go forward to Pittsburgh."

CHAPTER TWENTY-SEVEN

To Quaid Rafferty's eyes, things were going according to plan. The Mice were en route. They would arrive in the evening, after the factory shifts ended, when Jim Steed was known to work late—alone—in his office. They would infiltrate the premises using the security holes Molly had slipped them, and when they tried storming Steed's office, Quaid and Durwood would pounce.

Now they were monitoring video feeds from the back of the Vanagon.

"So, what's next?" Quaid said, threading his fingers behind his head. "After these hooligans are locked up, will you need time back in West Virginia to tend the farm? Or shall I proceed with booking us another gig?"

Durwood didn't take his eyes from the screens. "You count chickens, I'll watch the eggs."

Quaid groaned at the tired metaphor. "This could be a marketing coup, Wood—stopping the Blind Mice. We'd be fools not to capitalize."

Durwood switched between views, now pulling up Jim Steed at his desk, now towering cranes loading girders onto semis.

Quaid continued, undeterred by his partner's silence, "Now obviously you can't run TV advertisements about it, but word gets around. It'll grow the brand..."

Quaid was feeling optimistic. His and Durwood's spat at the hotel —over his treatment of Molly and the feeding of scraps to Sue-Ann, among other things—seemed forgotten. Both men were good forgetters. In the Mice's wake would be priceless art that needed recovering, and resistance movements in need of assistance (or quelling), and clients like Fabienne Rivard—who was still calling, still clamoring for Quaid's help—ready to hire them.

Though the Vanagon cabin was cramped, Quaid's loafers resting one on a bungee cord and two on a sleeping dog, his mind carried him away.

He believed Third Chance Enterprises should be more than a small-force private-arms outfit. Could they co-brand a line of spy gadgets? Content was king nowadays—might their adventures translate onto the printed page? Or the silver screen? Quaid knew plenty of Hollywood heavies.

As a boy, Quaid used to feel sad about all the people he'd never know, people in Namibia or Burma or the middle of Ohio whose paths his would never cross. Politics had been a balm for this regret, but it hadn't cured him.

Actually, it had been his downfall as governor. He and the woman had struck up a conversation at the bar around the corner from the capitol, Quaid wearing a wig, the disguise he used to get out among the people and gauge broader sentiments.

Her story of being laid off and evicted—which turned out to be true—had so moved him that, yes, he'd made an inquiry with city housing officials. Yes, he'd left voice mails on her home phone. Yes, he'd had a relationship with her—absolutely within his rights as a bachelor.

And yes, it turned out, she'd been a call girl: a fact his political opponents, and later Draktor Industrial, would exploit to maximum gain.

"Shoot."

Durwood's utterance took Quaid out of his reverie.

"What's the word?" he said. "Are the Mice here?"

Durwood shook his head. "Ten, fifteen minutes out still." He nodded to the feed. "But Steed's about to go."

"Go where? But we checked the logs—he never leaves before eight. Every Thursday, he works late, drinks one drink at the hotel bar, and falls asleep."

"That's the pattern," Durwood said. "But here, look yourself."

He zoomed tight on Steed's luggage, which was leaning against the office door. Beside his usual briefcase was a roller bag.

"Flying," Quaid said. "He's about to get on a plane."

"Appears so."

"Why's he flying? He loves the drive." Quaid dropped his voice: "'State police got bigger fish to fry, I floor it on I-76.'"

Durwood said he didn't know.

On-screen, Jim Steed stood from his computer and put on a coat. He furrowed his brow a moment, tapping his desk as though trying to remember something.

Quaid said, "If he's gone when the Mice get here, they'll call it off. They'll crucify Molly for giving bad info."

"Possible," Durwood said.

"We have to stall him, keep him there somehow."

"I could throw an alarm."

Quaid stood and began pacing the small bit he could in the Vanagon. "No, that throws things off. It needs to be normal when the Mice show, no sirens blaring."

Durwood nodded his agreement.

"I'll go, I'll keep him there," Quaid said, slipping into his sport coat.

"How?"

"I don't know, I'll get him talking."

Durwood shifted his hat on his head. "Steed doesn't know you're here—he thinks it's just me putting in extra security. What's your story?"

Quaid turned his palms up. "I'll improvise one."

One foot out the sliding van door, Quaid paused to scan the contents of the cabin. Stinger missiles. Crates of grenades. An array of chunky black cases that might've belonged to a marching band—but

Quaid knew actually contained enough firepower to take down a Central American government.

On the tailgate, stowed in a notched rack, was some disk-shaped instrument attached to a stick.

Quaid took it.

Durwood said, "That's not what you think."

"Doesn't matter." The object looked like a selfie stick, but Quaid knew it was probably capable of focusing the sun's rays into a death beam. "I just need a prop."

He crossed the parking lot and entered the factory using the contractor badge he'd gotten at the start of the job. The plant was dark at this hour, the sound of Quaid's loafers on the catwalk echoing about the machines and conveyor belts.

Jim Steed's office was the first door off the catwalk. Quaid caught him on the way out, locking up.

"Whoa there, amigo," Quaid said. "Don't tell me you were about to leave without saying hello."

Steed twisted his key from the knob. "What're you doing here, Rafferty? Thought you hated Pittsburgh."

"Nah, Pittsburgh I love. It's your stinking factory..."

Quaid stretched out the greeting, drawing on his full range of icebreakers and masculinity jabs. Steed was a chummy sort and happy to play along.

"Now you must have a girlfriend here," Quaid said. "One day a week here? Heck, you could have a second family."

Jim Steed turned his lunchpail jaw aside. "Connie and I have sixteen years under the bridge, this April. I'm proud of that."

Quaid pointed to the locked office. "I don't believe I've seen a picture of your wife. You have one inside, on the walls?"

Steed said he sure did. Setting down the roller bag, he inserted his key back into the knob.

The Steed family portrait was indeed on the walls, front and center, as Quaid had remembered.

"Fine-looking crew," he commented. The boy was wearing a Sidney Crosby jersey. "Your kid a Penguins fan?"

"Oh yeah," Steed said. "Got hockey tonight himself—that's why I'm blowing out early."

"You're flying home for a kids' hockey game?"

"It's regionals. It's a big deal." The executive drew up tall. "Maybe if you had kids of your own, you'd get that."

"Maybe," Quaid said. "Or maybe I'd leave the nachos and bleacher chitchat to my wife, and stay focused on the forty-billion dollar corporation I run."

Steed chuckled. "You're a jerk, Rafferty."

"No argument there."

Quaid kept up the banter, moving clockwise through the photo from Steed's daughter—*Lucky she got her looks from Mom*—to his dog —*Good God, what do you feed that thing, small children?*

Before he could formulate a time-sucking quip about Steed's own image, possibly something about that ribbed sweater, the CEO got a text.

"That's the airline," he said. "I need to go. Flight boards in thirty minutes."

As he started for his roller bag, Quaid groped for another stall. He'd have to raise the stakes—Steed wasn't going to risk missing hockey for more *Kings of Comedy* material.

"Er, I almost forgot," Quaid said, producing the selfie stick from behind his back. "I need to, uh...take care of a quick scan."

Steed reared back. "Scan?"

"Right. We told you our plant got promoted to Algernon, right? Well, she got some new intel today—that's why I rushed out here."

Jim Steed hadn't set down his roller bag.

Quaid continued, "It's not a hundred percent confirmed. I didn't want to unnecessarily alarm you. But there is some concern your office may be booby-trapped."

That word got his attention. Steed hunched in place—eyes zipping around like he was back in the Mekong Delta on the lookout for poisoned bamboo sticks.

"How'd they get inside?" he demanded. "Damn it, where was the breach?"

"We're not sure." Quaid raised the selfie stick. "Let me just run the scan, see what we see. Then we can figure out whether and when a breach occurred."

Steed was livid, his already ruddy complexion turning purple.

"I'm gonna tear somebody a new one for this," he roared. "*It's gonna run brown in front and yellow out the back.*"

Quaid walked around the office, extending the tip of his stick to the baseboards and upper corners. Steed dropped his bags, tore off his suit coat, and began tapping the walls for hollow spots.

In another minute, Quaid got a text from Durwood.

Mice arrived. Meet back at van and we take them.

Jim Steed was examining his desk drawers for false bottoms.

Quaid frowned at his selfie stick. "Shucks, I'm out of juice. Durwood's got spare batteries out in the van, though. Hang tight—I'll be right back."

Steed gave Quaid a thumbs-up from his knees, still looking at the drawers.

CHAPTER TWENTY-EIGHT

W e parked on side streets outside the American Dynamics complex, no more than two per block to avoid suspicion. I locked the Prius, blip-*blip*, and looked out over the vast, barren parking lots—built in the days when AmDye had needed five times as many workers.

I walked to the designated fence line where the other Mice were trickling in. In all, the group was about thirty—over Piper and Hatch's objections, Josiah had invited everyone at the cafe.

Now the leader bowed dramatically to me. "Show us the path, Miss Wixom."

I balled my fists, eyeing the barbed-wire fence. The factories beyond looked bleak and forlorn. Their rust-streaked smokestacks belched into the night sky, but the streams seemed thin—somehow diminished.

Durwood had said the weakened section of fence would be twenty yards due west of this point. I started that way. The sod was soggy, and I could hear the others' shoes behind me, sticking and unsticking.

Only a corner of the fence section was loose—Durwood had been subtle—but Hatch easily yanked the chain link back. His forearm hot rods bulging, he held it up so the rest of us could stoop through.

We continued to hug the fence line on our way around to the old steel factory, shying from the glow of towering light posts. The air got worse with every step, sulfur and standing water. I was holding my nose by the time we reached the side door Durwood had disconnected from the alarm circuit.

Piper glanced up the side of the building. "Which window is Steed's?"

"Seventh floor, middle," I said.

All eyes raised to a single pale-yellow square.

"He's there," Josiah said. "The felon."

To psych us up at the cafe, Josiah had rattled off a litany of charges against Jim Steed: the staggering salary, the outrageous carbon foot-print, the shameful temp-worker-ization of the workforce.

Josiah paused to do something on his phone.

Garrison sidled up to me and whispered, "*Who is he texting? Aren't we all here?*"

I whispered back that I didn't know, feeling Garrison's breath on my neck. I'd given him a ride here, but with two others in the car, we hadn't had a chance to talk about the near kiss.

Now didn't seem like a great time either.

He hunched closer. "Didn't he say something about 'friends,' texting 'his friends'?"

Again, I said I didn't know. Garrison seemed to think now that I was Algernon, I knew everything going on.

"Cool if I ride back with you too?" he asked.

"Sure," I said before remembering that actually, if tonight went how it was supposed to, I would be riding back with the guys in the Vanagon.

A spotlight's wide beam panned over our heads, growing suddenly huge on the brick building before veering away.

Josiah hissed, "Down, everyone *down!*"

We flattened to the ground. I tasted soil and some sort of grease runoff, and spat.

Josiah waved wildly for people to gather. Soon, we'd formed a pinwheel with our faces in the middle and our legs radiating out.

"This is the moment," he began. "We've nibbled their foundation.

Can't you feel them quivering? Can't you feel *the world* quivering? Think about three hundred fourteen *gigatons* of carbon dioxide last year. Keep that number. Keep it bright in your heads."

I was close enough to see the pink in his eyes, to smell that twisted mint on his breath.

He continued, "They've been spilling gasoline for years—*they've* provided the fuel. All we are is the match."

He asked Hatch for the knife. The giant man paused only a second before pulling the weapon from his ankle holster.

I peeked at the time on my phone. *Where were the guys?* Why hadn't they intercepted us yet?

Maybe they hadn't seen us. Maybe Durwood was waiting for visual confirmation Josiah was here.

Were we too early? The people ahead of me in the caravan had been pushing eighty-five miles per hour—the Prius had felt danger-ously rickety at that speed, but I'd kept up.

Hatch had taken a handheld saw from his backpack and was shearing off the face of a dead bolt. The screech was violent but quick. He twisted an inner mechanism, and the door fell open for us.

Josiah took the lead now, slinking through a tiled hall and up seven flights of stairs. I followed in the middle of the pack. The stairwell spilled out to a pair of doors: a rubber-sealed factory entrance and a regular door leading to the offices.

"Algernons with me," Josiah said, nodding to the offices. "The rest of you, go make a mess of the factory."

I found Garrison through the mass of bobbing heads. He was watching me. Maybe his eyes were quivering—maybe I was imagining.

Will I see him again?

Josiah waited for the last non-Algernons to disappear through the rubber seal.

"Now," he said to the rest of us. "Let's present our grievances to Mr. Steed."

As our group of six started up the hall, my lungs were taking double helpings of air.

Where were the guys? How far would they let this attack go?

What if something had gone wrong—like the last time, when Durwood had left the scene to rescue Quaid and Mayor Diaz?

We moved in single file, silent, hurrying. A low hum surrounded us, industrial, maybe the HVAC system. As we approached Jim Steed's office, the lone lighted one, I peered ahead with the small, desperate hope he'd be gone.

But he wasn't. From an angle, we saw Jim Steed standing at his desk with a stumped expression. Papers and manila folders were scattered as though he'd been searching for something.

Josiah stopped short, Hatch's knife poised in his hand. He looked playfully to me. "Somebody misses their Merry Maids."

I stared back dumbly. He kept looking at me. The others were looking too.

For a second, I took offense. Was he belittling me for having done cleaning work?

"Your source," he said. "Didn't your information come from Merry Maids?"

"Oh...yes. It did." I tried for a joshing eye roll toward the office. "He could use 'em, alright."

Josiah stared at me like I had mustard on my chin. For a second, I thought I'd blown everything—Josiah would smell a rat and lead us scampering back to New York.

Then a screech sounded from the factory.

We all spun that direction. In his office, Jim Steed jerked out of his thoughts and looked too.

Josiah said, "Now, we go *now!*"

We followed him ahead. I wondered what the noise had been—whether the guys were involved, whether Garrison was safe—but there was no time to worry. In the next moment, we swarmed the office.

Shock flashed in Jim Steed's eyes, then recognition.

"You!" he growled. "You bastards, what're you doing to my factories?"

He frowned up the hall, but Josiah and the rest of us were in his way.

"*Your* factories," Josiah said. "Not the shareholders'. Not the workers'. Yours, are they?"

Jim Steed extended an accusing finger. "Where'd you put it? Tell me where you put the bomb."

I dodged backward at the word, at the possibility.

But Josiah was grinning. "The guilt runs deep. So deep you begin imagining things." He squatted and spoke up from his haunches. "In your veins. In your organs. You can feel judgment coming."

Steed reared back dismissively. He seemed to be scanning our ranks, cataloging faces. He'd never met me, but he knew from the guys I existed—a female mole inside the Mice.

Was he trying to guess which was me? Would he call me out? If it came to a fight and the guys *still* weren't here, what should I do?

"Little snot," the CEO said. "Think you know something—something about what I do?" He bowed forward as if demonstrating his burden. "Go home to your parents' basement, loser."

Josiah stayed in a crouch, craning his neck in eerie, elastic moves. "Aren't we all losers compared with you?"

He launched a detailed critique of Steed's pay, comparing it to AmDye's abysmal environmental record. To the CO_2 number, he added—from memory—statistics about water consumption, deforestation, and plastic "fouling" the ocean.

Steed's square head got redder and redder until he yelled, "Friggin' shut up! It's commies like you lost us the Vietnam War—always nitpicking, never doing. I grew up in the fifties. We had real smog then. Was up to me, I'd ship you all to China and see how you liked—"

"It's not"—Josiah ran a black-painted fingernail along his knife's blade—"up to you. At this moment, exactly nothing is up to you."

The two were standing just a few feet apart. Josiah, extending his arm like some bony harpoon, pointed to Steed's shirt.

"The classic white dress shirt with blue collar," he said. "Perfect for the pig who pretends to be for the workingman. Ten dollars an hour isn't a living wage. Ten dollars an hour is rape—surely as you rape the planet."

As Steed looked at Josiah's finger, his mouth compressed to a pea. Rage filled his eyes. He swatted the finger away.

Now they fought. Steed emerged from the first collision with Josiah in a headlock—having taken and tossed the blade away. Josiah reached blindly backward and raked Steed's eyes. Steed staggered, roaring like a bear. He tried regaining his grip on Josiah but missed, clubbing his ear instead.

Scrappy as Josiah was, Jim Steed used his superior weight and skill to subdue him. They finished huffing, Josiah pinned to the carpet under Steed's knees.

Hatch stepped forward. "Let him up."

Steed's temple was caked with blood. He kept hold of Josiah's shirt.

He told Hatch, "You're gonna fit right in at Rikers Island. All those pretty tattoos? They'll just love you."

Hatch reached down and jerked Steed to his feet—easy as if he were one of Karen's baby dolls.

Josiah, gasping for air, scrambled to retrieve the knife. He found it under the desk, then recovered to poise it at Steed's throat.

"*Now*," he said. "Shut. Your. Mouth."

The image of Jim Steed at knifepoint gave me a terrible, vertiginous feeling of déjà vu. *It's Ted Blackstone all over again.*

I had to stop this.

CHAPTER TWENTY-NINE

R ight after texting Quaid the Mice had arrived, Durwood got the tickle.

The tickle always started behind his ears. Years back at the Vatican, talking to that fidgety cardinal who'd gone on to betray them. First time he'd rolled up in a dune buggy on Dr. Maxtor's dig, middle of the Sahara, which ended up being the epicenter of the Pestilence Project.

A small, instinctual discomfort. A chore you'd forgotten but couldn't place.

Durwood returned to the surveillance feeds. He pulled headphone cups over his ears. The audio seemed to have a new intensity, some shake or crackle below hearing range. Video looked quiet at first, but second and third looks showed pixels darkening, shifting.

Shadows.

Working a joystick with his calloused thumb, Durwood switched to a view of the engine factory—a half mile from the old steel factory and Steed's office. He panned to the corners, up along the rafters.

Was that door leaning ajar?

Hadn't that bulb been lit before?

He cycled through all twelve factories for anomalies. Surveillance was a patient art. Quaid Rafferty, on those occasions he actually sat with Durwood and did it, bored easily. If Durwood pointed out a curtain pushed too far on its rod, he'd say, *So? Curtain's gotta be someplace.*

Durwood didn't give coincidence such credit. He believed everything on God's green earth could be explained—if you took the time to study.

Now, in the tubing factory, there was a noise. Durwood switched to its video feed and saw shapes.

People.

Like the engine factory, this building was far from the old steel factory. These weren't the Mice.

Durwood zoomed out and switched to infrared. Two heat signatures came into focus. They were slinking around the perimeter, communicating by walkie-talkie. They squatted every ten yards to place small objects on the ground.

He checked the engine factory again, the lumber plant, the sugar refinery. Every last facility showed similar operations in progress.

Saboteurs.

The objects being placed were explosive charges. They were hitting all twelve AmDye factories and hadn't tripped one alarm.

Durwood, moving with urgency, found a frequency scanner in the overhead storage. He tuned through the ranges favored by clandestine/paramilitary forces. Sure enough, he found chatter.

The operatives' voices were rapid but assured. Hearing French, Durwood thought they'd stumbled upon a French outfit—but then he heard German. Then some Scandinavian language.

It was a coordinated team of foreigners preparing to blow these factories to kingdom come.

American Dynamics was half bankrupt as it was. Destroying the Pittsburgh facility, which contained—as Jim Steed would proudly tell it —"ninety-nine percent of our manufacturing, right here in the US of A," would finish the job.

Only the old steel factory differed. There, pipes were being played like bongos, and conveyor belts were being sliced. Loud, showy damage—but damage that didn't amount to much. He didn't see

Molly or any of the others he knew by name, but these must be the Blind Mice.

Durwood pulled up a view of Jim Steed's office. There they were—the leadership. Josiah stood nose to nose with the CEO.

Durwood pushed his hat up his forehead.

He couldn't intercede everywhere. How was the foreigners' sabotage related to the Mice's attack on Steed? Had Josiah contracted out for help? Were the foreigners some European version of the Mice, joining as brothers-in-arms?

Durwood didn't think so. They moved with the skill and precision of mercenaries. These boys wouldn't be pulling out their phones and tweeting during the op, he felt certain.

Sue-Ann was standing at the van's sliding door.

"That's right, girl. Time to move."

The question was, move where?

Durwood could take out the Mice, but if it turned out they weren't at the top of the scheme—these foreigners ran the show—then the unrest would continue. He and Quaid would deliver on the contract, but AmDye wouldn't be able to pay their lousy light bill after the destruction of its factories.

Durwood armed himself and strapped on his combat watch, which allowed him to monitor the video feeds on the move. He opened the van's sliding door.

Sue-Ann took a gimpy step after.

"Not tonight," Durwood said, showing her a flat hand.

On his way to the first factory, he called Quaid.

"Foreigners—they're wiring up the whole complex," he said. "I'll disarm as many as I can."

"What about the Mice?" Quaid said.

"You're close, you take care of it," Durwood said.

Quaid made a noise like a horse chuffing at flies.

Durwood said, "We're the ones teed Steed up. And Moll's there too."

"I know." Quaid sighed. "I'm en route."

Durwood had reached the tubing factory. He hung up and entered without breaking stride. He moved straight for the first man. AmDye ran its ventilation systems overnight to clear fumes, which was fortunate. The giant ducts' wheezing obscured the noise of his boots.

He slipped behind a rack of hard hats, then beside a twenty-gauge riveter. The first hostile was hunched over placing a charge and could not see Durwood coming.

Durwood drove his forearm into the man's neck, knocking him out with a clean brachial stun. He then squatted over the man's still body, drawing his M9. The second commando, across the factory, stood from his wiring—like a hare in a garden with a mouthful of lettuce.

There was no time for nonlethal force. As it was, Durwood doubted he could save all twelve factories. He centered the man in his gun's night scope and fired a kill shot.

The first commando was still unconscious. Durwood examined the charge he'd been setting: a double brick of C-4. The det wires showed no sign of fancy booby-trapping. These charges weren't meant to sit around exposed. They were meant to get ready, get set, and go *boom*.

He disabled the charge, left it where it was, and hurried to the next. The foreigners had wired up load-bearing structures for maximum damage—same as Durwood would have. He disabled all he found and moved on to the engine factory.

A single man was working this building, Durwood confirmed on his watch. He entered by a delivery port. The man was moving away from him, planting his explosives in a clockwise circuit. Durwood closed rapidly and dropped the man with another brachial stun. He disarmed the three live charges and proceeded to the lumber plant.

On the way, he looked in on Jim Steed. The image on the watch confused Durwood at first—looked like a tarp billowing over a pile of sticks.

Then he realized it was a fight, Josiah and Jim Steed.

Over the next minutes, Durwood checked in occasionally as he dispatched the foreign commandos. He cleared six factories in a similar manner to how he'd done the first two.

His boots became caked with mud. His nose went numb, either from a punch he took in the textile mill or the toxic mix of industrials smells.

(Probably the punch—Durwood had grown up in and around West Virginia coal mines.)

He continued to leave disconnected charges where they lay, for speed. The risk of them being rearmed was negligible. These folks were operating in a tight time frame. Half were dead anyhow.

As he fought, Durwood gained an impression of the enemy. The equipment was black-ops grade. Clothing and details of appearance—brands, styles of facial hair—suggested an international mix of mercenaries. An all-star team.

The man at the seventh factory must've been the weak sister—Durwood stopped him as he was removing his first charge from its packaging. Durwood kept moving, but did note a Styrofoam peanut on the ground.

Pink Styrofoam.

He checked his watch again to see what was going on in Jim Steed's office. The fight had escalated. Big Hatch had Steed up by the collar like a crappie on a fishing stringer. Josiah had a knife.

Steed was running out of time. With three factories still left to disarm, so was Durwood.

CHAPTER THIRTY

"Stop, I want to ask him something!" I called out. Hatch and Josiah both looked back to see who'd spoken. I had my hand raised, feeling strangely like I was back in Mr. Arnoff's psych 101 lecture.

"It's just that I...I blog a lot about American Dynamics, about the environment," I said. "I want to hear what they're going to do with the Utica Shale."

Josiah still wore a seething expression, but he'd momentarily lowered the knife. "I think we can safely assume they plan to *rape* it—like they rape all reservoirs of natural resources."

He turned back to Jim Steed, his fist tightening around the handle of the blade.

I said, "But it's a secret. American Dynamics said so at their last earnings call. 'We are not disclosing our development plans for Utica at this time.' We need to know, to stop it. We have to get it out of him!"

Jim Steed had a puzzled look on his face—I had no clue what was said at his last earnings call. Hatch and Josiah seemed to be weighing my idea, which vaguely suggested torture, against Josiah and the Bowie knife.

I was scrambling to come up with another follow-up, some

comment or question to eat more time, when the sound of whistling came from the hall.

A man in a gray janitor's uniform was cruising toward the office pushing a handled box sweeper. He stared straight down as though examining what lint his sweeper was about to pick up.

He turned into the office, head still down, coming several steps inside.

Hatch snorted. "This guy."

Josiah's eyes bulged, incredulous. The intruder had tied his sandy hair back with a rubber band, and his shoes looked wrong for the job.

Loafers.

With a start, the "janitor" looked up.

"What'n the heck?" he said in a whiskey voice I barely recognized as Quaid Rafferty's. "I wasn't informed of an after-hours gathering tonight."

Josiah, smearing blood from one nostril, waved Quaid away with his knife.

"We aren't here for you, friend." He nodded to Steed. "This man here, who's suppressed your wage for decades I'd bet, is the one we've come for."

Quaid stroked his chin ponderously. Then he pointed the handle of his sweeper toward the executive. "Is he gonna die?"

Steed's back went stiff. He must've recognized Quaid, who wasn't wearing a wig or any facial prosthetics I could see.

Josiah opened his mouth but garbled a reply—he didn't seem to know how to talk to the janitor.

Quaid said, "Or you're just spooking him? Because he looks plenty spooked now."

Though he was playing the situation as cool as ever, I wondered why Quaid had come alone—why both guys hadn't come with guns blazing and stopped this.

Would Quaid really be able to talk Josiah down?

Josiah said, "Those at the top *must* be held accountable. Until they are, until they pay a price *in kind* for the destruction they sow in the underclass, our attacks will continue to grow in violence. Indeed, they must."

Quaid pushed his tongue around his cheek. "So, die? What I'm hearing is I get to watch him die?"

The Algernons shuffled in place and looked among each other like kindergartners meeting a new class pet. What to make of this character?

Naturally, Quaid decided to plug the gas pedal.

"I'm in, brother." He let his sweeper fall against Jim Steed's desk and smacked his hands together. "They've skipped my Christmas bonus two years running, and everybody in the company knows the order came straight from the top."

He held out his knuckles to Hatch in solidarity. Hatch considered the offer a moment, then tapped him back.

Jim Steed snapped, "That's ridiculous. We're fair on wages. I worked in a plant myself after 'Nam, I know how hard men can—"

"You know squat," Quaid said. "My father worked in this plant. He died of emphysema years ago. Didn't smoke a day in his life, but the coroner said his insides looked like a fifty-year-old chimney nobody ever cleaned."

Josiah nodded along awkwardly. Steed got past his anger flash and now—maybe figuring Quaid's routine for an act—stood stiff-legged like he was awaiting some call to action.

Quaid gestured to Josiah's knife. "Mind if I do the honors? I told Mom I'd avenge Dad's death one day, pay American Dynamics back with interest. I was just blowing smoke—I never figured I'd get the chance." He licked his lips. "It's a dream come true."

Unconsciously, I'd raised up on the balls of my feet. Quaid was so convincing—the clenched mouth, the murderous gleam in his eye—that I almost wondered if it wasn't an act. I knew Jim Steed annoyed him. Whether it was tactics or the chintzy monthly stipend, or Steed's being a bore conversationally—Quaid was always grumbling about him.

He wouldn't.

Right?

Josiah, apparently picking up on the same cues, handed Quaid the knife.

Quaid bent his knees and began passing the knife giddily between his hands.

"H-hey, careful, bub," Steed said with a step backward. "That ain't Lysol."

Quaid raised the knife overhead. He mimed a few practice thrusts, growling audibly. I couldn't see his expression from where I stood, but judging by Steed's swirling eyes, it must have been convincing.

Steed held up both forearms. Quaid reared back with the blade, his uniform sleeve flapping.

Josiah, off to one side, began recording on his phone. He was probably thinking viral—*Watch what this janitor did to the CEO of his own company!!!*

At the last second, Quaid spun away from Steed. He flung the knife at Hatch, burying the blade in the big man's thigh.

"Aaaaooooww!" he cried.

Jim Steed rushed at Josiah, unarmed now, and slugged him in the jaw. Piper raced in to help, but the other Algernons hung back. I took a step forward and stopped.

Whose side do I jump in on? If I fight with Quaid and Steed, my cover is blown...but maybe the time's come for that.

Hatch reentered the fray before I could decide. He ripped the knife from his thigh and flung it aside. Heaving, his camouflage pants black with blood, he shoved Steed away from Josiah and caught Quaid in a half nelson.

Josiah, bailed out again, paced in front of his attackers.

"*Why?*" he spat at Quaid. "He doesn't care one dime for you, and you stick your neck out for him?"

Quaid squirmed under the yoke of Hatch's arm. "Guess I think a criminal's a criminal. Guess I'm just another simple working-class dummy."

It was a smart try—and Quaid sold it with a hangdog look—but Josiah wasn't buying. Off the carpet, he picked up the knife—gloppy with Hatch's blood—and poised it over Quaid's chest.

"Wait, stop!" I heard myself say.

Piper Jackson cut her eyes at me.

I continued, "Wasn't he just being loyal? He saw you threatening the leader of his company, this place he's worked for, for"—I glanced at Quaid, who smiled with his eyes alone—"for forever, and he tried to be a hero. We *punish* him for that? For loyalty?"

Josiah whirled on me—and I knew at once this interruption wouldn't work like my others. He was rabid. His torn T-shirt revealed one blue-red nipple and wiry armpit hair. His eyes glowed with pink fury and his teeth gnashed and I wasn't sure who he'd kill first between me and Quaid.

Before he could choose, a blast shook the building. The floor rocked underneath me, sending my knees opposite ways. Blaring noise stuffed the air.

The sky outside the window changed from black to flaming orange.

CHAPTER THIRTY-ONE

Six Months Later

T he international response to what was first termed "the data-storage software glitch," then "degradation of socio-civil struc-tures due to rapidly spreading infrastructure weakness," and finally just "the Anarchy" was slow. At the United Nations, Russia and China blocked resolutions calling for a coordinated worldwide response, unwilling to devote resources to what they saw as the West's problem. For their part, Western nations hesitated sharing intelligence with those it feared might use it against them. At every level of society, trust was low.

Finally, the Security Council agreed to convene an exploratory commission. The Copenhagen-based group took five months releasing its report, which contained the following conclusions:

1. The Anarchy began in the United States, triggered by the internet-based group known as the Blind Mice.

2. The Anarchy is worsening.

· · ·

3. Greater transparency and regulation might have prevented the Anarchy.

The commission pointed to the decimation of American Dynamics' factories as "an inciting event," the beginning of investor panic. The effect snowballed days later when NASDAQ began experiencing "irreconcilable packet loss." Millions of dollars in meat, fish, and temperature-sensitive medicine spoiled after Port Newark's container refrigeration algorithm failed. The loss of electronic deeds plunged several municipalities into territorial legal fights. Banks, desperate to shield deposit records against the wave of disappearing data, retained paper backups. Soon these physical sites became targets. How much the Mice directed versus merely inspired was unclear.

Capital markets ran dry. Nobody, neither lenders nor borrowers, had faith in institutions' ability to enforce future obligations. Building projects from Tucson to Vladivostok stopped. Vital maintenance stopped. A bridge span crumbled spectacularly in Jakarta. The Suez Canal fell into disrepair; a commercial fishing trawler tried one last run and ended up aground fifteen miles into Egypt, sunk in the sand, bluefin tuna rotting on deck.

News devolved to a kind of pointillist, unreliable info-cloud. Depending on which sites you read, you might believe any one of a dizzying array of fact sets: that overprotection of civil liberties was sustaining the Anarchy, that a school of dolphins in the Red Sea carried all the world's data in embedded microchips, that Kim Jong Un was in cahoots with evil corporations, that the richest 1 percent were being shuttled in batches to moon colonies via Richard Branson's personal spaceship.

It was a bad time, also, to be mayor of New York City.

"No. No, that is patently false," Sergio Diaz said into the phone now, pacing about his office.

The reporter on speakerphone pressed, "A number of city employees have gone on record saying their paychecks bounced. Is this true? Is the government insolvent?"

"I assure you, we're paying our people," the mayor said. "Everyone is struggling with logistics now. These kinks will get ironed—"

"Has NYPD ceded parts of Staten Island and the Bronx to motor-cycle gangs?"

"I have no idea where you would've—"

"There are multiple reports Hells Angels and the Bandidos effectively control the outer boroughs. Can you confirm or deny?"

Sergio walked to his mahogany sideboard, bracing himself by a carved elephant tusk. "Crime continues to be a challenge. My office makes no secret of that."

"What about the plume of smoke coming from the Waldorf Astoria? Has the source been ID'd? Is the building being evacuated?"

Sergio found a pen and jotted *Waldorf fire?* on a Post-it. He'd ask Ingrid to make some calls.

"All these issues are being addressed. We're doing the best we can with the resources at our disposal."

The reporter asked, "Is there a plan for getting the data back? What's the expected return date?"

Sergio dug a hand back through his jet-black hair. He would've given anything to blow off steam tonight by touring the Manhattan party circuit, but his security czar no longer allowed him anywhere unaccompanied by full SWAT.

"I am told it's like Christmas lights," he said. "One bad bulb ruins the string. You have to hunt through and find it, but once you do, the rest blink on."

The mayor delivered this metaphor by rote. He'd been using it for months, and the words leaving his mouth no longer registered in his brain. The reporter's guffaw was audible over the line.

Ten minutes later, Sergio received a visit from Bruce Delaney of Forceworthy Services—the next man up after Todd Finley, about whom the mayor had heard nothing after the Dakota. Delaney had talked his way past Ingrid a half dozen times for some high-pressure pitch, but today was different.

The mayor had requested today's meeting.

"Glad to see y'come around," Bruce said as they shook. "New York City is the beacon of civilization, and Forceworthy wants to be a part of its preservation."

"We are only talking," Sergio said. "I still have faith in my police, and Albany is promising national guard help soon."

Bruce Delaney unfastened his briefcase, spread out his materials. "Saw the plywood on my way in. Not super confidence inspiring when city hall can't keep glass in its windows."

Ruefully, the mayor began flipping through pamphlets. The Forceworthy rep pitched three security bundles. *Up and down the force spectrum, whatever your needs.* The Eliminator package was available at $80 million per day. MuniShield, which counted fence-line drones among its deterrents, was still extremely reasonable at $190 million. And, lastly, the top-of-the-line PoodleSkirt ran an even $500 million.

"PoodleSkirt?" Sergio repeated.

"Right, 1950s," Delaney said. "We turn the clock back. Pies cooling in every window, leave your doors unlocked. Forceworthy brings overwhelming force to bear and gives you back your city."

He delivered the slogan with a pearly grin.

Sergio said, "*Five hundred million?* The city doesn't spend that much across all services in one day."

"Which is why I'm flexible. We can slice and dice between MuniShield and Poodle, get y'a custom package, get us to a price point where everyone's happy."

When the mayor didn't respond, his head foggy at all those zeroes, Delaney went on, "Look, in these dark times, Forceworthy is the light. All the success stories, all the cities that're managing to beat off this awful, savage thing—they have one thing in common. And that's us. Forceworthy Services.

"Let's speak frankly, shall we? NYPD controls most bridges and tunnels, and major thoroughfares in Manhattan and Brooklyn—and not a helluva lot else. Our research indicates a thirty to thirty-five percent loss of territory. Forceworthy can give you the tools to regain that land."

The mayor turned from Delaney to hide his ashen face. He'd expected to hear a big dollar number, but the figures Delaney was floating were staggering. He couldn't have afforded these expenditures on a pre-Anarchy budget—when sales and real-estate taxes were being regularly collected. The cash flows they operated off now were down 90 percent.

"I simply can't," Sergio said. "The fees are a nonstarter. Who can afford this? Who's paying you?"

"Different municipalities are handling the expense in different ways. Forceworthy understands credit's tough at this historical moment, and we've designed some innovative financial structures with this in mind. The one I'm thinking could work here is called Equi-tySecure—it requires zero up-front cash."

Sergio narrowed his cocoa eyes.

Delaney rubbed his hands like he was making fire and continued, "Fantastic deal. And drop-dead simple. Rather than pay us outright, you grant Forceworthy an equity stake in your city or town." He flung an arm toward the skyline. "Obviously, city in your case. Then we come in, as primary stakeholders now, and determine a security package appropriate to your Anarchy-suppressing needs. Win-win all the way."

"An equity stake?" Sergio felt the floor sway under his wing tips. "As in, Forceworthy Services owns a piece of New York City?"

Bruce Delaney laughed out loud, smacking the thigh of his suit pants too grandly. "'Owns' is a strong word. The arrangement is loose. Your citizens keep the lion's share of rights. I believe there're provisions for votes on certain points of policy"—puffing his cheeks dismissively—"but we'd have to drag the lawyers in to understand all that. Nobody wants that, am I right?

"Bottom line, EquitySecure is helping mayors and governors in all fifty states. Nebraska has seen phenomenal results, reclaimed ninety-seven percent of its territorial integrity. Charlotte, great story—Charlotte restored its entire shoreline back to the rightful owners. We installed our satellite-based HotShield patrols, unmanned drones? Pirate scum didn't stand a chance."

The pitch continued several more minutes. As Delaney spoke, Sergio Diaz paced a slow circle around his office. He'd had hundreds of awful meetings here since the Anarchy had taken hold, but none quite so depressing as this.

He'd heard from other mayors—Carol Carruthers in LA, Dick

Madsen in Houston—that Forceworthy was the surest way to govern your city. The new threats couldn't be contained internally—you needed help, you needed firepower, and Forceworthy had it.

But good God, the price. Had Carol and Dick surrendered their cities' sovereignty in this crackpot EquityShare scheme? Had Forceworthy recently spiked its prices? Or had they just quoted Sergio high, knowing he was in desperate straits?

Sergio began shaking his head.

"This is not happening." He walked to the door and twisted its knob. "I won't be the mayor who sold off New York City."

A sly expression came over the Forceworthy rep's face. "You won't be the mayor *period*, if you can't maintain some semblance of order."

"Perhaps," Sergio said, though his people were telling him he was likely to stay in office past November—there was no way to conduct an election under the current conditions.

Bruce Delaney tapped his pamphlets into a stack, replaced them in his briefcase, and left—thanking the mayor and assuring him he'd be just a phone call away if he had a change of heart.

Sergio went to the sideboard and poured himself a scotch. The liquor singed going down but did not deliver its usual relaxing aftereffect. He poured a second. He was staring hard into the sideboard's gilt-edged mirror, wishing for Providence or at least the distracting company of Quaid Rafferty, when he spotted something awry at his temple.

A gray hair.

CHAPTER THIRTY-TWO

New Jersey

I pulled the kids out of school in December. Lots of parents were. According to the office ladies, who I still knew from my days as a counselor there, the district had no precise figures due to attendance records having vanished. The violence had gotten bad. Teachers were keeping guns in their desks. Well-off students were arriving with bodyguards. Rumors circulated that grades couldn't be stored—Zach claimed Mr. Bortles dropped their European history quizzes straight into the recycle bin every Friday afternoon.

"Are we homeschooled now?" Karen asked that first morning over breakfast.

I couldn't tell if she thought the idea was thrilling or a badge of shame. "Sure, I suppose you are."

"That means you're our teacher?"

"I'm always your teacher, honey—that's my job. I'll just be your teacher a little more often."

Zach sniffed through a bite of French toast. "Till you get a call from Cowboy and Slick."

I weighed my response. Fourteen was a tough age. Certain concepts Zach navigated with unexpected grace—he never brought up his father, for example, knowing it would bring me down—but others escaped him completely, like the difference between telling your pastor, *Thank you*, with your eyes and whole face rather than mumbling it.

"My obligations in this job are irregular, that's true," I said. "But on the plus side, it has given me lots of free time to be home. With both of you."

Karen smiled and took my hand over the table, and I felt blessed to be a parent.

Then Zach said, "Are you dating Slick?"

I jerked in my chair. "*What?* Where did you get that idea?"

"I dunno, he's around an awful lot." Zach reached for more syrup —his French toast had dried out. "I just figured."

Since Pittsburgh, as the unrest hardened into the full-blown Anarchy, Quaid had made a point of stopping by most nights. After dark, like most neighborhoods, ours thrummed with theft, arson, and worse. Quaid would show up and do goofy voices for Karen's dolls, or debate socialism with Zach (he could argue either way), or just pour himself a prairie fire and sit with us on the couch.

Sometimes he'd rub my shoulders. When I baked pork chops, I made sure to cook five.

Actually, now that I thought about it, I could understand Zach's mistake.

"We aren't dating," I said. "I have been seeing a lot of him, but I just... It's weird. It's a weird time."

Zach shrugged. "Whatever. As dudes go, I mean, Slick's not the worst you—"

"*Quaid*," I said. "His name is Quaid. You and he have had multiple conversations. There's no reason you can't use his proper name."

Zach raised his eyebrows and scooched back from the table like I was being unreasonable.

Maybe I was. Truthfully, I was struggling. Everybody was. The guys had cut my weekly stipend in half after Jim Steed made the job fully pay-on-completion—and who knew if my money, any of it, would be there when I asked the bank for it?

We'd stopped trying snatch-and-grab operations against the Mice. Catching Josiah wouldn't stop the Anarchy. The mission had morphed into intelligence gathering on the foreign connection that'd emerged in Pittsburgh. Jim Steed believed the entity pulling the strings must be an AmDye competitor, "somebody with a vested interest in cutting American manufacturing down at the knees."

To maintain my status in the Blind Mice, I'd shown up to a few meetings at the relocated Lewd Brew. I worried they would be angry I'd stuck up for that American Dynamics janitor, but nobody said a word. It had gotten lost in the factories' explosions and ensuing chaos.

Garrison and I had trouble talking. The aborted kiss, my Algernon promotion, Pittsburgh and all that followed—whatever delicate balance had made our attraction work had been thrown off. His texts felt sheepish. Times we'd bumped into each other, I didn't feel the same electricity.

I guess it could've been the shoulder rubs.

By the calendar, the holidays had arrived. But it didn't feel like the holidays. Nobody dared go caroling on strangers' front porches. The Salvation Army knew better than to send its bell ringers out. That feeling of good cheer and charity, of helping your fellow human, had been sucked from the world.

I shielded the kids as best I could. We found Karen a Santa at an upscale mall in Essex Fells with X-ray machines and five security "elves" with assault rifles. Granny dazzled us with tales of roaring 1950s Christmases, Macy's and bubble lights and Harry Belafonte. ("And old fashioneds all around, yes?" Quaid put in.)

They did remarkably well, the kids. Karen's complex inner world occupied her for hours in a row. Zach complained only minimally about restrictions on his comings and goings.

On Christmas Eve, I relaxed my no-noneducational-TV rule and said we could watch the Rockefeller Center celebration. Everyone snuggled into place around a heaping platter of fiesta chicken nachos.

I tapped the remote. Thankfully—cable worked roughly 40 percent of the time—an image appeared on-screen of the iconic Christmas tree towering over an ice rink.

Karen squealed, "Pepillo!"

She and Zach scrambled close to the television as the broadcast showed the sixteen-year-old footballer, whom commentators said "plays with the joy of a cheetah cub." Pepillo stood precariously on skates with his girlfriend, Jenna Jinson, the Disney actress-singer-songwriter. They made a striking couple, his chiseled face beside her rosy lollipop cheeks.

Karen said, "He looks cold."

"Duh, he's Brazilian," Zach said. "Of course he's cold."

"Zach..." I warned, but they were too engrossed in the show to fight.

Pepillo skated exactly like a boy who'd grown up near the equator, but the Disney starlet guided him gently by the elbow, ducking her head, those telegenic eyes drawing him forward.

The two had dominated gossip websites for months, since confirming the rumor that the young striker was seeing the pop star, whose multipronged contract rivaled his own with Real Madrid in total value.

Zach loved watching grainy YouTube clips of Pepillo guiding tennis balls along his instep or beating a whole beach of defenders. Jenna Jinson's face decorated lunch boxes and soda cans, her effervescent smile ubiquitous as any image in today's fragmented media diaspora.

Jenna had just accepted a microphone and seemed ready to sing when a knock sounded on the front door.

"*Somebody order an extra-large pie with double anchovies?*" a voice called from outside.

Granny was just pulling an afghan over her legs. "Why?" She made a gnarled fist. "Every time I'm ready for a moment of peace, that man appears."

Quaid backed his way inside, grinning, carrying two pizza boxes and a leather satchel bag over his shoulder. He laid one pizza on the coffee table and flopped it open with the panache of a five-star waiter.

I propped a hand on my hip. "I told you I was making nachos."

"Nachos are an appetizer," he said.

"But I added chicken, which makes—"

"Doesn't matter if you toss protein on top, the Platonic ideal of a nacho is supplemental." He picked out a gloppy chip and tasted. "Excellent flavors, no question. But an appetizer nonetheless."

From his bag, Quaid produced wine, a fresh sixty-four box of crayons, and a can of WD-40.

He tossed the lubricant to Zach. "Durwood says one squirt inside each wheel, and that skateboard of yours'll go like a bobcat chasing after a crooked Appalachian lawyer."

Zach squinted at the blue bottle. "He really said that?"

Quaid gave my side a squeeze. "Nope. But doesn't it sound like a thing he might?" He nodded to the television. "Did they find Santa's sleigh on radar yet? Which way's he coming this year, from the east or around west?"

Karen turned from the screen. "Santa Claus is make-believe, Mr. Rafferty."

Quaid's head whipped back and forth between me and the kids. "The whole thing's a fraud? You're kidding. Who eats all those milk and cookies I've been putting out?"

Karen answered, "Your parents."

As the banter petered out—Quaid tried engaging Granny next but got nothing but scowls—I settled in beside him and breathed deep. He shed his sport coat and pulled my legs into his lap.

I let him. In his touch, the cushions felt softer. The noises outside seemed less sinister.

Still, a voice within me said, *Don't trust it. He'll get distracted. He'll wander off sure as a toddler at Chuck E. Cheese, and there's nobody in a giant mouse costume to drag him back to you.*

Jenna Jinson belted out a heart-twisting version of "Hallelujah," the hundred-foot screen behind her cycling through images of Anarchy victims: the 577 members of the French National Assembly, the prime minister of Australia, popular musicians and writers, and child after child after child.

The song could have lasted a week, and there would've been plenty more faces to show.

Jenna Jinson finished, chopping backward off the carpeted stage and onto the ice, which had been cleared of all but her partner.

Pepillo took her hand, and the two skated around the oval rink. Whether he'd been faking before or simply had his natural athleticism click in, I didn't know; but Pepillo glided beside Jenna now with ease.

Granny jabbed a finger at the screen. "That's not him. *That's a double!* They can't skate."

I pulled a hand down my face and was crafting my response to "they" when Quaid muttered, "Leave it alone."

Pepillo and Jenna Jinson carved figure eights in the blue-tinged ice. A live audience watched spellbound from behind a rail, and millions more online or through their TVs. They spun. They knocked the other's hip. They embraced and shared a solemn, intimate smile.

My hand found Quaid's. Karen and Zach were rubbing shoulders and bopping knees like I hadn't seen them do for years.

From high in the camera shot, a puff.

Granny stopped rocking in her chair. The kids kept staring at the screen, rapt, waiting. I glanced to Quaid. His face had lost its ruddy glow.

A trickle of red appeared from the center of Jenna Jinson's forehead. The angelic smile slid off her lips.

Pepillo staggered to support her. His prior confidence gone, his blades scurried underneath and his arms flailed. Terror blared in his eyes.

For an instant, the pop star seemed to come to his aid. Her blood-smeared cheek nestled in the crook of his neck. Her limp hand draped across his waist.

Then a hail of sniper fire riddled their bodies. They were sides of meat hanging on hooks, getting pelted.

Although the live audience gasped and a news anchor broke in stammering, the reaction contained a certain grim familiarity. The anchor's ducked head seemed to say, *How stupid we all were...how silly to believe this, even this, was above ruin...*

Karen was a shivering ball in my lap. Quaid had shifted off the couch and laid a hand on Zach's head, which my son neither resisted nor protested. I could hear his sobs.

I found the remote and switched off the TV.

CHAPTER THIRTY-THREE

P er the typical arrangement, Durwood found Yakov's key in the bathroom of the Kingsland train stop. The Kazakh hid it somewhere different every time. Durwood checked underneath the tank, around back of the sink's rusty drainpipe. He found it Scotch-taped to the top of the last hand dryer, and stuck it in his blue jeans pocket.

Then he and Sue-Ann boarded a westbound train. The conductor took Durwood's ticket with a glance at Sue. He said nothing. Between the M9 bulging in Durwood's coat and having bigger fish to fry, the man wasn't quibbling over a dog.

Durwood watched out the window through cracks and bullet holes. Crumbling brick apartments. A whole block on fire. Husks of industrial buildings.

Sue-Ann drowsed against his boot. There was a catch in her lungs lately. Durwood suspected the air quality, which had gotten bad in the Anarchy. Could've just been old age.

It was Christmas Day. A day for celebrating Jesus Christ. Durwood shook his head, thinking what His world had come to.

They disembarked at the end of the line and walked eight dodgy blocks to the U-Store. Twilight had turned full dark. Bitter winds swirled up loose cardboard and chapped Durwood's face. He and Sue walked in the road, both sidewalks torn asunder by scrap-metal thieves wanting the pipes below.

Durwood circled to the back row of storage units. Several bays were open, their doors battered or ripped off. Contents long gone. He found the unit matching the key's imprinted number and inserted the key.

The steel door rattled up its track, slamming at the top. Yakov sat waiting in a canvas chair.

"Six grams of Novichok were not easy to find," said the man, wiry with a salt-and-pepper mustache. "I should have charged you a higher premium."

Durwood and Sue-Ann advanced into the storage unit. Durwood pulled the door down after them. The rattle was louder inside. The space, lit by a single bare bulb, smelled of sawdust and almonds.

Yakov said, "You should have secure transport. I can loan you a lead canister, but..." He trailed off as his eyes fell to Durwood's hands, which didn't carry a canister, or suitcase of cash, or anything. "What is this?"

Durwood folded his arms. "Need information on a sale you made."

"All my transactions are strictly private," the Kazakh said. "This is my rule, as you know."

"I do know. But your rule needs to break, this once."

Yakov's arm whipped behind his chair and whipped back with a pistol. "This was not intelligent, Mr. Jones. Not at all."

Durwood kept his arms folded. "Few months back, you woulda sold some charges to a merc squad. Foreigners. Significant job. Few dozen charges."

"I never have betrayed a buyer, and I—"

"Found your pink Styrofoam at the site." Durwood nodded at a large chute of packing peanuts. "They should've unpacked before. Lazy."

Yakov's aim was jittery. His muzzle danced like a firefly in a boy's jar. "We have done business many years. I have known you to be honorable, a man who keeps his word."

Durwood had no interest in this line of talk. "Who paid?"

"I'll ask you to leave now, friend. Later we will speak about payment for the Novichok."

"I ain't your friend. Never pretended I was."

He clucked at Sue-Ann, and the old coonhound began loping around the storage unit. She passed into shadow, her paws nicking the concrete floor.

Yakov said, "A dog? A dog can't go back there—I have chemicals! I have bombs with caesium, he will—"

"She."

"She, fine—*what in God's name?*" Yakov kept swiveling between Durwood and the dim recesses of the unit. "I deal with professionals, only with professionals! And this is not—"

He didn't finish saying what it wasn't, because Durwood—perfectly timing the man's movements—drew his M9 and cocked the hammer.

Yakov swore.

"Now," Durwood said. "Who paid?"

"You know what I know—they were foreigners. That's all I know."

"Who paid?" Durwood repeated. "I need names. Nationalities."

Yakov made a show of keeping his gun up, but his shoulders were shriveled toward his chest. His knees pinched like he needed the john.

"They didn't give me names."

"Like hell. You know who you deal to."

Yakov shook his head, pained, mustache twitching. Durwood knew his procedures to the letter. It was pointless acting otherwise and Yakov knew it.

"You have lost a supplier today," the arms dealer said. "We're done, you and I."

"Plenty others in your racket."

"If you are comfortable shooting and detonating *junk.*" Yakov sneered at the thought of his competitors' wares.

Truth be told, losing Yakov was a blow. Quaid and Durwood had no other leads on the Mice's foreign connection, though, and it had taken long enough already, months, to tease Yakov out with the Novichok request. Durwood hated losing access to Yakov's bleeding-edge technology, but finding the mastermind behind Pittsburgh—and maybe behind the whole Anarchy—was worth it.

"Last chance 'fore I start with a kneecap." Durwood gripped the barrel of his M9. "Who bought the charges?"

Yakov dropped his gun and began sniveling. Durwood knew what he was thinking. *I give up identities, I lose trust. And trust is the whole deal in this business.*

Durwood shifted his aim just over the man's ear. He would give him a close shave first, and do the kneecap if he had to.

A moment before he squeezed the trigger, Yakov croaked, "Rivard."

Durwood lowered his gun in a long breath. He called Sue-Ann.

Rivard LLC. The darn French.

He should've known.

PART THREE

CHAPTER THIRTY-FOUR

Switzerland - Five Weeks Later

Pre-Anarchy, Quaid Rafferty had enjoyed air travel. Flying between mission sites and his adopted home of Las Vegas, he'd liked hearing what Carly from Minneapolis thought about driverless cars, or giving Len from Pensacola his spiel on why you always, *always*, order the chef's special at restaurants. He hadn't even minded delays or layovers, which just gave life more chances to plant wildflowers in your path.

Post-Anarchy, he enjoyed it less.

The flight into Davos showed an arrival window of 3:13 to 5:43. Boarding, Quaid tipped his head to the pilots, who were conversing out the cockpit window with the F-16 pilot who'd be escorting them to Davos.

Quaid pressed through to their seats, followed by Molly, Durwood, and a thinner-looking Sue-Ann. Flight attendants helped passengers jam bags into overhead bins—checked luggage was almost unheard of, nobody in their right mind willing to hand over a bag to some stranger. Backs hunched. Eye avoided eye. Adults transferred guns from duffel bags into jacket pockets.

Quaid's boarding pass read *37-A*, window, but a large, mulleted man was there.

"Excuse me," Quaid said. "I believe we need to switcheroo."

The man gestured to his camo-pattern rucksack wedged tightly underneath the seat in front, and closed his eyes.

"I'm sure there's assistance to be had moving your bag," Quaid said. "What seat did they give you? Could be you got one of those fake tickets."

The man raised his middle finger without opening his eyes.

Quaid had scarcely registered the gesture when Durwood shot past and seized the man's knobby finger in his fist.

"*Ow!*" the man cried. "Hey, what're you—"

He stopped when he saw not Quaid's gregarious face but the drum-tight glare of Durwood Oak Jones. Before he could protest or start to comply, Durwood yanked the rucksack out from under the seat —jerking the man's knee unnaturally—and slammed the bag into his gut.

"G'on," said the ex-marine. "Find your right place."

The man looked at Durwood, then at Quaid, Molly, and the coonhound, and seemed to decide that whatever this motley crew was about, he wanted no part. He moved across the aisle.

Once tray tables were up and the wings' antimissile plating was affixed, Quaid perused the magazines in his seat-back pocket. Somebody had left a *Maxim*, and as luck would have it, the cover featured none other than the woman they were on their way to see.

"We Cook the Books With Fabienne Rivard," read the headline, across a shot of the French heiress-CEO straddling a boardroom chair.

Fabienne was the daughter of the legendary Henri Rivard, founder of Rivard LLC. Henri had built Rivard into a titan, dominating commerce across the Continent, defying United States sanctions to form lucrative partnerships with Mideast dictators, trading in murky industries—weapons, various "professional services"—that others shied from.

When Fabienne had taken the reins six years earlier amid reports of her father's deteriorating health, there had been speculation she would bring a feminine touch to the organization. She'd grown up in the media glare, spilling out of Hollywood clubs with famous actors at age fifteen, briefly hosting a reality show.

Would she start a charity arm of Rivard to fight Third World disease? Might she finally apologize for, or at least address, the allegations of atrocities committed by Rivard's *combattantes de contrat*?

She did nothing of the sort. Although it was said her merciless gender equalization policies had made Rivard's upper management team more diverse, nothing about the company's engagement with the outside world changed.

If anything, Rivard LLC became more aggressive. Quaid and Durwood had stopped two cataclysmic plots hatched during her reign —one involving space lasers, the other a mind-altering virus that nearly necessitated every human being on the planet taking BienVous, Rivard's signature psychotic.

"Is that her?"

The question, from Molly beside him, brought Quaid out of his thoughts—which had just begun veering into daydream, Fabienne's sharp legs making an inviting V across the magazine.

"Uh, right," he said. "The one and only Fabienne Rivard."

Molly scooted closer to examine the picture. Her nose wrinkled. "So we think she's the mastermind behind the Anarchy?"

Quaid looked to his partner.

Durwood's mouth set in a snarl. "I do."

Quaid was, by trade, more diplomatic with words. "That's what we're flying to Switzerland for. To figure it out."

The World Economic Forum had insisted on holding its annual Davos meeting despite the security challenges and hostile corporate climate, pronouncing that "now more than ever, leaders of all stripes must step to the fore." Fabienne Rivard, whose company investors had heralded as a fantastic Anarchy play for its continued financial success, was delivering the keynote address.

"I still don't understand," Molly said. "The Blind Mice hate corporations. Rivard *is* a corporation. Why are they working together?"

"Money," Durwood said, his voice thick with disgust. "Profit."

"But destabilizing the world—destabilizing commerce, destabilizing credit. How does that help Rivard?"

Quaid looked at the picture of Fabienne, the smoldering eyes, the brow ridge—heavy like Henri's, like a stiff rod from which hung the rest of her gaunt face.

"They're like vultures, Rivard," he said. "You see roadkill and think tragedy, but not them. They see lunch."

The flight over the Atlantic was more or less uneventful. The F-16 scrambled twice, booming off parabolically to check some threat, but mostly stayed by their side. As the pilot began her descent, she announced they would be maintaining altitude until the last possible moment—making a harder target for shoulder-fired RPGs—but managed to set them down with barely a bump.

Quaid, Molly, Durwood, and Sue-Ann deplaned to a horde of protesters. Signs bobbed from all directions.

GREED-con!

World Economic Farce.

You change the equation at the top, over a nose-eyes-whiskers symbol.

The conference organizers had arranged countermeasures. Snipers in black bodysuits stood atop building corners like antennae. Battalions of shield-thrusting police enforced a path to the limousine stand.

On the way to the hotel, Quaid saw further dissent. Crowds staggering through clouds of tear gas. In the distance, a mountain gondola dangling by one wheel. Sagging power lines, decapitated lampposts, buildings without facades—he'd heard rumors the richer countries were doing better, but it seemed not by much.

They met Jim Steed in the hotel lobby.

"Good, you made it," he said.

Steed looked like he'd just come off the graveyard shift, bleary-eyed, keeping himself upright by a lobby armchair.

Quaid asked, "What happened to you?"

"Ah, I'm behind—got the board of directors breathing down my neck." Steed waved his phone ambiguously. "Forget that. When do we nail these froggy cheats? I want this done."

"We need to take our time, do it right."

"Take our time?" the CEO said. "They sent that albino freak to assassinate me! I want scalps."

"To be fair," Quaid said, accepting a tapenade appetizer off a server's tray, "we haven't established exactly how that attack came about."

Rivard had a long history of subterfuge against American Dynamics, ranging from simple price manipulations to the more elaborate—like the time a Rivard agent posing as a sympathetic bartender at a watering hole near the plant stole AmDye's new fiberglass formulation.

Quaid felt that at this crucial juncture in the AmDye–Third Chance relationship, telling Steed the truth about who'd tipped the Blind Mice off to his Pittsburgh schedule would be unproductive.

Now Steed led the way to their bank of rooms.

He said to Durwood, "You got the evidence, right? We go public with the fact they're scheming with the Blind Mice, it blows a hole right through Fabienne's big speech."

Durwood didn't answer. He walked beside Sue-Ann, who was busy sniffing the hotel baseboards.

Quaid said, "I tipped a guy in the media pool. He can put it out there, but Fabienne will just deny. They've got their own puppets in the press who'll muddy up the waters."

"I know, I know," Steed conceded. They'd reached his room, which was littered with dossiers and stacks of manila folders. "I have to do something, though. Got my shareholders, everybody on the board of directors pushing me to retrofit our factories for military production. That's where Rivard is, and look at their results."

Quaid said, "They wanna start building tanks?"

"Yeah!" Steed fished through a pile of folders for one whose cover showed a hulking gray M1 Abrams. "I told 'em we should wait. The data comes back, we're stuck with the wrong products again. Giant manufacturing plants devoted to stuff nobody wants—Detroit all over again."

"And?"

Steed shook his head. "They think the Anarchy is permanent. They think it's 'the new normal'"—he used air quotes and a nasal corporate voice—"and the data's never coming back."

"Then we need to show them they're wrong," Quaid said.

"How?"

JEFF BOND

Quaid opened his shoulders to Molly, who was looking around the opulent suite. "We still have McGill here positioned inside the Mice. She has an intimate relationship with the key techie, Piper Jackson. We can use that relationship and find out more about the nitty-gritty of the data loss."

Steed kneaded his forehead. "Blind Mice are the B team now. They're barely relevant."

"Except they have this kernel, this thing that's zapping the data," Quaid said. "Molly's seen it in action. If she can pull the string—"

"Too much pussyfooting around," Steed cut in. "She's been dancing that jig for months."

"She's made progress. She's penetrated their inner circle."

"And a whole lotta good it's done. While she's been off—"

"Alright, *she*," Molly said, inserting herself into the discussion, "is standing right here. I don't see any of your methods panning out. I don't see either of you putting yourselves in the crosshairs, figuring out where the Mice are weak or might crack. All I see is ego."

Jim Steed pulled back as though dodging Vietcong sniper darts. "Where could they crack?"

Molly's brilliant-green eyes stayed hot. She paused before answering. "Piper has serious misgivings about all this."

"Misgivings? She told you this?"

Molly nodded, but Quaid detected some reluctance. "We've batted around misgivings."

"Can you turn her?" Steed asked with a glint in his eye. "Get her to switch sides?

"I...think so," Molly said. "If I reveal myself, she'll help us. We can figure out where the kernel started and what needs to be done to stop it."

It was audacious—a course of action she hadn't discussed previously with Quaid and Durwood. She was working off script.

Steed considered, palming his lunchpail jaw.

"Eh, feels like a Hail Mary," he said. "That's your whole plan?"

"Oh no," Quaid jumped in. "Third Chance Enterprises always has multiple avenues of approach. I'm working it from the other side. I have a tête-à-tête scheduled with Fabienne tonight, and I'm going to find out what their angle is."

"How? Why's she meeting with you?"

Though Jim Steed had asked the question, everyone in the room looked eager for Quaid's answer. Even Sue-Ann seemed to droop one bloodshot eye slightly lower.

Quaid straightened one lapel of his sport coat. "Because we have a special relationship."

The heat in McGill's face—which had ebbed since her outburst—came roaring back. The answer seemed to displease Durwood too. His bottom lip pushed past his top, jutting like a peeved horse's.

Quaid hadn't discussed his prior contact with Fabienne Rivard. Durwood knew Quaid did freelance jobs without him, sidehustles in support of either liberal political causes Durwood didn't support or clients like Fabienne with morally murky goals.

No good would come from expounding upon his and Fabienne's relationship—to Durwood, to Molly, to any of them.

Jim Steed said, "Special, huh?"

"Fabienne Rivard is the key," Quaid said. "If I can get inside with her, see where her head's at? This whole mess might unravel itself yet."

And he believed this, about 73 percent.

CHAPTER THIRTY-FIVE

Fabienne Rivard strutted onstage before a wall of high-definition monitors, a fifty-by-fifty grid of synchronized screens showing the Rivard logo—that muscular, sanserif *R*—superimposed over a spinning globe. Microphones carried the *clack* of her stilettos to every corner of the auditorium.

The sight of her made my stomach slide.

I shouldn't have come. The guys had given me the option of staying back in New Jersey, but I'd refused, wanting a piece of the operation, afraid of losing my role after the revelation the Blind Mice weren't pulling their own strings.

Now I was supposed to be "monitoring the crowd for unusual activity." There was nothing much to monitor: every eye in the room was glued to Fabienne.

She was everything I'd heard: hollow-cheeked and plump-lipped as a supermodel, powerful in the thrust of her hips. She strode forth from the wall of razor-sharp screens and seemed part technology herself—cyborg or augmented human.

I tried focusing on the heiress's feet, which in heels looked veiny and impossibly long, not cute and compact as men have complimented mine in the past.

Didn't help.

In Fabienne's wake, a panel of eleven women and one older man—sprawling white hair, aristocratic looking—sat in folding chairs, making a hemispheric frame about their leader.

"Welcome, leaders of industry, to Davos," Fabienne began in her smoky accent. "I have been asked to speak of the French perspective on this new world in which we find ourselves. But I fear there is nothing French in what I will say today. This Anarchy, all face equally. All must stand with strength."

I elbowed out space between reporters and cameramen to see. Quaid had used his connections to get a choice seat up front, better than mine or even Jim Steed's. Durwood was patrolling the perimeter.

Fabienne continued, "The time for glossing over has passed. Now we must reshape our institutions—as chief executives, reshape our product offerings—to fit this new reality. The reality of chaos. It can be managed, I promise you. And the correct place for this management is the private sector."

Gliding her forefinger up and down a presentation clicker, Fabienne laid out a stark vision for the future. Governments had proved incapable of protecting their peoples and peoples' property, too focused on assigning blame and gaining votes. If corporations failed to fill this leadership vacuum, criminals would.

"In this spirit, Rivard LLC is pleased to announce a new initiative." She pressed the clicker, and the digital wall erupted with images of armored vehicles and rifle-sighting commandos. "For some time, we have partnered with Forceworthy Services, the global security leaders. Today, Forceworthy joins the Rivard family as a wholly owned brand. We plan to expand the division aggressively—bringing peace to communities small and large, to homes, to schools, to all seven continents."

The wall of monitors switched to videos of neighborhood pool parties, men in leisure suits and women in sundresses pouring wine as fires raged in the distance, safely separated by razor wire and rows of Rivard-Forceworthy soldiers.

Listening, I got the same sensation I feel stepping over a dirty sidewalk panel and realizing—with a weak gag—that I'm not actually looking at dirt, but an ant swarm.

I glanced up front to see how Quaid was taking the speech. His eyes were locked on Fabienne Rivard, his mouth cocked in a dreamy smile.

His words replayed in my head. *We have a special relationship.*

I shouldn't have been surprised. He'd done it before, gone chasing after the next shiny thing once the thrill wore off.

I refused to be jealous. Already, I'd let the green goblin get me—back in Jim Steed's hotel room when I'd volunteered to "turn" Piper Jackson. Quaid had been gaping at that magazine during the flight...then he and Steed talking about the operation like I was some subhuman pawn...it had burned me. *I* had been the one putting my life on the line, assuming the big risks.

And now I was signed up to risk even more—to reveal myself to Piper.

I was terrified to imagine her face when she found out I had been a plant all along. How her eyes would boil down to points. Would she grip my arm and drag me straight to Josiah? Wreck the plan without giving me any chance to explain? And what sick revenge would *he* take?

Now Fabienne segued into different initiatives. Rivard saw itself becoming a provider of currency. A guaranteer of online connectivity. Currently, Rivard's network of high-speed routers was the internet's sole reliable backbone—

"Excuse, excuse, por favor," a reporter interrupted. "Manuel Aguilera, blogging for the Venezuelan people. What do you say to criticism that Rivard is profiteering off this terrible situation?"

Fabienne fixed the man with a cool glare. "I say nonsense. There is a need, and we are filling it."

"You've spoken ninety minutes," he said, "and not once mentioned efforts to retrieve the missing data. This seems strange, does it not?"

Fabienne sniffed. "I am a realist."

"There are those who claim Rivard's Enterprise Software division is compromised, that the very antivirus programs protecting the data in fact jeopard—"

"Further nonsense. Our competitors are waging a campaign to smear us, to conjure some grand conspiracy."

"Speaking of competitors," the reporter said, "it's been rumored your forces were involved in the attack on American Dynamics plants in Pittsburgh. Can you comment?"

The reporter peeked to one side, finding Quaid's eye.

At the same time, I felt a mobilization beginning around the reporter, a subtle but insistent closing of space. Men wearing sunglasses and earpieces advanced through the crowd.

Fabienne gave a breathy chuckle. "Ah *oui*, the mainstream media has made it their mission to slander the great company of my father. I have grown accustomed to these lies."

Manuel Aguilera scribbled in a pad. "How is your father? Does Henri approve of this turn toward militarism?"

"My father is gravely ill. He remains, sadly, far removed from our day-to-day operations."

"My organization has come into possession of documents"— Manuel waved a sheaf of watermarked papers I recognized from Durwood's research—"that show, several months *before* the Blind Mice began their attacks, large security upgrades to Rivard's headquarters in Paris."

Fabienne said, "I will not apologize for vigilance."

"Localized missile defense? Bulletproof office windows?" The reporter spread his arms, playing to the crowd's growing murmurs. "How is it you were so prescient, Miss Rivard?"

The heiress dragged her tongue across her upper lip. "The fraying of society is not a new phenomenon. Roche Rivard was built during my father's regime. The idea of having a fortress for a corporate head-quarters dates back forty years—to the height of socialism when my father chose to chisel Roche Rivard from trillion-ton limestone in the Boulogne Woods. I have merely expanded upon his vision."

When a second reporter jumped in with a technical question, Fabienne deferred to the older man on her panel, introducing him as Yves Pomeroy.

Pomeroy tottered to the fore and was immediately hit with a hailstorm of suspicion. Why had Rivard's software permitted such data loss? Was it true Singapore had banned computers running the Rivard operating system? Who was leading the effort to restore the data? What were their qualifications?

The man addressed each challenge in measured terms. His hands palsied at the sides of a sleek glass podium.

When the questioners seemed to have him pinned down on time-lines—"*Before or after the report, Monsieur Pomeroy?*"—Fabienne seized control.

"Yves, who is a holdover from my father's time, suffers from Parkinson's disease as anyone can see. I will allow no further cruelty against him."

Pomeroy receded to his chair with a bewildered air, cutting his eyes repeatedly at Fabienne. I was reminded of Granny, how she never quite trusts it when I tell her to load plates into the dishwasher without rinsing—it'd never worked like that with her Kenmore.

I hoped she was doing okay with the kids. After Pepillo's Christmas-night slaughter, there had been a period of scared-straight behavior, but it had passed. Zach had been pushing to rehab one of the junked motorcycles you could find on any major highway—and though I'd been firm he was *not* authorized to ride any vehicle whose repair he was responsible for, Granny didn't always stay current on my rules.

Fabienne Rivard was wrapping up.

"We have been given an awful situation—by these Blind Mice, by the American government that has failed to stop them. They are a cancer, and that cancer has metastasized." Despite the gravity of her words, an excited purr entered her voice. "Many of you may be discouraged upon hearing my assessment. You wish for a return to the previous state of affairs."

She pivoted on one stiff leg, showing the audience a new side of her face. "If you look inside your people—if you look inside yourselves—you will know that this is not possible. The Anarchy has brought out a darkness in the world. A darkness that always existed in the hearts of man.

"It is surprising, perhaps, that it stayed covered for so long. Oh, it lived in the patriarchy and other repressive norms. Now this force, this *power,* has become diffused. An energy has been unleashed, and this energy can even be positive—if structures exist to channel it in a positive direction."

The wall of monitors began a slow fade back to the Rivard logo. The auditorium lights rose. As the reporters around me stuffed notepads into pockets, I tried looking inside myself.

Do I have darkness? Has the Anarchy changed me?

I realized, with a mix of fear and grit, that it had.

I was just thinking ahead to how I might start the conversation with Piper Jackson—*Okay, I haven't been* entirely *honest with you*—when fingers clamped my upper arm.

"Have we met before, miss?" said a British voice.

I flinched away, but the fingers stayed clamped. The man who owned them had a cruel face and muscles galore—cords and ropes of tanned, glimmering muscle.

"I—no, you must be confusing me with someone else."

His eyes were still. "Florence. Or was it Spain, San Sebastián?"

My arm was turning white, and my mind reeled with panic.

"This is my first time out of the States," I managed. "You—you must be mistaken."

The man yanked me, forcing our faces together. "I don't make mistakes, lass."

I was just deciding whether to knee him in the groin or scream when my arm came suddenly free.

CHAPTER THIRTY-SIX

D urwood had been slow. He'd been casting about for trouble, for odd or too well-coordinated patterns of movement. People who looked out of place, either by dress or behavior. He'd been noting the crisp, professional performance of her security detail.

Then he'd heard the chirp of pain.

Molly.

The muscle-bound thug had a grip on her. Durwood had covered twelve feet in two strides. He seized the thug's arm at the elbow—so hard the fingers loosened and Molly came free.

"Stand down," Durwood ordered.

The men faced each other. Durwood felt an ugly rumbling in his loins, recognizing his old nemesis, the British mercenary Blake Leathersby.

"Bugger off, Jones." The man flexed his arm, but Durwood's grip held. "Why are you in Davos? It's for corporate leaders, not some livestock show."

Durwood said, "Guess I just showed up."

"You shouldn't have, mate. Where's Rafferty hiding?" Leathersby, his brawny neck swiveling, used a homosexual slur. "Ain't seen him round yet."

"I couldn't say."

"How about that flea-ridden mutt of yours? Sally Mae, yeah? She finally kick the bucket?"

Sue-Ann was back at the hotel, nursing a bad cough.

"She's purebred," Durwood said. "Her ma and pa were blueticks both."

Leathersby laughed—deep, boorish. "The bird here, she's with you?" His eyes traveled Molly's curves. "Right decent, Jones. Got all her teeth, I see. I thought you backwoods types liked 'em dirtier..."

As he prattled on, Durwood thought. Thought about that tickle back in Pittsburgh. That thrum in his mind, watching the foreigners wire up charges in the factories.

Leathersby: Durwood was sure of it now. The job fit his style, methodical and unexpected, the use of multiple nationalities. He must be working for Fabienne Rivard.

How did he recognize Molly?

Maybe Rivard had the Mice under surveillance. Maybe from one of the other jobs Molly had done for the guys? Durwood couldn't recall whether Leathersby had been part of the enemy force in that Florence gig of theirs or not.

"Don't know her from Eve," Durwood said. "I see a man threaten a woman, I stop it."

He kept a stiff hold on Leathersby, who tried without success to flinch free. Durwood's farm strength against Leathersby's swollen gym muscles.

"Whatever you came for," Leathersby said, "you'd best steer clear of me."

"I came to restore law," Durwood said. "To mend this broken world."

Leathersby scoffed. "Mend? Yeah, take out your sewing needle and find plenty of thread, mate. Law is over."

Durwood squeezed. "I beg to differ."

The Brit, who had Durwood by a good five inches, struggled to get free. "So bloody simple, Jones. Boots, blue jeans, and God. I know every thought in that pea-size brain of yours."

"What am I thinking now?"

Men in *Davos Security* windbreakers had noticed the fight. They hustled through the crowd, talking in headsets.

The confrontation was about to end, but Durwood knew it would resume at some later point. Likely a more dangerous one.

Leathersby said, "I expect you're wishing you had what hangs in my right trouser holster: a Webley top-break .455 caliber revolver."

Durwood nearly smiled as he let go of his foe's forearm, security having reached them.

"Man with a US Army M9 semiautomatic has no envy of that," he said. "But I'm sure it serves you well on fox hunts."

CHAPTER THIRTY-SEVEN

There was a certain aptness to the Rivard LLC delegation staying at Hotel Zauberberg. The lodge—built into the side of the mountain like their own headquarters, Roche Rivard—rose skyward in terraced levels that became narrower and more exclusive the higher they climbed. Dormers and spare white arches gave the hotel a haughty old-world feel.

Quaid entered by ten-foot farmhouse doors and immediately heard the fuzzing of Geiger counters. A guard in a suit checked a computer screen and waved Quaid through. Inside, concierges were loading skis onto a brass luggage cart for a man wearing a cape.

The lobby contained an inviting bar area—marbled wood décor, teardrop chandelier. Quaid decided to wet his whistle before starting out after Fabienne.

The entire facility would be under surveillance. The heiress might at this very moment be reclining on some velvet chaise, watching him on closed caption.

Quaid had oversold his "tête-à-tête" with Fabienne to the others. It wasn't, in fact, scheduled, and their last contact had been months ago. Still, he felt sure that when she saw him—and remembered the night they'd spent in Bucharest together—she would respond with enthusiasm.

The server brought Quaid something that didn't deserve the name "prairie fire"—did he taste grenadine?—but he drank it without complaint and ordered another.

As he loosened up, Quaid gauged Hotel Zauberberg's security. It was ironclad as expected, but showed a level of technical sophistication beyond anything he'd seen in the States. Liquor bottles had digital pourers to detect poisons. A red-pulsing laser net below the ceiling morphed with his and the server's movements.

It made Quaid think of his friend Manuel's question about missile defense at Roche Rivard.

How long does a thing like that take to pull together?

That Rivard had conspired with the Blind Mice seemed clear, but there was more to know. Were the Mice unique as instigators, or had Rivard contracted with other similar groups? How tight was the coupling? Had Rivard merely ridden a wave the Mice had set in motion, or engineered it themselves?

Quaid finished his second drink—grenadine, definitely—then joined a waiting group at the elevator bank. The car arrived and all shuffled on. As others disembarked at lower floors, he checked his sandy hair by its reflection in gold plating, re-mussing a spot on the right.

Quaid had charmed a range of women over the years, but Fabienne Rivard was a category unto herself. Her rumored trysts were outrageous—Stephen Hawking, Cristiano Ronaldo, Princess Charlotte of Monaco. He needed to be at the top of his game.

At the elevator's *ding* for Twenty-Two, Quaid smacked his palms and strode forward with conviction.

Here goes nothing.

He hadn't taken three steps when a voice called, *"Arrêtez!"*

Three men emerged from a door, aiming assault rifles at Quaid's forehead. They wore dark, trim-fit clothes and gloves.

"You guys looking for the gym or business center?" Quaid asked. "I believe the pool's on seven."

None of them cracked a smile.

"*Quelle est votre entreprise?*" asked the middle one, who despite the choice of language had a Spaniard's look. "*Personne n'est autorisé ici.*"

Quaid nodded past them, up a corridor. "I'm here to see Mademoiselle Rivard."

"*Bof,*" said another guard. "You? And Miss Rivard?"

"We go way back. Tell her Quaid Rafferty is here. Tell her I'm ready to discuss terms."

Without lowering their guns, the men shared a dark look. They spoke in low tones for a moment, then one stepped forward to clamp cuffs roughly on Quaid's wrists.

As he was shoved forward by the small of his back, Quaid recalled the reports that Fabienne had recently built an oubliette—French for "dungeon with only a trapdoor in the ceiling for entry"—into Roche Rivard.

What if they locked him up? What if he never even got an audience with Fabienne? People disappeared all the time now, easy as poker chips.

Quaid was led through two hallways, one door with a pair of heavy-gauge combination locks, and a short passage smelling of incense.

The handcuffs had just sawed a scratch of blood across one wrist when he was dumped unceremoniously into a suite fit for Cleopatra. Inside, sitting cross-legged on a Louis XIV couch, was Fabienne Rivard.

"*Relâchez cet homme,*" she ordered, standing and approaching Quaid.

Each stride crossed her body at a severe angle, as though the leading line of hip-knee-foot were a machete slicing air.

The Spaniard uncuffed Quaid. Fabienne sent the guards off with a sneering jerk of the head. Then she led Quaid wordlessly to an adjoining room with a four-poster bed.

He followed warily, feeling lured in, coaxed onto the tendrils of a silken web. The smell of incense became stronger. When his eyes strayed from Fabienne's rear—the top third of which was exposed by her backless dress—he noticed two others in the room: a buxom blond woman and an African wearing ammunition across his bare chest on dual bandoliers.

Fabienne spoke briefly to the woman, who returned a cheek kiss and left. The man stayed.

Quaid gazed about the frescoed ceiling. "Nice digs. Who's the gal pal?"

"Thérèse Laurent has a PhD in organizational behavior." Fabienne's voice seemed to waft forth from the room's smell, which Quaid saw now originated from a hookah in the corner. "She was President Macron's chief of staff before I hired her away."

Quaid raised his eyebrows, impressed. "And I suppose this guy"—nodding to the African—"negotiated the rebel peace treaty in Sudan?"

The heiress laid her hand on the man's shoulder, her vermilion nails standing out against his skin. "Maha intrigues you?"

"I'm open-minded as the next guy," Quaid said, "but no, not like that. Those bullets look like they'd chafe."

She left Maha with a pout and walked to the couch, beckoning Quaid to join.

"Our correspondence has fallen into arrears," she said. "When we last spoke, you said you were busy with other projects. 'Booked solid,' as I recall. I found others."

Quaid did sit, the velour fabric smooth under his palms. "Third Chance Enterprises is in great demand."

Fabienne scoffed. "That idiotic name of yours."

"It's called branding. I know *you* know about branding—that's what the Forceworthy move was all about, right? Branding Rivard as number one in security?"

Fabienne didn't answer. Out the sprawling windows, moonlight reflected off the Alps turned her neck a bloodless blue. Together with her liquid eyes, the color made her seem aquatic—like some mermaid or sea nymph.

Now those eyes bore into Quaid.

He continued, "I wanted to take your gig, honestly. But Durwood wasn't keen on it. He tells me they're predicting ten thousand people could be killed this year *for their tooth fillings*."

Fabienne batted her eyelashes. "Terrible."

"Right. Though I must say, based on your talk today, it seems like nobody at Rivard is gonna mind much if the Anarchy keeps right on rolling."

"The world is complicated," she said. "Each day, women die like dogs in childbirth. The price of corn rises two cents, and how many starve? One cannot know."

Fabienne's dress was a deep, lusty purple, and the body inside was lithe and muscled. The hollows of her unshaved armpits were deep—skeletal almost.

Quaid was helpless against Bucharest memories. The essential oils, the papaya slices, that wrought-iron balcony whose imprint Quaid's back had borne for weeks.

He asked, "So who were these 'others' you hired instead?"

Fabienne lightened her voice. "Freelancers, much the same as you."

"The Blind Mice?"

She laughed. "First, tell me who you are working for. Then perhaps we can have an open discussion of associates."

Saying this, she swung a leg over Quaid's thigh. The inner bone of her ankle hiked the cuff of his pants up.

He said, "We work for whoever'll write us a check."

"*Peut-être* our friend Sergio."

"Sergio?" Quaid said. The three had once partied together in Ibiza during Carnival. "He can barely afford to keep his bridges standing."

He glanced up and saw the African staring intently at his hand, which had settled above Fabienne's knee.

The heiress, noticing the two men noticing each other, began working her fingers through Quaid's hair. "What have you come for? To propose a fresh partnership?"

"I'm proposing...an exploration," he said. "It would depend on terms, of course. And what exactly needed doing."

Fabienne, in a single coordinated motion, whipped her far leg over Quaid and pinned him to the couch by the hair, straddling him. "There is much that needs doing."

Quaid was already aroused—now he felt himself coming to the brink. "I'm sure there is."

"Much of the work is...*eh bien*, unsavory." Fabienne leaned in concert with her winding words, making friction between their bodies. "I wonder if you have the stomach for such work."

As if to check, she dragged her long forefinger from the middle button of his sport coat down his belly, then under his shirt and beyond.

In a flash, her palm was around him.

Quaid's mind was a jumble. Swirling around inside were nights with Molly and days chasing Mice, and what besides grenadine had been in his drink, and incense, and which side of the razor wire he ought to angle for.

"Might be I'd have to"—Quaid struggled for breath—"have to— have to cut Durwood out. He can be quite the moralist."

Fabienne had his zipper undone. "The rate would be lower, *oui*? Without Mr. Oak Jones?"

She was teasing—budget never mattered to Rivard LLC. As their physical entanglement progressed, Quaid felt burgeoning danger. There was menace in Fabienne's actions—a display of power, a seizing of will. Quaid was a red-blooded man: he could no more stop this than a desert castaway could walk past a puddle without falling to his knees and drinking.

It means nothing. Part of the job.

"Let's hear about this unsavory job of yours," he panted. "How dirty are we talking?"

Fabienne had a Vulcan grip below, while higher, her gaunt thighs and arms pinned him like iron rods to the couch.

She bit his earlobe. "*Assassination.*"

Quaid moaned at the combination of stimuli—nice, painful, slow, sudden—and found his field of vision rolling away.

He managed, "Government or civilian?"

Fabienne pulled aside her dress. Hair bristled against hair.

"*Civilian.*"

She joined them with a frank thrust that sent Quaid wild—to a place of violence and unconstrained pleasure, a private anarchy unleashed on every inch of the couch's velour.

It was a good while before his next intelligible thought.

When Quaid regained sense, he was propped by an elbow. The

African remained at his post. The bandoliers across his chest shimmered, moonlight reflecting off individual shells.

Fabienne was pulling on her purple dress, using the guard's bare torso for balance.

"So this civilian you want eliminated," Quaid said. "I take it he or she's outgrown their usefulness to Rivard?"

The heiress had the guard zip her up in back. Then she returned to the couch to whisper, "You are out of your depth, Mr. Rafferty."

Then she strode from the room. Through the open doorway, Quaid saw her meet Thérèse Laurent.

He called, "Should we be firming up particulars? It's still early, we could hit the town..."

But the two women were gone.

Quaid briefly thought he'd been left to fend for himself—maybe he could snoop around and see whether any dastardly Rivard plans were lying about—but in the next moment, the African yanked him off the couch and dragged him out of Hotel Zauberberg.

CHAPTER THIRTY-EIGHT

New York State

Piper Jackson used her phone to pay the rideshare driver, stepped from his burnt-orange sedan, and looked at the jail. The Windhorne Correctional Facility loomed over its barbed-wire perimeter, squat, made of beige bricks. It didn't have any chunks missing. That was unusual.

Piper confirmed the envelope in her pants pocket. She asked the driver, "Are you cool waiting here? I'll pay."

The bearded man had put his earbuds back in. He cupped a hand to his head.

"Are you cool to wait?" she said. "I'll be out in twenty minutes, half hour tops."

He took out his buds and, after making her repeat herself a third time, said nope, he couldn't wait.

"It'd screw me in the app," he said. "I need to keep taking rides or my rating goes down."

"So? I'll pay you three hundred."

"Can't. I got my rating up to four-point-eight-nine-nine."

Piper thought about telling him she could make his rating a damn twelve if she wanted, but decided exposing her identity was too risky.

The driver, noticing her annoyance and probably afraid *she'd* rate him badly, scratched his beard. "But you can schedule a ride. Here, schedule me for twenty minutes." He showed her where the icon was. "I'll accept right now, then we're all set."

"And you can wait?" she asked.

"No, I still gotta go get other rides," he said. "But this way I'm back in twenty minutes guaranteed."

Piper wondered how guaranteed "guaranteed" was, but she scheduled the ride anyway. There wasn't time to fuss. Windhorne's evening guards came on duty in forty-five minutes, and her plan had a much better chance against the lighter afternoon shift.

The driver slipped his burnt-orange car back into city gridlock.

Piper turned toward the jail, smoothing the sleeves of her mother's blazer, balling her hands to fists.

Busting Marcus out should've been easier. Prisoners escaped all the time now. Jails were understaffed, and the cops had too much craziness going to bother rounding anybody back up.

The problem was Windhorne Correctional Facility. The warden was some kind of stickler. He'd gotten written up online—*Hudson Valley prison bucks trend, warden credits "culture of neatness and duty."* Windhorne had experienced zero inmate loss during the Anarchy.

Piper could've pulled other Mice into the job, made it easier. Hatch would've been game. Molly McGill was always eager to help. Piper could never tell if Molly was trying for a bigger role in the group, or wanted to seem woke, or what.

In the end, she decided to do this Marcus thing solo. She didn't want the other Mice in her business. It was hard to explain. When she imagined meeting up with her brother again after a year and half, the thought of standing there next to all these bloggers, all slapping Marcus on the back and congratulating themselves, bugged her.

A woman in a gray uniform worked the guard booth.

"How may I direct you?" she asked through a speaker hole in her Plexiglas.

Piper took the envelope from her pocket. "I need to speak with Warden Hufnagel about a release."

The woman said, "You're in possession of the proper documents?"

Piper showed a letter embossed with the New York State seal.

217

The woman raised a corded phone. "And what's the prisoner name?"

"Marcus Jackson."

The woman tapped a lighted button. As a dial tone began, Piper's heart jumped.

Piper added, "An official letter went out from the governor. You should've got it a couple days ago."

The woman looked around her space and frowned. She flinched when a voice came through her phone.

"Warden Hufnagel, yes!" she recovered. "I—I have a person here, an official, with release documents for Marcus Jackson."

She listened a moment and said, "Certainly. Yes, of course."

The woman hung up and told Piper with a saccharine smile, "The warden will be able to assist you shortly. He handles each transfer and release request personally."

Piper already knew. It'd been in the online write-up. She faced the beige-brick building to wait.

Nothing happened for five minutes. Maybe the warden had a long walk—she couldn't see how deep the facility was. She worried that twenty-minute estimate of hers had been too optimistic.

What if it takes longer? Would her driver stick around? Maybe she should schedule a different ride, with a different app, for thirty minutes. Or forty.

Before she got to the point of doing it, a man emerged from the building. Very tall and very bald, he was a chopstick in a suit. His long strides devoured the distance between him and Piper.

Before he was really in hearing range, he called, "What's this about a release? Name was what, Jackson?"

In another second, he'd reached the booth. Piercing eyes shifted between Piper and the woman in gray.

Piper held out her letter. Warden Hufnagel snatched it from her like a loose twenty off the sidewalk. His lips burbled silently as he read.

Piper said, "That's just a copy. Your office should've got the original in the mail."

Hufnagel glared at the woman inside the booth. "Well, did we? I'm not letting one of my inmates go based upon a single sheet of paper."

The woman picked up and set down binders, looked underneath her keyboard.

The warden said to Piper, "Anybody can make a printout. *Ooh, here—here's my order for a million bucks. Can I get my million bucks now?*"

He crumpled his tall body, pretending to beg.

Piper said, "It wasn't anybody who made this." She pointed to the signature at the bottom, a digital twin of the real thing. "Governor of New York."

The warden pulled a handkerchief from his breast pocket, shook it out vigorously, and polished a smudge on the booth.

Piper slipped a finger down to her cell phone and found its volume button. She held it down three seconds.

The computer inside the booth dinged.

The woman checked the ding. "Um, Warden?"

He seemed reluctant to take his eyes off Piper, but did. "What do you have there, Officer Munoz?"

He squeezed into the small booth and bent to look over Munoz's shoulder. His face soured as he considered the incoming message, whose recipient address—Piper knew—belonged to the office of the governor.

Hufnagel flung his arm out, whirling from the screen. "Why? What happened that this Jackson's getting out early?"

"No idea," Piper said. "I'm just transport."

He looked past her to the street. "If you're transport, where's your vehicle? I don't see a paddy wagon."

Crap, Piper thought. She'd answered without thinking.

"Yeah, budget cuts." She decided to stick close to the truth. "They got us using rideshares."

The warden pulled back distastefully but didn't challenge further. The government outsourcing rides was no stretch. Most bridges had gone pay-as-you-please. The city couldn't afford to staff them, and E-ZPass had been toast for months.

"Alright. Fine," Hufnagel said. "Let's go free Marcus Jackson."

At this, Piper felt she might soar up out of this bland place and join the sky.

The deal's not sealed yet, she reminded herself, following the warden and Officer Munoz toward the prison.

Inside, Piper's joy turned to anger. The joint smelled awful but not how she'd expected. As Warden Hufnagel grinned proudly over his shoulder, Piper tried figuring out the stench. There was a body undercurrent, that earthy too-much-humanity smell from the subway, but covering it was a wave of antiseptic. Dizzying, sharp in Piper's nostrils.

Fans were blowing pink spray from the corners of the ceiling. Now that she saw, Piper recognized the mist falling on her skin. Cells lined the corridor on either side, packed with prisoners—so, *so* many. The cells had fans too, blasting the same disinfectant or whatever into the living quarters.

"Can you—er, can they breathe?" she said. "That pink stuff's strong."

Piper thought a sympathetic look crossed Officer Munoz's face, but it vanished.

Warden Hufnagel raised his nose savoringly. "They get used to it. It's necessary. Germs are rampant in places like this—germs are what kills. You must be proactive."

Piper coughed, scanning left and right for the face of her brother. Inmates were lined up three deep behind the cells' bars, like crowds waiting to get in a show.

Where did they all sleep? *How?* Stacked on top of each other?

After Piper's coughing fit, the warden stopped short.

"Officer Munoz," he said, "see if you can't reach the governor by the phone. I'd like to get verbal confirmation on this release if possible. The whole thing smells fishy."

He smells fish? Piper thought. *How can he smell anything?*

As Munoz headed back to her booth, Piper considered. She didn't figure the governor's office would pick up. If they did, it would be some clerk who'd have to go find a superior. The superior would be clueless—the state had zip electronically on Marcus Jackson or anybody. By the time they figured out the governor'd had nothing to do with that email or Piper's embossed letter, she and Marcus would be long gone.

She hoped.

Piper blanked out her face, closed off her nose, and refused to accept the mounting danger.

She wasn't the same girl who had seen her brother taken into custody at Harvest Earth. She was almost nineteen now—Marcus's age that day. She'd become known across the globe. She had power. The Blind Mice had made change just like they'd said they would the night everyone got inked at Lewd Brew.

Why doesn't it feel better?

Warden Hufnagel stalked past shower stalls, more cells, the mess hall. Workers in orange vests scrubbed floors and walls with stiff-bristled pads. In the mess hall, empty now, upside-down chairs lined the tabletops at perfect intervals.

The warden stopped halfway to the end. He looked to his right, into a cell marked *TW4X7*. Piper tensed. She'd been so focused on pulling off this scheme, then on the weirdness of this place. She wasn't ready.

But here he was. Marcus looked scrawnier, and tired. He was still Marcus, though—the playful eyes, the ears too low on his head. *So I can hear you yapping all the way down there,* he'd always teased.

Piper hadn't visited him at Windhorne. At first, their mother wouldn't allow it, and then, once the Mice got rolling, she figured she might end up doing this and need to be anonymous.

As their eyes met through the mass of bodies now, Marcus surged another inch taller. Piper's face froze, then he got it and froze too.

Hufnagel said, "Which one of you fleabags is Jackson? Marcus Jackson?"

Marcus shimmied past his cellmates. One elbowed him and cracked a joke. He said, *I see you, boy,* and raised a fist back, grinning.

The sight made Piper happier than she'd thought possible, that Marcus could still joke after a year and a half in this freaky place.

"Right here," he said. "I'm Jackson."

The warden's gaze moved from Marcus to Piper. Harsh light from overhead tubes glinted off his shiny head as it tipped one way, then the other.

People in the neighborhood said the Jackson kids all got the same nose. Now Piper raised a hand over hers, covering a fake yawn.

Warden Hufnagel clapped a hand roughly onto Marcus's shoulder.

"Somebody important decided it was your lucky day." He peered up the corridor. "We'll just need to retrieve your personal effects, bleach out your locker so it's ready for the next fleabag."

Marcus said, "Sounds like a plan."

"Do you recall what you were admitted with?"

Marcus shrugged. "Just clothes, I think."

Piper offered, "I could take him like this." She nodded to his jump-suit. "The governor's office doesn't mind."

Again, the warden clapped Marcus's shoulder. He rubbed the suit's fabric between scalpel-thin fingers.

"*I* mind," he said. "These getups cost money, straight off my bottom line. Money we dearly need for brushes and antibacterial soap."

Marcus was handcuffed for the walk to the storage room. He and Piper stayed a step behind the warden. Even though they weren't looking at each other, she could tell he wanted to bump her with his hip.

Like everywhere else, in storage, cleanliness was the Windhorne Correctional Facility's top priority. Warden Hufnagel squirted sanitizer into his palms as he entered the tiled room of wall-to-wall lockers.

"What's your inmate ID, Jackson?"

Marcus recited from memory, "M77-324."

As the chopstick drifted along the wall of lockers, reading laminated tags, Piper again felt her brother's love. She wished she could've thrown both arms around him and squeezed, taken him home to Mom and eaten her ranch-chicken enchiladas until none of them could move.

The warden disappeared to an auxiliary room and reappeared with an armful of clothes. His nose kept twitching.

"Were these laundered when they took you in?" he asked.

Marcus looked around uncertainly. "Maybe? Or not."

Warden Hufnagel's jaw clenched. He muttered to an attendant about needing to upgrade intake procedures.

Piper glanced back to check Officer Munoz. She couldn't see the booth across the yard.

"Cool, I saw a bathroom down the hall," she said. "Can he change there?"

The warden allowed it.

Marcus's cuffs were removed, and he left for the bathroom. Hufnagel followed him a few steps into the hall. Piper thought he might insist on watching, making sure Marcus didn't let his jumpsuit touch the floor or something.

What an odd duck. Maybe this obsessive neatness was how he dealt, how he stayed sane during the Anarchy. You control this tiny piece of the world, then the big stuff feels separate—just bad news on TV.

Hell, everybody had hang-ups. Piper hated using laptop trackpads. The problem was, when people in positions of authority had hang-ups, a crap ton of others paid the price.

Example number one of that was Josiah. Now that word was out among the Mice he wasn't acting alone—those "friends" in Pittsburgh made it pretty obvious for anyone who hadn't caught on—he had a major chip on his shoulder. The attacks needed to go beyond the Despicable Dozen now. They needed to be about *changing the culture*. He had this big idea to hit Shop-All, the last remaining chain super-store, to "drive a stake through the heart of consumerism."

None of the Mice cared about Shop-All. Neither did those "friends."

When Marcus came out of the bathroom dressed, it was like a time warp. The Giants sweatshirt he'd always worn at Harvest Earth. The ratty leather belt that barely kept his pants up now. Piper wanted to cry for the days they'd lost together.

Marcus handed his folded jumpsuit to the warden. "It's all yours again."

Hufnagel turned the bundle over, frowning at a spot.

"Indeed, it is," he said. "Windhorne wishes you well. You're young, with a long life ahead. Live it well."

Marcus looked surprised when the man extended a hand, but he recovered to shake it. "Thanks. I'll try."

Warden Hufnagel gestured forward and walked them toward the exit.

He continued, "If you should ever be contacted by an independent survey firm, I would appreciate it if you kept in mind the high standard of cleanliness we enforced here."

Marcus said he would. Piper thought, *Seriously? Is there anybody not obsessed with their own rating?*

Speaking of ratings—when Piper and Marcus got to the street, there wasn't any burnt-orange sedan.

Piper gritted her teeth. "The rideshare guy's supposed to be here."

The warden peered both ways up the block. "Do you...need to call him?"

She checked her phone, which showed *GERALD P.* six minutes away. "Nah, he's coming. We'll just walk some. I bet we run into him."

Giving the warden a stuffy nod of thanks, Piper started up the sidewalk with her brother. The jail was on a busy street. If they could get a block or two away, they'd blend into the crowd and be clear.

Marcus waited until the warden was well back to ask, "How'd you do it, sis?"

Piper peeked back at the booth without moving her head. "Fake order from the governor."

As they hurried, he squeezed her arm below the elbow—spontaneously, the first place his fingers found.

They hadn't quite made the corner when an air horn screeched.

Piper knew what she would see before she turned around: whirling blue lights on the prison fence line.

"Move, *move!*" she said.

They bolted into the intersection, which was jammed up, its signals all dark.

Behind them, Warden Hufnagel came sprinting from the booth trailed by officers in orange vests.

"Stop them! That's an escaped inmate!"

He was too far away for anyone near Piper to hear clearly or understand who he meant. She and Marcus hunched low and ran. She wasn't sweating bystanders. Chases on foot were no big deal these days.

Marcus tripped on a fire hydrant.

"Dang, *ow*." He hopped on one foot and tried running again. "I'm good, go."

But he wasn't good. The injury slowed them down. Warden Hufnagel began gaining, pointing wildly ahead, shoving pedestrians out of the way, screaming for his guards to follow.

The next intersection was jammed up too.

Marcus said, "What's up with the lights? Why are they out?"

Piper cut between idling cars, pulling him by the wrist as drivers honked and cursed. "They just are."

The warden's head bobbed above the crowd, shiny pink, coming hard. Two blocks ahead, a city bus lay smoking on its side. Firefighters and paramedics were gathered around, people who might actually do something about a shouted plea from Hufnagel.

Then, from the next side street, a burnt-orange flash.

"Here, come on!" Piper waved overhead and bolted across traffic to meet the sedan in its lane.

Marcus hobbled after, drawing more honks and curses.

The sedan screeched to a halt, its tires smoking.

"You changed the pickup location," the driver complained through the window. "You're supposed to be two blocks over, the app's not gonna count—"

"Screw the app!" Piper said as she and Marcus tumbled into the back seat. "Drive."

The man, palming his beard, glanced at his phone. Then he glanced back at their faces.

Then he drove.

Piper, keeping low in her seat, looked down the block where the warden was talking animatedly to the firefighters. He hadn't seen their detour.

Marcus was looking outside too. His bloodshot eyes glazed around the chaos—plumes of smoke, pocked storefronts, charred remnants of abandoned cars. His fingers found Piper's arm again.

"Man," he said. "When did this happen?"

CHAPTER THIRTY-NINE

New Jersey

The house was a wreck. The family portrait at Niagara Falls, the only trace of Karen's father I'd left up after the divorce, hung at a thirty-degree skew, and Game of Life money was strewn across the coffee table. The cat was chewing the corner of a fifty—she'd puke it up in approximately an hour.

It was Sunday, seven a.m. Nobody was awake. I collapsed onto the couch, adding my suitcase to the clutter, and for just a moment, I gave in to despair.

As if my meeting with Piper Jackson later today weren't reason enough to cry, now this. I couldn't keep leaving Granny in charge of the kids. There was a time when I would've come home to immaculate cabinets and a vinegar-scrubbed sink, but that time had passed. Every trip I took with the guys or mission with the Mice was a roll of the dice, and with the Anarchy raging, one of them was bound to come up snake eyes.

Zach came downstairs first in boxers and a T-shirt.

I hassled him into a hug. "I missed you guys! So, how was your week? Looks like you had board game night?"

He mumbled past to the kitchen and found cereal in the pantry.

I asked six positive questions before saying, "You might've helped

Granny pick up. You and your sister are old enough now—old enough to take on responsibilities."

Zach raised a spoonful of Cinnamon Toast Crunch, watching milk drip through the grooves. "Um, who prepared this healthy breakfast? Pretty sure it was *moi.*"

Karen came prancing down in her panda pajamas, hopping two-footed down the stairs. She must've heard.

"That cereal isn't healthy," she said. "It provides zero protein."

"Says she who has no clue what protein is," Zach replied. "You're just copying Mom."

This was accurate—I had said that verbatim, several times—but Karen was undeterred.

"Just because it's copying doesn't mean it isn't true. *I* want a balanced breakfast. Eggs maybe."

"Yeah? Try eating a nest."

"Stop it!"

"Stop what?"

"Nests aren't food, you're making fun." Karen blushed fiercely and frumped her arms.

Now Granny shuffled in, slippers whooshing over linoleum. Her hair, up in curlers, had a new purple tinge.

"Whole time you were gone, like this." She flung out a hand dramatically. "At each other's throats."

Quickly, Karen was tattling on Zach for sneaking out after curfew on his skateboard, he was needling her about how many Easy Reader books she'd *actually* read over the weekend versus how many she'd been *supposed* to read, and I felt my sinuses start to throb like boils in my face.

I wanted to yell, *First time seeing me in four days and all you do is fight, really?* But I restrained myself. I knew I should be thankful they were squabbling like this instead of joining the riots downtown or dealing with rolling blackouts. They were still in the bubble of adolescence—annoying at times but better than today's alternatives.

Badly as I craved sleep, I unpacked my bag and announced we were going to church.

"You're joking," Zach said.

"No joke." I hustled upstairs and brought back Karen's favorite dress and a tie, which I tossed to Zach. "I did a lot of thinking on this trip, and I want to bring faith back to this household. It's easy to neglect church when things get tough. But that's exactly when we need it most."

The congregation was sparse but spirited at Blessed Sacrament. Glancing around the pews, I felt cheered by the collective will. We'd all risked cross fire and highway IEDs to be here. We'd pulled knee highs up our weary calves, taken the time to tuck down our collars. The simple acts of listening to a sermon as one and clutching our fellow parishioners' hands during the Peace felt like victories—small defiances we might stitch together and use to shield ourselves.

Back home, I felt better. I couldn't control when the world returned to sanity, or what Quaid had or hadn't done with Fabienne Rivard in Davos. ("Her style is very direct, refreshingly so," he had told me and Durwood during the debrief.) I couldn't make Zach and Karen appreciate how lucky they were to still belong to a family, imperfect though we were.

I didn't need to force any of this. I just needed to keep going, giving my best.

CHAPTER FORTY

I rode five different trains and buses to Mott Haven. Public transit had suffered—no connection was as close as forty-five minutes, each wait a white-knuckle situation. I kept one hand on my gun and tried to look impatient like everybody around me.

Lewd Brew, or Lewd Brew II, had only gotten rattier since my last visit. The splintered door hung by a single hinge, and the east wall was four-fifths plywood. Somebody had lined up chunks of fallen plaster smallest to largest on the espresso counter.

I ordered a coffee. As it was prepared, I picked up the exercise I'd begun in Davos, imagining my conversation with Piper. Imagining how I would tell her.

I need to come clean about something, something you won't like...

So we have this term in psychology called "perspective-dependent truth"...

I've been meaning to tell you about this guy, who I'm sort of seeing? He's actually the former governor of Massachusetts. He and I, and someone named Durwood Oak Jones, are small-force private-arms contractors...

There wasn't a good opener to be had.

Maybe I should've accepted Durwood's offer to back out. *Sure about this, Moll?* he'd asked during the transatlantic return flight. *We can go a different way.*

But I had said no, I could swing this.

Durwood was averse to emotional displays, but I'd seen those steel-colored eyes soften. He'd understood what was going through my head after Hotel Zauberberg.

Coffee in hand, I was just turning toward the tables to find Piper when a blast sounded from aboveground.

I dove to the floor, losing my drink. A few others did too, but most just glanced up. Of course, they didn't know what I knew about Rivard LLC. They hadn't heard Fabienne's grand speech or had Blake Leathersby's tourniquet grip around their arms.

Garrison brought me a replacement coffee. "No worries, probably just bikers. Bandidos are occupying that old bank on the corner."

I thanked him and gulped half the cup, getting in my caffeine before the next disruption.

"How was your trip?" he asked.

"Good, pretty good," I said. I'd told people here I was visiting my cousin in Baltimore who ran a sustainable living co-op on abandoned land. "It's amazing—they get everything from the earth, one hundred percent renewable."

"That *is* amazing," Garrison said. "What do they do for shoes? Like hemp?"

"The shoes...might've been foraged."

He nodded eagerly. "Lemme know next time you go, okay? I'd be psyched to join and see their process."

"Sure. Yeah, that'd be fun."

For weeks, he'd been trying to reconnect, to get back that flirty we're-in-this-craziness-together vibe we'd had before Pittsburgh. I didn't really think that was possible. Too much had happened. I'd become an Algernon. He hadn't. Everything had gotten more grave—society, my kids' situation.

But maybe I'd been premature. Looking into his mellow eyes now, hearing about the offshoot work he'd been doing with the homeless, I wondered if I should reconsider. I thought about this morning's sermon, which had been about protecting hope and small joys in the face of adversity.

Maybe this was exactly the time for a little low-commitment romance.

We found a table. Garrison smelled great, brisk and nautical. His foot wandered into my space over the next several minutes. My heel nestled in his instep, nonchalant. The contact was thrilling and warmed me throughout. We kept chatting about rumors, personal updates (mine were mostly fabricated), not acknowledging what was happening below.

But Garrison's crooked smile and occasional fumbled word made it clear he felt the same heat.

I excused myself when Piper finally showed—though I didn't want to.

She was in a group with Josiah, Hatch, and a few other Algernons. They were sitting at a corner table, Josiah ranting and pinwheeling his arms.

"It's the same-ass consumerism as ever!" he was saying. "We have to beat it down, keep sledgehammering until it dies."

Hatch was kneading his tattooed skull. There was a blueprint laid out across the table, a bowl of jerky, and Skittles.

I asked Piper quietly, "Do you need to finish with them?"

She stood and snapped her laptop shut. "Nah, they're good. They can do it how they want."

"Do what?"

"Shop-All. It's not my thing."

Josiah continued ranting about how the Anarchy was making commerce local again, crippling the multinationals' supply and distribution chains. *If they could just break Shop-All, they'd be on the verge of honest neighbor-to-neighbor barter.*

His voice fading as we left for a table of our own, Piper said, "It's dumb. Shop-All won't last. Busting up one store doesn't do a thing."

I nodded along, feeling lucky to catch her at a moment of disillusionment. "It just looks like looting."

"For real." She laced her knuckles in front of her. "You had something to talk about?"

I laced my knuckles, too, and confirmed Josiah and the others were out of earshot. "Right. I just—I'm just worried about where this is all going. It seems like our goals...aren't...I guess I don't understand exactly where we stand on goals."

"Join the club."

"Social justice was a big motivating factor for me," I said, "and it's getting hard to see how these attacks—like this Shop-All mission—move us forward."

Piper looked at me with a flat, world-weary expression. Her corn-rows had started growing out, fuzzy between the tight ridges.

I pressed, "Should we really be following Josiah blindly? Now he has these 'friends,' whoever helped us in Pittsburgh. What do we know about them? Are they the ones pushing for Shop-All?"

"No, they don't want Shop-All. That's a hundred percent Josiah."

"Do you believe he's stable?"

Piper chuckled grimly. "You've been here. Nothing about him's stable."

"Should we try to stop him? Reel him in? I wonder if there's some way we could, I dunno...reclaim the movement."

Piper's jaw worked side to side.

"It ain't perfect," she said. "Things ain't fixed, but maybe we scrambled them just enough. Show people what it feels like to be arbitrarily screwed with. Like the nobodies who get screwed with twenty-four seven, three sixty-five."

The Anarchy had a weird mix of supporters. Some on the left saw the instruments of oppression going away, wealth obliterated, playing fields leveled. Luddite types, craving a return to hunter-gatherer times, saw a just reckoning for a civilization that'd come to value technology above people.

Supporters on the right saw the Anarchy as an experiment in pure laissez-faire, allowing the fittest to prevail without the nanny state butting in. Personal responsibility was back—from staking out land to educating kin to protecting one's self by group affiliation or firearm.

Most moderates wanted yesterday back. They saw skyrocketing crime, felt afraid on sidewalks and at stoplights. Musicians refused to tour, sports matches were being played in venues closed off to the public.

Maybe these people had been in for change at the beginning—

different bangs, a new part for their hair. They'd ended up with a purple Mohawk and nose ring.

I had thought Piper might be drifting into this last camp, but apparently not. The phrase "arbitrarily screwed with" wasn't promising.

I argued, "But these 'friends'"—I made air quotes—"don't care about the underclass. They're professionals themselves. They're corporate. Rivard LLC, right? Everyone says it's them."

I hadn't meant to name Rivard. It had just slipped out.

Piper said, "What if it is."

"Well, then it's awful," I said. "Rivard isn't interested in causes. They're interested in one thing and one thing only: money."

This seemed to affect Piper. She bit her lip and gripped the edge of her laptop, as though for security.

Was it enough of a crack?

I kept arguing, waiting for that perfect moment when our eyes locked and wordless understanding could pass between us, paving the way for my admission. Piper didn't trust easily, but I felt I had made headway during eDeed and times we'd talked since.

Are her shoulders opened wider toward me? Is she leaning forward?

I said, "How will we know when it's too far? When we've crossed the line?"

Piper glanced to the table where Josiah was still ranting. "Maybe we won't."

We sat in silence. The clock was literally ticking—that weird clock with the counter-spinning circles. Its psychedelic swirls got into my thoughts, warping, urgent.

It has to be now. You told the guys you'd do it—you told Jim Steed. So do it.

Now.

The Blind Mice's importance to the mission was fading. Zach was slipping out after curfew—who knew where he'd really gone with his skateboard while I'd been off in Davos.

If I didn't make something happen soon, the guys would have no choice but to work their only other angle: the connection between Quaid and Fabienne Rivard.

I took Piper's hand across the table. "Hey Piper, I...this is awkward, but there's something I need to explain."

I combed back through my rehearsals for one of the gentler wordings, but drew a blank.

I said, "My story is more complicated than you know."

"Complicated how?"

Her hand felt cold, like the stainless-steel handle of a refrigerator.

"You know I have a little brother, right?" I said. "The one who showed up at eDeed?"

Piper nodded.

"See, protecting him is my number-one priority." I was straying off topic, but I thought I could bring it back. "Everything I've done, it's with him in mind."

"I get you," Piper said. "It's family. You protect your family, that's cool."

Before I could move into my disclosure, she lowered her own voice and said, "I just saw my brother. First time in a while."

"Really, Marcus?" I said. "Did he get out of prison?"

Piper nodded. "Yeah, he got out."

She didn't elaborate, but her eyes were hard. I could tell she was thinking about him.

"How is he?" I asked. "What did he say? You joined the Mice because of him, right?"

Piper picked my first question to answer. "He's been better. Eighteen months locked up messes with you."

I wondered what she meant. Did her brother have mental problems? PTSD? Was it possible he didn't see the world—didn't see the Anarchy—the same way Piper did?

None of these were questions I could ask just now.

I said, "I'm sorry he had to go through that ordeal."

She raised her lip in what I took for grudging thanks, then shook her head.

"Should've never been there," she said. "People sold him out. People he helped, supposed to be his friends."

I still had hold of Piper's hand. Now it felt even colder, like the inside of that fridge. Like the freezer.

"That's rotten," I said.

Our hands slipped apart.

She asked, "So what's complicated about your story? Just your bro, that you're trying to protect him?"

"Uh...pretty much." I faked a bright expression. "I just worry about him, that's all."

CHAPTER FORTY-ONE

The Vanagon was parked in section green-19, tract C, of the Shop-All parking lot. From the passenger seat, Quaid just could make out the mammoth Shop-All logo, the *S* overlapping the *A* inside a spinning red circle. The structure underneath was ten stories high. Steady streams of eighteen-wheelers crept along in designated loading lanes.

"I never could get into the big-box thing," Quaid said. "I go food shopping, I want to be traipsing through the aisles and discover something new. Something in season."

Durwood, back in the cabin, was working a steel needle through a fine-mesh suit. His hat sat crooked on his head.

Quaid continued, "I don't want to worry a crate of Hamburger Helper's gonna fall on me. I don't need fifteen spreadable butter options. I want to be delighted."

Durwood firmed his brow at a knot in the suit, which was stretched tight over the lap of his blue jeans. In a nearby cup holder sat micropliers and a tweezer tube that smelled like okra.

"Tell me," Quaid said. "When were you last delighted?"

The question was met with a low growl—which Quaid might've mistaken for Sue-Ann's if she hadn't been sitting up front with him, watching Shop-All from the driver seat.

"Need to get those headaches checked out," he said. "How long have you been getting them? Months, right?"

Durwood didn't look up from his work. "I'm healthy as a horse."

He probably was. Most days his diet consisted of eggs, either raw or hard-boiled, and unadorned green peppers. He drank water exclusively and must've been walking ten miles a night on those crime patrols of his.

"Headache can be a symptom of tumors," Quaid said. "They obstruct your cerebral fluid, create pressure—"

"How about we get square on this mission?" Durwood eyeballed his partner over the mesh. "You gimme your diagnosis later."

Quaid didn't take the rebuke personally. "Fine by me. What can I do to be useful?"

Durwood checked his watch. "It's three fifteen." Molly had told them the attack was to begin at three o'clock. "You get visual on the Mice yet?"

Quaid glanced outside. Seeing nothing by naked eye, he climbed back to the cabin and took control of the camera joystick, cycling through the feeds Durwood had placed throughout Shop-All early in the week.

He scanned for the Mice, homing in on large groups of young shoppers. No luck.

"What if they're flaking? Or somebody talked sense into Josiah and he canceled?"

Durwood shook his head. "Moll would've called us."

"Unless they sniffed her out and she can't. What if the Jackson girl gave her up?"

Molly had assured the guys that Piper Jackson was "on board," but Quaid hadn't liked the way she'd said it. Her eyes had been too bright, and she'd seemed eager to change the subject.

"Only fifteen minutes late," Durwood said. "Not out of character, this nut."

Quaid wondered how things would go once they had the Grand Nut himself, Josiah, in hand. The hope was that after snatching him today, they could debrief him and Jackson and gain a clearer picture of the Anarchy—the exact role of Rivard, how or whether it was possible to reverse the damage caused by the kernel.

But would Josiah talk?

Durwood thought so. *We'll loosen up his lips*, the ex-marine had said during prep. *Few ways to go about it.*

Quaid had left that one alone.

Now he asked, "What if Rivard beat us to the punch? What if Leathersby already took care of Josiah?"

Durwood finished a last repair of his mesh suit. "Leathersby's in Europe."

"He was last week."

Durwood, ignoring the comment, stripped and began pulling on his mesh suit. Quaid futzed with the joystick, looking for the Mice, zooming alternately too close and too far. Once Durwood had the mesh gloves and hood on, and pinched them securely to the rest of the suit, he took control of the camera feeds.

Together, they cycled through ten stories of retail bacchanalia. Shoppers considered sleeves of paper cups as big as their own arms. Kiosks tempted passersby with cherry bratwurst, loaded eggnog, while-you-wait silk screening.

After five minutes, Durwood switched to the exterior cams. On camera number three, a fifteen-passenger Ford cargo van—black— idled near the entrance.

Durwood lingered on the vehicle, narrowing focus on the windshield, trying to resolve the driver.

Quaid said, "Leathersby wouldn't be caught dead driving a Ford."

Durwood made a noise almost like chuckling. The hatred between him and Blake Leathersby ran deep. It wasn't just that they'd shot at each other across the Vltava River, or fought wearing crampons on a Greenlandic glacier. The rift had deep cultural roots.

Though the two men had ostensibly fought on the same side in Desert Storm, Britain being a United States coalition partner, they had come to their service differently. Where Durwood had risen up the enlisted ranks, Leathersby had been special forces. "Big SAS boy," Durwood had once said. "Missions with code names, politicians watching from situation rooms."

Now, as the passenger van cruised off, Durwood switched back to a view inside the fifth floor, which contained the Shop-All management offices. They figured Josiah would end his spree there, finding some unlucky executive to lay blame upon—as he had with Blackstone and Steed.

Using a feather touch on the joystick, Durwood hunted the fringes of the fifth, fourth, and third floors. He peeked behind racks of cut-rate coats and stacks of car batteries. His steel-colored eyes traveled the entire monitor, rising to the corners, flitting to the bottom.

Then stopping.

"There."

Quaid scooted closer to the screen. "Where? What am I looking at?"

Durwood pointed to the display's left side. A dozen tiny figures were huddled near an emergency-exit staircase around a wiry figure with upswept blue hair. It was a wide view—the camera position was on the other side of the floor. Durwood dragged his thumb along a separate wheel control to augment the shot.

There was Molly, with the jet-black bob and wearing that tight blue sweater Quaid loved. There was a big guy that must've been Hatch, his face tattoos concealed with makeup.

And the wiry figure? Josiah. Wig or not, those erratic movements were unmistakable.

They were in Pickles and Olives.

Quaid said, "Where's Jackson?"

Durwood inched the camera view along a wall of condiments, over food-court-style seating, into the kitchen of a burger counter advertising sixty-nine-cent steakburgers.

There, wearing a boat-shaped paper hat, was Piper Jackson. She was twisting dials on deep fryers and reaching around back of soda fountain dispensers, slinking from one machine to the next, out of sight of the register.

"Huh," Durwood said.

Quaid crossed one tasseled loafer over the other. "Does that look like somebody getting ready to betray her compadres?"

Durwood didn't answer. He reached down to activate a switch on the heel of his suit and slipped quietly outside.

CHAPTER FORTY-TWO

The air felt oily on Josiah's skin, and a casino of sound assaulted his ears—registers ringing, specials singing over the PA, an indeterminate *zzzzzip* every fifteen seconds from Home Electronics. Any direction you looked, Shop-All had cheap junk to fix your life.

Fifty-quart coolers for ten dollars! Tins of pressed ham, free with the purchase of any deep fryer!

When Josiah separated from the other Mice to begin the mayhem, a greeter stepped in his path.

"Welcome to Pickles and Olives." The elderly woman spread her arms like she was presenting Shangri-la. "The tastes may be sour, but our deals are sweet as cherry pie. Have yourself an amazing afternoon!"

Josiah countered with his own excruciatingly wide grin. He felt his wig clips stretching away from his sideburns. "You do the same, sister!"

He spurned her offer of a cart and started up an aisle at random. His pink-tinged eyes bulged at the obscene volumes. His calves spasmed with rage.

Shop-All pedaled a nauseating breed of good-old-days nostalgia.

No guns. (Confiscated at the entrance.) No casual shoplifting. Products stacked orderly instead of spilling from ripped-open cardboard.

The average American weight had dropped 35 percent during the Anarchy, but you wouldn't know it here. Necks had folds—and folds within folds. Arm fat jiggled. A third of the customers drove motorized scooters.

An overhead banner proclaimed, *Experience the Shop-All Difference: Security, Savings, Serenity.*

Josiah snickered. *Serenity.*

Choosing his first act, he boosted up on his tiptoes and fought the urge to squeeze or bite the people streaming by, to grip them by the shoulders and shake, and shake, and shake—until he'd shaken the urge to shop right out of them.

They are merely the symptom, he reminded himself. *You don't punish the pawns.*

He emerged from Pickles and Olives to stand at a point equidistant from Leather Recliners and Giant TVs. He reached into the pocket of his cargo shorts and tapped the button of a remote.

An uneasy stitch passed through the mass of shoppers. Something had changed—they felt it but hadn't yet identified the source.

A woman pointed to a blank LCD display next to an eighty-three-inch TV. "The price! What happened to my price?"

Another television was being admired by a teenager crinkling a bag of potato chips.

"Momma, why does it say 'out of stock'?" he asked. "I see like fifty of them."

Shop-All employees rushed to address the situation, checking coaxial connections, pressing reset buttons, calling supervisors on red phones. Nothing helped.

Josiah pushed his remote again, and the prices returned—all reduced to one penny.

The chaos fed Josiah's growing glee. He popped four pills into his mouth and chewed them to minty dust.

He stalked to the food court next. The smell staggered him. Trans fat, yellow dye #6, GMO sludge—the sort of chain food that'd mostly been eradicated but stuck around here.

A maple syrup bar. Nonperishable cheese food. Meat on toothpicks.

Josiah tapped his remote again. A stereophonic hiss began, affecting many kitchen areas at once. Diners leaned off their hard-plastic seats to look. Food workers hopped back from stations, rubbing their arms.

"The fries are possessed!" yelled a kid in a paper hat.

Chicken tenders, corn dogs, funnel cakes—all burned to a dark caramel as digital temp readings over wire baskets climbed higher and higher.

Next, Josiah superheated the griddles. Pink patties seared black. Onions shriveled to crisps. Eggs bubbled like exploding eyeballs. Soft serve dispensers spurted milky jets.

As messes ran together on the tile, Josiah felt giddy with revulsion.

Who needs Rivard LLC anyway?

Rivard hadn't wanted the Shop-All attack. That steroid jock Leathersby had told him it wasn't a priority. "Does bugger all good for us, mate." Fabienne Rivard had other sites she wanted to see hit.

They could both kiss his ass. From now on, the Blind Mice made the mayhem unassisted. Au naturel.

Josiah rode moving walkways through other sections, frazzing out Shop-All systems like some vengeful god. At checkout, he made the rubber conveyor belts run triple speed. He changed the SuperSaver siren from a hopeful *bring-bring* to a low, dull cattle moo.

When the confusion had reached a fever pitch, he made his way to the management offices. A man in a supervisor's vest stood at a podium receiving updates by earpiece.

"Everyone, please remain calm," he said into a loudspeaker mic. "We're experiencing a malfunction, clearly, but it will be resolved soon. I assure you."

Josiah strode jauntily up to the podium and clapped the man on the shoulder.

"You think?"

The man looked at Josiah's blue hair, then out across the deluged food court, overrun sackers, and panicked shoppers. Security guards were rushing ten ways at once.

"Uh—er, stay where you are," the man continued to his customers. "Don't abandon your carts. We'll get this straightened out in a jiff."

This was too much for Josiah—that the pig's primary concern was lost sales. He ripped off the wig, revealing his ghost-white hair.

Everybody around gasped, recognizing the notorious leader of the Blind Mice.

Before the man at the podium could react, Josiah ran a knifepoint from his temple down through the thick cauliflower stem of his ear.

The earpiece, and the ear inside, dropped to the floor.

Josiah took the microphone. "Attention, consumers," boomed his voice through all ten floors. "I have an important announcement to make. Your way of life is over. I hereby declare this"—he felt his face curdle as he groped for a word—"this grotesquerie over. The Blind Mice are here, and we've brought you deliverance—free of charge!"

CHAPTER FORTY-THREE

The shrieks were awful. As parents pulled their children to the ground and wrapped them in their arms, I lay on the tile with palms pressed over my ears. We were supposed to pretend to be regular customers—dumb, horrified—and, for me, this was no stretch. It's possible I was screaming myself.

A woman behind me whispered, *"Why is this happening?"*

I glanced back. A jar of pickles had shattered, and its juices were running into the pants of her young son.

"Don't move!" she told him. "You'll roll into the glass."

I crawled back and picked up jagged chunks of glass from out of the briny puddle. "Let's stay down. Probably it'll be over soon."

But the boy kept squirming. The woman smothered him with her torso, which only made him squirm worse, both of them sniveling.

I took the boy's hand and looked directly at him with a smile—the warmest, quietest I could manage. It was a calming mechanism that'd worked with Karen. (Though not often with Zach.)

The woman repeated, *"Why is this happening?"*

In my periphery, I saw Piper looking our way. Her brows were knit. Was she fighting regret? Angry at Josiah for going off script?

I was ready for Durwood to rush in and end this helter-skelter. The plan had been to stop Josiah before he could hurt anybody, but he'd acted too quickly.

Up on the podium, Josiah gripped the microphone. "Are we all feeling the savings *now*? Who's ready to reconsider their life? To think deeply about the impact their choices have on the rest of *humanity*?"

Four security guards converged on the podium, hunched low, deliberate. Shoppers watched from the floor with a measure of hope.

Josiah caught Piper's eye in the crowd. She gave a subtle nod.

He reached into his cargo shorts, and by a twitch in his forearm, I knew he'd tapped the remote inside.

Low, brittle noises sounded. The guards all clutched their sides where their tasers were holstered.

"That's a warning zap," Josiah said, eyes wide. "We can go hotter, baby! We can go a whole lot hotter."

The security guards stopped advancing.

The man who'd lost his ear was back on his feet. Using his vest to stop the bleeding, he staggered toward Josiah. He was broad-shoul-dered, maybe a college athlete. A patch on his vest read *Pasternacky*.

"*You're* the despicable one," he said, rushing forward and knocking Josiah down.

Josiah bared his teeth, hyena-like, and hurled himself at the man. As they grappled, I wished Pasternacky would go for Josiah's remote, but he seemed unaware of it.

They fought for a bit before Hatch, with what might've been a reluctant air, stepped in to subdue Pasternacky.

"Do *not*," Josiah screamed, "*mess with me!*"

His white hair whipping about, he scanned the floor around him. He spun several times in search of...what? The only thing he found was the severed ear, which he snatched up and held to his mouth.

"*Do not mess with me!*" he repeated.

Nobody reacted—the ear didn't project his voice through the PA system.

Josiah, looking frustrated at the nonresponse, bit hard into the ear. He shook his head like a dog with a chew toy until he'd managed to gnaw off the earlobe. He spat it toward a display of juicers.

Pasternacky urged toward Josiah again, but Hatch held him back.

The concealer had rubbed off one side of Hatch's face, showing his green tattoos—and a deflated expression.

Piper, lying not far from me, held her head low.

"Playing with Mom's knives again, little Joey?" boomed a voice from the next aisle. "We really need to get you in art classes, redirect these antisocial urges into more constructive channels."

It took Josiah a moment to realize he was being heckled. He looked around, wiping his mouth, smearing blood across one cheek, before finding Quaid.

"Hey, what—" His eyes moved quizzically to Hatch and Piper. "You're that janitor. That...weird janitor from Pittsburgh."

Quaid kept approaching. "I get around."

Josiah scowled. "Something's cranked, you shouldn't be here. I'll give you one chance. One chance to leave."

"Thanks." Quaid stopped and folded his arms. With one thumb, he smoothed the breast of his sport coat.

Another Shop-All employee rose now and took a step toward the podium. Several people had their phones out, recording video.

Josiah seemed to realize the effect of Quaid's words. "Everyone back, *back*! I have no desire to punish pawns." He lurched toward a family with young children. "But I will, janitor dude—I absolutely will if you don't take off now!"

"You're over," Quaid said in a sober tone. "History will judge you however it's going to judge you, but for my money, you should stop. Cut your body of work off right here."

In the space between the two men, I perceived a disturbance. Not movement exactly, more like energy. Like gasoline rippling the air behind a jet engine.

I lost it, then squinted and got it back. Then lost it. Then thought I got it again, but maybe those ultra-high-definition televisions in the background were confusing me.

Meanwhile, Quaid kept Josiah talking.

"...because I'll tell you quite honestly, I enjoy greeters," said the former politician. "I do. Are they helpful? Do they add much to the shopping experience? No. But their presence is comforting, just the knowledge that older members of society still..."

Now I definitely saw the presence. Quaid saw it too—while his mouth motored on, his gaze moved ever so slightly that way. The presence moved closer to Josiah, flowing from cover to cover, behind a pillar, around a six-foot cardboard Mr. Peanut, between two racks of slippers. It was hard to fix in my field of vision—tiny imperfections of color, a shadow where it shouldn't be.

Josiah interrupted Quaid's rambling, "All of you need to back up, or this goes next level. I'm *serious!*"

He spun about 540 degrees around, scanning the frightened onlookers—looking half spooked himself. His eyes settled on a gangly tween wearing her hair in a single plait.

"Everybody gives me space *now*," he said. "Or Sarah Plain and Tall pays the price!"

Quaid raised one finger for calm. "History. Think this one forward."

The presence—which could only be Durwood—had maneuvered to within five feet of Josiah. As Josiah took the tween's arm, yanking her up to the podium, the presence closed the gap further.

Piper called, "Jo! Watch out from beh—"

Before she could finish her warning, I scrambled around in front of her. *"It's okay!"* I whispered. *"Those guys are with me."*

I was kneeling in front of her on the hard Shop-All tile. Piper was lying on her tummy, her face blank. The whites of her eyes were perfect jails around each dark pupil.

I was still facing her when a gasp ripped through the crowd. We both turned.

Josiah's knife was raised in the start of a slashing motion, but it wasn't going anywhere. He strained and grunted and twisted his hips violently, but the knife stayed up.

After several seconds of animal exertion, he realized he was being restrained and flailed backward with his free arm. He whipped about at random. One blow caught the presence, ripping the material of its suit.

Durwood's right arm and half his face were exposed.

Josiah fought furiously, but even with the ex-marine half occupied getting free of his camouflage material—or skin, or suit, whatever—it was over quickly. Durwood ducked Josiah's looping stabs easily. He sidestepped a spinning sunglasses display and foam from a fire extinguisher—Josiah was hurling anything and everything.

With Shop-All employees and customers rising cautiously, Durwood countered with short, efficient blows. I imagined him trying to catch the reins of a feisty colt.

Finally, Durwood had taken Josiah's knife and detained him in a half nelson. The girl with the single plait was rubbing her arm, crying with her family.

Pasternacky recovered his ear from the floor.

The food court fry buckets had stopped boiling, leaving behind the smell of burned breading.

Josiah bucked against the steady pressure from Durwood's forearm. "Get him off! We are the righteous—we are not defeated, we *can't* be defeated!"

His eyes zipped around for help, but none of the Mice seemed to want a piece of Durwood Oak Jones.

"*The foes of progress are upon us,*" Josiah continued, "*but our mission of justice shall—*"

"Enough."

Durwood snarled and forced Josiah's head down. He seemed on the verge of worse when Quaid stepped in.

"Let's move," Quaid said. "Quicker we go, the fewer the witnesses —and the less chance this gets back to you-know-who."

With an intense blink, Durwood came back to himself. He bound Josiah's wrists with plastic zip ties.

Hatch said, "You aren't police?"

"No, sir," Quaid said. "What we are is your best possible outcome."

Hatch didn't seem to believe Quaid, but neither did he seem eager to have a go at Durwood. He raised his hands in surrender.

Quaid found me and Piper in the crowd. "Okay, you two, tell us: Who's important enough to take?"

Piper was glaring at me—a hot, terrible look. Garrison came rushing from the 3D printers aisle, openmouthed, strands of hair whirling the wrong way from his part.

My long nightmare embedded with the Mice was over.

CHAPTER FORTY-FOUR

Durwood drove. With seven people in back, plus its usual payload of weapons and gadgets, the Vanagon handled like a pregnant mare.

He steered them through the Shop-All parking complex. Cars squealed in front of them. There were several wrecks, folks scrambling from the scene. Durwood weaved through it all to the interstate.

Sue-Ann sat on the passenger seat. Around her paws were fragments of the invisibility suit. Bent nanocameras. Ragged mesh. Several wire ends remained stuck in Durwood's neck where the suit had adhered too strongly to his skin.

It was beyond repair. And he'd yet to find a replacement for Yakov.

Voices raged from the cabin.

"This is garbage on a galactic scale!" Josiah went on, swearing colorfully. "Are we hostages? Is that about what we are?"

"Not about," Quaid said. "It's exactly what you are."

"What do you even *want*? You've been jocking us since Pittsburgh. You had a spy."

Durwood glanced in the rearview. Molly's face burned. The Mice they'd taken were spread about the cabin, handcuffed by one wrist.

Quaid said, "We want information. For starters, we need to hear about this kernel. Or virus—whatever it is your nonverbal friend here built."

Piper Jackson hadn't said a word, hunched below the Stinger missiles. A ball of anger.

Josiah said, "Why should we tell you *a thing*?"

"Because we're in charge," Quaid said. "You started this mess, lost control. Now the grown-ups have to clean it up."

"By *clean*," Josiah hissed, "you mean stop. You mean retard the march of progress."

"Gimme a break," Quaid said. "I voted ninety-five percent with the progressive caucus as governor of Massachusetts, and I didn't see one thing that even remotely resembled progress back there..."

Then he went into grandstanding mode. Telling about responsibility, and the trap of self-righteousness.

Josiah argued back.

Quaid said, "You won't cooperate? Then it gets simple. We pass you off to the feds. They don't control much, but they sure would enjoy trotting you out for the press, tossing you in some ultra-max detention center."

A new voice said, "This cuff is cutting off my blood flow! I can't feel my hand."

The voice was young but husky. Molly's friend Garrison.

Quaid said, "Ah, you'll be fine. Handsome guy like you? Bet you can make purple work."

"Release us!" Josiah roared. "Right *now*, or we unleash the hounds of hell, the worst there is. Our followers will find us."

Durwood was having flashbacks to rearing his own children with Maybelle.

"Sue," he said.

The dog's milky eyes ticked up.

Durwood raised his right hand, fingers curled in an exaggerated claw. He commanded, "Scare."

Something like a tired sigh issued from Sue-Ann. Still, she climbed over the center console and got to work.

"Roo *roo*! Roo roo, ruff! Roo roo rrrrrrrruf!"

In the cabin, shoes scampering over metal. A *toink* that might've been bone on titanium. Then a scared squeal.

The squeal was Josiah's.

Now it got quiet. Durwood was able to hear a conversation between Molly and Piper Jackson, who sat closest to the cab.

"...really believed what I was writing," Molly was saying. "The blog entries, MollyWantsChange.org. I bought into it, even though I— you know, was trying to..."

Piper wouldn't answer. Durwood peeked in the rearview, found her pupils still as a hawk's.

"...and I realize you feel betrayed," Molly continued, "but we can help. We really can."

Piper muttered something Durwood didn't catch.

Neither did Molly. "What?"

Piper said, "Who's *we*? These dudes you're with."

Molly met Durwood's eyes in the mirror. "They're...well, they call themselves 'small-force private-arms operators.'"

"The hell is that?"

Molly tried to explain, but the message wasn't getting through.

She said, "Their names are Quaid Rafferty and Durwood Oak Jones."

"Durwood?"

"Right. He used to be a soldier in the marines."

"And Quinn?"

"Quaid. He was a politician, but then he got arrested. Now they're partners."

"Mercenaries," Piper said. "And you too."

"I mean, I guess in a way. I guess I am." Molly's voice cracked. "But don't you think it was time? Don't you think it's time to stop the kernel?"

Piper said nothing. Durwood checked her expression. Was that shame? Or emptiness?

Molly seemed to sense an opening. "Maybe it's hard because you built it—it feels like your child. Your instinct is to protect. I know I do, I'll argue back if one of Zach's teachers says he isn't applying himself.

But after I go home and sit with the knowledge, after I've cooled off and applied some rational thought, I realize—"

"I didn't build it," Piper said.

Durwood pulled off to the shoulder and braked.

Molly's face was still twisted with emotion from talking about her son.

She asked, "Who did?"

The hacker looked across the Vanagon cabin to Josiah and Hatch. Their six eyes were a single falling weight.

She said, "Somebody French."

CHAPTER FORTY-FIVE

Three Weeks Later

Quaid watched flight crews carrying out their prep from the helipad lobby. He wore a suit like the other men here, business travelers. He helped himself to coffee from an urn, sampled scones and sculpted melon balls from complimentary platters. Once sated, he ambled back to his corner chair.

Toward the white-haired older man reading *Le Monde*, he displayed complete indifference.

Helicopters were fast becoming the preferred transport for those who could afford it. The kernel had crippled public air traffic control, with a byzantine patchwork of private parties taking its place. The red tape involved in passing from one airspace to the next could be murder, but choppers traveled low enough to skirt these issues.

A text arrived from Durwood.

Rivard helo gassed up, any second now.

Quaid thumbed away the message and looked out across the pad. He couldn't tell which of the blue-gray maintenance uniforms was Durwood's.

The man reading *Le Monde* flipped the page with his right hand.

Yves Pomeroy's left hand rested against the leg of a female companion. The hand palsied constantly, two fingers skittering over the brunette's thigh, then skittering back.

They were accompanied by two obvious security personnel, brawny types with guns and shades.

Durwood wrote, *still just two guards?*

Quaid left a heavy roller bag at his seat to refill his coffee at the urn —though he would've preferred a nip from the flask, given what they were about to attempt.

Three other groups were waiting to board. Quaid didn't see anyone floating about the lobby or lingering in the restrooms, all clearly associated with departing passengers.

Still two, he tapped back.

Durwood's response took several seconds coming.

I don't trust it.

Quaid didn't understand why his partner was being such a nervous Nellie. They'd chosen to go after this chopper flight specifically because it was the weakest link in Rivard's security chain. Overground, Pomeroy traveled by bulletproof convoy. In satellite offices, he enjoyed a phalanx of muscle. (At Roche Rivard, of course, he and everyone else were as untouchable as goblin's gold.) For transcontinental flights, he took one of Fabienne Rivard's custom-built personal jets, whose countermeasures were on par with those of a B-1 stealth bomber.

So what if Yves Pomeroy only had two guards? Why look a gift horse in the mouth?

Piper's "French dude" must work for Yves Pomeroy, Rivard's vice president of Enterprise Software. Something like 80 percent of all offices worldwide used its antivirus software—US and European officials were regularly bribed to ignore antitrust concerns—and Piper's descriptions of how easily the kernel had slithered into systems guarded by Rivard's CyberSafe suite strongly suggested it had originated from Yves's group.

The fact that he'd been at Fabienne Rivard's side in Davos, in the firing line of technical questions, further proved his importance.

Quaid found "M McGill" in his contacts and texted, *Piper close to the phone in case?*

Molly took a while answering, and Quaid wondered whether she and Sue-Ann were having trouble keeping all the Mice in line at the hotel.

Finally, her response came.

yep, she's here. we're ready.

Quaid wrote, *everyone behaving?*

more or less.

Translation? Any escape attempts?

not really.

Quaid sent three questions marks in response.

Molly wrote, *it's under control.*

Having witnessed "under control" in the McGill household, he was less than reassured.

They were detaining Hatch, Piper, the longhaired kid who had the hots for Molly, and Josiah. The first three had been mad after Shop-All but were persuaded to cooperate by Quaid, who'd recounted Fabienne's Davos speech and apocalyptic vision of corporate dominion over all.

They'd been ready to concede—Quaid had read it in their postures. Josiah's cruel, nonsensical violence had carried them to that point.

Josiah himself was a different story. He'd been persuaded of nothing. Luckily, he flinched every time Sue-Ann as much as looked at him.

Now a mellifluous voice called over the public address, "Yves Pomeroy, please report with your party to the flight deck for departure."

Pomeroy struggled up, using his shapely companion for balance. As they flashed their tickets and left by accordion doors for their helicopter, Quaid bussed his food.

He texted Durwood, *coming to you.*

Stretching tall, Quaid extended the handle of his roller bag and gave the Rivard foursome a healthy lead before heading for the exit himself.

The gate agent poised her scanner. "Ticket?"

Quaid held his tie busily against his chest, producing his document. This and Durwood's mechanic credentials had come from Quaid's buddy, the former head of the Federal Aviation Administration with whom Quaid had once pedaled a bar trolley down the streets of New Orleans.

The agent pointed out that he didn't depart for another hour.

"I like to get myself situated," Quaid said, pulling a neck pillow from his bag. "I slept exactly twelve minutes, gunshots outside my window all night long."

The agent twisted her mouth in sympathy and scanned his ticket.

Quaid strode surely across the helipad. A half dozen choppers were about, making it easy to veer close to the Rivard group without arousing suspicion. Their chopper was large, squat, and dark—a crow with rotors. The logo, R over the spinning globe, was painted black on black and barely visible.

Pomeroy boarded the cabin by a rail, assisted by his companions. The female took his briefcase. The guards supported his wrists and elbows like teacup handles before joining him aboard.

Across the helipad, a lone man in blue-gray emerged from an equipment shed.

The Rivard pilot conferred with controllers by corded microphone. Then he started his engine. Rotors roared alive, their wind whipping Quaid's hair and pinning his suit pants to his shins.

The man in blue-gray approached and knocked on the nose glass.

The pilot sprung his ladder hatch.

Quaid hastened his steps in order to hear the exchange.

"...good look at that altimeter," Durwood was saying. "Should read six-forty, give or take."

The pilot crinkled his brow.

Durwood gestured for permission to mount. The pilot nodded. Durwood dropped his head with a put-upon air, simultaneously reaching back for the gun tucked into the waistband of his pants.

Quaid jogged to follow him inside.

He only lost sight of Durwood for a few seconds, but by the time he'd climbed the ladder and made the cabin, Durwood had incapacitated one guard—slumped diagonally in his jump seat—and taken the other's firearm.

Yves Pomeroy threw an arm gallantly across his companion. "What is the meaning of this? Identify yourself!"

Durwood ignored the demand, leveling his gun on the pilot. "Take 'er up. Now."

The pilot blubbered, "Wh-where? Where are you taking us?"

Quaid said, "Same destination, don't worry. All we want is information. Everything's gonna turn out fine."

The pilot did as he was told, throttling up, pulling his stick. It seemed an unsteady takeoff—Quaid wobbled like a honeymoon surfer—but they kept gaining altitude and soon cleared the city skyline.

Yves Pomeroy had begun inching toward a red button on the wall.

"*Non, non, monsieur*," Quaid said, producing his own pistol from the roller bag. "One more move and this baby gets some brand-new ventilation."

Pomeroy inched back to his companion, his palsy newly violent. "This will not stand." His accent turned every *th* into a flamboyant *z*. "The price will be high."

Durwood, continuing to ignore the man, tore through Quaid's bag until he found the infrared scanner. He waved it above Yves's and his companion's heads, along a solid wall. The cabin's interior size didn't match its exterior. Clearly, there was a compartment behind the wall.

The scanner remained silent.

Durwood said, "What's back there?"

Yves Pomeroy glared back with contempt. "It is an empty bay."

Durwood cut his eyes to the woman.

She blinked and nodded and blinked more. "*Oui*, empty, as he said!"

Durwood looked between them. "Maybe a sleeping chamber." To Yves: "See you wear a wedding ring. Guess it don't mean much to you."

The old man reared back in offense.

Quaid said, "We could have company any second—let's not waste time getting our moral hackles up." He told Pomeroy, "Don't sweat Maude back home. As long as you cooperate, your secret's safe with us."

Pomeroy's eyebrows shook. "You cannot scare me. I will tell you nothing."

The helicopter banked, providing a view of several subdivisions and a lake.

Durwood said, "Long way down, person were to fall."

"Threats, *boff*," Pomeroy said. "I have endured far worse. In February, I was kidnapped by Dutch students who blamed Rivard for the Anarchy. Knowing of my weakness for foie gras, they force-fed me corn boiled in fat until I agreed to talk. What did they receive in return? Nothing but my contempt and a mess in their bathroom."

As the helicopter continued ascending, Quaid touched his stomach.

"This is different—we can protect you." He pulled a device from his bag and extended its antenna. "We're scrambling all wireless microphones. Nobody can hear a word you're saying. Not Fabienne or anybody else at Roche Rivard."

Yves Pomeroy shuddered at his boss's name. "I am not sure I believe this."

Saying this, he shied ever so slightly from his female companion. He was worried she'd report back to Fabienne.

Quaid offered the woman his hand. "Come, let's have you assist the pilot up front. I didn't see a copilot, which seems like an oversight..."

He ushered her to the cockpit before returning to Pomeroy.

"Now. Let's discuss this kernel."

"I do not know this word, kernel," Pomeroy said.

"It's a piece of software that's infecting data in your systems."

His nostrils wriggled, showing stray white hairs. "We are having a translation issue, I fear. Perhaps you can give your meaning in a different way?"

Quaid did his best to recall specifics from Piper Jackson's account, but Yves Pomeroy continued to stare at him like he was speaking gibberish.

Durwood cut in, "*You understand fine.* Rivard's in the middle of this data loss, and you're in charge. Start talking."

"I—*non*, you misunderstand," Pomeroy said. "I am only in my position due to my association with Henri. Now I am surrounded by his daughter's lackeys. I am undermined at every turn."

The flesh of his neck quivering, he launched into the tale of how

ANARCHY OF THE MICE

Fabienne had decimated the old guard—how she'd fired half her father's management team her first week and missed no opportunity to humiliate Yves himself. She had taken away his expense account. She'd subjected him to demeaning career reviews, at which every innocent gesture and politeness came under scrutiny.

"Henri was a great man whose leadership is sorely missed," Pomeroy said. "We are not told of his whereabouts. Has he died? There are rumors he is held underground at Roche Rivard. Maybe he is vegetative, maybe not. One is filled with sadness."

Quaid knew for a fact Henri Rivard had been no saint in his younger days, when he was in charge of the company, but saw no advantage in debating the point. They'd scared Yves off his red button, but who knew what the pilot had access to? A squadron of F-18s could be five miles out and closing.

"Let's shift gears," Quaid said, beginning to fear they'd taken this giant risk for nothing. "How *could* it work? Presupposing the data loss originated in Rivard systems. If somebody wanted to sneak in with a Trojan horse, where would they put it?"

Pomeroy's eyes lost focus.

Durwood gripped him by a starched shirt collar. "Quit playing the old goat, we saw you talk in Davos. Now think!"

"It is not a matter of thought," Pomeroy said. "Even if I wanted to help, I have not read a line of code in decades. I know nothing specific of my team's work."

Durwood's fist continued to tighten at Yves Pomeroy's throat—shrinking, whitening, until Quaid pulled him off.

"Forget code," Quaid said, "forget the whats and hows. Let's start from the whos. Who manages CyberSafe, the antivirus software? You must know that."

Yves massaged his own shoulder, recovering from Durwood's grip. "Of course."

"Who?"

"CyberSafe is the responsibility of Thérèse Laurent."

Quaid swished the name around his brain. "I feel like I know that name..."

"She is the closest *amie* of Fabienne," Pomeroy said. "There is nothing at Rivard LLC in which she does not have a hand."

In a flash, Quaid remembered that night at Hotel Zauberberg: the buxom blond with a PhD in organizational behavior.

Pomeroy said, "You do not suspect..." Horror blanched his face. "It is not possible! You cannot believe they have conspired to sabotage CyberSafe."

Quaid looked to Durwood, then back at the Rivard executive. "Can you?"

A fresh wave of palsy overtook Yves Pomeroy, great spastic jolts. He tried covering his own eyes but poked himself instead. Then he flailed to one side in despair, his right arm shooting out.

Quaid and Durwood lunged to stop him, but too late: he'd hit the red button.

With a mechanical wheeze, the wall behind them split. Armed fighters poured into cabin.

CHAPTER FORTY-SIX

D urwood stopped the first fighter with a chop to the face. He
dislocated the second's elbow with an arm bar. The Rivard men
seemed reluctant to fire, though the cabin of the chopper—a modified
Aerospatiale SA 3—wasn't pressurized.

This was to their detriment.

Numbers three and four rushed Durwood. He picked an ax off the
wall and swung it like a scythe.

The ax head lodged deep in the first man's ribs. Durwood had
swung with such force that momentum carried the man through his
squadmate.

Toppled, but not done.

Pain pounded in Durwood's head. He fought toward the hurt,
nursing it, using it. God's wrath lived in his fists.

Across the cabin, Quaid was pinned beneath a fighter with a Croat
look. Durwood collected guns off the men he'd downed and yanked
Quaid's attacker off by the neck of a Kevlar vest.

The man raised his hands and whimpered for mercy.

Durwood drove a knee into his nose. *Mercy. Sure, till I turn my back.*

The very last enemy plowed into Durwood from behind. His face rang off the steel edge of a jump seat. Durwood felt the swelling begin immediately—like Grandma Jones's sourdough in a hot oven.

He stayed on his knees, controlling the fury in his muscles. Then he jolted backward. His skull hit soft tissue.

There was a groan and the sour tang of blood.

Durwood spun and attacked. The man's eyes fluttered. His mouth hung slack.

Durwood's headache rose to a terrific peak. He rammed his chin into the man's Adam's apple—a move suggested by no training Durwood had ever received. The impact resounded above the helicopter's rotor wash.

The man's eyes closed.

"*Mon Dieu!*" Yves Pomeroy gasped. "These are paid contractors—whatever you believe of me or my company, they do not deserve to be brutalized!"

Durwood said, "Tell it to the United Nations. Now talk. Won't be long before we have more company up here."

On cue, two attack choppers rose in the west horizon. Apaches. Missile tubes squared, like fangs mounted on wings.

Quaid picked himself up off the ground. "Tell us more about Thérèse Laurent. How long has she been running CyberSafe?"

Yves considered. "Fabienne appointed her last fall, *eh bien*...perhaps a year."

"About how long the Blind Mice have been zapping data."

"I have begged for resources to fix the data loss," Yves said. "I am rebuffed. Fabienne believes the goal is unattainable—the data is forever lost."

"Unattainable? The woman built a space laser capable of annihilating enemies from twenty thousand miles up."

Yves stroked his chin. "One is puzzled by it, *certainement*."

Durwood said, "Nothing puzzling about it."

The Apaches were closing in.

Quaid tried Pomeroy on several technical points but only managed to confuse the aging executive. *Did he mean the CyberSafe partner interface? Or server-side processing?*

Quaid winced. "I think we need outside help."

He found his phone and called Molly. She answered and must've started right in because Quaid said, "I'll explain later—we're plugging away up here—but right now, I need Jackson on the phone."

As Quaid talked to Piper Jackson, Durwood watched the Apaches. They were in firing range, easy. Would they fire with Yves Pomeroy inside?

Probably not.

He squinted to see inside the nearest Apache. Looked like they were preparing a rappel line.

They intend to board us.

Quaid tried relaying Piper's tech information to Yves Pomeroy. A question about encryption. Some port number in the seven thousands.

The old man only got more confused.

Quaid said, "Here—she wants me to put her on speaker."

He tapped his phone and held it up.

"Everybody hear me?" came Jackson's voice.

Pomeroy leaned near the phone. "I can hear, yes."

"Cool," she said. "Listen, I think it has to be in that partner gateway API."

Yves Pomeroy bit his lip.

Piper went on, "Right? When a system wasn't using CyberSafe, I could still get the kernel in—but it took finagling. The other antivirus programs all have that gateway so they can talk to Rivard, y'all got so much of the market."

"CyberParle," Pomeroy muttered. "Yes, the gateway API could conceivably... I—I never considered this but it... One might..." He gained vigor suddenly. "If what you say is true, it makes perfect sense —CyberParle!" He clutched Durwood's sleeve. "*Oui, oui*—it is installed everywhere, it would be the perfect delivery mechanism for a piece of malicious code..."

He kept on, telling how Thérèse had overhauled this gateway deal her first week on the job.

Durwood was glad the Einsteins finally had an idea, but he wasn't sure where it got them. It sounded like Yves Pomeroy was out of the loop in his own company. Two minutes ago, he hadn't known what "kernel" meant. Now he figured he understood the whole kit and caboodle?

Quaid said, "Will you help us? Fabienne railroaded you, but we can make it right—if we work together."

Yves Pomeroy's wiry eyebrows acted like they were fighting each other.

Quaid Rafferty had a gift for catching a man just right—just when he was ready to make a change. Would Pomeroy change? It was one thing to be disgruntled. It was another to turn traitor.

Durwood had dealt with informants in the marines. He knew such people were vital to mission success. Still, he could never look one in the eye without growling—a little, to himself.

Finally, Yves declared, "I will help, *oui*! For Henri, for the world. For this company I have given my life to, Rivard LLC."

Quaid looked enthusiastically to Durwood.

Durwood's mouth was straight.

A heavy clap sounded from the nose of the aircraft. All three looked.

One of the Apache's rappel lines had attached to the cockpit. The attack chopper hovered twenty yards out, starboard side. The two crafts, tethered now, tugged and tore and strained against each other.

Durwood looked down. They were over water.

Quaid staggered to keep his feet. "Don't say a word back at Roche Rivard. Got it? Act like nothing's changed. We'll contact you."

Yves Pomeroy gave a stern nod.

Two figures were moving along the rappel line. Black-clad and dangling through space like a couple spiders hurrying after their dinners.

Quaid drew his gun and started for the cockpit.

"Nope," Durwood said.

Quaid's eyes went wobbly when he saw Durwood tightening the waist and shoulder straps of a parachute.

Durwood tossed a second chute at his partner's chest.

"Check your rip cord," he said. "Quickly."

Quaid closed his mouth. "We are *not* going in the drink."

Durwood gave his straps a final cinch and twisted the portside hatch. Air screamed in around the seal.

"This is nuts," Quaid said. "The whole operation was nuts on the drawing board, and it got nuttier when he hit that red button—and now we're ten miles into Loonytown."

But he was putting on his chute.

Durwood looked down again. The river was brown with slow-frothing peaks. About a mile wide, he judged, though only the middle three-quarters would be survivable.

The packs were Yakov's, the last two Durwood had. Small and featherweight, reliable.

A commotion sounded from the cockpit. Metal clanging, orders shouted.

The spiders had arrived.

Durwood swung the hatch up and muscled it into its catch, making a four-foot maw in the side of the helicopter. The sky reached for them, livid and loud.

Quaid gave his partner a last sullen look. Then he jumped.

Durwood followed into the void.

Free fall washed over his body and brain, cleansing his headache and all previous thought. His cheeks rattled. Organs clung to his spine.

The air cracked with tracers from the Apaches' guns. They didn't stay in range long, the choppers shrinking to pinpoints above.

The jump was short, maybe fifteen hundred feet. Durwood counted one-thousand-four and pulled his cord.

The chute lines unspooled and a second later the canopy filled. Durwood's shoulders felt jackhammered from inside their sockets.

Deceleration was immediate. He floated toward the river, on perfect course for the center.

Quaid pulled later.

As the chute below unfurled—low, too damn low—Durwood experienced a pang of regret.

Had he told Quaid they were only at 1500? No. He'd been annoyed. It was their default, Quaid complaining and Durwood annoyed. It was habit.

In his brusqueness, Durwood had been negligent. Negligent with the life of a man who'd pulled him out of his life's deepest trough.

His discharge complete, his wife and eldest son dead, Durwood had been living on the West Virginia property. Johnsongrass grown up everywhere, the barn in disrepair. He'd had no will for work. He hadn't seen the point.

The man in the sport coat had stood there fifteen minutes, knocking on his pine door, before Durwood finally answered. He talked another three hours. Said he wasn't taking no for an answer. Said he believed in Durwood—he'd heard the facts and believed the good outweighed the bad. *Who among us doesn't slip?*

Hell, he was done with government work too. Why didn't they build a thing from scratch? Make it whatever they wanted. What did they have to lose?

Durwood couldn't see his partner's splashdown. The chute was in the way. It did manage to open fully, but not for long. A beat later, the white fabric billowed flat across brown water.

There was a lump in the middle.

Durwood pulled his steering lines, adjusting course. He floated toward Quaid. His heart swelled up his chest. He tensed his arms to his sides and pointed his toes to go faster. He watched for movement.

A breeze caught Quaid's chute. The river started pulling it downstream. The fabric snagged and tumbled over whitecaps.

Quaid's chute cleared the lump just before Durwood plunged into frigid water. He didn't register the temperature shock, digging for the surface, orienting himself.

He spotted Quaid ten yards away. His own chute pack still on his back, Durwood knifed forward in a perfect freestyle stroke toward his partner.

Quaid bobbed in the water, slumped to one side. He'd drifted such that Durwood couldn't see if his eyes were open.

Durwood swam faster.

He reached Quaid and plucked him from the water, panting, ignoring the lines strangling his wrists.

He spun Quaid around. The eyes were closed.

"Quaid!" he shouted. "Quaid, *talk*—tell me you're good!"

The eyes did not open, but Quaid's hand moved to a strand of hair over his temple, reshaping it into a soggy curlicue.

Durwood gazed up, heavenward, and exhaled.

CHAPTER FORTY-SEVEN

Paris - Two Weeks Later

As my limousine wound through the rubble-strewn boulevards of Paris (talk about words I never expected would apply to me), I distracted myself from the ridiculous danger I was walking into with polite chatter. I asked the driver if he missed the Louvre. Were these hot temps about typical for the season? Did he have any children?

"*Ah oui*, four sons." The man raised so many fingers over the headrest.

"That must keep you hopping," I said. "How do they get along?"

He wagged his hand side to side. "This violence everywhere, it doesn't help. But my wife has some tricks for making them..."

He slicked his thumb and forefinger together, searching for the word.

I said, "Behave?"

"Yes, yes. To not kill the other." He smiled and switched lanes. "*Et vous*? You are American—it is said that American children are loud. Is it true? Are your children quite loud?"

I wasn't thrilled about his assumption I had children, but I reminded myself the wig and brow prosthetic were *supposed* to make me look older.

"You get used to it," I said. "I'll bet they're in the same decibel range as your boys."

The driver huffed lightly, accelerating toward a tunnel marked *ROCHE RIVARD*.

My breezy answer notwithstanding, I did worry about Zach and Karen. It was my second international trip in a month. As we were saying goodbyes, Zach kept asking when my flight was—*Closer to two? When're you probably hitting the road?*—like he had big plans for my absence.

Karen hugged me hard but was preoccupied with finishing her dolls' "safety fortress"—a cardboard-and-tape structure that already encompassed one whole corner of the living room. It still needed a boudoir and beading room, and a bulletproof roof for the second story.

Granny insisted they were fine.

"You aren't meant to know every little drip dropping through their heads," she'd said, putting her hair up in curlers. "We never did, and look—we raised the Greatest Generation."

The limo emerged from the tunnel, out of Paris now and in the Boulogne Woods. Even in the climate-controlled car, I felt immediately cooler. Heavy limbs draped over the expressway—several literally across the road, such that we had to drive around on the shoulder.

Six winding miles later, the road straightened and a hulking tower rose before us. It was primarily black glass, with stone shoulders and a barbed-wire skirt. Small crafts hovered about its upper reaches like flies buzzing a stallion's head.

My veins seemed to clench. "Is that..."

The driver didn't look back. "*Oui, madame.* This is Roche Rivard."

I took several breaths, visualizing oxygen flowing into my brain.

This is the best lead you've got, I reminded myself. *The best lead anybody's got.*

Roche Rivard had security like Saturn has rings. A quarter mile out, I was required to show identification at a guard tower. This permitted me through an electrified fence and into a labyrinth of lanes winding through various sensors—like an automated car wash, only with infrared and invisible rays rather than suds and water jets.

The driver said, "Nothing in your bag, one hopes?"

I clutched my leather satchel, thinking of the time Zach had slipped an Xbox game into my purse and the supermarket exit bleated at us.

"One hopes," I agreed.

I passed through the final checkpoint on foot, paying my driver— "*Bonne chance,*" he said—and providing the name of the Rivard person I'd come to see. A severe woman in epaulets had me wait in a window-less room with foam cream-colored walls.

Soundproof? Bug-proof?

Five tense minutes later, Yves Pomeroy tottered in.

"*Excellentement!*" he said. "So thrilled I am to show you Rivard LLC in action."

I'd worn a navy blazer and snug but professional jeans—an outfit that, together with auburn hair and the older face, we hoped would pass for a Silicon Valley executive.

Yves Pomeroy led me from the windowless room to the Roche Rivard lobby, which was as big as a train station—a hive of rushing men and women, walls adorned with live video feeds and bright electronic charts.

Yves approached a receptionist—the most attractive one, I noted. "I have Mademoiselle Jansen here! Her company is considering a large purchase of CyberSafe, and we are touring the facility."

His palsy became violent, knocking my elbow. I thought his nerves would give us away, but the receptionist paid no mind. She entered information off my passport, a high-quality fake the guys had obtained, and used a 3D printer to produce a badge.

Yves pinned the badge on my chest.

"I could've done that myself," I said.

He bowed from the waist, oblivious. "Not at all."

The badge was wafer thin, flexible, electronic. Its face showed my name—*Denise Jansen*—and a timer that ticked down from sixty minutes.

We needed to go, but I was mesmerized by a display that took up one entire wall of the lobby. The gigantic screen tracked various revenue measures, the company's stock price (ticker symbol: RIV), and dozens of *objectifs centraux* in a stunning holographic display, some-thing right out of *Star Wars*.

Yves saw my gaze. "The Grand Planifier," he explained. "One's progress is constantly monitored and reported upon."

He raised his own badge, which showed four red lines flashing *EN RETARD*. The lines seemed to bend off the badge toward their wispy representations high above.

There were other marvels—drones carrying manila folders, virtual-reality cubicles for communicating with satellite offices like Beijing and Mexico City. If Willy Wonka had built a corporate headquarters, this would be it.

Yves tapped my badge. "We have just fifty-eight minutes to conduct our, eh...our tour."

"What happens if we go over?"

"The badge will emit a deafening beacon," he said. "Security officers will respond in a matter of seconds."

Yves started us toward the elevators, but the receptionist called after us.

"*Excusez, excusez-moi!*" She paused to listen to a sleek silver earbud. "Miss Rivard requests a word at the beginning of your tour, Mr. Pomeroy. With you and your Californian guest."

Yves and I froze. Had she put snark into the word "Californian"? Maybe it was just her accent.

"Of course, of course." Yves quickly masked the alarm in his face. "It is an honor, yes, an honor to receive a moment of Mademoiselle Rivard's time."

I bobbed my head in agreement.

As we boarded an elevator going up—rather than down where Enterprise Software was—Yves whispered, "It cannot be helped. Scrutiny is high."

The plan had been for us to probe, using this marketing tour as cover, the low-level Enterprise Software staff on CyberSafe. Had their recent work introduced any known vulnerabilities? How significant had Thérèse Laurent's involvement been? Were the changes reversible? Questions that would've seemed suspicious coming from Yves but maybe not from an outsider.

This was dangerous enough, fishing for intel in a building Human

Rights Watch had designated "a de facto detention center." Now I had to bluff Fabienne Rivard face-to-face?

What if she recognized me from Davos? What if she'd intercepted the guys' coded messages to Yves Pomeroy?

The elevator zoomed skyward, trees blurred in the glass sides.

In a hushed tone, Yves said, "Total confidence is required when one deals with Fabienne Rivard. The woman can smell dishonesty. It is her gift."

I set my jaw as the floor indicator climbed. I'd convinced Hatch at the Nowhere Tattoo Parlor. I'd survived the eDeed mission with Piper Jackson.

I could do this.

The elevator stopped at Eighty-Three. I was surprised Fabienne's office wasn't on the top floor—there were 117—until Yves explained that its precise location rotated every six weeks to thwart assassination plots.

We found Fabienne reading a slim novel.

"Yves, *bon*," she said. "I was told you had a visitor. Please introduce us."

She laid her book facedown, cracking its spine, to take my hand. Fabienne was every inch as tall as she'd looked in Davos. I felt like I was shaking the foreleg of a praying mantis.

Once names were established, Fabienne said, "Tell me about Blap-Blap.com."

I joined my hands formally. "Right, that's what we're calling it. The name polled well with eighteen- to twenty-five-year-olds."

Fabienne looked to Yves, then back to me. "Your company is in Silicon Valley, where the best programmers in the world live. Yet you are considering outsourcing antivirus protection to Rivard. Why?"

"Well, CyberSafe is the leading product in the space. Our programmers don't—that is, they aren't virus experts."

Her angular face shifted, looking purple in the new light. "What is your strategy for the data loss?"

"Obviously, we hope to avoid it," I said. "So far, our code's been kept strictly in house and we've had no issues, and ideally CyberSafe would keep it that way."

I liked the answer—it'd felt smooth off my tongue, like a line from a commercial—but Fabienne did not relent.

"Doubtless you've heard rumors," she said, "that our software plays some role."

"Role?"

"*Oui.* In the data loss."

I hadn't been expecting her to come out and articulate this, but it was a perfectly valid question. I needed an answer.

"I—I was told by Mr. Pomeroy"—opening my shoulders, inviting Yves to chime in—"these were slurs propagated by competitors jealous of Rivard's growth and dominant market position."

The answer seemed to please Fabienne. She circled back around her desk, an oval of some semitransparent alloy, and picked up her novel.

She read for three minutes.

Yves said, "If there is nothing more, perhaps we will begin our tour..."

Before Fabienne could answer, the door opened and an impressive woman with platinum-blond hair entered.

"My apologies," she said, "it couldn't be helped, I have just learned—"

She stopped at the sight of me and Yves Pomeroy. "A tour, Pomeroy? You are giving a tour?"

Yves took a step back, as though physically intimidated. The woman had three inches on him. "Yes, Thérèse. A tour."

"As the director of technical operations," the woman said, "I should be included in all client tours."

"You declined several invitations last week, so I only thought—"

"*Last week,* yes," Thérèse Laurent said. "My schedule has freed up since then."

Yves quivered. He balked for another moment, then seemed to buck himself up.

"We were just speaking of CyberSafe. I was preparing to explain our recent improvements, which have made the suite more secure than ever—but I am sure you know the technical aspects best." His eyes twinkled. "Being, as you are, director of technical operations. *Oui?*"

Thérèse shifted weight between her legs. "We've closed many vulnerabilities, it's true. I won't bore the woman with details."

"Bore her!" Yves insisted. "She works in Silicon Valley, she will understand..."

He pressed her to say more about the tech details of CyberSafe. It seemed like one of those passive-aggressive office exchanges where one person is trying to make a point about another.

Thérèse said, "You are the man, Yves. Naturally, you are correct and know what's best."

Yves blushed furiously. "No, that is not fair, I merely—"

"Attempt to humiliate and discredit me before a client?" Thérèse finished.

Fabienne walked slowly from her desk to stand behind Thérèse. Both women looked at Yves Pomeroy as though his billowy white hair were a toxic cloud.

A chime sounded from somewhere below my chin. When I glanced down, my badge had changed color to yellow.

Yves, seeming thrilled for the distraction, said, "*Eh bien*, one carries on! The tour must begin. Will you be joining us, Mademoiselle Laurent? Or do the two of you have more pressing business?"

The women shared a look, then Thérèse Laurent made a brush-off gesture.

We turned to go.

Fabienne called after us, "I trust you will be impressed. In these times, no company can match the power and reputation of Rivard LLC."

I pivoted at the threshold to smile my anticipation, or under-standing—whatever I needed to do to escape this bizarre situation—and didn't see the stocky man until we slammed into each other.

CHAPTER FORTY-EIGHT

Blake Leathersby was in workout clothes, spandex shorts and a ribbed Union Jack tank top. Colliding with his chest was like having an airbag deploy in my face—a stiff, sweaty one.

"Oh!" I said, barely keeping my feet. "Sorry, I didn't see you."

As he stepped back to consider me, one of his trunk-like legs hit Yves Pomeroy—and Yves wasn't able to keep his feet.

"*Excusez-vous*," the older man snapped, a jumble on the floor. "One should watch where one steps."

Leathersby didn't offer a hand up. "One should be sturdier than a blade of grass. I'm coming from the gym. Might check the place out yourself. Add some muscle mass, Colonel Blimp."

I didn't get the reference, but Yves puffed up like it was a slur. I hung back and let them argue—not wanting Leathersby to get a longer look at me.

Yves said, "We French place less value on brawn for brawn's sake."

Leathersby sniffed. "Could be that explains why we English paste you every time it comes to war."

Fabienne Rivard, witnessing the commotion, walked to her door and jerked it closed with evident irritation.

Yves fixed the lay of his shirt. "As vice president of executive security, you should know: I was kidnapped again. In America this time."

"No kidding? Get force-fed any corn?"

The Frenchman refused to dignify the questions with a response. "You and your brutes are paid to protect me."

Leathersby chuckled—gruff, cruel. "What can I say? We do our best, but it's a lot of nutjobs want to see your old bones gone."

Then he resumed up the hall, emitting a gust of odor from his armpit. Yves and I went the other way.

"He's awful," I said.

"Quite," Yves agreed.

"The guys told me he was a mercenary—he only did certain jobs for Rivard. What was that talk about vice president?"

Yves steered us around a corner. "Fabienne has recently installed him in a full-time role. In meetings, the man is a bully. He makes crass gestures when a decision goes against him. He is the worst of his country—and each day this Anarchy continues, his stature grows. He thrives like"—Yves's face curdled—"like mold. Some poison mold which feeds off darkness and ignorance."

We reached the elevator bank. Yves faltered at the button panel, still flushed from the confrontation. He took several seconds finding and pressing *Down*.

I expected Enterprise Software to be some space-age facility, machines with neon-colored innards or something, but it was unspectacular. The computers looked like any old PC I might've worked on through Rainey Personnel, and the kitchenette was nothing fancy: a chips-and-candy-bar vending machine, drip coffee maker with a stained pot.

The engineers seemed run of the mill too. Yves introduced me to his principal software architect, Gaspard, a spindly man who kept honking into a tissue.

"This is it, where we make the software—*achew!*" He waved an arm around the floor. "Every day, we receive eight hundred new virus reports. We're lucky to get half in the patch—*achew!*"

I nodded, feigning interest.

Yves said, "I was hoping to introduce Mademoiselle Jansen to Marie, who typically leads the tour. Where is Marie?"

Gaspard and his colleagues looked at their shoes.

Yves said, "As the primary engineer in the CyberSafe revamp, Marie would be best for speaking of the recent changes."

Gaspard, still looking at his shoes, said, "You have not been present much, sir."

"I—yes, I am required to travel," Yves said, "to defend our department in public. This cannot be helped."

Another worker said, "Something has happened to Marie—some harm. We all know this. She has not been here in months."

"*Months?*" Yves repeated. "Then who is running CyberSafe?"

"Thérèse," Gaspard said. "Thérèse Laurent has taken direct command."

The workers' body language clamped shut at the name—as clear a nonverbal cue as I'd ever seen. Yves's face turned ashen.

He asked a few more questions to keep up the ruse—Fine work, *bon, c'est ça!*—then thanked his team and hustled us away to his office.

"This is not good," he said as the door closed. "Thérèse is a businesswoman, a lackey of Fabienne's. She cannot direct a software product—much less one under siege, as CyberSafe is."

"Do you think she's hiding the kernel?"

"I did not want to believe," Yves said. "But...we must consider it."

As he brooded on how deep his company's ties to the Anarchy ran, I scanned Yves Pomeroy's office. Like the rest of Enterprise Software, his space was modest—even dingy. His desk was particleboard, and four folding chairs were his only furniture. The space got no natural light, though there was a dim glass pane behind him—like a window in front of a brick wall, only not brick.

"Your office isn't great," I observed.

Yves got a forlorn expression. "Under Henri, nothing but the best." He kissed his fingertips. "Under his daughter, I am punished. Her Gender Council has dug into my actions decades ago—when France was a different place—and decided I need 'rehabilitation.'"

His pouty tone and air quotes didn't impress me. I was no Fabienne

Rivard fan, but in the brief interactions I'd had with Yves so far, I felt like her council was on decently solid ground in that estimation.

I gestured to the glass. "What does your window overlook? *Is* that a window?"

Yves squinted a moment in confusion before twisting abruptly. "The shaft! *Oui, oui*—a window of sorts."

"Shaft?"

"The inner shaft." He stood and approached the pane, raising its sill, craning his head through.

He explained that the rock Roche Rivard was built into had been tectonically active—remained so to this day. When geologists had discovered this during construction, they had advised Henri Rivard to seek another site. Henri demanded they build anyway. Most of the scientists and project leaders refused, but he found one young Turk who believed drilling deeply through the Earth's crust in the precise center of the building—a kind of release valve—would mitigate the risk. Henri ordered it done. Now a handful of offices on each floor overlooked the inner shaft.

"Sounds hazardous," I said.

Yves shrugged. "Some claim they can smell sulfur. I am a recognized sommelier by the region of Bordeaux, and I never have."

"There's never been any kind of explosion?"

Yves shook his head and told the story of the Algerian nationalists who seized two floors of Roche Rivard in 1983, stole Rivard's experimental sonic agitator, and threatened to discharge it straight down the inner shaft—directly into the fault line—unless Henri agreed to pay reparations.

Yves smiled admiringly at the memory. "Henri told them, 'Do your worst!' I was at his side—it was beautiful. 'I am done apologizing for *le colonialisme!*' They killed hostage after hostage. Henri backed down not a centimeter. 'Did Rivard profit from past abuse? Indeed, we did— handsomely. Accept this and abandon your terror now, or die like dogs.'"

I wasn't loving Yves's hero worship. "And?"

"Die they did," Yves said, "at the hands of our very best sharp-shooters."

Before he could say anything to further lower my opinion of him, my badge blipped. I looked down. It was orange.

"Fifteen minutes!" Yves said. "We must get to the records, to the bowels! I'd hoped to avoid them, but one cannot always choose."

"The bowels?" I said.

"All software changes, to CyberSafe and otherwise, are logged in a separate floor deep within the rock of Roche Rivard."

"You can't just look them up on your computer?"

Yves was standing, taking a cashmere coat off a rack. "I'm afraid not. Did you bring a coat?"

"No, I..." I was having trouble focusing on the question, thinking about lava. "It's spring, I didn't think I would need one."

Yves gallantly handed me his own coat and retrieved a V-neck sweater from a desk drawer for himself.

"Outside, *oui*, it is spring," he said. "It is not spring in the bowels."

CHAPTER FORTY-NINE

I t took three separate elevators to reach the bowels. The first bottomed out at a level marked *B2*. The second was a kind of freight elevator, lined with knotty boards, much colder. We rode with a crew in hard hats.

The third required us to walk a path of fine gravel. We passed construction sites with cage-lantern lights and hydraulic diggers. Grit and sawdust clogged my nose. Wood-paneled walls gave way to bare rock—the limestone skeleton of Roche Rivard.

In another ten feet, the path ended in a void of blackest black.

Yves twisted back, wringing his hands. "The car will arrive shortly."

I inched up to the void, keeping my nicest work clogs safely on gravel. This close, I could see the shaft better. It was irregularly shaped, wider on the left than the right, with a thick cable running down its center.

During prep, Quaid and Durwood had mentioned the bowels: the partially developed foundation of Rivard LLC's headquarters that was rumored to house the darkest of the company's many dark projects. Fabienne Rivard's controversial oubliette. Exotic plasma weapons. Dalliances in genetic engineering.

All the James Bond stuff, Quaid had said. *I don't buy half of it.*

Durwood had cleared his throat.

I was just thinking about Durwood—his doubts about Yves Pomeroy and belief the man would turn on us the moment he saw a benefit in it—when a *clank* from the shaft startled me.

Then, far below, grinding sounds.

I stepped back in line with Yves. Together, we watched a heavy, irregularly tarnished platform ascend. The platform wobbled and whinnied and knocked against the short side of the shaft.

When it stopped in front of us, the gap was three feet.

"One must jump," Yves said, staggering his stance.

He dashed sprightly to the platform, causing it to dip and the cable to creak. I jumped next. My shoes' impact echoed up the shaft, coming back at us in a gloomy cacophony.

Yves found a knotted rope dangling beside the cable. He pulled it left. Soon, the platform began descending—low, jerky, uneven.

With every drop, the air was colder. I pulled Yves's coat tight around my shoulders.

There seemed to be only one stop, which took us ninety seconds to reach. The platform settled to a wobbly rest. The distance to the limestone seemed a little farther than where we'd boarded, but Yves and I both managed the leap.

Next, we found ourselves in a narrow tunnel—dark and sloped, spiraling deeper into the earth.

"*We must hurry,*" Yves said, taking my wrist. "It is another six levels to the archives."

We ran. Cold stung my face—the tunnel's corners showed either frost or cobwebs. Distant plops seemed to come from above and below us at once.

We passed several chambers without doors. Inside one, I saw a table-mounted scope or laser. Other chambers had irregular openings and seemed freshly blasted.

"What was *that?*" I asked, glimpsing a room that pulsed red from some central orb—an intense, monochromatic disco.

"Many even I do not know," said Yves. "I, who have been here five decades."

When I shrank at his volume—the acoustics amplified all sound here—he said, "Discretion is not necessary. The bowels have no cameras or microphones."

"Why?"

He called back, "Deniability."

We hurried lower. The air was filmy, oppressive—curtain after curtain of grime. My breath made crystals.

I thought about Karen and her dolls' "safety fortress." As richly as she'd imagined it, it was nothing against the realities of Roche Rivard.

I was just losing sensation in my fingers when Yves stopped at steel doors. They looked more permanent than most of what was here, recessed in the limestone and paired with a lighted badge reader.

Yves waved his badge at the reader, which blipped green. The doors split and disappeared into the walls.

The chamber beyond was dark, but the moment Yves crossed the threshold, a brief *fzzz* sounded from his badge and three aisles of file cabinets lit from above.

"Those are yours?" I asked. "Enterprise Software?"

Yves nodded. "I am also cleared to access Robotics"—he nodded to the last aisle—"due to my former role. But these we do not need."

He opened the first drawer, his fingers quick but shaky on the tabs. The chamber's walls looked like green-brown coral by fluorescent lights. Craggy ceiling overhangs made me think of taking Zach to Laurel Caverns when he was little.

Yves raised a page triumphantly overhead. "Here, the revamp of CyberSafe!"

His seamed face glowing, he scanned the document. His eyes zagged wildly down the page while I glanced back at the steel doors.

"If there is something about CyberParle, the gateway...then we will know..."

It was quiet except for those faraway plops. Water? Lava? It was the kind of ambient sound you might miss completely—but once you'd heard it, you couldn't unhear it.

Yves's exhilaration changed to a sigh.

"Redacted." He pointed to blacked-out sections of the page.

"Indeed, there is a piece of the code which Rivard engineers altered. A nook, if you will. The margin note indicates it has been moved."

"Moved where?"

"It does not say."

The folder contained other documents beyond Yves's code print-outs—emails, PowerPoint files, loose sheaves of memos.

I pointed to the memos. "What do those say?"

"Meeting notes," Yves said dismissively. "The idle doodles of secretaries."

I was tempted to yank the pocket square from his fancy shirt and swat him. I've taken my share of meeting notes as a temp. It isn't easy, scrambling to jot every comment or objection, and it's important work: compiling the official record of what was discussed and by whom.

As Yves sought further clues in the code printouts, I read through meeting notes. My French isn't flawless, but it was good enough now. Whoever had taken these had done a nice job—solid penmanship and grammar, consistent abbreviations—and I covered weeks of notes quickly.

"Here, they talk about it!" I said, coming to a meeting named *Cyber-Safe Rewrite*. "'This secret core, if it is to be incorporated, must be made available in full for review.'"

"Who said this?" Yves asked.

"The entry is from *Marie Bu*. Looks like she and Thérèse Laurent were on opposite sides of the issue."

"Marie, *ma chérie!*" he exulted. "What was decided? Did she win out?"

"I...am not sure," I said.

As portrayed in the notes, Thérèse was adamant that her *coeur secret* not be exposed. She believed it was too valuable to the company, "such a revolutionary step forward," that allowing eyes on its source code—even internal Rivard eyes—was too great a risk. It must be destroyed.

When Marie and others explained that CyberSafe would not operate without the full source code being present—somewhere—Thérèse had relented. The source code would be preserved.

Yves drifted near to read over my shoulder. "Where? *Where did they put it?*"

We read forward in the meeting notes. The conversation veered into procedural details and complaints by Marie and others about not being allowed to attend industry conferences.

My badge blipped again. I looked down to find it red.

"Five minutes!" Yves said.

We split up the remaining notes. Mine contained a detailed discussion of which parts of the software were affected by the CyberSafe revamp, which felt like more unimportant detail until I came across the term "CyberParle."

"Wasn't that the gateway to the other systems?" I asked Yves.

"*Oui!*" he said. "What do the notes say? Was CyberParle part of the revamp?"

"Apparently a big part."

Yves Pomeroy's expression caught between revelation and horror. "This is proof! CyberParle is the perfect delivery mechanism to non-Rivard systems. The only reason for Thérèse to be meddling with it is to expand the data loss!"

As my last minutes ticked down, we continued speed-reading notes. The far-off plops were driving me crazy. I hit a dense stack of tech talk that ground my progress to a halt.

Yves was flipping through his pages furiously. His face alternately bulged and shriveled and twisted and grew tall.

"*Mon Dieu,*" he said, holding the final pack of his stack aloft.

"What did you find?"

He said, listless, "Thérèse changed her mind about the source code."

"About preserving it?"

He nodded and gulped at once. "She proposed another solution."

"What?"

He steadied his hands in front of him as though preparing to deliver a terminal diagnosis.

"Obfuscation," he said.

The melodramatic reticence was annoying me. "Let's skip the twenty questions and you just tell me what it means."

"To obfuscate software is to scramble its underlying source, to reduce it to binary form that only computers can read."

"Now is that..." I was scared to ask. "Reversible?"

Yves shook his head. "If the source code was obfuscated, it is beyond recovery."

A pulsing light began below. I glanced down and saw it was coming from my badge—which now displayed a countdown underneath the message, *YOUR ACCESS TO ROCHE RIVARD IS ABOUT TO EXPIRE.*

58.

57.

56.

I asked, "So, did they do it? Is this all moot?"

Yves looked at the final page again.

"This is unclear," he said. "Marie offered a counterproposal. She argued there was a way the source code could be both preserved—in case small alteration became necessary—and also kept hidden."

"How?"

Yves croaked, just above a whisper, "The Great Safe."

Before I could ask where or what this was—visions of hissing snakes and Sanskrit riddles and Indiana Jones–style booby traps swirling through my head—my badge started to wail.

CHAPTER FIFTY

Via closed-circuit display, Fabienne Rivard watched security guards eject Pomeroy's visitor from the lobby. The woman wore the drab uniform of an American businesswoman: dark blazer, denim pants, flat shoes. Chosen to minimize sexuality and emphasize one's fitness to do battle with male peacocks.

Yves Pomeroy pushed through the guards for a final clutch. Then he watched her disappear into a limousine with a lingering smile. No doubt he was erect.

Fabienne tracked him back to his office, switching cameras by swiping her finger through midair. The man looked spent, even for his age. He rested his head atop crossed arms. His skin, usually well bronzed from the frequent Côte d'Azur jaunts he used to stave off depression, seemed sallow.

What difference a decade made.

Then, he and his wife had entertained teenaged Fabienne at their sixth arrondissement flat. This had been at the height of Fabienne's adolescent wandering when she'd been merely the daughter of Henri Rivard, tabloids snapping her every night stoned or *accouplé* with a different American actor.

Yves had persuaded her to seek a more constructive happiness. The night had ended with tearful embraces and Fabienne's promise to act in a manner that respected her father, her father's company, and most importantly herself.

When her father's health had forced Fabienne into the CEO role, Yves had been her right hand. Even as her diversity initiatives were knocking him down several pegs, Yves confided fresh takes on the Latin markets and how best to handle the Sarkozy transition—two strategies that became pillars of Fabienne's early success.

Last year, when she'd needed a wise hand to lead Enterprise Software, a division for which she had great ambitions, he'd surrendered his more lucrative role as chief operating officer without a peep.

The man had been a reliable doormat throughout.

She checked her clock.

Twenty minutes.

Yves and his visitor had spent twenty minutes unobserved in the bowels.

Fabienne tapped a sequence of buttons on her desk phone, initiating a conference call.

"In my office *maintenant*," she said simply, and terminated the call.

Thérèse Laurent and Blake Leathersby appeared in under a minute.

The English bore—still dressed for weight lifting—could not stand still, rocking between his swollen legs.

Thérèse took a step away. "You are new to the corporate world, I realize, but perhaps a shower before meeting your superiors would be advisable."

Leathersby smirked. "That an invitation, lass?"

Thérèse wore a red dress, plus-size and gorgeous around her derriere. "Is his presence absolutely necessary?"

Fabienne's top lieutenants despised each other by design. She believed conflict drove achievement and perfectionism.

"I quite wish otherwise," Fabienne said. "But yes. I need you both. We are losing control of Yves Pomeroy."

Thérèse insisted they weren't. "I have the old man in hand. He is still useful for attracting media attacks."

"They're tiring of him," Fabienne said. Only four reporters had shown up to his last presser—his evasive answers were essentially worthless. "If he becomes disgruntled, he could do us harm."

"How? He knows nothing."

With a pen, Fabienne traced the sharp lines of her kneecap. "You're certain?"

"I believe he's in the dark," Thérèse said.

Blake Leathersby rounded on her. "*You believe?* Well, cheers, then— I'll tell my men to leave off watching his house and tapping his phones because Mademoiselle Pork Chop here—"

"You little boy," Thérèse hissed. "I suppose your solution would be killing him, *oui?*"

"Not a bad idea."

"A man of Yves Pomeroy's stature can't simply disappear," she said. "What happened to Marie is bad enough."

Thérèse glared at Leathersby.

"That bird from Enterprise Software?" he said. "Did something—"

"Terrible," Fabienne cut in. "Let us discuss the matter no further."

She'd told Thérèse that Marie had died when Leathersby's men had applied overzealous force detaining her. In fact, Marie was safe and sound in the oubliette—or as safe as one can be in a dungeon built thousands of feet deep in limestone.

"Since his most recent kidnapping," Fabienne said, "Yves has been different. His heart rate is elevated. He visits the archives more."

"He's just jumpy," Thérèse said. "He nearly got thrown out of a helicopter. It's natural."

In his debriefing, Yves Pomeroy said the Americans, Quaid Rafferty and Durwood Oak Jones, had been after competitive information on Rivard product launches. This matched with the working theory they were on the payroll of American Dynamics. The two men did many jobs for the lumbering dinosaur.

Still.

"Things are rarely what they appear when Rafferty and Jones are involved," Fabienne said. "I'm told information is leaking from Enterprise Software. Is Yves the source?"

"He can't be," Thérèse claimed. "As I said, he knows nothing to leak."

The leaks didn't worry Fabienne per se. Rivard could assail the new sources, ascribe the rumors to jealousy and xenophobic tendencies in the United States and Britain.

If Yves felt emboldened enough to leak, though, what else might he try?

"He must be watched more closely." Fabienne turned to Blake Leathersby. "Are the surveillance flies operational?"

"Yeah, good enough," he said. "We had 'em buzzing around the bowels, transmitted just fine."

"Whenever Pomeroy visits the archives, you will inform me. I will personally observe the live feed."

Leathersby fattened his lip in submission. "If he goes for the Great Safe, I think we should neutralize the coot."

Fabienne did four hundred planks on each side daily; none burned her core more than unsolicited advice from Leathersby.

"Do. Your. Job," she said. "Your job and nothing else. There is no thinking component to your role at Rivard LLC."

Leathersby fell silent. He was like the Rottweiler one finds bullying a pack of strays: terrible but damaged, easily cowed by superior strength.

She hadn't wanted him in a permanent role. Since the beginning of time, he'd been threatening to take his services elsewhere "unless I get broader responsibilities, management-like." Fabienne's general course had been to look into the man's oxen face, nod, and then proceed as though the exchange had never occurred.

This summer, though, his whines had become threatening enough —"MI6 keeps asking me back, figure they'd be interested to hear what I been up to..."—that Fabienne had been forced to promote him.

Thérèse said, "Perhaps the leaks are coming from the other side of the operation. Josiah."

Leathersby took umbrage—he handled all interactions with the Blind Mice's leader. "That one ain't the leaker. He wanted to tell what he knew, it'd be all over his Twitter."

Fabienne took out her phone and checked the josiahTheAvenger handle. "He is quiet. Only one post in three weeks."

"Ah, he's just sulky," Leathersby said. "Turned out he didn't own the Anarchy, after all. Big baby's all he is. Wouldn't be surprised if he offed himself."

Fabienne asked if they had corresponded recently.

"Here and there." Leathersby sniffed. "We've discussed next targets."

"Has he acquiesced on Morganville?"

"Ain't settled yet. He'll come around and do her, I think."

Only two data storage facilities could still protect their data. One was in Morganville, New Jersey.

Fabienne stood and walked to her window, gazing out at the Boulogne Woods. "We cannot launch the second strain until Morganville falls. Thérèse, is your man ready?"

"He is," Thérèse said. "The strain has been tested, its hypervirulence confirmed. The injection will occur from an untraceable internet cafe in Plovdiv."

"Where are we on the Otaru facility?"

"Goes dark tomorrow," Leathersby said. "We got them other nutballs"—the Japanese version of the Blind Mice called themselves Konton, or "Chaos"—"all ginned up. Then it's down to Morganville."

Fabienne dismissed them.

She felt pleased. Her suspicions of Yves Pomeroy had waned. The man was an unlikely traitor. Josiah was witless as any of his countrymen—he could be steered toward Morganville, easy as shaking a hive of bees into a bear's den.

Fabienne gazed farther out her window—beyond the woods to Paris—and imagined the world in another ten months. A sensation of onrushing power swirled in her body, a dreamy shudder like the onset of club drugs at four a.m. when one has just conquered the night and must now train her sights on the morning sun.

How rapidly will society decay?

What bottoms of human nature might emerge? What gremlins? What furry black sludges?

The species had been devolving for a century, pulled by the tractor trailer of American culture, but modern technological advances had masked the decline. No more. Without their traffic lights and thermostats and welfare *chèques*, and policemen to stop them from eating each other's hearts, what would people do?

How savage might they become?

CHAPTER FIFTY-ONE

New York City

Of the many persuasions Quaid had attempted with Third Chance Enterprises—turning Sigrada the Serpent, talking the Sri Lankans into letting the Bay of Bengal stop that wave of hydrofluoric acid—bringing Josiah into the fold rated among the most challenging.

For days, the kid barely spoke. When he did, it was to rant about reactionary jackals and bovine hordes, nonsense babble spewed to nobody in particular. Quaid let him vent. It was an understandably rough comedown, going from Bad Boy Crusader to captive in a boarded-up tanning salon on the Lower East Side.

He refused to post to Twitter, so Quaid had had to channel his inner josiahTheAvenger for a 280-character screed assuring his followers the Mice were biding their time and would be "resuming the mAYhEm" shortly.

It didn't help that Josiah was in withdrawal. The kid was hooked on amphetamines at a minimum, and suffered from dry heaves and insomnia.

Today, as he did each morning, Quaid brought Josiah Saltines and ginger ale in the tanning chamber that served as his de facto cell.

"You can turn this around," he said. "It's crap from your perspective, I get that. But your story isn't over."

Josiah remained on his side on the mattress they'd set up on the tanning bed. "The microsecond you get what you want out of me, you're gonna turn me in to the FBI."

Quaid scoffed. "First of all, nobody's getting prosecuted. If the government ever gets control back, they'll grant some blanket amnesty."

Josiah didn't answer, flopping away from Quaid the little bit he could. Quarters were regrettably cramped. The tanning salon had been the best Quaid could swing on short notice. An old flame, the promoter and MMA trainer DJ Lilja, had run it pre-Anarchy and said he was welcome to the space.

Now he kept on: "Helping us stop Rivard is not capitulating. *They* co-opted the Anarchy, and now *you're* co-opting it back. It's part and parcel of the same struggle."

Josiah sniffed violently, either from the missing drugs or wariness about Quaid's pitch.

"Pro wrestlers do it all the time." Quaid stood and began gesturing as though he were in some candidate forum. "Switch sides, go from bad to good. If you're seen as stemming the tide, wresting the Anarchy from corporate interests? Hey, you're right back to the A-list."

Josiah looked up. "What a swell dude you are, looking out for me."

"Absolutely not," Quaid said. "I think you booked your spot in hell months ago, somewhere between Ted Blackstone's throat and that ear you sliced off. But I work for American Dynamics, and they'd like to not fight World War III against Rivard. That goal just happens to dovetail nicely with the rehabilitation of your image."

Quaid wheedled and reasoned and brought tastier crackers, and finally convinced Josiah of the truth: cooperating was his only play.

The specifics of the plan were devised by Piper Jackson. She knew Fabienne Rivard was gunning for the data facility in Morganville. If Josiah agreed to hit it but said the Mice needed the kernel source code in order to tweak the attack for Morganville's security, Rivard might hand it over. Then Piper could reverse engineer an antidote.

She thought.

Durwood had been skeptical. "If I'm Rivard, why do I give it over?"

"Because we did it before," Piper had said, explaining she'd had to alter the source code in the early days to beat a certain version of Norton's security software.

Everyone had agreed the phone call should come from Josiah, who'd so far initiated all communications with Rivard.

Four days after Quaid's "pro wrestler" pep talk, the whole gang—he, Molly, and Durwood, plus the other Mice captives—gathered around Josiah's cell phone in the lobby of the tanning salon.

Quaid said, "Don't act overeager. You're just tossing out ideas. You're spitballing. Keep it cool, nice and easy, relaxed."

Garrison burst out, sweeping his hair back in a flourish, "But if he's all chill and relaxed, that's a giveaway too! Josiah wasn't like that before."

Molly's boy toy was always doing this, trying to score gnatty points against Quaid. He seemed to perceive a rivalry.

"Thanks for your input," Quaid said. "Great insight. Really."

Now he produced Josiah's phone from a sport coat pocket and laid it on the table they were all sitting around.

"Are you game?" he asked their reluctant star. "You're all in, ready to play your part?"

Josiah slicked a fingernail on the table's edge, jittery. His eyes gleamed with, what, anticipation? Loathing?

For whom?

"All in," Josiah said through a tight mouth.

Quaid didn't love his disposition, but there was nothing to be done. If the kid laid an egg today—if their ruse was sniffed out—then the Mice were out of the game. Their last tie to Rivard LCC and the kernel would be severed, Molly's year of deep-cover work down the drain.

Josiah found the contact and tapped. The phone dialed, starting with the France country code.

The lobby was dim despite the afternoon hour, its plywood windows allowing only slivers of light. Molly was hunched over joined knuckles. Durwood stood at the door on lookout, Sue-Ann lying against his boot. Piper Jackson had her laptop ready; Garrison hovered near Molly; Hatch towered beside Quaid—the two had become friendly sparring partners across a range of public policy debates.

A voice answered, "*Allo?*"

Josiah said, "This is Narwhal One."

Durwood turned from his post to catch Quaid's eye.

Narwhal?

"No," Josiah said into the phone. "No, I'm not holding for Blake Leathersby. I need Fabienne Rivard."

He grinned wildly around the lobby, seeming proud or confident or both.

The other end answered.

Josiah said, "Yes, Fabienne Rivard, *now!*" He chomped the air, livid. "Because we need to discuss a mission of vital importance." A film of spittle appeared on the phone. "Of vital importance!"

Quaid had a sinking feeling as the exchange continued. Rivard wasn't biting. They were going to tell Josiah to buzz off. No matter how badly they coveted a Morganville attack, they weren't going to expose the kernel source code—if it even existed.

"Only Fabienne!" Josiah roared. "Don't *dare* put someone else on the line."

Fifteen seconds passed. Garrison laid his hand on Molly's back.

Startlingly, Josiah resumed, "I told you nobody but Fabienne!" He held the phone two-handed up to his face, like a sheet of paper he wanted to break with sound waves. "I have emails typed up to *Huff-Post*, Drudge, and the *New York Times* confessing the whole gig! *Just try me!*"

The threat was pure improvisation, probably overdone, but it fit the kid's style. He fidgeted as Team Rivard considered its response, hopping in place, digging his fingernail into the table.

Thirty seconds later, his eyes danced.

"Yes! That's right, it's me, Narwhal One," he said. "We're ready to take out Morganville, but we need the kernel source code. Binary Two says we'll never get in without adjusting it some."

Piper cringed, either disliking her code name or nervous—but the conversation seemed to proceed well enough. Josiah repeated various dates and times, and whoever was on the line for Rivard—Fabienne?— kept answering.

At one point, Josiah waved frantically for a pen. "We could hit it then, sure. As long as you get us the code ahead of time, at least a week."

Durwood hurried up with a ballpoint pen. Josiah shook it to get ink flowing and scratched furiously on a piece of paper.

"I'm ready, yeah," he said. "What day?"

He poised the pen over the paper...and kept it poised. For thirty seconds.

For a minute.

Piper chewed her lip. Quaid palmed the elbow of his sport coat.

Josiah covered the microphone. *"They aren't going for it—she says they never transmit the kernel electronically! It needs to stay on their servers."*

Quaid looked to Piper.

"That's bull," she said. "I got it sent to me before, woman named Marie."

Josiah's eyes zipped between them. "What am I supposed to say?"

His knee, bouncing under the table, knocked its underside.

"You're fine, you can handle this," Quaid said. "Tell her...look, say if she wants you to go ahead and attack without adjustments, fine. Binary Two thinks it's about a ninety-nine percent chance of failure, but you'll go ahead. Maybe Morganville goes dark and maybe it doesn't."

Josiah got back on the call. He delivered Quaid's general message, then waited out a long response.

Off-mic again, he whispered, *"Still negative on giving it to us electronic, but she'll do a physical handoff."*

Durwood thinned his lips. Molly looked up from her knuckles.

Quaid didn't love the idea of a physical handoff, but he also doubted the getting would get any better.

He flashed Josiah a thumbs-up.

CHAPTER FIFTY-TWO

I made it back to New Jersey in under two hours, pushing the Prius hard and paying the bikers' two-hundred-dollar ransom to use the left lane of the turnpike. I swerved between asphalt craters in the neighborhood and pulled into the driveway in time to make pasta with jarred sauce for dinner.

I had one foot out of the car, preparing for whatever lesser anarchies awaited me inside, when a figure came creeping around the side lawn.

Wearing skater shoes and a hoodie, looking back over their shoulder as they went.

Zach.

I cut through the pampas grass to bar his way. "Where do you think you're going?"

He flinched hard and sighed his annoyance. "I'm just going out for a sec."

"Out where?"

"To a...like, a meeting."

"A meeting with whom?"

Zach scratched his ear, reaching up inside the hoodie. "Just Reggie and some of the other Spiders."

The word crawled up my neck like a real one. "And who are the Spiders?"

"Okay, look, I will tell you? If you promise not to overreact."

I breathed and said, "I promise to react in perfect proportion to your answer."

He puffed his cheeks. "The Spiders are sort of an affiliation."

"Like a gang?"

"Not like a gang, definitely not."

At my skeptical expression, he added, "Spider's one of the good ones! If you're not in Spider, people are gonna assume you're in Reich or Spree or Deathfinger. It's like prison—you have to declare your alliance."

I was speechless for a moment. Then I wanted to hug him right here on the lawn. Then I recovered to ask—in the most reasonable tone I could manage, "How long have you been a Spider?"

He shrugged. "Two weeks. Ish."

How did he swing this? He was only allowed out of the house for an hour at a time—and never after nightfall. With me homeschooling them, I had eyes on him constantly.

Except those three days I'd been in France. Which had been about two weeks ago.

I'd felt like things were improving with Zach. He'd been having fewer fights with Karen and wasn't defying me at every turn. As I thought about it now, though, it occurred to me he'd been spending more time in his room, hiding long stretches of his days. Rolling his eyes instead of arguing.

He was withdrawing.

"Thank you for telling me," I said. "Thank you for being honest. It's hard now. Everything is hard."

When I stepped forward to hug him, he didn't squirm away—and even hugged me back a little.

"But you're not going to your Spider meeting." I pointed at the sky. "Too dark out."

A scoff started in his throat, but he swallowed it and followed me back inside.

In the living room, Karen was at work on her expansion of the dolls' safety fortress, which now covered two-thirds of the carpet. She had her little tongue sticking out the side of her mouth, draping a small blanket painstakingly over the tops of four structures.

"What's the blanket for?" I said. "A roof?"

"No, a *shield*," she said. "It protects them from enemies."

I gave a long, slow nod. With Karen, I'd been trying to deemphasize the crime stories that dominated the news, to divert her back to dance or dinosaurs—subjects that'd interested her before the Anarchy.

"It'll probably keep them warmer too," I said. "Do they sleep upstairs? Which are the bedrooms?"

Karen pointed to their tiny bedrolls, made of quarter-sheet paper towels, but then returned to the shield.

"It can't be too low or the enemies can shoot inside," she explained. "But if it's too *high*, then they—"

She broke off when the blanket's weight caved in one of the cardboard structures underneath, starting a domino effect that toppled half the fortress.

On her knees, Karen began to whimper.

"Oh, honey," I said. "Let me just put the pasta water on, then I'll help rebuild."

CHAPTER FIFTY-THREE

The date of the source code handoff with Rivard was Sunday: five days away. I spent all four in New Jersey with the kids.

I let Zach attend a Spider meeting—with me waiting outside in the Prius, listening in by secret microphone. That word he'd used, "affiliation," did seem accurate. They mostly talked about bands and the best apps for lip-syncing on their phones.

Karen added a moat of quicksand (marbles) and sharks (plastic, Hasbro) to her safety fortress. I suggested expanding the moat into a whole aquarium section, and spent big chunks of two days cutting eels and jellyfish out of colored construction paper.

"There!" I said, placing the last in the pool. (Sky-blue beanbag stuffing.) "Now the dolls can relax and watch the fish."

Karen asked, "Are the red fish the enemy fish?"

"No, I just liked that shade," I said. "There aren't really enemy fish, I don't think. They all live together and get along."

She crinkled her downy eyebrow at me as though she pitied my naivety.

Quaid texted throughout the week. Tuesday, he wrote, *planning the Rivard exchange today. coming in?*

I answered, *swamped at home.*

Wednesday, he said, *Durwood's worried you'll lose your base tan...in today?*

Can't, sorry, I said.

The guys could handle the kernel source code exchange themselves. I'd exposed myself to more than enough danger, poking around the bowels of Roche Rivard with Yves Pomeroy. The kids needed me here.

Saturday, the day before the exchange, was my fourth straight at home. It started out smoky when I burned an omelet, distracted by the cat's pre-vomit hacking in the hall. Then Zach and Granny had a pointless argument about when an egg became a chicken. Then containerizing leftovers turned into a project.

Granny held a blue and a clear Tupperware top in either hand. "What's your system? Does blue go on the shorts or the talls?"

I was busy prepping the kids' social studies lesson on the three branches of government. Karen would be learning their names and functions while Zach filled out worksheets tracking an example bill from passage to enforcement to legal challenge.

"I don't really have a system," I told Granny. "Either way."

She frowned at the blue lid. "This one's got crusties. That dishwasher of yours is junk."

I kept working on social studies.

Granny said, "Lid's cracked too. Do you put the cracked lids away separate? *What's your system?*"

I tried printing Zach's worksheets, but the printer refused to wake up. "No system. Just use your judgment, okay, Granny?"

She didn't answer, glaring between the two lids.

I walked to the printer and tried pressing every one of its buttons. The small rectangular display remained dark. I confirmed it was plugged in—to the outlet and the router. I said, *"Please, pretty please,"* and threatened to go paperless with my curriculum.

"Stop, you're *ruining* it!" Karen shouted from another room.

I left my stubborn printer to see what was wrong. I found Zach in the living room, standing over a jumble of Matchbox cars and cardboard.

He said, "It wasn't overly stable."

"It wasn't finished!" Karen said. "I didn't have it all-the-way taped, I couldn't find more tape in the art drawer."

"I just, like, brushed against it." Zach was barely keeping a straight face, which was making matters worse—minimizing his sister's outrage. "The wind would've knocked it over eventually if I hadn't."

Karen crunched her eyes at me, appealing for justice. Granny may have asked another question from the kitchen.

"Zach," I said evenly, "you should know better. She's been working hard on that."

"*What?* I did nothing! You didn't even *see* how it—"

"And Karen," I cut in, "you need to handle these setbacks better. The fortress is gigantic—it's going to get bumped."

Both kids were livid at my response. They shouted at me, then at each other. Then Zach faked pinching Karen's arm and stormed upstairs to his room.

Karen turned to me with a helpless expression, expecting me to fix her "parking garage." I had a flash of anger and doubt.

Am I doing too much? Am I solving her problems too quickly?

Karen said, "Now they can't escape when the bad guys come. If the bad guys get past the shield and the moat? Then they'll just..." She sniveled. "...just die!"

I draped my arm around her and pulled Janey, her favorite doll, into our embrace.

I noticed now that the hospital—adjacent to the parking garage—was collapsed too. All the miniature creations inside were crushed or displaced, a toothpick-box bed flattened, a nurse (Popsicle stick in a paper dress) snapped in two.

"It'll be alright, honey," I said. "I have more tape in the hall closet."

She clutched Janey to her chest. "Thanks, Mom."

Grandma yelled through the walls, "*I need to know your system!*"

I felt my teeth grind.

Karen said, "You can go help her." She gestured to the ravaged hospital and garage. "Don't worry, I'll get us started."

Her eyes were tender pools of green. I squeezed her hand and had to force myself to let go.

Granny stood beside the range with arms akimbo. "You got a whole 'nother drawer with *round* lids..."

The afternoon went similarly, one challenge after another. I'd planned to make stew for dinner but found I was out of onions. I tried bringing some semblance of order to the garage and discovered a dead chipmunk.

Zach came downstairs ten minutes before my thrown-together macaroni casserole was ready to say he had another Spider meeting.

I asked when.

"Now," he said.

"We're about to eat," I said. "You'll have to tell them you can't go."

Zach's eyes bulged. "It's important. They're not cool with members missing important meetings."

I took the green beans out of the crisper. "Maybe Spider's not right for you. Maybe you need to pick some different associates."

"Oh, cuz you're *so* good at picking associates."

"What's that supposed to mean?"

He scoffed. "Quaid? Durwood?"

As I looked up from setting the table, a crack formed in my conviction. "What about Quaid and Durwood?"

"They totally kill people! Which is something my Spider friends totally don't do—"

"Zach!"

"Am I wrong?" he said. "I've seen Durwood staring into the hallway mirror, holding his head for, like, *many minutes*. That dude has serious demons."

I couldn't argue with this. Before I'd stopped showing up at the tanning salon, Durwood had been taking longer and longer patrols around Manhattan. Every morning, his hands had some new scrap or gash. Some days, Sue-Ann wouldn't move at all from her spot by the door.

Zach continued, "And no offense, Mom? But I think you're getting played by Quaid."

He said this in the icked-out voice of a kid discussing their parent's love life.

The chances of me engaging on *that* subject were exactly zero.

"Those are some interesting observations," I said, "and it's possible you notice more than I give you credit for. But it's still a no on the Spider meeting."

This set a chippy tone for dinner. Zach sulked through the meal. Karen picked the ground beef out of her casserole, which had come out bland, and complained about the green peppers. Granny kept staring at the cabinets—I could just see her wheels spinning about what combination of lids and shorts/talls would be the optimal Tupperware for leftovers.

At quarter past six, I was gathering the last of the silverware from the table, feeling like a boxer trudging to her corner after the sixteenth round, when the doorbell rang.

I walked to the living room window and pulled back the curtains an inch to see who it was, following our custom now.

Standing on the porch were Quaid and Piper.

What are they doing here? With the Rivard handoff tomorrow, they both should've been deep in prep work at the tanning salon.

"Hey, guys," I said, inviting them in. "What's going on?"

Quaid squinted into the kitchen, up the stairs. "*Where are the children? Are they watching? Can you speak freely?*"

"If form follows," I said, "they should be sticking hot pokers into each other's voodoo dolls right about now."

He smiled at Piper. "Sounds like we're right on time."

The smile almost caught to Piper, one corner of her mouth raising.

I asked, "What're you here for?"

"A date!" Quaid said, offering me his hand in a flourish.

It took me a second to process this. "Date" felt archaic, a word from a different era—for me, for the world. When I caught his meaning, I laughed reflexively.

"Good one," I said. "We'd come back and one of 'em would be swinging from the ceiling fan."

"Nope," Quaid said, "it's under control." He extended his arm toward Piper. "I couldn't find a flower stand open, but I did bring a babysitter."

The hacker didn't look thrilled with the label but nonetheless took another step inside. My kids, having heard us, were coming downstairs hesitantly.

Zach and Piper weren't so different in size.

I hedged, "I—well, let me just finish cleaning up dinner and we'll see if—"

"I know how to load a dishwasher," Piper said. "What time they go to bed?"

Quaid snagged my purse from the coffee table and looped it over my shoulder, then began guiding me toward the door.

"Uh, about ten usually..." I said. "Karen should read twenty minutes, and I like Zach to do something constructive..."

"Zach'll be busy." Piper helped Quaid push me out to the porch. "This day and age, every teen should know how to code a simple bubble sort."

Before I could ask what a bubble sort was or caution her about Zach's "combative learning style" (his old principal's term), Quaid was ushering me into the Vanagon.

I asked where we were going.

"It's a date," Quaid said. "We're going where everybody goes on dates: to the movies."

And like that, we were leaving the neighborhood, Quaid driving through dark stoplights and past abandoned cars, some smoldering, chatting idly and making liberal use of the horn.

He updated me on the situation in Manhattan. The handoff was still on for tomorrow. They'd taken the whole gang on a scouting trip to the rock quarry where they would be meeting Rivard—a sandy, open space where neither side would be able to conceal much.

"Any more debates with Hatch?" I asked.

"Plenty," Quaid said. "He's a delight. I told him once this thing blows over—once elections start back up—he should run for office. Fix it from within."

He'd taken a hand off the steering wheel to gesticulate. I motioned him to put it back on. "Sounds like you're having fun."

"I enjoy a good dialogue." He shrugged. "When you're used to conversing with Durwood Oak Jones, it's a low bar. Heck, I even had a discussion with your admirer. Darryl is it? Gary?"

He knew the name, but I supplied it anyway.

"That's it, Garrison," Quaid said. "Did you know he's a graphic designer by trade?"

"Yes. He makes digital art."

Quaid pulled a face. "Let's not get carried away, McGill. He does website logos. They ain't clamoring for his stuff at the Guggenheim."

I had no desire to pursue this line of banter. "How's Durwood been?"

"Cheerless as ever. Last night, he made us all sleep in the cellar. He's convinced he's seeing 'irregular surveillance activity' on those patrols of his. Thinks Rivard is planning some sneak attack."

"What if he's right?"

Quaid shook his head dismissively. "We've been careful, kept the Mice out of sight. He's just being paranoid."

We were exiting the highway now, joining a knot of traffic at the rear. I peered around the cars and spotted a giant white canvas on the horizon.

"You weren't serious about going to the movies," I asked. "*Were you?*"

Quaid cocked his tongue in one cheek. "Didn't you hear drive-ins were making a comeback? It's a thing."

He explained the phenomenon, which he believed to be a sort of communal defiance to the dangers they all faced now.

"You travel to an isolated field and park among strangers, you make a sitting duck of yourself, and why?" he said. "To prove it can be done. To prove we're not all animals."

After waiting out the traffic, Quaid eased the Vanagon over softly crunching grass and around a jagged line of bumpers. He parked beside a speaker at the end of a row. To our right, a field of sweet corn stretched away, gray and restless by the glow of the hundred-foot screen.

To our left sat a Buick with a half primer, half burgundy paint job.

The previews began. Quaid reached back to the cabin and produced a six-pack from underneath a crate of bazookas. He twisted one off for me and a second for himself.

That first gulp was heaven.

"Durwood didn't mind you taking the van?" I asked.

"He wasn't thrilled." Quaid tuned the radio to the drive-in audio. "What can he do? My name's on the title, same as his."

He reached across the center console for my hand as the movie started. As my fingers loosened to permit his, a warm jolt passed through my whole body. The towering screen hung slightly crooked, and one corner was badly tattered—but the picture and sound were otherwise great. *A Summer Without Regret* opened at the ocean, twentysomething characters standing in a frothy surf, speaking into a pink sunrise.

The film, which had been number one at the box office for months, told the story of recent college graduates hanging out before departing for far-flung jobs. It was tame, bland even, a lot of gossip and awkward silence with a little infidelity mixed in.

"Alright, I'm calling it," Quaid said. "That guy there"—pointing with his free hand—"ends up with the redhead. Notice how he can't catch a break in act one? Textbook reversal of fortune."

He commented throughout the film—on acting technique, on lighting and camera angles, everything. As governor, he'd ridden shotgun on the filming of a PBS documentary on Boston Common and considered himself an auteur.

During the ten-minute intermission, he asked what I thought.

"I like it," I said. "It's...soothing, somehow, watching people worry about relationships and rumors. That stuff nobody has time for now."

Quaid looked into my eyes. "You could have a future in criticism." His palm seemed to get deeper, letting my hand farther inside. "But I believe your true calling is operative work."

I broke our shared look, flopping my head toward the van's ceiling. "If you'd witnessed the last four days at my house, you'd understand the impossibility of that."

"What, the kiddos?"

"Yes. The fourteen-year-old who's just becoming active in gang culture. The kindergartner who's developing a danger complex."

Quaid brushed these concerns away. "The only way Zach's going to learn is to make mistakes, take his lumps. You can't smother him. And

I'll tell you how you help Karen: you stop the danger. Stop the Anarchy, like we're doing."

He cracked another beer and closed my fingers around it.

"What you have, McGill," he continued, "is a childcare problem. Those are fixable."

As Quaid talked on, I set the beer in a cupholder. Zach's words echoed in my head. *No offense, Mom? But I think you're getting played.*

I said, "You don't need me tomorrow. You and Durwood can handle it."

"Wrong," he said. "We can handle the remote piece, watching from a mile away. But Rivard knows us—we can't be there on the ground with the Mice. What if Josiah panics? What if Darryl pees his pants? They're amateurs."

I opened my mouth but didn't say the answer that came to mind.

Quaid said, "That's right, you're *not* an amateur. Could an amateur have sneaked into the most secretive group on the planet? Could an amateur have won the trust—then *kept* the trust, after revealing herself —of Piper Jackson?"

I felt a blush coming into my cheeks. Quaid kept talking—about their strategy at the handoff, about Mayor Diaz's road map for the restoration of law. His words and touch together breathed excitement into me.

Could it really end?

Had this mission I'd gotten rolling with MollyWantsChange.org actually save the world?

When I turned and looked into Quaid's pleading face, I felt like I wanted to be a part of it. I had to be.

He recognized the decision in my eyes, and we kissed. First slowly, then kicking off shoes and pulling at each other's clothes, then tumbling back to the cabin over Kevlar body armor and crates of grenades—fevered.

We forgot about the Buick and the sweet corn. We missed the second half of *A Summer Without Regret*, just like teenagers on a date.

CHAPTER FIFTY-FOUR

The tanning salon was being cased. Durwood knew this and didn't care if Quaid thought he was nuts. As he walked the neighborhood, the hairs in his ears felt wrong. Details stuck out in the background. A bystander taking too long to move. Discolorations in high windows. Durwood took care to act natural and not let on he was noticing.

But he noticed.

He extended his nightly patrols, covering more city blocks, sweeping up greater numbers of offenders.

On the eve of the kernel exchange, Durwood left the salon at nightfall intending to find the people watching them—once and for all.

He cleaned and holstered his M9, and roused Sue-Ann.

"Well, ole girl." He touched a boot to her ribs. "Let's see what we see."

With a phlegmy wheeze, the dog struggled to all fours.

They left by the alley door. Durwood charted an impossibly wide perimeter. A solid mile, from Times Square to the East River. Man and dog walked a steady hour, pausing only to stop large thefts—autos, cargo trailers—and free obvious captives.

At the Queensboro Bridge, Durwood pulled microbinoculars from his coat. He started hiking stairs for the upper deck.

Sue-Ann balked.

Durwood said from the fourth step, "Been taking stairs since you were a pup. You scared?"

Sue-Ann stayed in her sit. That bum hip was quivering.

Durwood felt sympathy but knew the moment you accommodated such a thing, you finished a dog.

He fished a tab of venison jerky from a pocket. "C'mon already."

Sue's eyes bulged, and she did scamper up now.

"So you know," he said from the stair above, "this isn't turning into a habit."

From the upper deck, Durwood surveyed the tanning salon through chain-link diamonds. He tried placing himself in Blake Leathersby's head. He considered angles and lines of sight, where Rivard might set up. The sun's path through skyscrapers. The effect of low-lurking smog.

He identified five likely spots.

Sue liked going down stairs even less than going up, but she managed. The patrol resumed.

Durwood felt invigorated by the night air. They walked progressively tighter circles. Curfew came and went. Pedestrian traffic dwindled, not because anyone feared law enforcement but out of simple good sense.

Durwood enjoyed the extra room on the avenues. Often he and Sue had the cross streets all to themselves. When they did encounter another in the rubble- and trash-strewn road, it felt like the Old West— violence humming in every glance. No government to tell you not to cross until the sign beeped. Nobody to cover their eyes if your dog killed a stray cat, as Sue might have in better days.

A man could make his own way, with Christ the Lord as his only judge.

Though he accepted Rivard's role in creating the Anarchy, Durwood believed the modern world deserved some blame too.

Maybe He doesn't think much of our slick technology and bickering.

It could be the Anarchy was a trial. A lesson. Durwood didn't know if the world would be different once order was restored. (It *would* be restored.) Part of him believed it wouldn't be. Funny thing about His lessons, though: they worked on their own schedule. It mattered how people responded. He was watching.

Now Durwood approached the first possible surveillance spot. A mixed-use building, about thirty stories. He crept along its face. It scanned clean, both thermal and infrared. He left Sue on the street and climbed the fire escape.

He identified the window with the best vantage point and found the position clear. He removed his microbinoculars from his coat and had a look for himself.

Two thousand feet out, the tanning salon appeared harmless. Windows boarded and grates down like any other storefront. Was there a car too many parked out on the street?

Maybe. Nothing much, though.

He descended the fire escape. Sue-Ann fell in beside him up Sixth Avenue. They cleared two more surveillance spots, walking smaller and smaller circles, moving closer to the salon.

At midnight, Durwood stopped at a diner tucked back from the sideway. He bought a roast beef sandwich and tore off a third for Sue. She nibbled some bread but left the beef.

Something was wrong, either the dog or the beef.

Afterward, they cleared the final two surveillance spots. They found no sign of Rivard or anybody else.

They slipped back into the tanning salon how they'd left—by the alley door. Sue took a noisy slurp of water, then she curled against the radiator. Out for the night.

Durwood stopped outside the tanning booths, listening for breath. He confirmed each booth had one and only one breather before moving on.

Piper Jackson's booth was too quiet. Durwood lowered silently to his knees and pressed his ear to the door. He heard nothing. He listened harder, holding his own breath. His head hurt.

Finally, he did hear a soft exhalation—she must've been back in a corner.

At three a.m., Durwood bedded down. He drank a glass of water, brushed his teeth, and kept his blue jeans on. Bone tired, he dropped off the moment his head hit the scrap of foam he used for a pillow.

He didn't sleep long.

The noise came from the storeroom. A crackle that might've been the door or a floorboard.

Durwood sat up, considering what was in the storeroom. Food. Certain weapons he'd relocated from the cabin of the Vanagon.

He slipped into boots and left his booth. Tiptoeing toward the storeroom, he noticed Sue-Ann still sleeping at the entrance.

She was slipping.

Durwood found the storeroom closed, door flush to its jambs. He did not draw his M9. The intruder had intelligence value. Captured alive, they might roll over on Rivard.

No light escaped around the door's edges. The noises inside were furtive. A seal unsticking. *Shppt*. A *pip* that could have been a canister top or valve.

Chemical agent? Biological?

Whatever it was, the person doing the opening was keen to keep quiet.

The storeroom had a single window. High, too small for an average-size male. Meaning this door was the only means of exit.

Durwood considered waiting. Apprehending a suspect leaving through a door was simple. No question of positioning. Little opportunity for the suspect to respond.

The trade-off was time. How long would this storeroom phase of their operation last? What if information was being transmitted back to France? What if Josiah was already blown?

Maybe it wasn't even Rivard. The Anarchy was great cover for revenge—maybe another party he and Quaid had foiled previously was settling a score. Draktor would've loved a piece of Quaid. The Iraqis, after Tikrit, surely wished a bad end for Durwood.

He decided not to wait.

Durwood tested the doorknob. It was locked. He staggered his stance and loaded weight to his front shoulder. He prayed briefly, then he barreled through the door.

It pancaked forward. He bulled inside over the splintered door, crouched like a wrecking ball accelerating toward its target.

Approximately four chopping steps later, his skull connected with a soft abdomen. Durwood plowed the intruder off his feet—it was a he, and big—to the tile.

He pinned his knees onto what felt like elbows and punched, punished, incapacitated. He couldn't see, but his fists found the large man easily. The skin might've been dark. Leathersby used mercenaries of all creeds.

The man reached through Durwood's flying fists for his neck. Durwood gripped his wrist and snapped it.

The man was trying to speak. "Gorrm*mmm*...off, *dang*...ooAAAIY..."

Durwood kept at him, straight rights and straight lefts in the dark, extinguishing all resistance. If it moved, he hit it. If it made noise, he silenced it. A night's worth of coiled fury poured out of him.

Durwood heard voices dimly at the door.

The lights came on.

He turned his hands over. His palms looked like instruments of meat grinding—warm, gummy red.

The intruder had dark skin, Durwood saw. But not naturally. It was intricately mottled and green.

They were tattoos.

"Get off, *damn*!" Hatch slurred, a pencil-width gap in his upper lip. "I'm g-tting a beer, you w-nna *kill* me?"

Durwood stood back. Quaid and Molly, Piper Jackson, Josiah, Garrison—all of them stood looking at Durwood in their bedclothes. Looking with slow, concerned eyes.

Durwood offered Hatch a hand, but the giant stayed down and covered his bloodied face.

CHAPTER FIFTY-FIVE

It was a two-mile hike from the quarry parking lot to the rendezvous point, and it seemed longer over the sandy terrain. I walked between Piper and Josiah over the dunes, climbing one gray rise after another.

My arms were shivering. I'd worn a paper-thin hoodie in an attempt to look even younger than usual, creating the biggest possible gap from the CIO persona I'd used at Roche Rivard.

"Cold?" Piper asked.

I nodded. "How much farther?"

Josiah had his phone out, watching our GPS icon on a map. "We should be ju-uuust about on top of it."

"Didn't you guys come earlier and scope it out?"

Piper looked around the barren landscape. "Yeah, it was the same then. Bunch of flat nothing."

We walked a few circles, Josiah waving and tilting his phone for a better signal, before deciding this was the spot.

"What up, are we early?" he asked.

Piper said, "Not by much."

The rest of us settled in to wait, swiveling around, scanning the empty horizon. Hatch, straggling at the back, winced at the effort. His wrist was splinted and ribs taped after Durwood's accidental pummeling last night.

This was the first time the Mice had been out together since Shop-All. I recognized the same nervous jitters of previous missions, but also a dourness, people kicking rocks, facing away from each other. There was a palpable feeling of things ending.

For five minutes, I stood shivering.

Garrison was off by himself. I walked up to him and said, "Drawing anything cool these days?"

He raised one shoulder. "Not really."

"Do you have gigs lined up for after the Anarchy, or...?"

I trailed off at his detached expression. I had thought he was being a little sulky today, that maybe he'd caught wind of my date with Quaid.

Now I knew he had.

"Garrison," I said, "I'm sorry if signals have been sorta mixed from me. I—you know, it's a weird time. Obviously. I know it's weird for you too."

He brushed his hair back. "No worries. Nothing happened, right?"

His voice had a twinge that seemed part accusatory, part wistful. Looking at him now—toes turned in together, handsome—I couldn't deny my own what-ifs.

I nodded and moved off to wait alone.

The prearranged handoff time came and went. Rivard was ten minutes late.

Fifteen.

Twenty.

Durwood's voice crackled in my ear, "How're they holding up?"

I took fresh inventory of the group. Piper squinted at the setting sun. Hatch was muttering under his breath, holding his lower back. Josiah's rawboned arms swayed slowly in what might've been tai chi.

"Mixed bag," I said into my hoodie's collar. "Do you have Rivard on radar?"

"Negative," Durwood said.

I looked distantly to the southeast, the direction of the lot where the guys had parked. "You're sure they won't spot the Vanagon?"

"I pulled her in underneath this shed," Durwood said. "Their birds can't see us."

I wondered if Rivard had other ways of seeing. We weren't supposed to linger on this frequency, though, so I swallowed my concerns and signed off.

As the wait stretched on, the other Mice started looking over to me —as though it were my fault we were stuck in this cold, dusty purgatory. Every grimace of Hatch's felt like an indictment. Piper had her laptop out, ready to receive the source code, rolling her head between her shoulders to stay loose.

Josiah said, "Now what's the plan? Just stand around and wait forever?"

I was going to ignore this, but his pink-tinged eyes kept boring into me.

"I...I mean, I don't know how far away Rivard is coming from," I said. "Maybe they ran into the police? Or air traffic was bad?"

This satisfied exactly nobody.

Piper closed her laptop.

I said, "They could be here anytime."

She nodded. "I'm saving the battery."

I walked closer and, squatting, lowering my voice so only she could hear. "Thanks for last night, with the kids. I really needed a break."

"No biggie," she said.

"I hope Zach didn't try sneaking out."

She shook her head. "If he did, he got back before I noticed."

I forced a smile. The quarry's chalky air stung my throat. "Was Karen okay with me being gone? I told her I was going to help with her fortress—"

"It was good, it was all good," Piper said.

I could tell I'd annoyed her, but I wasn't sure how. Last night, Piper had seemed on board with the plan. *What changed?*

My thoughts must've shown on my face because Piper said, "This sucks, is all."

She tucked her laptop in her armpit.

"It does," I said.

I realized my instinct to distract with small talk in anxious moments—developed at doctor appointments and dance recitals—was doing me no favors. I willed myself to a better mindset. I thought about what life might look like post-Anarchy. Would the guys ask me to join Third Chance Enterprises permanently? After what Quaid had said last night at the drive-in, I felt like it was possible.

I wasn't sure I would accept. Reviving McGill Investigators might be better—for my family, for my own safety. If our role in foiling Rivard got reported around in the press, if *my* role did, it could be a huge publicity boon.

I looked toward the sun, only half visible now, hazy orange through the sulfur pollution.

I tried to imagine order. Not riding my brakes through every stop-light. Smiling at strangers on the sidewalk instead of fixing my gaze straight down. Would people treat each other more kindly after a reprieve? Would they appreciate the blessing of peace? Would they cherish it?

A rumble began, low, groaning through the quarry. Soon after, black shapes rose on the horizon. They grew in size to giant, steel-winged locusts.

Helicopters.

As the lead craft approached, I made out dark face shields in its cockpit glass. Noise blotted out all thought in my head—it sounded like air was being ripped, one atom at a time, from a reluctant sky.

The Rivard pilots fought the wind. The long, sharp landing skids bucked during descent, and I thought for sure they would have to pull up—but somehow they steadied themselves and landed in formation.

My hair whorled five inches off my head. A fine mist pelted my face.

The first man out of the first helicopter was Blake Leathersby. The mercenary-turned-vice-president stepped jauntily down. His buzz cut moved not one inch in the rotor wash.

Durwood in my ear: *"Who's that, Leathersby?"*

I nodded in the blaring noise and wind before remembering that Durwood couldn't see me.

"Right, Leathersby," I said.

A half dozen commandos emerged next.

Durwood said, "He bring a package?"

I squinted. "Something in his right hand."

"Small?"

"Very."

"Good. Small's better than big."

Durwood had been skeptical about the exchange following Josiah's call to Rivard, mistrusting Fabienne and fearing a double cross. After last night, though, what he'd done to Hatch, his objection seemed to have lost its force.

Quaid, for his part, believed the exchange made perfect sense. Rivard wanted the Morganville facility hit, and the Mice had said they needed the kernel source code to get inside and do said hitting. Simple. They'd given the code to Piper Jackson once before; why not again now?

You're overthinking it, Wood, Quaid had said. *Stop looking for a shooter on the grassy knoll.*

As Leathersby stepped toward Josiah, though, his high-lacing boots pulverizing stone underfoot, I wondered why he was the one handling the pass off. Why not a subordinate? Why not Yves Pomeroy, who would've had the technical expertise to discuss with Piper if some issue arose?

Maybe Fabienne didn't trust subordinates with the kernel. She certainly hadn't seemed to trust Yves much when I'd seen them together in France.

Josiah and Leathersby were five feet apart now. The Brit began talking through a tight grin. He held his beefy arms out ten permanent degrees from his sides.

What's he saying?

I moved closer to hear over the rotors, Piper on my heels.

"...beat you up, your boyfriend?" Leathersby jutted his chin toward Hatch, several yards away. "You American queers must play rough."

Josiah said, "What're you even *talking* about?"

"Got all them tattoos," Leathersby said. "That's a gay thing in the States, yeah?"

I watched the small box in his hand, which he held by his thumb and pinkie finger.

It was black. The size of a matchbox.

Piper said, "Cut the trash talk. Just give us the kernel. Give it over and go."

Again, Leathersby grinned tightly, tendons bulging in his neck. He eyed each of us in turn. Josiah. Piper. Hatch. Garrison. And me.

He raised the box in front of his cruel eyes. As he considered it, he tipped his head and quirked one eyebrow. The box seemed too big for a flash drive—how Piper said she'd gotten the kernel before.

Is there some secondary container inside? Could it be rattling around loose?

Leathersby thrust the box at Josiah, knocking him back.

"All yours, mate," he said. "Enjoy."

Josiah recovered and, tightening his thin fingers across the box, held it to his chest.

In my ear: "He make the pass?"

I didn't risk a response. I was holding my breath, stretched up on tiptoes, eager for Piper to get the kernel and start reverse engineering the antidote.

We're so close. It's almost over.

Josiah shot a fierce look at the Rivard contingent. Then he glanced hesitantly at the box in his hands.

Leathersby said, "Go on. Scared it'll bite you?"

Blushing furiously, Josiah flicked the box open with his thumb. He looked inside and whatever he saw made him flinch. The box fell. It landed crookedly, and out crawled a white mouse, eyes the same pink as Josiah's.

"What *is* this?" he said as the mouse scampered past his shoe and away over the sand.

Blake Leathersby was holding a gun. "This is you getting what's deserved, traitor."

He raised the barrel and shot Josiah in the face. I spun away from the grisly sight—like a balloon of blood popping—and felt wet flecks on my cheek.

The noise and sudden gore stunned me. I couldn't breathe.

Piper, ducking, shouted, "We had a deal! We were gonna do Morganville—"

"Bollocks." Leathersby made a tactical hand gesture to the commandos, two fingers spread and thumb twisting. "Boss Lady's having me and the boys handle Morganville ourselves, that's our next stop. Might be we could use a hand."

One of the men seized Piper and dragged her toward a chopper. They were taking her captive—the sight lifted me out of my shock. I thought back to Roche Rivard and the rumored oubliette, that dungeon in the bowels.

This is our fault. The guys and I, we put her up to this.

I rushed the commando, dislodging his grip. Piper ran. So did I.

We only managed a few steps before other men caught up and jerked us back. Hatch hobbled to our defense, but Leathersby dropped him with a swift round kick.

Then the Brit aimed his gun at me. "Not wise, lass."

I felt an exploding panic, thinking of Zach and Karen and this steady black muzzle. "Why—what're you...but you...you can't, I wasn't—"

"Oh, I think I can."

He cocked the hammer, and my head swirled with dances and graduations and heart-to-heart talks I would never have with my children. Seconds ago, I'd been mentally rebooting McGill Investigators. *How did things go so wrong so fast?*

Now Leathersby's face changed, a glint piercing the thickness.

"Davos," he said. "I remember...you were with Oak Jones."

My brain froze. Was this a good or bad development? I was still alive, at least. My overriding worry had been being recognized from Roche Rivard, my most recent exposure to Leathersby. I'd almost forgotten that run-in after Fabienne's speech in Davos.

Leathersby told a subordinate, "She's mixed up with Rafferty and Jones somehow."

He dropped the gun to his side—*thank God*—and peered out across the horizon.

"Where the bugger are they, I wonder?"

Leathersby swiveled around in place, boots pulverizing sand, looking from one dune to the next. He identified the highest—which actually was where Durwood had planted a microcamera—and tugged his crotch.

"Cheers, mates!" he called. "I got your woman now!"

He gripped my hoodie and pulled me toward the chopper. Other men were wrestling Piper near the landing skids, forcing her aboard.

Garrison rushed in and took my free hand. "You are *not* taking Molly."

Leathersby laughed as they tugged me in opposite directions like a rope at field day. "You just saw me shoot a bloke point-blank. You rate your chances any better?"

Garrison's hot hand pressed mine. His throat gurgled.

He repeated, "You're not taking her. I won't let you."

Leathersby raised his gun at Garrison, the blocky weapon inches from my face. "Suit yourself."

Piper screamed from the helicopter. I saw Leathersby's forearm twitch and his trigger finger start to move.

I lunged forward and bit.

"*Oww!*" Leathersby shrieked, shaking his hand. The gun had fallen to the sand. He picked it up with his left—unbitten—hand and slugged Garrison across the mouth. Garrison fell and didn't get up.

Next, he shoved me in the chest, a vicious open-fisted blow. I joined Garrison on the ground, sand grit in my mouth, but a second later, Leathersby jerked me to my feet and resumed taking me to the helicopter.

Piper and I resisted, but there were too many strong hands and arms. Eventually, our flailing limbs were folded through the chopper doors, which Leathersby then pulled closed, making a snap-circle gesture to the pilot.

The rotors roared to life. I lost my stomach as we pitched forward.

The pilot asked, "Do we need to sweep for hostiles?"

Leathersby squinted at the maelstrom of dust below. "Nah. This is their battlefield." He turned to me, eyes on my snug harness straps. "They'll come to us now."

I closed both arms across my chest.

He said, "Ah, loosen up. Your uncle Blakey's got you now. This is where the fun starts."

PART FOUR

CHAPTER FIFTY-SIX

Pittsburgh

Jim Steed drove a rental car up to New York to meet the guys. The hunk of junk had a bum serpentine belt, which started yipping in Altoona and never stopped. He chugged through the Lincoln Tunnel and got to Cusser's Last Stand, Quaid's bar, by ten thirty.

Parking was a mess. Half the cars on the street had no tires, rims rusting into the curb. Finally, Steed found a spot. He cut the noisy motor, unstuck his butt from the vinyl seat, and walked to the bar.

Cusser's Last Stand was mostly rubble inside. The "bar" was a wood plank laid across stacked cinder blocks. The stools looked like fire salvage—chipped, singed black.

Quaid sat on the center one, Durwood to his right. That ancient dog sprawled out underneath, asleep.

"Slick place," Steed said, fitting his trick knee around the cinder blocks.

Quaid sat before a tumbler of gold splashed red with Tabasco. Judging by posture, Steed guessed it wasn't his first prairie fire.

Quaid said, "Did you bring the cash?"

Jim Steed sucked in a breath. "About that. Bad news."

Durwood's eyes cut over beneath the brim of his hat.

Steed explained, "Someone snitched to my board of directors. They

red-flagged all the Third Chance Enterprises line items in the budget."
He tossed an envelope onto the plank bar. "It's about a fourth of what
you asked for."

"A *fourth*?" Quaid said. "I thought you were the CEO."

"For now," Steed said. "The rest of the executive team thinks I'm
nuts to be spending a dime on you guys."

"But American Dynamics is on fire. Stock's up something like three
hundred percent, right? You're flush with moola."

"That's true." Steed raised three fingers to the bartender. "Pittsburgh's back to max utilization, and we just added a third shift in
Akron. It's all Anarchy segments. Guns. Fortification. Extra-legal
security."

Durwood said, "Same as Rivard."

"Not the same, *damn it*." Steed slapped the plank, waking the dog
below. "We're responding, is all. It's an arms race."

"You could just...stop," Quaid said. His blue eyes were airy and full
of booze.

Steed looked between the two, incredulous. They didn't get it. They
hadn't walked through the rebuilt AmDye factories and felt the morale
—surging like a tidal wave. They hadn't seen machinery operators
wearing pieces, proudly thumping the giant missile tubes streaming
off the assembly line.

They hadn't heard the chants from the catwalk, "*Steed, Steed, Steed,*"
and felt the workers' rumbling, rocking energy through the grate.

The workers, who thought Steed was the architect of AmDye's mili-
taristic resurgence. If they only knew the dread in his heart.

Jim Steed had started the Vietnam War a green eighteen-year-old
and ended it believing his government had failed him. For as long as
he lived, he would smell the fetid jungle air of Khe Sanh and feel—in
his flat, arthritic feet—the twenty klicks he and his squadmates had
hiked into Vietcong territory that October night.

They'd camped under a harvest moon after taking two sniper casualties. Steed and a squadmate carried a possible third—pulse strong
but with a nasty gut wound—between them on stretched bamboo.
They laid the injured man at the foot of a towering jackfruit tree.

Steed felt half dead himself. Sweat had made a stinking second skin of his clothes. He couldn't tell if the deafening insect noise and giant fruits overhead were real or hallucinated.

His lone touchstone to sanity was the other men.

Though exhausted, none of them could sleep. They had orders to attack a VC stronghold upriver in three hours. It'd been a daring, costly mission already, but it was almost over. One way or another.

At four a.m., the comm crackled. Greggie from Omaha, the radio engineer, tuned his dial and listened at the earpiece. His sigh told the squad all it needed to know: *mission abort.*

They sat around and bitched. Mad, relieved, frustrated—they felt it all.

Ricketts, a Mississippi kid who'd joined the Fifth straight out of boot camp, said, "Can't anyone stop this?"

For a while, only the insects answered.

Then Steed—youngest in the squad—said, "LBJ could. Right? Couldn't LBJ if he wanted to?"

The rest looked at him with eyes as black as bullets.

Forty years later, here was Jim Steed: not a president or wacko dictator, but the leader of a corporation—holding the same awesome, paralyzed power.

"Sure," he said now. "I could try to stop it—step in front of the runaway train. Say we refuse to profiteer. Say we're staying outta the Anarchy segments. They'd just run over me. Board of directors.

"They got this one jerk, guy wears a bow tie. Says I'm being too timid. Says if I don't step on the gas, go even more aggressive, he'll gin the unions up against me. Believe that? The unions. I started out a stamper, Quaid. *Goddamn stamper on the line.*"

Quaid edged his thumb around the rim of his glass.

The three men, and dog, sat in silence. Bar silence, anyhow. Cusser's Last Stand featured the steady din of the homeless, the alcoholic, and a few stray hipsters braving the chaos.

Jim Steed understood Quaid and Durwood had their own reasons to despair. The source-code-for-Morganville exchange had flopped. Josiah, their most valuable asset, was dead, and Rivard had captured the McGill woman, who—you had to figure—Quaid had a thing with.

Steed rubbed the corners of his eyes. "You guys think there even *is* a source code? This kernel deal."

Durwood's steel-colored eyes fixed on the plank.

Quaid said, "Yes. Yes, I do. And I believe it's locked up tight at Roche Rivard."

"Tell me that's not what you wanted the cash for," Steed said. "*Roche Rivard?* That's a suicide mission."

Quaid lifted the envelope. "We'd have a lot better odds if you'd've gotten us the amount we asked for."

"You kiddin' me?" Steed said. "I put my butt in a sling to get you *that* much."

Durwood interrupted, "We're going."

The ex-marine's face was stone.

He said, "Don't matter about the money. Don't matter about the kernel either—if it's there or the bottom of the ocean. Moll's there. The Jackson girl too."

Jim Steed nodded. He wasn't surprised to hear Durwood Oak Jones take such a stance. Unfortunately, it made his second piece of bad news all the worse.

"Well," he said, "you're gonna have to go quick."

Quaid stopped his drink just shy of his lips. "Why's that?"

Steed palmed his jaw. "The board wants me to hit 'em. They think it's only a matter of time before Rivard engages us directly."

"*Engages?*"

"Our weapons face off against theirs in the field every day, through different proxies. There's a school of thought that, one day, the proxies'll go away."

Steed had never seen Durwood scared—possibly no one had—but as the West Virginian mulled these last words, the whites of his eyes grew.

"Hitting Roche Rivard..." Durwood's head ticked side to side. "Defenses they have in place... Kinda firepower you'd have to strike with..."

Steed sighed. "I know."

"They've got drone patrols...missile defense... How would you even..."

Steed explained the board had brought in outside consultants to analyze thousands of satellite and seismic surveys. The consultants had concluded Roche Rivard's inner shaft was vulnerable: a tactical nuke straight down the chute would take out the whole facility.

"Board thinks it'll be just like the Death Star," Steed said. "Win the war in one shot."

Durwood's mouth took an ugly line. "Board of directors. Consultants. Bunch of chicken hawks in suits."

"I won't argue that," Steed said. "They're telling me we gotta go. Gotta go now, can't afford to squander our 'window of surprise.'"

Quaid, who'd been quiet through the last stretch, polished off his drink.

"Their own little Pearl Harbor, huh?" he said. "Except this time it's the good guys dropping bombs."

CHAPTER FIFTY-SEVEN
Paris

I sat in one of the cell's two stainless-steel egg chairs, staring through a pane of crystal-clear glass. At waist height, a pentagram-shaped icon pulsed blue at regular intervals—the spot where guards pressed their hands to enter. The icon didn't have to be illuminated to work, fuzzing out as quickly as my eyes could register it.

The mechanism was one of many high-tech riddles that tormented us, intentionally or not, in Fabienne Rivard's oubliette.

Phosphorescent tubes modulated between eerie yellow "day" and black-purple "night," shifting imperceptibly by the hour. Mechanical insects traipsed through our cell, passing in and out by a small gap in the glass below the ceiling. An incessant far-off beeping reminded me of the microwave back home complaining that it'd finished heating my tea water, I could take it out anytime.

An insect buzzed in now. Piper scooted deeper into her egg chair. She thought the eyes were cameras.

The gizmos zipped two circles around the cell, never more than six inches below the ceiling, and left.

Piper said, "When're your boys busting us out?"

Her voice was thick with disdain.

"Let's just stay observant," I said. "If there's an opening, we have to be ready."

She huffed and closed her eyes. The tubes' brightness seemed to indicate midday, but I had no idea what time it was. Neither of us had been sleeping.

I'd expected different cruelties when Blake Leathersby first shoved us down the winding limestone tunnel, ankles shackled and wrists zip-tied, to the subterranean jail. We'd suffered no torture here. The amenities were top-notch. Last night's dinner had been veal and petits pois. In addition to the egg chairs, we had desks, writing supplies, and a private bathroom with a door.

The deprivations were more psychological—the regimented light, the constant thrum of electronics, the impersonal décor. Machines handled all cleaning and maintenance.

Together with the general hopelessness of our situation, it was fertile ground for depression.

I walked to the glass. As the feathery blue pentagram faded in and out, I stared at my reflection. My eyes were puffy, deep crow's-feet at the corner of each.

"I'll say it again—I'll say this a million times." I turned to Piper. She didn't open her eyes. "I'm sorry."

Four days in the oubliette had hardened my cellmate. She'd retreated deeper into herself, into bitterness.

I said, "It's not enough, I know. But I am sorry the guys...you know, that we got you stuck in here."

Her eyes opened to a squint. "Which one?"

"Which what?"

"Is it *we* or *the guys*?" Piper swiveled her chair to look at me square. "Who's calling the shots?"

I opened my mouth to speak, but she went on, "And what's this history y'all have with Rivard? What am I caught in the middle of?"

I was encouraged by her questions. The answers weren't easy, though. "It's complicated."

"Uncomplicate it."

Beyond the cell glass, the maddening beeps continued. A gate crunched open. Piper's eyes stayed on me.

"This is my third job with the guys," I said. "The roles and relationships aren't one hundred percent clear..."

The Mice had gotten a sanitized version of the truth after Shop-All, that we were contractors—more or less—working for American Dynamics. Now I told Piper everything: the wild story that led to my second divorce and introduced me to Quaid and Durwood, about battling Rivard in Florence and ending up strolling the *strade* arm in arm with Quaid, about space lasers and artifact heists and my failed run as a private investigator.

Piper said, "I'm supposed to believe that?"

The *clunk* of the main oubliette entrance saved me from having to respond. In another moment, Blake Leathersby appeared in the cell glass. He was at the guard station.

"What's that bollocks noise?" he asked.

The on-duty guard, whom I couldn't hear, raised his palm and five fingers, shaking his head.

"So turn the idiot things back on," Leathersby snapped.

The guard seemed to be saying he couldn't, or it wasn't so simple—

"That *noise!*" Leathersby gripped his own buzz cut above the ears. "I'm about to punch something. Could be you, mate."

The guard tapped a hurried series of keys at his station. A cool chime sounded, and the beeping stopped.

"Finally." Leathersby corkscrewed a knuckle into each ear. "Now. Where you keeping the two American birds?"

The guard gestured to our cell, one of maybe a dozen arrayed about the oubliette's receiving area. Leathersby spotted us with a lewd sneer and stalked to the cell glass. He laid his hand against the blue pentagram.

The mechanism blipped harshly.

He replaced his hand on the spot, taking care to press the palm perfectly flat.

It blipped again.

Leathersby rounded on the guard. "Idiot thing won't let me in."

The guard explained that, as he'd started to say before, the palm sensors had been finicky lately. That's why they had been disabled.

Leathersby lifted his hand. "It's a damn hand. I got clearance. Why's this hard?"

The guard said one's entire vascular network factored in—the shape and size of veins, rates of constriction and expansion. *Had he been doing anything that might've affected his veins?*

"Pumping iron, yeah." Leathersby smirked. "Expect that makes about everything on me bigger."

The guard said that must be it.

Leathersby ordered the man to disable the lock and let him the hell in already.

The beeps resumed.

He muttered, "High-tech junk."

The English mercenary stalked into the cell. "Bloody waste of space. I coulda kept twenty of my Desert Storm towelheads in here."

Piper and I stayed in our chairs. As Leathersby swung his thick legs about, I smelled his body—strong, sour.

He began, "Tell me about New Jersey. And I don't mean the traffic, or that wanker Bruce Springsteen."

I looked across to Piper.

She said, "You screwed us over. Shot Josiah in the face."

Leathersby grinned. "That was brilliant, wasn't it? But what I need cleared up now is what you two got going with Jones and Rafferty. Why you wanted that kernel."

As a mechanical insect whispered by overhead, I scrambled to figure out how much he could logically know. He'd recognized me from Davos, so he was aware I had *some* connection to the guys. He still hadn't said anything about the fake CIO persona I'd used snooping around with Yves Pomeroy, though.

"Morganville—the data facility," I said. "We needed to modify it to take out Morganville."

Leathersby crossed his arms, looming over me. "Same as Josiah told us up front, yeah?"

I nodded.

"Weren't planning no double cross?"

My stomach felt like it was trying to flip over in place, but I managed, "Nope."

He stepped closer, flexing his biceps one after the other like some musical instrument. He glared at me.

Piper said, "Their AV software's tweaked. If we'd'a hit them with the regular kernel, they'd be back up in a day."

Leathersby faced her with a vacuous expression.

"'AV' stands for 'antivirus,'" she said. "As in, the stuff that keeps data from—"

"I know what goddamn AV means." An ugly twist came into Leathersby's mouth. "On your feet, you."

When Piper didn't budge, he yanked her up from the egg chair. Bolts in the floor underneath rattled. "You need to be searched."

"They searched us day one."

"Not properly," Leathersby said. "Let your uncle Blakey have a look. Might be you smuggled in some'a those American street drugs."

With a glance up—no insects were hovering at the moment—he started patting Piper down roughly, kneading into her armpits, gripping between her breasts. He spun her around twice and ripped her from the cell into view of other prisoners.

"*I like an audience*," he growled.

He reached to undo Piper's belt. She bucked against him, and I bolted forward to help, but the guard stopped me before I could get close.

Leathersby gripped both Piper's wrists in one hand and forced her feet wide apart. He was just pulling up his own shirt when a hiss settled over the room.

Leathersby continued hotly another few seconds until the hiss rose to a crackle and, in the middle of the oubliette's common area, a holographic image of Fabienne Rivard appeared.

"*Arrêtez*, now!" it commanded in a voice no less withering than the real thing. "Rivard LLC respects the Geneva convention. Any employee who flouts it will answer to me."

Sheepishly, Leathersby released Piper. "Right, of course. I was only making a show of it. Scare 'em, see what they really know."

The hollows of Fabienne's digitized face deepened. "And? What have you learned?"

Leathersby stumbled over a bin of mechanical insects, loose on the floor. "They ain't saying a thing. They been disappointing me."

"As you disappoint me," Holographic Fabienne said.

The 3D image flickered at the edges, giving the heiress's black hair an electric quality and her body a barbed angularity. The floor underneath was discolored from the rest of the limestone—darker, mirrored.

The image persisted until Leathersby turned down his eyes submissively. Then, in a collapsing vertical blip, it vanished.

"*Bitch!*" Leathersby said, kicking the bin of mechanized insects on his way out.

The devices clattered across the floor, whirring to life and rising to the ceiling.

The guard returned us to the cell.

For the rest of the afternoon, as the disabled locks beeped on, I thought about the dynamics at play above us in the offices of Roche Rivard. Leathersby's cruelty and Fabienne's cunning—how they fit or didn't fit together, whether the conflict between them could be exploited. I thought about what Quaid and Durwood were up to, if their breaking us out was imminent or if we needed to be making a plan of our own.

Piper was for making a plan.

"Check this out," she said, reaching into the toe of her shoe.

Upon the silver platter the mechanized food wheel had brought us earlier, she placed one of the mechanical insects.

"*Where'd you get that?*" I asked. "They always stay up by the ceiling."

She peeked out to the common area and confirmed the guard was busy on his computer.

"When Muscle Head kicked over that bin, I caught one."

Camouflaging the device with her plate and utensils, Piper showed me its detachable terminal—a kind of fat twist-off tail with steering controls and a display from its camera eyes.

"Does it work?" I said. "What can we do with it?"

She shrugged. "Take it for a spin."

We waited for nighttime—for the phosphorescent tubes' deepest purple. The oubliette had a number of corridors radiating off the main detention area that contained our cell, spokes leading deeper into the limestone. Piper detached our insect's tail terminal and tapped a control to send its body aloft. As it fluttered to the ceiling, she shifted to one side of her egg chair so I could see over her shoulder.

Enough insects were about, passing in and out of cells seemingly at random, that ours wasn't conspicuous. Piper took a minute getting familiar with the controls, sending the flying spy through nearby cells occupied by various bruisers muttering in various languages. The cameras were equipped with night vision, any moving object showing up stark white against the dim backdrops.

"*The corridors,*" I suggested.

Piper nodded and wordlessly navigated our insect from the cell of a husband-wife pair of Norwegian dissidents. She probed several dark corridors and found more of the same, cell after cell after cell of prisoners, hundreds, some sleeping, some up scheming like us.

Our spy kept moving, skimming below ceilings, beaming back images of fellow prisoners. I tried to think how else we could use the insect. Could it slip out into the main limestone tunnel, maybe during a guard shift change? Observe a typed password?

How long would its batteries last? When we finished, how would we return the tail terminal without being found out? Should we hide the whole thing in one of our beds?

As the minutes stretched on, it seemed the oubliette's massive scale was the only thing we'd learn. My questions began repeating, and my eyelids had just started sagging when Piper said something.

"Huh?" I sat up—we were sharing a single egg chair now. "You find something?"

"I dunno," she said. "But this hall's weird. Empty."

I peered at the terminal screen, no bigger than an inch square, and saw screen after screen of nothing.

"No prisoners here?" I said. "Are the eyes still working?"

She angled the insect up, bringing the phosphorescent tubes in the ceiling corners into view.

"Weird," I said. "Why wouldn't they be using this space?"

"Maybe it's to keep something separated," Piper said. "Something they wanna keep secret."

"Like what?"

She mused out the corner of her mouth, "An exit."

I was suddenly wide awake, pulse pounding in my wrists. Had any of the guards or previous interrogators left that way? I wasn't sure. The viewing angles weren't great in the oubliette. It was hard telling one corridor from the next, especially working from memory.

Piper guided the insect on, and on, and on. The vacant corridor might have been a half mile long.

How far can they drill before they hit the fault line?

Finally, the phosphorescent tubes ended and the limestone walls turned full dark. The insect's display wobbled.

Piper, who'd started talking to the device at some point, said, "Sorry, guy, I think we ran you into a wall. End of the line."

Our hopes sank as she backed the insect up and swiveled it around, panning, rising, lowering, finding nothing but shades of black.

Then, a flash.

It was quick—if we'd both blinked at the same time, we would've missed it.

"*Back up!*" I said. "Did you see?"

She had. Quickly, pinching and swiping her fingertips on the tail terminal, she steadied the insect's eyes in front of the light source: an oblong yellow slit in the limestone.

"Window," she said.

Our shoulders were pressed together. The cavity of the egg chair felt hot. "You think? Can you zoom?"

"No zoom, but..."

She inched the insect closer to the slit until it grew to encompass the entire display. The camera exposure changed—the yellow turned bright white for an instant, then it resolved to a scene of what lay beyond the slit.

Four walls. A bed. Stainless-steel egg chair like the one we were crowded into.

"Darn." Piper gritted her teeth. "Just another cell."

I was disappointed we hadn't found an exit, but I felt a twinge of hope too.

"Not just another cell," I said, gesturing to the figure sleeping on the cot. "Henri Rivard's cell."

CHAPTER FIFTY-EIGHT

F abienne stepped out of the holo-chamber and called into the air, "Geoffrey, I need the American president *par téléphone.*"

A speaker on her desk crackled, followed by her manservant's voice. "What shall I give as the reason for the call?"

Fabienne frowned. "Give none."

"Understood," Geoffrey said. "At once, mademoiselle."

Scurrying was heard over the speaker. Fabienne approached her window—bulletproof, four-inch aluminum oxynitride—and looked out. Beyond the blurred headlights of Boulevard Périphérique lay Paris. Even from a kilometer out, the great city showed the toll of anarchy. Building facades had gaping holes like some risqué dress she might wear to the Oscars. Burning slums upwind had turned the Eiffel Tower black from its usual brown.

Geoffrey appeared at the doorway. "I have the president on line two."

Fabienne extended her palm backward. Geoffrey hurried and placed the handset there.

"Hello, Edward." She pronounced the name like bland bouillabaisse.

The president said, "What's on your mind, Fabes?"

The heiress grinned hard into the folksy nickname, which the Texan had bestowed upon her at their introduction years ago.

"It has come to my attention," she said, "that an American corporation is plotting to attack Roche Rivard."

"You're kidding," said the president. "Who'd be dim enough to try that?"

As clearly as if it had appeared in the holo-chamber, Fabienne saw Jim Steed's jowly face in her mind.

"American Dynamics," she said. "They are drawing up battle plans as we speak."

"How would you happen to know that?"

"We employ a broad portfolio of information-harvesting techniques at Rivard LLC."

The president, whose last campaign slogan had been, "Simple Man, Simple Solutions," said, "Bet you do."

Then he whistled in a feeble attempt to evoke sex.

Fabienne ignored the misogyny. "I trust my organization can count on your full-throated cooperation in preventing this ruthless, unprovoked attack."

The president wheezed. "Half of California seceded last week. I got national guardsmen deployed to Mount Rushmore, trying to keep Honest Abe's forehead from crushing Teddy Roosevelt's mustache. You think I have the wherewithal to preempt some corporate attack?"

"You will not stop them?"

"I *can't* stop them. No money, no men. Hell, some days I beg Canada to keep tabs on Seattle for us."

Fabienne gave a breathy sigh at the answer, which she'd anticipated. "Then I must warn you that Rivard does not accept an attack on its headquarters. This will be considered an act of war."

"The whole damn mess is war, isn't it? How do you separate the mud from the pig's slop?"

"I don't understand your farmspeak," she said. "But know this. We reserve all military options when a foreign entity threatens our very existence."

"What's that mean, all military options?"

"All means all. In our French, the word is *tout*."

She explained that not only the Pittsburgh plant but American Dynamics facilities in Reno, Pensacola, Mexico City, and more would be in scope as retaliatory targets.

The president barely objected. Fabienne understood he had zero leverage over Jim Steed or—more importantly—Steed's board of directors. She merely needed to establish American Dynamics as the aggressor, thus minimizing the inevitable backlash to Rivard's devastating response.

Next, Fabienne had Geoffrey reach the prime minister of Germany, and after her, the crown prince of Dubai. Some heads of state she pressed similarly to curtail rogue actors in their country. Others she lobbied for larger Forceworthy spends.

She was in the middle of needling Zimbabwe's strongman leader —"Congo siphons five thousand barrels each day, and you do nothing?"—when Thérèse Laurent entered.

Worry spoiled the blond's face.

"Excuse me, Kufar," she said into the phone. "I must go. We will talk more about your weakened stream."

As she hung up, Thérèse clutched her Grand Planifier tablet over her chest. "What have you learned about New Jersey?"

Fabienne looked neutrally at her *amie*. "Nothing more."

"Did Leathersby interrogate the hostages?"

"He did. It was a waste."

"How? We must find out if the kernel's truth is known outside the organization! The risks, if we are exposed..."

Thérèse shivered at the thought—or perhaps at the twelve-degree-Celsius office temperature, which Fabienne insisted upon for the health of the planet.

Though Fabienne herself had little fear of whatever Rafferty and Jones had brewing, she would not say so and blunt her friend's paranoia. Paranoia bred vigilance—the two matched like blue cheese and a Sauternes with apricot notes.

"Our Neanderthal colleague," she said, staying on the topic of Leathersby, "is done being trusted with female detainees. He may be done altogether here."

She'd thought this dig at her rival would codify Thérèse, but it did not.

"If the data loss is connected to CyberSafe..." Thérèse fretted. "If people find out..."

"Words do nothing. Rumors." Fabienne flopped her svelte wrist, bored. "We can deny plausibly enough."

"What if an attempt is made on the kernel itself?"

"*N'importe quoi*," Fabienne said. "The Great Safe is impenetrable."

"But Rafferty and Jones have interfered before. With the space laser, with the virus—"

"The laser was my father's failure." Fabienne heard a crack. Looking down at her hands, she found she'd snapped a pencil in two. "The Americans cannot stop us."

Thérèse licked her full lips. Her Grand Planifier tablet chimed, informing her that some task had slipped behind schedule.

"We have their associate, the dowdy woman," Fabienne continued. "They are cowboys. They are powerless *not* to come for her."

When Thérèse's tablet chimed again, Fabienne suggested she leave and address the issue. Thérèse did as told.

Alone again in her office, Fabienne had Geoffrey get the leader of Argentina on the phone. She secured another ninety million euros in security outlays from him and other world leaders over the course of the next hour.

When she'd tired of this, she summoned Geoffrey again. He took back the phone and started for his cubicle. Then he stopped to face the heiress.

"Permit me to say," he began, head ducked, "that your father would be proud. Henri himself could not have done better."

Fabienne's mouth made a long, bent line. "My, Geoffrey. What a compliment. How revealing to hear the wonder in your voice— wonder that I could do a thing as well as my father."

"I—*mais non*, I only meant to say you're doing a fine job, you increase the company's stature each day, none can possibly question your fitness in regards to..."

She didn't speak up or otherwise relieve his consternation.

Geoffrey Dubois had been a top lieutenant under her father. His womanizing had been notorious, surpassing even Yves Pomeroy's. The complaint hotline Fabienne had established fielded no fewer than fifty calls regarding Geoffrey its first week. He had used a company yacht as a spider's web, luring women aboard with promises of advancement, pouring them champagne on the Seine while tugging relentlessly toward the captain's quarters.

Fabienne had listened to many hotline accounts personally.

Geoffrey's first task, upon being reassigned as her personal assistant, was to handwrite apologies to every female he'd managed during his eighteen years at Rivard.

When the man had sputtered out, Fabienne said, "You cannot let go of my father. This loyalty he inspired—it amazes me. I lived with this man. Mother and I did not see this side of him."

Geoffrey's hands wrested over his belt buckle. "I miss him, it's true. He was a great man. I don't suppose he—er, would be"—the manservant gestured down, through the floor—"capable of visitors? Where he is held?"

Fabienne arched her eyebrows. "Why do you look down?"

"I—*eh bien*, it is said he may be kept, or may reside, I should better say, someplace in the bowels..."

Fabienne remained stolid.

"...but perhaps this is nonsense and I'm talking rot! I apologize, I apologize, please don't take this as a reflection of—of anything at all..."

After some time, Fabienne asked, "Do you believe that if my father were capable of visitors, I would deny him?"

"*Non*, certainly not."

"Do you believe I erred when I removed him from public life, Geoffrey?"

"I do not, mademoiselle. I'm sure the decision was correct."

"Were you there to hear him repeat the same story to investors during earnings calls, one quarter after the next?"

"Indeed, I recall that he often struggled with—"

"Did you ever speak with the aide who ferried him to the bathroom? Who buttoned his Vuitton jackets for him when he could not manage himself?"

"Yes, I—well no, I never personally met the aide—"

"Then shut up," Fabienne said. "Shut up, return to your cubicle, and ask no more of my father—else you may find yourself reunited. *Permanently.*"

Geoffrey, like Thérèse before him, did as told.

The heiress returned to the bulletproof window, Henri on the mind. She thought of him in his remote corner of the oubliette—of which none knew save for a single jailer.

She thought of being a girl, standing beside him at their large wall map of La France as her father narrated the family's holdings.

We own factories there, and there—pointing to Reims—and there aussi, my little Fabi.

Awestruck, she would follow his finger around and ask what they owned in Germany or Switzerland or Spain, since those were the countries at the map's periphery.

Not yet, little Fabi. Nothing there yet. But soon.

Fabienne smiled at the memory. Perhaps when the kernel had finished its work, she would visit her father in the depths of Roche Rivard with a globe, and show him their domain then. Allow him to spin the model in his frail hands and feel the oceans, the mountains, the landmasses over which they ruled.

Every last meter of it.

CHAPTER FIFTY-NINE

New Jersey

Quaid listened to the grandmother's voice mail, phone in one hand and flask in the other.

"...looking for the louse—I don't know as I got the right number. Quaid? Quaid Rafferty! Listen up. My granddaughter's missing and I know it's your doing. You got one shred of decency in that degenerate body of yours, you'll come out and tell these children what's become of their mother..."

She ranted another full minute, casting aspersions on Quaid's upbringing, threatening various Depression-era banes.

Something clattered in the background. A fallen pot? Zach's skate-board off the stair rail?

Durwood was busy scouring the Roche Rivard blueprints Steed had passed along, plotting a rescue mission. The Garrison kid had ventured chez McGill once, reporting back, "They don't, like, listen to me," and complaining his concussion symptoms—which had started with Leathersby's punch at the rock quarry—had recurred.

So, on this chilly Sunday afternoon, it was up to Quaid to drive the Vanagon out to the New Jersey suburbs. He actually had been to the house twice—a fact that'd seemingly slipped Eunice's mind.

Karen answered the door.

"Mr. Rafferty!" she cried, pigtails bouncing. "Did you bring

Mommy this time?"

Quaid patted her shoulder on the way inside. "Ah, no. I didn't."

She stayed in the open doorway, squinting out at the van. "Mommy enjoys surprises. I'm going to watch so she doesn't sneak up and trick me."

Zach stood at the foot of the stairs, arms crossed.

Quaid said, "No tricks today. But hey, it's cold out—she'd want you inside out of the weather." He gestured at the pink ribbon in her hair. "Tell me about that pretty bow. Where'd you get it?"

It was a move he'd learned in politics, handy at rallies when dealing with constituents' small children. You pick out the most vibrant part of the kid's outfit—ask a question, give it a light tap.

Karen pulled at her bow, unraveling one braid. "For sure no Mommy?"

"For sure. Sorry. But I promise she'll be back soon."

Quaid pulled the door closed, gently nudging Karen—still looking out—back by the tip of her nose.

Unpaired shoes dotted the living room, and a teetering stack of *Reader's Digests* made a Leaning Tower of Pisa atop the coffee table. No fewer than a dozen of Karen's dioramas lined the fireplace. Quaid smelled socks and furnace and—deeper down—that skunky-piney scent of marijuana.

He turned toward Zach.

The boy, reading his mind, said, "It's legal now."

"Not at fourteen, it isn't," Quaid said.

"I'm fifteen."

Quaid crimped his brow.

"My birthday was last week," Zach said. "The day after Mom stopped coming home."

Quaid opened his mouth to say pot wasn't legal at fifteen either, but Zach was already stomping off up the stairs.

Karen said, "Is Mommy with Mr. Durwood?"

"Not right this second," Quaid said. "We're getting her soon. Ju-uust about to go get her."

A smile bloomed on Karen's face, and Quaid figured he was clear.

The girl said, "Can I come?"

"Can you come?" he repeated. "Afraid not. It's a special trip. A one-person kind of trip."

"So Mr. Durwood isn't going?"

"No, he—" Quaid had taken too many pulls off the flask in the van, psyching up, and lost a measure of verbal acuity. "I misspoke, Durwood is going. We're getting her together. But it's just grown-ups."

Karen twirled on the ball of her foot, seeming to ponder what kind of trip would be off-limits to kids.

Now the marijuana smell rose to distraction, and Karen curdled her face.

"Zach's friends are stinky," she said. "I think they always forget their baths."

"I'm sure that's true," Quaid said. "Say, I haven't seen your great-grandmother. Where is she?"

"Napping."

"At four in the afternoon?"

"She gets tired. She is old as the hills."

Quaid would've chuckled if not for the heavy sense of besiegement settling over him. The household felt like a sputtering plane on autopilot drifting down after its human pilots had parachuted out.

He left Karen in the company of her dolls and hiked upstairs to Zach's room. Pressing his ear to the door, he heard video games intermingled with a cacophony of dopey giggles.

He plowed inside.

"The hell?" Zach said, fumbling a plastic-and-aluminum-foil contraption as two puffy-eyed pals snapped out of slouches.

"This is how you step up when your mother's away?" Quaid said.

Zach hurriedly passed the contraption to a friend, who recoiled at the hot foil.

Quaid smeared his nose at the foulness. The three slack-a-teers had left microwave pizza crusts on the bedspread. A soiled sweatshirt hung from one blade of a ceiling fan, rotating overhead like some dingy bird.

"Is Eunice losing her sense of smell too?" he said. "She lets you get away with this?"

"She thinks it's a science project," Zach said. "For homeschool."

Quaid disentangled one loafer from controller cords. "You guys need to get outside. I don't know what the teen social scene looks like in the Anarchy, but this? Sitting around Mommy's house getting high? Not how you break out of virginhood."

One of Zach's friends piped up, "Who says we're virgins?"

"Nobody. Nobody has to—your actions say it loud and clear." Quaid stepped closer to Zach and lowered his voice. *"Your little sister is probably out in the hall listening to every word. She sees you. She soaks things up. For her sake, you need to man up."*

"Like you?" Zach said.

"That's right."

A friend said, "A man like you?"

"Again, yes." Quaid snapped his fingers before the kid's face. "Are you processing? Did a plug get pulled back there, a cortex or two blow a fuse?"

Before any of the three managed a comeback, the grandmother's warble sounded through the bedroom door.

"Is science class almost over in there? You woke me up with that smell. The candle wicks must be about burned through, aren't they?"

The teenagers erupted in chuckle-snorts. One tumbled off the bed.

Zach called, "Sorry, Great-Grandma. Just a couple experiments left..."

Quaid opened the door.

Eunice, after a double take at his presence, turned out the wrinkled points of her elbows. "Why, will wonders never cease? The louse showed up. The louse who lost my granddaughter."

"Take it easy," Quaid said, lowering his eyes for discretion. "Nobody lost Molly."

"Then where is she? Why isn't she here?" If anything, Eunice was getting louder. "Where'd she go?"

Quaid guided her to the hallway and confirmed Karen was downstairs. "Durwood and I know where she is, where she's being held. We'll get her out soon."

"Shouldn't have gotten her *in* in the first place. Shoulda done your own dang dirty work."

Quaid couldn't argue there. "Look. We will make this right."

Eunice wasn't appeased. "*You* put my Molly on the hook. She would've never joined up if it weren't for *you*. If *you* weren't involved."

At every "you," her dimples—which were so cute on Molly—deepened starkly, turning her face into a pocked tableau of loathing.

"We're doing all we can," Quaid said. "I don't know what else I can say or offer."

"I'll tell you what you can *offer*." Eunice thrust a bony finger toward the front door. "You can get right on outta here."

"You asked me to come. I came."

"And now you can go!" She bared her teeth, a sliver opening between her gums and denture plate.

Quaid backpedaled down the stairs with hands raised. Karen and even Zach, peeking out from his room, were watching the confrontation.

Quaid felt lousy. He'd been sleeping poorly—awakened every night at two a.m. by Durwood, returning from his patrol—and had precious little will to navigate Eunice's wrath.

That soft couch in the tanning salon lobby would feel great right about now. Plus a nip or three from the flask? Send him right off into dreamland.

Quaid was just sizing up an adieu along the lines of, *Call me when some measure of sanity reappears at this address*, when he caught sight of the pictures in the hall—a framed sequence of Molly with big hair in high school, then at her humble wedding (the first one), then holding Zach as a baby.

The photographs transported Quaid. Molly's looks and fashions changed through the sequence, but the one constant was hope. At each of these big moments, she had believed happiness lay before her. He thought of how hard she'd fought to be accepted by the Mice. How hard she fought for her kids. The ordeal she'd endured with Karen's father.

Biographers might never line up for the privilege of telling Molly McGill's life story, but she'd scrapped for every inch of it.

Those big green eyes bored into him. *This is my life. This: this mess you're knee deep in the middle of.*

Quaid stopped backpedaling. Eunice's invective continued, but he closed his mind to it. He walked to Zach's room, swept up the drugs and associated paraphernalia, and dumped them in the trash—all but one bong.

"This," he told the grandmother, showing her the apparatus, "is not a candle. No more of these allowed."

Zach and friends reached forward weakly as Quaid chucked it too.

"Karen." He marched downstairs and pointed to the fireplace. "We're done with dioramas, okay? You need something to do, I want you reading those Curious George books."

The girl nodded, eyes wide at Quaid's vigor.

"When your mom comes back, I want her to see how hard you've been working." His phone buzzed in an inner pocket of his sport coat. He ignored it. "Now. Before I go, we're going to eat together. We're going to eat a regular family sit-down meal."

He looked at Zach's friends. "The word that should've jumped out from that sentence there was 'family.'"

The slack-a-teers looked back blankly.

"Scram," he said. "Go home and eat an apple. Don't return."

They slinked off. Zach bolted up as though to object, but stopped when he saw Quaid's face—which had lost any trace of playfulness.

The front door closed, Quaid walked to the TV and switched off the reality court show Eunice had just started watching.

"You all need to hear a few things," he announced. "Your mother—Eunice, your granddaughter—is in a bit of a pickle."

With the kids hugging their elbows tight, Quaid talked. He fielded every concern. *Was Mom in jail? Was she alive? If she was coming back, would she bring souvenirs?*

Why was Mr. Durwood always so quiet when he visited now?

Quaid answered with wit and selective candor, drawing on his extensive repertoire of evasions.

Then he asked Eunice if she had dinner thoughts.

"Roast is always nice," she said forlornly.

Quaid smelled nothing from the kitchen—it was almost four thirty. "Got any quicker ideas?"

The old woman shrugged. "Pasta. Sauce from a jar."

"Sold," Quaid said. "I'll start the water boiling."

CHAPTER SIXTY

Paris

Yves Pomeroy watched his own hand fluttering his badge before the lobby sensor. Many days, he could master his palsy with a concerted effort, mentally tunneling into each knuckle's movement and wrist's turn, willing himself through simple tasks.

Many days, he could. But not this one.

A female guard rushed to his assistance. "Allow me, monsieur."

Her two warm hands wrapped his one, guiding the badge toward the sensor's infrared beam.

The contact exhilarated Yves—she was a comely brunette with a chest like Mont Blanc—but he managed to blunt his urges and proceed inside. He felt something upset in the exchange, some pocket or cuff.

Bof, it is nothing, he decided. Sensations couldn't be trusted when one was aroused.

Yves strode past reception with manufactured assurance, mouth puckered, shoulders out. He well knew they could be watching via closed circuit.

Had they been watching forty minutes ago when he'd been in the first arrondissement, the heart of Paris, answering Durwood Oak Jones's questions about this very building, Roche Rivard?

American Dynamics had provided Jones a formidable intelligence cache, but it contained blind spots and was somewhat dated due to the speed at which Fabienne was redoubling her defenses. Yves had clued the American in to the latest procedures and told what he knew of recent excavations in the deep, wet limestone.

"This is yours, *oui*?" a voice called behind.

Yves whipped about, his aged back cracking.

The guard held a scrap of paper. Even five meters out, Yves could discern the diagram he'd sketched of supply tunnels radiating eastward from the building's bowels.

"It is, yes, *merci bien*." He shuffled to retrieve it.

The woman seemed to hold the scrap overlong, forcing Yves to rip one corner.

He walked the incriminating paper rapidly to the elevators. Fear screamed through his thoughts, for which he hated himself. As a young man, indeed even as a not-so-young man, he had stood tall with Henri Rivard. They had faced down Somali butchers together. Israeli poisoners. Greenpeace propagandists.

Now he cowered before a woman guard. Under a woman CEO. He'd been thwarted at every turn by a woman—Thérèse Laurent— who should be taking orders from him, but did not.

Quelle disgrâce.

Yves boarded a waiting bullet car and pressed the button for the Enterprise Software floor. The doors began closing, but several sets of fingers appeared in between before they could finish.

The doors reopened. Yves looked past the supplicants who'd lunged for the door to see who they'd stopped it for.

Naturellement: Fabienne Rivard.

"Ah, Yves." She flashed a dark smile. "My favorite elevator *ami*. You are heading up?"

"Yes," Yves said, then deeper: "Up, that is correct."

Fabienne smirked and boarded. The supplicants followed hesitantly, but a look from the heiress sent them scampering off—leaving her and Yves alone.

The doors closed. The car shot skyward.

Fabienne said, "Myself, I am going down."

Yves glanced over queerly. "This car...is going up."

"I have time. My engagement in the oubliette is not for another two hours."

She left these words hanging in the cold, still air.

Though he felt wary, *politesse* compelled Yves to ask, "What is happening in two hours?"

Her gaunt cheeks seemed to applaud. "The Americans are being executed."

"*Executed?*" He checked his shock and tried: "Which Americans? The moto riders who were discovered defacing the French embassy?"

Fabienne watched him coolly. "*Non.* The Blind Mice."

His hand jerked, slamming a brass rail. "Piper Jackson?"

"And Molly Wixom."

"Right, right. And you said t-two hours?"

"That will depend on the speed of the cocktail. Pancuronium bromide metabolizes at different rates in different individuals."

"Of course."

In a blink, the elevator reached the Enterprise Software floor. Yves nodded perfunctorily to the heiress, disembarked, and paced to his office with a bellyful of dread.

Time was short. Yves had pledged to look in on the captives for Durwood, to ensure they were treated humanely until a rescue mission could be attempted. Yves had given his word.

If the two women were executed, Durwood and Quaid would call off their plan—and any associated attempt to retrieve the kernel source code and restore the world's data. All possibility of salvaging Rivard LLC's legacy in this regrettable phase of history would be lost.

Yves told his secretary to hold all calls and returned to the elevators. En route, he grabbed a file folder to use as a prop—in case it became necessary to invent some cover story.

His nerves jumped. His head throbbed, had been throbbing for days. These secret collaborations carried a crushing burden, an inner pressure that jangled Yves's very bones and fibers.

He rode to the bottom of the main shaft, B2, then took the coarser basement elevator, then—after huffing hard over the fine gravel path— the teetering final platform to the limestone depths.

The air became dank and thick with static. A slow, indeterminate crumbling played about Yves's head.

He moved down the grade, hurrying, worrying.

How long was the execution protocol? When would it start? Who would administer the cocktail? Not Leathersby, one hoped. The brute was known to keep the condemned writhing at the precipice for hours —from cruelty or incompetence, none knew.

By the time Yves reached the oubliette, he felt his legs might be ten thousand years old.

He showed his badge. The jailer asked which prisoner he was visiting.

"I *visit* no one," Yves snapped. "I've come to interrogate the Americans."

The man consulted a ledger. "I don't find any interrogations in the schedule. You'll need to put a request through—"

"They're to die in minutes!" Yves slammed a quivering fist on the desk. "To the devil with schedules—if they don't talk now, their information is lost forever."

The jailer groused about the lack of notice but did finally admit Yves, ushering him through various X-ray and weapons-detection systems.

Inside, Yves quickly appraised the detainee population. It had exploded in number since he last visited mere weeks ago. *Is this simply booming demand for Forceworthy's EverLock product? Or are these all Fabienne's enemies?*

The jailer led him to the Americans' cell and stood.

"Yes, well," Yves said. "I have it from here."

The troll grunted his disapproval but did return to his station. Yves pressed his palm to the pentagon phasing in and out of the glass. The lock disengaged at once.

"*We must hurry,*" he hissed a step into the cell. "You're to be executed in two hours!"

The women looked stunned. Had they not been told?

The Jackson girl recovered first. "What's the plan?"

Yves scrubbed in his white hair, thinking. "There are lower floors— deeper in the limestone, which have been excavated but not developed. These you can hide in. Some perhaps contain nuclear or chemical waste. One cannot be choosy."

Molly lost her grip on the side of a steel egg chair. The Jackson girl's eyes stayed deadly still.

"Fine, then—*fine*," Yves spat. "Stay and meet your maker!"

After conferring briefly, they slipped on shoes and joined Yves at the cell door. He peered out at the jailer, who'd returned to his computer and was watching a monitor.

Yves yelled, "Talk! Tell now of your role in the conspiracy, or it will get worse. Much worse..."

He barked more demands, communicating with his wiry eyebrows they should play along, before bursting from the cell with apparent annoyance.

"They say nothing, *rien*," he complained to the jailer. "I must take them to the Answer Chamber."

The guard knocked his computer mouse on its pad, deactivating the screen saver.

"I see the chamber is not reserved," he said, "but you should know the bone saw is inoperable."

"What happened?" Yves said. "Did you burn through the rotors again?"

"Eh, I was on holiday yesterday. But I heard we were busy. The peacenik Swedes were processed."

Yves closed his mouth against a gag reflex. "I will make do with the tweezers and fire-hose."

The guard shrugged and let them by.

Yves charged into the frigid limestone hall. Their three sets of footsteps echoed about.

It would take twenty minutes to reach the undeveloped floors, then Yves would require another twenty getting back. Perhaps he would be discovered and need to improvise some story explaining his loss of the prisoners.

He could claim they overpowered him or received help from another party.

Neither would be believed. Perhaps he should flee with them, melt into the murky roots of Roche Rivard and await rescue. Durwood believed the rescue operation would go soon, possibly within a week.

How long could he evade capture? How would he subsist? Where would they find food and water?

None of these questions would matter if they didn't move quickly now. Yves reached back for Molly's hand, but the woman shook him off.

He was still smarting from the rebuff—women had appreciated his gallantry in younger days—when a voice sounded ahead.

"What have we come upon here?" Fabienne said. "Playing the white knight, Monsieur Pomeroy?"

The air became colder still. Yves blinked hard in disbelief. *Does she make copies of herself?* Some of the technologies in Roche Rivard were not far from it.

"I—I was taking them away for interrogation." Yves realized there was no reason his cover story to the jailer shouldn't be equally valid with Fabienne. "To extract what information we can before you...er, before the executions are carried out."

At the word "executions," Blake Leathersby bounded forth from Fabienne's shadow.

She said, "Rest your small mind, Blake. The Americans are not being executed. Not today."

She said to Yves, "I had Miss Wixom's biometrics checked against the Roche Rivard visitor logs from the last six months. What a surprise to learn you two are previously acquainted."

Yves shuddered. He'd been found out. Fabienne knew Molly and the Silicon Valley CIO were one and the same.

Zut! Of course all incoming prisoners were swabbed for DNA. Of course Fabienne would have compared the two databases and made the connection.

Why the ruse of the execution, though?

She must've read all this in his face. "To be certain," she said. "To know the extent of your betrayal. I had hoped you might be of further use to us, like an old *chemise* with many holes, which one cuts into strips for kitchen rags."

She looked down Yves's tired form with contempt. Then she faced Molly.

"A third cot will be installed in your cell," she said. "I suggest sleeping with one eye open. Monsieur Pomeroy is aged and weak, but a weak, aged pervert is a pervert still."

CHAPTER SIXTY-ONE

Durwood couldn't find a place for his boots. The cafe table had fancy wrought-iron legs that took up twice the space they ought to. Sue-Ann was under his chair, finally asleep. Her lungs had been giving her trouble, and he was not inclined to disturb her.

He tucked one boot awkwardly forward. The other he pulled up onto that knee.

The Seine flowed, black, out beyond the sidewalk. Trash bobbed along, some flaming, some just smoking. The crime sounds here were similar to those in New York. Sirens. The *shtock* of fists hitting chins.

Durwood had done a double patrol here last night. He'd done doubles every night since what he'd done to Hatch.

How many bad men had he dispatched?

Not enough.

He had prayed for forgiveness. He'd sat with Hatch when the doctor took out the stitches and fixed up the big man's Harley, which had been bleeding oil.

None of it was enough.

Quaid sat beside him across the frilly tablecloth.

"Let's go tomorrow," he said. "Monday morning. Every office in the world is sluggish on Monday morning."

Durwood tapped his bootheel. "Plan's not ripe."

"Not ripe? We've been in Paris a week, how much riper can it get?"

"Rivard's still doing construction on those tunnels."

"So we get in another way."

"We talked about that. Tunnels are best."

"You don't always get the best!" Quaid flung one arm toward Quai Saint-Bernard. "It's time, Wood. Time to play the cards we have."

They'd gone around and around on the point. After tunnels, their next option was a surgical strike though the visitors center. Some faked fire or health emergency. If they'd had the Jackson girl to disrupt electronic surveillance, maybe. But they didn't have her.

Rivard did.

Also, the pattern bothered Durwood. They had used similar tactics against Blake Leathersby in previous missions. Leathersby might be as arrogant as the men who'd built the *Titanic*, but he knew tactics. If he smelled a pattern, they were sunk.

This argument didn't sway Quaid. No, sir. Quaid was ready to waltz in with a wig and plastic nose, pull the cord on that motormouth of his, and let her rip. Like always.

But all the talk in the world wouldn't do Molly and Piper one whit of good—not if Durwood didn't beat Leathersby on tactics.

"Need those tunnels." Durwood glanced at the cafe entrance where Parisians streamed in and out. "Everywhere else, Roche Rivard is buttoned up tight as a tick."

Quaid puffed his cheeks.

A businessman entered carrying a newspaper. He looked at the line with a put-upon air. These French took their time when it came to coffee.

Quaid said, "That him?"

Durwood, aiming his head a different way, looked from under his brim.

"Yes."

The man shifted weight from one wing tip to another. Checked his watch. Squeezed his newspaper into a thin tube.

Durwood took out his notebook.

Quaid gestured to the other customers writing or sketching. "You fit right in. All you need's an earring and a beret."

The businessman ordered a croissant and drink, ate at the counter, used the john, and left.

Durwood finished jotting a note.

"Next question is scope," he said. "Is this strictly a rescue mission? Or are we goin' looking for the kernel?"

"Where would we look?"

Durwood answered flatly, "Pomeroy says it's in the Great Safe."

"You don't believe him?"

"Doesn't much matter. He says the safe's someplace in the bowels. Even if he's telling the truth, that's ten tons of limestone to search."

Quaid twisted his mouth. "Seems like a waste to blast in for Molly and Jackson but leave the kernel. Like breaking into the candy store for taffy and leaving all the fudge in the case."

Durwood didn't favor sweets himself, but he agreed with the sentiment.

Quaid asked, "Is there anyone inside we could lean on for the safe's location? What about that Thérèse Laurent, could we nab her?"

"Pomeroy said it's just immediate family that knows. The Rivards. If you buy that."

Quaid grinned. "You don't believe a word that comes out of Pomeroy's mouth, do you?"

Durwood reset his boots underneath. "The man's a known philanderer."

"So am I," Quaid said.

"There's plenty I don't trust about you either."

"Touché."

Pomeroy was more than a philanderer. He'd been a cog in Henri Rivard's immoral regime, allegedly the company's go-between with Saddam Hussein when they'd been flouting international sanctions.

"Well," Durwood said, "I figure he's right about the safe. Makes sense they'd keep that information circle small."

They talked through the pros and cons of getting just the hostages, or the hostages and kernel both. Durwood was surprised to hear

Quaid leaning toward a straight rescue. Normally, he was a home-run type. *Believe, Wood!* he'd say. *There's nothing on God's green earth you can't accomplish without belief.*

But not today. Today, he seemed to think discretion was the better part of valor.

Durwood knew Quaid had been visiting Molly's place in New Jersey. Said something about a spaghetti dinner. Might be that spaghetti dinner had something to do with it.

Women could change a man's arithmetic.

Back in West Virginia, Durwood kept a scrapbook file of keepsakes from their most daring operations—the real humdingers. Ticket stub from the Trans-Siberian railcar they froze with liquid nitrogen. Glove he wore disarming the booby-trapped Olympic torch. Quaid's scribble of that Tunisian madman's lair, which he'd drawn while blindfolded and drugged.

The most treasured item in Durwood's file was from a failed operation: an orange stocking cap. The cap his wife, Maybelle, used to hunt grouse in. She'd generally worn it in the field in Iraq, underneath her camo-helmet, but had not the morning of her capture.

Durwood had tucked it into his Kevlar, planned on pulling it snug over her ears once he had her safe.

That situation hadn't been so different from this. The Tikrit warlord knew the value of his hostage. Knew they were coming, fortified his defenses. Flat desert terrain was darn near impossible to cross unseen.

Durwood's commanding officer had reservations about a rescue. Wanted to wait for a darker moon. Wanted auxiliary extraction support from Charlie Company. Wasn't satisfied with Durwood's initial plan, insisted on seeing three-fork contingencies starting at minute one. Final document ran twenty pages.

After all that, the warlord killed her the night before the raid.

Durwood said, "Just hostages, then."

Quaid nodded. "How about tomorrow morning?"

Back to this.

"If they finish up the tunnel work," he said, "sure."

"We can only wait so long."

Durwood shifted again—his legs kept going stiff. He nudged Sue on accident. She snorted out of her doze.

"That's true," he said. "Too true."

CHAPTER SIXTY-TWO

Claude Friloux sat with his espresso and *pain au chocolat* at the counter, newspaper spread out before him.

The Stabilisation Act would pass, eh? Of course it would. The leftists loved the Anarchy, the chance to spook the calves back to Mother France's teat. Rent controls, curfew, the mandated wage. By all means, seize every choice one has!

Claude's parents' properties—which had been his grandparents' properties before, and their grandparents' before that—were bringing roughly a third of what they would have in a free market, and cost a minor fortune to secure besides. Likely, Claude would be forced to sell the ninety-foot yacht, leaving him to entertain his wife's German cousins with the forty-foot weekender.

One might as well hoist bedsheets up a canoe.

Claude picked at his gray-streaked sideburns, nursing his annoyance. Finally, he gave it up to nibble the pastry into its chocolate core. Then he sipped, savoring the bitter coffee over the firm confection—that first heavenly demi-melt in his mouth.

The caffeine set his knee twitching, his Rivard LLC badge bouncing in his pocket.

What the criminals didn't take, the socialists would. It could not be denied: his lifestyle was headed for the crapper.

Now the diuretic effects of the coffee set in, and Claude contemplated his daily trip to that literal place.

Eight a.m. Right on schedule.

He rolled *Le Figaro* into a tube and stood. *One day, I won't even have to wipe my own ass. The government will do it for me.*

Two steps into the restroom, a blow struck Claude between the shoulder blades. He crumpled to the tile.

Quick fingers raced through his pockets for ID and badge. He raised his head, wincing. Through the blurry pain, he saw a man dressed for business pressing false sideburns into his temples.

A second man bound Claude's wrists as the first pulled a wig over tousled blond hair and clipped on the stolen badge.

"How do I look?" the first said.

The second pushed his lower lip forward. "'Bout right, Mr. Friloux."

In the man's dialect, some American underclass variety, Claude's surname sounded like the croaking of a toad.

CHAPTER SIXTY-THREE

Quaid, adding Claude's usual ten-cent tip to the nine-euro tab, exited to Quai Saint-Bernard and walked two blocks to the man's Aston Martin. He found the briefcase and propped it open on the passenger seat, replacing pens and memos with more useful items.

Roche Rivard was a straight shot through the seventeenth arrondissement, but gridlock and bombed-out pavement made it an hour's drive. Quaid, still cooling off from the bathroom encounter, took advantage of the time to get into character. He raised his chin at lesser vehicles, chortled when a teenager tried carjacking him and got zapped by the silver beauty's high-end security system.

Finally, escaping Paris proper, Quaid joined the first of several feeder roads through the Boulogne Woods and into Roche Rivard. This leg of the drive was placid, the roads immaculate thanks to the automated laser turrets discouraging crime.

In another ten minutes, he crossed into the fortress's shadow. The temperature dropped precipitously. Quaid fastened another button of Claude's suit coat and angled his sportster to the first of a dozen security tollbooths set into rock.

"*Glisser votre badge,*" a guard ordered through smoked glass. Beyond his booth—beyond all the booths—lay black nothing.

Quaid reached Claude's badge out the window and pressed it to a reader.

The reader blipped green.

In his booth, the guard consulted a screen. "*Le deuxième prénom de votre sœur?*"

Quaid scanned the list of security question-answer pairs Durwood had taped to a free patch of dashboard.

"Jennett," he said, pronouncing the *t*'s, though he wasn't sure he ought to. McGill would've known.

The guard remained impassive, but a mechanism clicked in the void ahead. Simultaneously, the Aston Martin's tires were seized from below and the car jolted forward without Quaid's having moved a muscle.

He gripped the steering wheel, but it wouldn't budge. A pillbox attached to Claude's visor blinked red. The gas and brake pedals began moving independently, taking the car on a blind ride into the rock.

Quaid sensed other vehicles converging on either side.

Were they being guided by some central controller?

The temperature became even colder—he rubbed his arms and blasted the heater. The Aston Martin's speedometer showed twelve kilometers per hour. Whether he was being taken up or down, left or right, Quaid couldn't tell.

Heavy thuds sounded within the rock, mixed with the piercing shriek of an air ratchet. The dark was thick and total. Quaid had ridden Space Mountain once during a governors' convention, and this felt like that—if you added the possibility of Mickey Mouse wringing your neck with piano wire at any moment.

The car accelerated. After a minute of steady ascent, they descended rapidly. Quaid's stomach flipped. The briefcase slid to the passenger floorboard.

A sliver of blue appeared ahead. Sky?

"Not good, not what I was expecting," he muttered, wrestling the wheel again, again having no luck.

Did they already sniff me out? How?

Are they ejecting me out the side of the mountain?

As the sliver of blue broadened—it was sky, no question now—it seemed they were doing exactly that. The car vroomed down an even steeper grade. Quaid's shoulder restraint pinned his chest.

The sky came closer and closer, bigger and brighter.

A lake came into view, a speck far below. Quaid wondered in a flash if he still had control of the door locks, if he stood any better chance jumping.

Just before he reached for the handle to try, a row of license plates materialized in the darkness. There was a gap in the line of cars. The Aston Martin's winged hood ornament pointed itself for this gap as the car twisted clockwise to match the others' orientation. The front bumper screeched to a stop in a perfect row between a Renault and a Mercedes.

Quaid's heart was beating an inch outside his chest.

As the Aston Martin's engine stopped, more cars zipped into place above, below, and to either side, filling out a honeycomb-like parking structure. Quaid realized that the layout was maximally efficient, packing five times as many cars as would've fit into the same space elsewhere.

Breathing deeply, he picked up the briefcase and joined a group walking to the elevators. He didn't know which floor Claude Friloux worked on and decided not to press any buttons. He exited with the first large group disembarking, at Forty-Eight.

In a private bathroom, he spread the briefcase open and used its contents to transform again—this time into Jesse Holt.

Quaid had boned up on French in case he needed to converse as Claude with some coworker, but felt happy now to waste the prep. He much preferred living in Jesse's English-only-thanks skin.

He pulled off his Claude wig and false sideburns, installed Jesse's buckteeth and beer-belly girdle. Donned the Caterpillar vest and ball cap.

He pulled the cap snug in the mirror.

"Why, hello there," he said, trying on the Midwestern accent. "I'm with the excavation crew. Understand y'all have a few rocks need moving?"

The accent improved with each phrase. Quaid's back cracked in protest but gradually adjusted to the belly.

Jesse Holt was Quaid's favorite character. Others he'd used in his Third Chance work were more colorful, like Anatol Drachmonovik, the Russian oligopolist/hip-hop mogul, or suited him better, like Cape playboy Bret Barnaby, who was essentially Quaid with an Irish brogue.

Jesse had an easy, affable manner, able to wriggle out of trouble with a bear hug or lawyer joke. The regional touches weren't perfect. Durwood objected to the fat-lipped diction, which seemed more Southern or just plain hick than Midwestern, but Quaid contended that so long as the basic esprit was right, peripherals didn't matter.

Now, toting a toolbox, cinching his belt, Quaid left the bathroom. He nearly plowed into a woman in glasses.

"*Excusez-moi.*" She did a double take at his appearance. "*Puis-je vous aider à trouver quelque chose?*"

Quaid rubbed a knuckle in his ear. "Come again, miss?"

She tried another query in French.

Quaid said, "Thanks, but I ate my breakfast already. Éclair from the buffet. Chocolate, crème filled."

At this non sequitur, the woman crinkled her nose and walked on.

Quaid mopped his brow. *Nelly, I'm hot all of a sudden.* He returned to the main elevator and rode it to its bottom, B2. When Rivard employees looked sideways at him, Quaid raised his toolbox or gave one nostril a quick pick—both were effective at deflecting curiosity.

Riding the second freight-like elevator, he encountered various workmen. One whose hard hat bore a telecommunications logo. A team of four wearing gas masks and gloves, carrying a crate with smoke billowing from its seams.

"Gents," Quaid said, touching his cap.

Everything was going according to Hoyle. The gun was ready in his toolbox. Quaid's biometrics had not been taken. They'd chosen Claude Friloux in part for his security clearance, which had presumably spared Quaid greater scrutiny. (Even if the parking privileges had almost given him a heart attack.)

So long as Durwood held up his end of the plan—and there were few surer bets than Durwood Oak Jones on a military mission—they would meet up at the oubliette. Spring Molly and Piper Jackson. Then beat it.

Quaid almost wondered if he should be dragging his feet. He'd heard no booms or exploding charges. What if he reached the oubliette first? Would he need to overcome the guards solo, or just hang out and wait?

He crunched his work boots deliberately over gravel, thankful for the thick Caterpillar gear. The walls changed from wood paneled to raw limestone. The smells, which Quaid couldn't quite peg, were making him feel a little floaty.

The third elevator, he knew from Molly's first trip to the bowels, lay around another bend or two.

Quaid began mentally preparing his script for the oubliette guard. Ideally, he would be permitted through initial security before drawing his gun. Could he claim there was excavation work to be done in the dungeon itself? Was it complete or still being developed? Pomeroy hadn't known.

He could say a particular cell needed repair. Or that one of the automated systems—nutrition, hydration, waste removal—was on the fritz.

But would Caterpillar really handle those? More likely, Rivard would use electrician or tech types, probably local.

Quaid began to feel a more intense cold—rigidness in the hairs of his inner ear—and knew he was nearing the final shaft. He edged around a corner.

A party of three riders preceded him. They stood in front of a void that was full black except for a thick, lilting cable.

Quaid planted his foot to retreat, but too late. The lead figure—in a midthigh skirt that must've been impossibly cold—whirled.

"*Bonjour,*" Fabienne Rivard said.

Now the others turned, Blake Leathersby and Thérèse Laurent—whom Quaid dimly recalled from Hotel Zauberberg.

Leathersby said, "Where do you think you're going, mate?"

They didn't seem to recognize him. Jesse was a thick disguise, after all. Clearly, Quaid was in a pickle, though. He combed through Jesse's stock phrases, one-liners he'd dropped in previous high-pressure situations. None seemed to fit here.

"Repairs." He scratched underneath his ball cap. "Supposed to be repairing some facilities down in the...whaddaya call 'em, bowels? Down in them bowels."

Leathersby and Thérèse looked to Fabienne.

The heiress asked, "And who is your point of contact?"

Quaid shifted in place, the gravel sounding sinister underfoot. He and Durwood had prepped for this question, but somehow he felt the answer they'd agreed upon wasn't going to fly now.

Able to think of no alternative, he said, "Yves Pomeroy."

Leathersby chuckled derisively.

Fabienne said, "That will be a problem."

CHAPTER SIXTY-FOUR

Stuffing the last explosives in a shoulder bag, Durwood heard a whimper. The box cart was packed and ready, ten flights down at street level, dressed up like a food cart. Anyone peeking under that tarp wouldn't find coffee and croissants. He needed to get rolling.

Durwood zipped the bag. He heard another whimper.

"Nope." He started for the fire escape. "No room in the cart, girl."

Sue-Ann stood in the middle of the hotel room, eyes droopy.

"Y'be fine," Durwood said. "Rest your hip."

The dog scrabbled forward a step. Her leg hitched, face pained. The overseas trip had been hard.

"Well," he said.

She urged hopefully toward him.

Durwood rubbed the base of his neck. If he rejiggered the frag grenades at the bottom, she might fit. Just. It wouldn't be a pleasure cruise.

"Alright," he said. "I'll carry you."

Ten flights would've taken her an hour, and he couldn't risk boarding an elevator with all these explosives.

Durwood controlled his breaths under the strain of the dog and bag. He hated to reward a beg, but he hadn't liked the idea of leaving her behind either.

This mission had a great chance of failure. Sue-Ann was old and unlikely to take a new master. This way might be better.

They reached the street. Parisian kids were poking around the box cart. Durwood lowered the dog gently and, shooing off the kids, ducked underneath the tarp.

He knew the configuration of items by feel. Swiftly, he added the charges and made Sue a space, hoisted her in.

She yipped when her haunch knocked against a rifle scope.

"Sorry," he said. "Gonna be rough going."

He had double-cased anything combustible. The frags, the breach charges, full loadouts for the shot, sniper, and assault guns. A few other goodies.

The entry point he'd chosen was on Rue Leclair, six blocks up. Durwood released the wheel brake and pushed. A man in a chartreuse coat asked him for something. He kept his head down, kept pushing.

The entrance to Rivard's tunnel system looked like a regular subway vent. Wide grate, steam wisping up. He bent until the knees of his blue jeans touched the heavy-gauge metal, then peered down into the chasm.

He took a crowbar from the box cart. Sue-Ann, curled in a corner, raised an eyelid.

He whispered, "'Bout ready to take a ride?" and felt glad she'd come.

Durwood waited for a lull in traffic before spinning out a half dozen bolts and prying up the grate. Then he lowered a pair of two-by-fours into the void until they stopped with a *thunk*.

Each board had a magnet drilled into its end. He leaned hard to be sure they'd anchored to the rails. Then he pulled the box cart around and eased its treads onto the boards, guiding it down the makeshift ramp.

The box cart grooved nicely onto Rivard's track below. He twisted on a microlight in his belt. Where the street grate was coarse and weathered, made to look antique, the track was gleaming steel.

Durwood shoved the boards back aboveground, abandoning them, and replaced the grate. He took a seat on top of the weaponry and reached down for the pull cord.

The box cart felt steady. Durwood had given her firm axles and minimal suspension. Three sides were built of walnut and the fourth brown maple, all reclaimed from street furniture. He'd teased out the grains with fine sandpaper, foolishly. Odds were this contraption would meet its end as a pile of splinters.

He yanked the cord. The pinions caught, and the old Bendix drive began chugging.

He tracked their position on a handheld GPS device. The precise layout of Rivard's tunnel system was unknown. Whether it was a grid or hub and spoke. American Dynamics didn't know. Jim Steed had given him what maps and coordinates they had. The Anarchy had crippled shipping routes—thieves took half or more of all cargo—and the tunnels allowed Rivard to get its products through safely.

It figured this Leclair track led back to Roche Rivard, somehow or other. Did it pass through checkpoints? Were the cars that rode it controlled autonomously so a lone vehicle like his—dumb, unconnected—was at risk of crashing?

Durwood didn't know.

He had walked the tunnels a bit, scouting. Not nearly the number he would've liked to. Tunnel construction had already pushed their operation right up against AmDye's planned attack on the inner shaft. Luke Skywalker flying into the Death Star.

Steed said it could come any day. Today, even.

The box cart moved west. Dank air whistled by, rippling Durwood's hat. Pebbles glanced off his face. The cart's engine ran quiet—for gas, anyhow—and zipped along decently. Every ten-odd yards, a purple LED tube gave off just enough light to suggest the tunnel's sides.

They were close. Eighteen, twenty inches from the box cart either way.

The cool temperature was ideal for a variety of shipments. Durwood detected the hum of various electronics behind the rock. These tunnels weren't built slapdash. Not in six months. Not in a year, even. They'd been planned for a while.

Durwood worked a throttle and hand brake. He moved slower through turns, faster in straightaways. Quaid—or Claude, or Jesse, whoever he was at this moment—could only talk his way so far. At some point, he would need what Durwood had in the cart.

Firepower.

Ten minutes along, Sue-Ann sat up. Durwood heard her fingernails on the box-cart floor.

"Sue? What do you have?"

Her mottled nose twitched. Now Durwood felt it too. A slight pressure behind his eyes. The air different, sharper. Compressed. He felt moisture on his neck.

A light came into view. Just a pinprick but growing. With it came a faint fizz. Like the bacon Maybelle used to sizzle up on Saturday mornings.

The light got bigger. A headlight.

As the noise became thunderous and the lead car resolved, Durwood saw it was, like the box cart, nearly as wide as the tunnel itself.

There were turnouts, recesses every so often where you could get off the main track. The last one had been a minute or two ago.

Should we head back for it? Or go forward and try catching the next?

He hit the throttle.

The oncoming car bellowed toward them. Bigger. Fizzing louder, angrier. Durwood felt sure it was unmanned and would thoughtlessly slam them to kingdom come.

The wind pinned his ears as they accelerated. Sue-Ann mewed—a high, pitiful sound.

At the last moment, a break in the rock wall appeared. Durwood forced his boot down through the ammunition and charges, finding the rudder pedal, squeezing the hand brake as hard as he dared.

The cart decelerated quickly and veered into the turnout. Rubber catches in the track stopped them altogether, smelling like an inferno in the Michelin factory. Durwood slammed forward into a crate of C-4 cartridges.

The train rushed by, deafening. Durwood felt like some raccoon was digging through his shirt to his innards. Displaced air rattled guns and grenades. The noise Dopplered ten seconds past the turnout, after the train's butt end had disappeared.

Durwood shut his eyes and relaxed.

It became routine, pulling aside every few minutes. Each train had its own unique sound. One shorter train gave off an urgent *zing—a-zing-a-zing*. Another came up behind them with a low grumble that put Durwood in mind of cattle at the trough—if you imagined some real hungry, insistent cows.

After this last turnout, Durwood checked GPS. They'd been moving a while, and the rock seemed changed. More porous. More fully muting the sounds of the Bendix engine.

The GPS beacon put him smack underneath Roche Rivard.

Their slope had been downward, Durwood felt confident. How sharply, though? How low had they gone?

According to schematics provided by AmDye spies, there were four possible chambers in this latitude-longitude range. Three were not good.

The topmost area was marked "experimental nanoblade." Durwood tapped into a note and read that Rivard was developing blades one atom thick, capable of slicing O_2 molecules into two single oxygens. This was presumed to be military tech, since "any single oxygen that didn't react with its mate would immediately react with the nasal passages of anyone who breathed, causing severe burns or asphyxiation."

The next level down held a grow house of carnivorous plants. Fabienne Rivard had given a TED Talk predicting ore-based weaponry would be history within three hundred years, and this research was thought to be her answer. Man-eating plants with constricting chutes and leeching tendrils and enzymes that could melt skin. The AmDye notes speculated the area would be recognizable by humidity and a low green light.

Below the grow house was the hyperdark chamber. Intel was scant here. "Characterized by extreme lack of light, owing to unknown (subatomic?) forces. Future applications: Unknown. Survivability: Unknown." Night-vision goggles were useless. There was no ambient light to enhance.

The fourth possibility was the oubliette.

Durwood leaned an elbow into the turnout wall, head propped. His forearms quivered from the work of steering the box cart. Sue sat up.

They could keep moving, follow the track to wherever it spilled out. Durwood had hoped exit would be possible straight from the rock, underground, but no. Most likely the track spiraled up aboveground.

Where there would be sentries. Scanners.

"What do you say, girl?"

He knuckled the rock. How thick were these walls? Three feet? Four?

He reached into the cart for Sue-Ann, lifting her, setting her on the track side of the box cart. The box cart would shield her some.

Next, he removed a charge from the cart. A four-inch-wide frame charge. He had used such weapons to breach militant hideouts in Iraq.

He squinted at the limestone.

Is that sucker rebar reinforced?

He put back the frame charge, took out a demolition charge instead. A full foot across.

He took out a second.

Using duct tape, he attached both charges to the wall at waist weight. Any higher risked a cave-in. Much lower, and the floor would sap the explosion of its full force.

He wired six feet of det cord to the charge, draping it around the cart and squatting by Sue. Under less dire circumstances, Durwood enjoyed explosives. As a boy, he'd watched the coal outfits blast chunks out of the West Virginia mountainside. He used to set off his own firecrackers to coincide with theirs.

Later, in the army, it had fascinated him that a little bridgewire and powder thrown together could wreak such havoc. He learned anything he could. When to use a granular versus a gelatin charge. The proper length of fuses. How you went about predicting projectiles.

No matter how far his skill progressed, his fascination stayed. His awe for the big boom.

He struck a match. *Pffft.*

The det cord became a hissing snake of orange. Ash traveled up the charge, dropping fine dust to the limestone floor.

The hiss ran to the end of the det cord and stopped for a pregnant quarter second. The sinews of Sue-Ann's neck stuck out.

Then: *GOOOOOMMM.*

The concussive impact hit Durwood like two tons of water. The box cart, thrown off its track, compressed his knees and boots. Watermelon-size chunks were falling all around, and a terrible ring spiraled in his ears.

He crawled free of the cart and looked over its top. The wall was no more. A giant crater started halfway up, taking much of the ceiling too. The rubble below stacked up nicely like stairs.

Durwood outfitted himself with shot and assault guns, an ammo vest, electrostatic monitor, among other equipment.

As he climbed into the bowels of Roche Rivard, exact point of entry unknown, Durwood heard nothing but ringing.

Did I blow my eardrums?

He would need his hearing in this fight. His hearing, and plenty more.

He punched out a last shard of limestone and stepped through, Sue at his heel. The light was low and green. His skin felt creepy-crawly and the base of his throat furry.

His ears continued to ring. He snapped thumb and forefinger hard, flush to the side of his head—and heard fine.

It wasn't his eardrums. It was the alarm.

CHAPTER SIXTY-FIVE

The noise was piercing, like a fire alarm at Karen's school if you had your ear pressed right up against the bell. I wrapped my arms around my head and waited for the siren to stop.

It didn't. It wailed on and on.

I looked to Piper. She'd tucked deeper into her steel egg chair, face bitter.

Only our new cellmate, Yves Pomeroy, rose with the noise.

"*L'alarme primaire!*" he cried. "I cannot believe! I thought never again in my lifetime would I hear it."

He canted his ear as though he were listening to the Vienna Philharmonic.

I asked over the screech, "What's the *alarme primaire?*"

"It means the building has been breached," he said. "There is but one explanation: Roche Rivard is under attack!"

Now his excitement caught to me because I knew exactly who must be responsible. Quaid and Durwood. I didn't know how, or where, or have the faintest idea what their plan was, but it had to be them.

I looked to Piper. "This is it. This is our chance."

She was nodding, already out of her chair and fetching the mechanical insect from behind the toilet. She detached the tail controller and got it aloft. I hurried to watch the terminal display over her shoulder.

Yves's expression was dumbstruck as the insect skittered below the ceiling, out of our cell, and into the oubliette lobby.

The guard didn't notice, typing busily at his computer. Did *he* know what to make of the *alarme primaire*? Was he trying to disable it?

We lost sight of him as our insect veered from the lobby, down a hallway we'd scoped out in advance. Piper worked the joystick with a steady practiced thumb, guiding, the insect skimming below the ceiling, farther, farther...

"There!" I said, pointing.

Piper had already seen and started backtracking, spinning the insect around and aiming its camera eyes at the discoloration.

It was a thin horizontal line, orange, bisecting one of the cutouts in the limestone just below the ceiling.

Piper said, "Do it?"

I nodded.

She jabbed her thumb forward, accelerating the insect into the line. The orange beam got bigger in the terminal screen, then very big, then disappeared as the insect passed through it.

I rushed to the glass to check the guard. He'd left his computer and was moving toward the limestone cutout—just as he had other times an insect had inadvertently tripped the light beam.

"He bit!"

Piper dropped the controller in her egg chair and joined me at the cell glass. I slicked my hand along the glass, waiting for the feathery blue pentagram to show itself. It did a moment later, and I aligned my palm.

The security sensor, disabled at the insistence of Leathersby and others annoyed by its frequent malfunctions, flashed green. The cell unlocked. I pushed through.

Piper cut her eyes back at Yves Pomeroy. "We taking him?"

I looked at Yves—scrambling to put on shoes, fighting his palsy. "I think so. We might need him."

We sprinted through the oubliette lobby. Other prisoners were backed into the corners of their cells against the earsplitting *alarme primaire.* One man lay naked on the ground, his butt in the air, trying to squeeze through a gap by the floor.

I kept my eyes forward and steps quiet. We probably weren't the only ones who'd figured out the locks were disabled, and I didn't think we should advertise the fact that we were choosing this exact moment to exploit the weakness. It's like those kids movies where all the dogs escape from evil animal control. Karen always hops up to her knees and yells, *Get away, doggies, run!*

Springing all *these* prisoners, I felt, might not deliver a feel-good ending.

At the empty guard station, Piper pivoted for the limestone hallway.

"No," I said. "Not yet."

I took a step toward the darkest, longest tunnel in the oubliette.

Piper said, "We gotta hurry. You said yourself."

"I know, we do," I said. "But first we have to try."

I bulged my eyes meaningfully. Piper growled into her shoulder—but did follow me. Yves Pomeroy followed too, though he quickly fell behind our pace. We scampered down the tunnel, deadening our footsteps as best we could, counting on the distraction of the alarm.

Now we'd probably have to overcome the guard. He was going to investigate the disturbed sensor, find nothing amiss, and return to his post. We wouldn't be able to slip by and disappear into the bowels—like we could have if we'd gone straight.

Still, I believed this was right.

A healthy hike later, we reached the end: a thin, oblong window. I laid my palm against a reader mounted in the limestone. The cell door opened. Piper and I walked forward into sickly yellow light. A figure was shriveled in one corner beneath either rags or a blanket.

Is it moving? Are we too late?

Piper and I approached the figure cautiously, as though it could be booby-trapped, filled with explosives or a den of tarantulas.

"*Mon Dieu!*" came a voice behind.

Yves Pomeroy had caught up. He rushed forward, unsteady on spindly legs, and hunched beside the figure.

"Henri, you live!" he cried. "What have they... How did this... Why, *why*?"

He wept and clawed the air beseechingly.

"No time for waterworks," I said, dropping to my knees next to the Rivard golden oldies. *Ninety seconds*, I thought. *If he can't tell us in ninety seconds, we have to bolt.*

Henri Rivard was sleeping, or dead, or in a coma; it was hard to tell. A rats'-nest beard reached halfway down his chest. His unshod feet were cracked and withered.

Yves shook him by the shoulders until his eyes opened.

"Henri! Can you hear? It is me, your great *ami*!"

The wasting man gradually began tracking Yves's face. He registered the merest shock, then a smile spread across his lips.

Then, with the cunning of a scorpion, he looked up to me.

I wasted no time. "The Great Safe, where is it? What level? How do we get there?"

Yves reared up at the question—at the audacity of our plan, which we hadn't shared with him. Henri's eye glazed, going to some inward place.

Piper said, "Let's beat it. There ain't nobody home."

I had to agree. Henri would show flashes of recognition but didn't seem to have the comprehension or stamina to carry on a conversation. I wondered how much could be blamed on the dementia begun when he was still CEO of Rivard versus the brutality he'd endured here.

How does Fabienne sleep at night?

Yves insisted, "Give him time! He's been rotting here who knows how long? He deserves time to—"

"No," I said. "From what I've heard, he doesn't deserve anything— and we have no time to give anyway. Escape is our first objective. The kernel is just a bonus, if—"

"Shaaaaafft."

The interruption was barely audible over the bleating alarm. Piper, Yves, and I all bent to Henri, who grimaced from the effort of speech.

"Shaft?" I said. "The inner shaft, you mean? The Great Safe is in the inner shaft?"

He managed a feeble head shake. "Elevator...b-bottom...shaft."

He clutched his throat as though these words had parched him of his last moisture.

The bottom shaft? I thought back that lowest elevator, its car dangling in the irregular void. Quiet. Damp. Fathomless. So very black.

"The Great Safe is underneath the third elevator shaft?"

Henri Rivard bobbed his head.

"But that's— How deep does it..." I tried to remember, the two times I'd taken it, what the shaft looked like beyond the car. "How would you get down there?"

Using two gnarled fingers, Henri simulated a running jump.

"Hell no," Piper said. "I'm supposed to dive down an invisible hole because some evil mastermind says so?"

Yves Pomeroy quivered with excitement. "No, no—it is brilliant! *He* is brilliant! Below the bowels, one reaches the water table. The greatest secrets encased in water, of course!"

I said, "So you swim to the Great Safe?"

Henri joined his hands and, weakly, split them in a breaststroke pantomime.

"Hell no," Piper said again.

I rubbed my eyes vigorously. The thought of retrieving the kernel was tantalizing, but I wasn't wild about diving blind into an underground reservoir—then swimming for who knew how long, then facing whatever else security Rivard had installed around the Great Safe. Swinging scythes? Killer bats?

"We don't have to decide now," I said. "Let's get out of the oubliette first. We need to surprise that guard—if he sees we're gone, he'll be ready for us."

Piper and I stood to go. Yves tried boosting Henri by his elbow.

"No chance," I said. "He's gotta stay, he'd slow us way down."

"We must save him," Yves said. "Look, you can see his condition is beastly!"

I glanced around, thinking of all the horrors in these bowels—many of which Henri had dreamed up. "What goes around comes around."

Yves protested further, but even Henri seemed to understand the impossibility of joining us. He patted his friend's cheek.

"Go," he croaked.

Then Henri looked to me. "At the end...at the very end...it will be dark."

I squinted. "Dark. Okay, got it."

The old man wished us *bonne chance.*

Yves kissed his own fingertips. "I will never forget the Rhône valley, spreading jam over fresh baguettes with those twins, the farmer's daughters. They were from heaven, *oui?*"

Henri smiled at the memory.

"Spare us the sex-plunder bromance," I said. "We're going, Pomeroy."

I led the way back to the oubliette lobby, moving rapidly in a stoop. The purple tube lights fizzed in and out. The *alarme primaire* continued blaring, and now faint rumblings and sharp pops—gunfire?—sounded in the distance.

Reaching the hall the guard had taken to investigate our mechanical insect's distraction, I stopped. I edged up to the passageway and, exposing just one shoulder and half my face, peered in. I saw no guard.

"*Damn,*" I heard behind me.

Piper was looking past me, straight through the lobby to our cell. A group of people was standing at the entrance, examining the door, eyes roaming to every corner of the empty cell. Fabienne Rivard. Blake Leathersby. Thérèse Laurent.

And behind them, bound and gagged, Quaid and Durwood.

Even at a distance, I could see Durwood had been roughed up. His face looked like the last eggplant in the supermarket bin, and one shoulder seemed to sag. His hat brim was charred.

The oubliette guard was inside the cell, gesturing defensively to Fabienne.

Piper said, "We can get by. They're arguing, let's go."

She began scampering low to the ground. There was no time to debate—I hugged the far wall through the lobby, past other cells, past the guard's vacated computer.

Out the corner of my eye, I saw Leathersby holding the insect controller we'd left behind, twisting it in his hands with a thick expression.

The oubliette exit was swinging open. We made it there unseen and dashed out to the limestone hall. I pulled the door quietly shut behind us. Piper took a step uphill.

"Wait!" I said. "We have to help the guys."

"How d'you figure?" Her eyes zipped up the ramp—aboveground to freedom, or to the elevator shaft Henri had said contained the Great Safe.

"*They came for us*," I said.

"And? I don't owe them a thing."

I argued we had to do something—signal to them, leave a weapon they could discover, something. If they hadn't tripped the alarm, we'd still be captives.

"And if I'd have turned and run the first time I saw 'em," Piper said, "I would've never been here in the first place."

Yves chimed in, "People are not perfect. One accepts the good with the bad."

Piper and I looked at each other.

She said, "Guess he's the expert on that."

Before we could agree on a course, the sound of rustling pebbles interrupted. Instinctively, I flattened to the limestone. Piper joined me. Wet moss seeped between my fingers.

The pebbles' noise had a rhythm to it—slow, halting. It was getting closer.

Sue-Ann trotted up. She was carrying a bag in her mouth.

"*Sue!*" I whisper-shouted.

She doggie-smiled, even as her whole body crimped toward the bad hip, and dropped the bag at my feet.

I unzipped and looked inside. It was stuffed with guns, grenades, ammunition cartridges.

"Oh. My. *God!* How did you even carry this, Sue?"

She kept smiling. Smiling and panting.

Piper said, "This is some weird Benji stuff, but it doesn't change a thing. I'm going."

When she started up the limestone, Sue-Ann unleashed a low, deep howl.

I knelt and rubbed under the dog's jaw. "Aw, Sue. What is it? What do you want?"

She limped toward the oubliette, shaky but resolute. She wanted her master.

CHAPTER SIXTY-SIX

iper tried to keep moving up, but I knew she wouldn't get far. With every step she took, the dog's moans became louder and more plaintive.

"Mmm-nnn. Nn*nnn*."

The sound seemed to come from deep in Sue-Ann's chest, pleading, soulful.

Piper turned around. "No."

Sue dipped one droopy ear like she hadn't quite caught that. "*Mmm?*"

Yves Pomeroy and I stood in a line with Sue.

Piper's wheeze was audible ten yards away, even over the alarm.

We divvied up weapons. I took the biggest pistol, black with a skinny cylindrical scope. Piper took the second biggest—silver, wood handle. Both were loaded.

We weren't sure whether or not to arm Yves. Between the palsy and his split loyalties, it seemed chancy.

He argued, "If I get a shot at the Brit"—meaning Leathersby—"I assure you, my aim will be true."

We gave him a gun.

I worried Sue-Ann would run ahead to the oubliette before we'd made a plan—she wore no collar, I had no leash—but she seemed to grok the situation, staying out of sight in the small recess we'd found in the wall.

Piper voted to shoot first and ask questions later. "Three bad guys, three of us, three guns. Simple."

I said, "If we can rescue the guys without killing, let's not kill."

Squatting knee to knee, we talked through the options. A furious firefight or a tense showdown—which favored us? Which gave us the best odds of survival?

Voices at the oubliette door stopped the argument.

We retreated deeper into the wall recess. Sue-Ann's tail stuck out into the tunnel; I pulled it in. We packed in tight. I was using my gun and two knees as points of balance. Yves almost sneezed, raising up with a huff, but he pinched his nose at the last moment.

"...*obvious they have escaped,*" Fabienne Rivard was saying at the head of her group. "You disabled the palm locks, imbecile that you are, and the Americans took advantage."

The guard who was being dressed down pulled a big-bellied version of Quaid after him.

"People always complained!" The guard pointed to Leathersby. "He said they were a nuisance, they annoyed him. So I turned them off—"

"Quit passing the buck," the mercenary said. "You screwed up, mate. Own it."

Leathersby pushed Durwood ahead in a painful-looking half nelson, his forearm coiled about Durwood's neck.

The group spilled out to the limestone hall, bickering and glaring at each other. Fabienne scanned left and right. Thérèse, a step behind, parroted the movement.

Sue-Ann growled beside me.

I looked to Piper. She nodded.

"*Freeze!*" I said as we both burst out, aiming our guns.

Yves Pomeroy tottered out too. "By article six-point-two of the Rivard bylaws, I seize control of this once-great company!"

Leathersby rolled his eyes, giving Durwood a needless jab to the ribs.

"Stop, *let them go*," I said. "Right now!"

Piper stuck the barrel of her gun in Leathersby's face, digging her fingernails into one of his biceps. When he didn't release Durwood, she gripped the gun overhand and—quick as milk boiling over on the stove—drove it into Leathersby's teeth.

Durwood scampered away as Leathersby spit blood and swore.

"You *bitch*, Goddamn it!" he roared.

"That's for touching me," Piper said. "Gimme a reason to shoot. Just one."

As she kept her sights on Leathersby, I trained mine on Fabienne. Her hollow-cheeked face showed no sign of panic or distress. In fact, she was smiling.

"The woman will save the cowboys this time, eh?" She licked her lips. "A different script."

I flicked my gun toward Quaid and the guard holding him. "Tell your man to let him go. Let him go or I shoot."

"I think not."

"I *will*." I brought my offhand onto the barrel, steadying. Every nerve in my body twitched. "And you'd deserve it for all you've done to the world."

She sucked in, making a noise like rattlers at the bottom of a pit. "Perhaps you would. But not for that reason. Not for the world."

I felt my brow crimping. "You've destroyed society. You've destroyed our civility."

"Mmm*mmmm*, yes. From you, though, I've taken more. Haven't I?"

She took a hip-jutting stride toward Quaid. Through his Caterpillar vest, she stroked his chest.

"Your man," she said. "I took your man."

"I—I don't know what you mean," I said, scrambling to understand what all Fabienne knew. Clearly, Quaid's Cat cover was blown. "Er, what're you even referring to—"

"In Davos. On a Louis the Fourteenth couch." She ran her fingers through Quaid's wavy hair. "It was enjoyable, though not our best."

Quaid's face was hard to read—those giant false teeth didn't help—but the former politician looked queasy. He tried moving his head away, but the guard held him in place. Fabienne continued to fondle his hair, pressing her fingers roughly about his ear and temple.

"Let him go," I repeated.

My voice cracked. I felt like I'd been slugged in the heart, but I refused to be distracted.

To Piper, I muttered, "We could lock them up in our old cell."

In the instant she took her eyes off him, Leathersby whipped his own pistol from a holster.

"Ah-ha, there we are." He ran his thumb lovingly over its hammer. "My good friend, the Webley top-break. Finest revolver known to man."

Sue-Ann loped up to Durwood and dropped yet another gun at his boots.

Durwood picked it up with a grimace. "Could be. If that man forgets about the M9 semiautomatic."

Now four people were armed, one on their side and three on ours. The two professionals—Leathersby and Durwood—were locked onto each other, wrists stiff, mouths ugly with hate.

Purple tube lights fizzed from ceiling corners. Far off, water dripped slowly.

Plop.

Plop.

Plop.

Quaid, still in the guard's grip, was staring intently at me, his blue eyes desperate to send some message.

I wasn't accepting.

I looked at Piper to see if she had any ideas.

Piper looked back with the same question in her eyes.

Fabienne said, "I am bored."

Now Sue-Ann, who alone in the standoff seemed free to roam around, trotted back to her bag and picked up a clay-colored block.

She dropped the block on the limestone ramp and sniffed it thoroughly.

Quaid said, "Hey Sue, that, uh...that's no chew toy."

She kept sniffing. After several curious moments, her milky eyes raised to Durwood. His steel-gray eyes looked back. Some meaning passed between man and dog.

She picked the block up, carried it to a point between the two factions, and dropped it.

Leathersby said, "Control your animal, Jones. The mutt may be at death's door herself but she don't have to take the lot of us with her."

Durwood took a calloused finger off his M9.

"I told you before," he snarled. "Sue's no mutt. Her ma and pa were blueticks both."

Seeming to sense she was the topic of conversation, Sue-Ann approached Leathersby and began licking his boot.

"Git, *git off!*" the Brit said.

He kicked, missing her at first, then connecting with Sue's head.

The sound was sickening.

"You're despicable," I said.

"That's no way to talk to your uncle Blakey," he said. "We shoulda spent more time getting to know each other in the oubliette."

Sue-Ann's gait, which had hitched to the right for as long as I'd known her, zigzagged now. She tried walking to Durwood but staggered, veering toward the Rivard side of the ramp. Then she fell. Then she stood weakly and turned in a circle.

"Oh, Sue," I said, starting for her.

She fell again. When she recovered to stand, her eyes shone with new wildness. She darted away from me.

She's confused—she must see me as a threat. Leathersby knocked the sense out of her.

I stopped at the clay-colored block and raised my hands, trying to look nonthreatening.

Fabienne performed a breathy sigh. "The dog show has run its course." She gestured to Piper and me. "They will not shoot. Blake, kill them."

Durwood poised his finger on the M9 trigger. "Go on, Blake. Try me."

Leathersby bristled, clearing his throat, seeming ill at ease.

Fabienne was wrong about the dog show: it wasn't over.

Sue-Ann lurched and wobbled and fell again, and stood, and fell, and took three ferocious bounds—a greyhound would've been proud —and bit the guard.

"Owww!" the man shrieked, losing his grip on Quaid.

Quaid sprinted to our side, his beer belly swinging. He pushed me away from the clay-colored block and toward the recess in the limestone.

Piper ran there, too, bumping Pomeroy into the recess as she went.

Durwood called, "Sue, *come!*" and, waiting no more than a two-count for her to join us, fired at the block.

CHAPTER SIXTY-SEVEN

Q uaid made it into the wall recess last, and felt the explosion as some leviathan's belching of force and debris. Limestone fragments showered the group. He wrapped Molly in his arms and they held on tight, heads in each other's chest. Gritty smoke stung his eyes and filled his nose.

Once the air had settled, a quiet whistling could be heard. Molly looked down. Quaid's eyes followed.

A rock shard had pierced Jesse Holt's belly.

Quaid shrugged off the girdle and dashed back to the tunnel to check whether it was still passable. Visibility was poor—the blast had taken out most of the purple tube lights.

The ceiling and walls were caved in, forming a barrier of rubble where the charge had gone off. The jagged, freshly exposed limestone showed a film of green sludge that made Quaid wonder what got released into the earth below Roche Rivard.

Voices penetrated the rubble.

"Clear it, *immédiatement!*"

"That could be five bloody yards thick."

"That's not my concern, find a way. Make a passage!"

It was Fabienne and Blake Leathersby, shouting at each other. She'd get her way sooner or later and they would make it through.

Molly and Durwood had joined Quaid in the tunnel. The trio twisted from the rubble up the limestone ramp, the only direction open to them.

Quaid asked, "Will we run into the supply tunnels going this way?"

Durwood shook his head. "They're lower."

Molly and Piper were already hustling up, with Yves Pomeroy tottering after.

"*The Great Safe is this way*," Molly urged. "It's at the bottom of the third elevator shaft!"

Quaid looked between her and the rubble, through which *chinks* could now be heard. He wasn't sure about this Great Safe business, but up did seem to be their only option.

So up they went—over the same ground Quaid had covered not twenty minutes ago, bullied ahead by Leathersby after Fabienne Rivard had seen through his disguise. The distance felt longer now. He kept stepping wrong in the dark. The frequent tunnel switchbacks surprised him. Once, he ran into Yves Pomeroy's back. Then Piper ran into his.

Sue-Ann intermittently howled as if answering the alarm. She kept losing her balance and veering sideways, aftereffects of Leathersby's brutal kick.

Durwood slipped back to the rear. They'd only been moving a few minutes when he called ahead, "They're through."

Quaid kept scrambling higher, running beside Molly at the head of the group. Far back, he heard cursing and rock-slapping stilettos.

Something hard poked his back. He turned and found Piper Jackson trying to give him a pistol.

"Your boy's passing out guns." The hacker held up a silver one. "I already helped myself."

"We'll assume the French have some Second Amendment equivalent," Quaid said, taking the weapon and continuing to move.

Popping, cracking echoes surrounded them in the tunnel—wave after wave of sharp sound. Durwood was taking fire. And returning it.

Yves Pomeroy flinched continuously. Piper squatted at Durwood's bootheel and squeezed off more suppressing fire. The walls trembled around them.

Do not think about the fault line, Quaid told himself. *Do not think about the fault line...*

The ascent seemed endless, but finally, they reached the third elevator shaft. Quaid rushed to the precipice before skidding to a stop.

"Whoa now," he said, peering down into the void.

Molly joined him, brushing shoulders, her breaths quick and hard in his ear. "Okay, we made it."

"Lucky us." Quaid poised his finger over the single unmarked button. "You sure about this Great Safe? Might be easier to—"

"No!" Molly yanked his finger away, burying it against her thigh. "I mean yes, but we're not taking the elevator up. You have to go down."

Quaid felt a crease appear in his forehead. He pulled a hand through his wavy hair, having lost Jesse's wig a while ago.

"How? Do we climb down or something?" He gestured to the cable, which would've required a good seven- or eight-foot leap into the chasm.

Sue-Ann's paws worried at the edge of the shaft. Durwood called her back. The air here was biting and made Quaid miss Jesse's bulk.

Molly said, "You have to get to the very bottom. It's water down there."

"Meaning..."

"You jump. Then swim."

As Quaid acclimated himself to this information, Durwood peered down and asked how she'd found that out.

Molly explained Henri Rivard had told them.

"Wait—you talked to *Henri Rivard*?" Quaid said.

Questions rushed to mind. Where had she found Henri? Why should they trust a single word out of that crook's mouth? Before he could put any of these into words, their pursuers' footsteps—which Durwood had temporarily silenced—got loud.

The ex-Marine said, "We need to go. Or try something else."

Meantime, he removed three grenades from his shoulder bag, which was caked stiff with dust. Threading the pins between the knuckles of one hand, he pulled all three in a single jerk and hurled them around a switchback.

The blasts came in succession, three gigantically amplified pinball *plings*. The footsteps stopped—for now.

Quaid said, "If Henri Rivard told you to take a running leap off a cliff, which isn't far off from what's come to pass, would you?"

Molly slid a hand up her hip.

Yves Pomeroy said, "Henri is a man *extraordinaire*, a man of his word!"

Durwood scowled. "Man buddies up to Saddam Hussein, his word doesn't mean much."

"The sanctions were ludicrous!" Yves said. "Iraqi citizens were paying the toll, only Henri recognized this."

"Hm. Real humanitarian."

Before they could delve deeper into Henri and Rivard LLC's past morality, the cable in the center of the shaft flexed tight and a whirring sounded, followed by the clatter of many feet.

"Reinforcements," Durwood said. "Coming at us from above and below."

Molly spread her feet shoulder width apart at the shaft's edge. "I'm jumping. If you guys are too scared, fine. I'll go myself."

Her knees flexed, and Quaid saw she wasn't bluffing. What kind of food had they given her in that oubliette? Spinach and nails?

He'd expected to find her terrorized, despondent after her captivity. Instead, she'd turned into an action hero.

"Nobody's scared, McGill," he said. "But look, Henri Rivard could've been feeding you a line of bull. Or left out some important stuff—like whatever's down there is laced with acid or full of man-eating fish."

Molly was having none of it. "The kernel source code *has* to be there. I believe it. I believe there's hope for the world." She found his eyes in the darkness. "I believe."

And she jumped. The shaft's dearth of light swallowed her with startling speed—her green eyes and upturned nose were there one second, gone the next. Quaid held his breath, expecting to hear a splash.

Where was the splash?

He lowered to one knee, dirtying his pants, listening. *Where was the splash?* Had Henri lied? Was the shaft a bottomless pit? Or solid ground below—and Quaid had just missed the dull thud of her landing?

A rattling *clang* started above, the car descending.

Reinforcements.

At last, impossibly far down, Quaid heard:

Plop.

He felt a mix of relief and dread—dread because he knew what had to be done now. He closed his eyes and sucked in a deep breath. A breath to last.

I believe, she'd said. Quaid hated when people turned his own catchphrases around on him.

He jumped too.

CHAPTER SIXTY-EIGHT

Durwood took stock. Piper Jackson's mouth was twisted like she'd bitten a bum peach. Yves Pomeroy had been gung ho a second ago, but now he hung back from the shaft's edge.

They heard a second splash below.

Durwood said, "Looks like Henri had it right."

Pomeroy crowed, "It is precisely as I said, he is an *homme d'honneur!*"

Memories of his dear old boss must've stirred something in the man's bones. He pinched his nose, closed his eyes, and jumped.

Piper Jackson watched him disappear. Then she said to Durwood, "Too far, man. Y'all got me captured by Rivard, locked up in a dungeon. Now I'm supposed to jump blind into some underground cavern?"

The cable stiffened in front of them. The whirring moved closer.

"You got worse in the Blind Mice." Durwood removed his coat and laid it on the limestone. He secured his guns and weapon satchel. "Did plenty yourself too."

The hacker glared back, but her feet were shuffling forward.

She pointed to Sue. "What happens to the dog?"

"If we swim," Durwood said, "she'll swim."

The bottom of the elevator car above came into view, clanging and knocking—the enemy was upon them.

"On three," Durwood said.

Piper sniffed.

"One..." He took his boots in hand. "Two..."

Sue-Ann picked herself up off the limestone.

Durwood bent his front leg, making his blue jeans tighten at the knee.

"Three!"

He jumped feetfirst toward the center of the shaft. Sue-Ann flailed after him. And with any luck, Jackson went too.

Durwood lost his stomach. He lost all orientation. Cold air knifed up his nostrils. He saw flashes of the elevator cable for fifteen-odd feet, then it was gone, everything was gone. He was falling through a vacuum.

He didn't see or hear Jackson.

Durwood drifted near the shaft's side and something like a nail raked his forehead. He couldn't see Sue in the full dark, but he heard her rasping.

Durwood made a straight line of his feet and toes, shrinking his landing profile. Of course Sue would have no such strategy. Most likely she was flying through the air spread eagle, like a baby deer on ice.

Durwood clenched his body, waiting.

He waited a while.

Finally, the water's surface arrived like a brick floor. Uppercutting his chin. Jolting his spine. When he'd recovered his sense, he gripped his boots and used them like flippers to swim.

The initial plunge had probably taken him twenty, thirty feet down. Was he above or below the others? Had they survived the impact? It'd felt so violent—was it possible he'd hit one of them instead of the water?

He swam about. He tried opening his eyes, but the water stung awful and he pinched them tight again. What little he'd seen had been black anyhow.

After several moments of struggle, Durwood learned ruefully that his partner, Quaid Rafferty, had been right.

About the man-eating fish.

Dagger teeth gnawed him six places at once, quick, eager. Durwood kicked the teeth off, but others latched on. He swatted and elbowed and snatched. He got hold of one. Piranha, judging by shape.

Murkily, Durwood heard bubbling below. Then he made out screams. Then the screams started coming from the sides, from above, everywhere.

He opened his eyes again, ignoring the sting. Now he could see a little, shapes and colors, by a far-off watery light.

Here was Yves Pomeroy, flopping like a channel cat hooked through the gills. Frizzy hair floating out from his head in white strands.

Durwood swam that direction. Transferring both boots to one hand, he caught the Frenchman's wrist. Every action took twice as long through water as it would've on land.

Paddling with one arm, Durwood propelled them both down. His lungs burned. The piranhas kept biting, but he left them be. He'd smack them off if they went after an artery.

Ten feet more, and the watery light got clearer. Some sort of spotlight. Next to it was a round portal, rubber-rimmed and three feet across.

Durwood angled for the light and portal. His clothes felt like an anchor. Yves's struggling kept pulling them off course. Durwood's muscles were on fumes, oxygen starved. The water at this depth felt heavy on his brain.

With the tip of one boot, he caught the portal. He reeled himself through and now saw—in the underwater passageway ahead—the bottom of Jackson's sneakers.

It must turn up at some point. Turn up, get dry.

He pulled Pomeroy through the portal next. The going was easier here—their knees could contact the passageway sides.

Durwood looked back and saw Sue-Ann struggling at the portal, the whites of her eyes frantic. She had three legs through and the fourth stuck, jammed between her ear and the rim.

He treaded water back to help, yanking her stranded paw through. He was sure his lungs would burst any second. At last, they reached a ladder. Durwood muscled up hand over hand, passing Yves. Their heads cleared after six rungs into sweet, sweet air.

"What took you so long?"

This voice had vexed Durwood often through the years, but he welcomed it now.

Quaid Rafferty stood with folded arms, suit coat dripping, grinning beside Molly McGill.

Durwood answered, "Fish."

They moved quickly to tactics. Quaid said he'd scouted ahead: the passage ran another forty yards before descending to more limestone tunnels.

Durwood checked his handheld GPS. "We're near the supply tunnels. Might be we could blast out."

"No—*no blasting!*" Molly said. "The Great Safe is this way."

Durwood ran his thumb along the rock. The surface felt hot, with a sort of brittle intensity.

"Maybe," he said. "And who knows what else."

CHAPTER SIXTY-NINE

The crew assembled and regrouped. Sue-Ann shook her short coat dry, but the rest were drenched. The hood of Piper Jackson's sweatshirt was plastered to her neck. Molly's shirt left nothing to the imagination—Quaid kept peeking between strands of sopping hair. Pomeroy looked like a roll of paper towels run through a car wash.

Durwood felt twenty pounds heavier himself.

GOOOOOM.

The crash scrambled all their footings. Durwood looked back down the ladder and saw the water level sinking.

"Fabienne's draining the pool," he said. "Won't be long before they're after us."

Durwood put his boots back on and hurried ahead—away from the suck of the vortex. The way got narrower. The walls became craggy and irregular. In another ten yards, they reached a door bearing a logo of two green leaves, serrated, drawn to look like a mouth ready to chomp.

"Carnivorous grow house," Durwood said.

The others looked at him like he had corncobs sticking out of his ears.

Durwood explained, "American Dynamics had a dossier. They believe Rivard is weaponizing vegetation."

Quaid gave the door a long crooked look. "So it's...a bunch of over-grown Venus flytraps?"

Durwood raised a shoulder. Before fear could take hold in the group, he gripped the door handle. "Follow me."

The air inside beaded on his skin, which was already wet. Phosphorescent light came from recessed orbs in the floor. The life-forms themselves were beyond exotic. Giant red-veined chutes rose from a vine that crisscrossed the room like Grandma Jones's sprawling squash plants. Sections of the vine bulged like food through a snake.

A thick green cube, could've been six feet square, had fibrous roots coming out the side. The roots' ends sat in a black pool of, what, motor oil?

From a center strip, tubular tentacles waved in the air—high as a man. To the left, some sort of pure-white albino ferns. To the right, a mat of kelp fibers that looked like less mature growth.

Durwood opted for the right. He stepped that way. His boot sank six inches into the kelp mat.

He looked down and found the fibers had somehow reformed across his boot's leather. When he tried raising his toe, they didn't yield. He kicked, he dragged, he stomped. The fibers only toughened around his boot.

Finally, he pulled a blade from his ankle holster and cut himself free.

Molly's eyes were big as saucers, and Quaid suddenly couldn't find a place to stick his hands.

Durwood said, "Let's give those ferns a try."

He circled back to the left. The middle tentacles seemed to be following him, swaying with his motion. Maybe that was just Durwood's imagination.

The ferns were planted in two long rows. Closer in, Durwood saw they weren't pure white. Near the leaves' feathery edges, some brilliant-yellow substance moved within a translucent skin.

Durwood ripped a piece of his shirt's cuff—already dangling from their flight—and tossed it between the rows of ferns.

From their feathery tips came a fine yellow spray.

Fzzzt.

The cuff, which Durwood believed to be flannel, disintegrated faster than corn bread at a church potluck. The soil underneath became parched and dark, ashen.

Quaid said, "What's option three?"

Durwood shook his head. Those middle tentacles were getting friskier by the second—he wanted no part of them.

"This is it. We'll make it work."

He tore off his whole sleeve and tossed it forward. The first ferns sprayed only faintly. The fabric kept moving and got zapped by the next section of ferns.

Durwood looked to the others. "We're gonna need more clothes."

Quaid sacrificed his Caterpillar vest. Yves Pomeroy gave his suit and cravat, Durwood and Piper their blue jeans, and Molly—with Quaid's enthusiastic support—her shirt.

Durwood led the way, tossing articles of clothing ahead as decoys. The ferns spent their corrosive loads. The air bristled with heat and chemistry. Once, Durwood followed the clothes too quickly and got singed—an army of fire ants attacking his face.

Now he passed the last ferns and reached the exit. He turned to watch the others. The plants stiffened and convulsed at the intruders, but their nasty was all gone.

The giant tentacles seemed to lose interest in Durwood—but gain interest in Yves Pomeroy. Maybe because he was last, or because they tracked motion and he had that palsy.

Whatever the cause, the tentacles swelled as Yves passed the halfway point. The biggest started kinking itself like a barn cat about to hock a hairball.

Yves noticed. His palsy got worse.

"*Non!*" he cried. "Go away, I am not ready to die!"

The tentacle's opening stretched wide. It seemed to be positioning itself to bite.

Durwood drew his M9 and put six rounds into the thing's mouth, or head, or face. Take your pick.

All the plants in the room seemed to shriek together—a tense, redoubling protest. Durwood would've sworn the floor breathed.

"Out, move!" he said, banging through to the hall.

The rest tumbled after him. Before the door sealed, Durwood heard the not-too-distant clatter of footsteps. Hostiles. Coming up on the plant room in a hurry—and the plants inside gassed.

The group sprinted ahead. The hall twisted. Their pounding strides brought pebbles from the sides. They reached another door. Black metal with a serious seal: a wheel like a ship captain's, but encased in glass. Freezing smoke bled from the door's top and sides.

Computer servers, Durwood knew, needed low temperatures.

Could this be the Great Safe?

A sign read, *RESTEZ BAS.*

Durwood didn't speak French.

He opened the glass case and spun the wheel. Reckless, sure, but there was no time for finesse. Icy mists billowed over his face.

The wheel caught. Durwood pulled and pushed and pulled again. Couldn't budge her. He put his shoulder into it and heaved, managing another quarter turn.

Finally, the door gave. Smoke poured out—thick and opaque with blue crystals—along with a depressurizing wheeze.

Durwood's right hand crossed the threshold first and met immediate, searing pain. His skin began blistering like tomato sauce in a hot skillet.

At the same time, his lungs felt gored—as though the air were unfit. His chest swelled instinctively to take in more, and the sensation got worse.

Backing out, he closed the door.

Yves Pomeroy said, "Nanoblades. Beginning ten inches from the floor, they cut oxygen molecules into single atoms, which one cannot breathe."

Durwood's esophagus felt like fifty-grit sandpaper. He was unable to speak. He squatted and held his good hand like so, questioning.

"*Oui*, ten inches," Yves said. "Years ago, I witnessed a prototype. The high-powered fans and a temperature gradient keep the bottom ten inches clear."

Nobody seemed eager to go. Piper Jackson stood with her hands tucked in her armpits. Molly kept looking, then looking away, from Durwood's bad hand.

He waved them forward. The hostiles might've beaten the plant room by now.

"I'll go last, cover our rear," he said. "Long as everyone stays on their bellies, nobody'll get hurt."

Ten inches wasn't much. They had to shimmy with arms flat to their sides—getting up on your elbows boosted you up too high.

Visibility was good. Overhead panels bathed the room in crisp, sterile light. Everything above ten inches had a slight blur to it, seen through the nanoblades.

It was hard to hear much over the fans, which were built into the walls. They blew the poisoned air sideways and up.

In the middle of the room was a computer terminal with an operator chair.

The nanoblades can't be active there, Durwood reasoned. *Not if the operator can sit.*

The group crawled on. Quaid and Molly reached the other end and left by another wheel-hatched door. Then Pomeroy. Then Piper, who was helping Sue-Ann.

By creeping, Sue just could stay under ten inches. The top of her skull caught it once—Durwood heard the mew—but she did okay otherwise.

The tile was murder on Durwood's naked knees. His lungs hadn't fully recovered—and this air, even the safe stuff by the floor, didn't seem regular.

He'd almost got to the computer terminal when noises sounded behind. He peeked back.

Blake Leathersby stood at the threshold of the nanoblade field barking orders to goons in Kevlar vests.

The goons raised their guns.

Durwood needed the cover of that terminal. *Could he dive for it?* Nah, it was a good ten feet still. He was a sitting duck. The goons had ample light and clear line of sight. Cross fire was no issue.

Muscles in Durwood's backside squeezed, braced for impact.

But the goons didn't shoot.

He scrambled the last stretch and threw himself behind the computer. Raising up gingerly, he felt no stabs of pain.

Durwood sucked in all the air he could and sat in the operator chair. Machinery hummed around him. He looked through the blurred expanse to Blake Leathersby. The Brit looked stumped. Stomping about, gesturing angrily at his team.

They pulled strap-on respirators over their mouths and noses, and dropped to the tile. Durwood thought they might be scared to shoot near the nanoblades, but soon bullets began flying low to the ground. They were shooting prone, chins on the tile.

What happened if one misfired and hit the nanoblades? Could it upset the air flow, send nanoblades flying everywhere and poisoning the whole room? Would everybody die?

Durwood hiked his bare legs up, knees to his chest. A bullet nicked the chair and spun him around.

The goons would shoot, then advance, then shoot, then advance again.

Durwood couldn't stay here—they'd be upon him soon. He toppled the chair and set it on its side for maximum spread. Then he drew his M9 and made for the exit.

The gunshots came faster. Durwood twisted occasionally to return fire and keep the hostiles on their toes. Mostly, he kept moving.

Finally, he reached the exit. He cleared the nanoblade field and stood. The relief in his back was exquisite.

Bullets whizzed his ankles. The only means Durwood saw of clearing ten inches was the captain's wheel. He propped himself upon it. In just boxers, he felt like he was sitting on the john reading the *Coal Valley Times*.

He watched the hostiles from his awkward perch. One by one, they came off their sights, bewildered. The respirators hid their lips but not their eyes.

And Durwood looked into every one.

Blake Leathersby—and Fabienne and Thérèse Laurent, Durwood saw—hadn't entered the nanoblade area. They stood shy of the field.

Leathersby saw Durwood aiming his M9 and swore.

Durwood shot the fans. After his bullets hit the first two, the rest quit spinning. They must've been on the same circuit. The blades' steady whir stopped, replaced by the goons' agonized shrieks as single oxygen atoms rushed into their lungs.

Durwood saw the closest man gagging and writhing on his back, clawing at his gear, and left.

The rest of the group awaited him in the limestone tunnel.

Quaid asked, "Are they still coming?"

Durwood nodded. "Some of 'em."

They clambered ahead. This stretch of the bowels had rapid switchbacks and seemed to be taking them lower, deeper into the rock. The switchbacks made it impossible to hear what was happening back in the nanoblade room, whether Leathersby had found a way through or remained blocked.

The next door they came to looked like solid glass but seemed opaque. Not a speck of light seeped around the jambs—neither top nor bottom, left nor right.

It was the blackest black Durwood had seen.

A sign read, *DANGER EXTRÊME: CHAMBRE HYPER-GRAVITÉ LUMIÈRE.*

Durwood took out his GPS again. Now they were right on top of the supply tunnels. If he gave this wall to the west a strong kick, they might stumble in. No question a simple frag would do it.

"Let's beat it, then," Quaid said. "Wire up the *bang bang*, and let's boogie on home."

Yves Pomeroy agreed, dropping his head in shame like a conquered Napoleon. Piper wanted the hell out too. Durwood reached in his bag for a grenade.

Then Molly spoke up.

CHAPTER SEVENTY

"The Great Safe is this way," I said, pointing to the sign warning of extreme danger.

Durwood was wedging a grenade into a groove of the limestone wall. "Could be another dozen rooms, one worse than the next."

"Right," Quaid said. "We've been lucky, but it's time to cash out." He was using his undershirt to stop a bloody cut in his neck. "You keep rolling the dice, eventually the house wins."

I asked Durwood, "Didn't the schematic from AmDye say four chambers? Oubliette, plants, nanoblades—this is the last one."

"Also said they'd be vertical," the ex-marine said. "Not horizontal like it turned out."

But I heard acknowledgment in his tone. Once a matter of honor was put to Durwood, a matter of bravery, he was incapable of refusing. It just wasn't in him.

I still had three more to convince.

"Henri told me it would be dark at the very end," I argued, pointing at the blacker-than-black glass in front of us. "See? The Great Safe is *right here.*"

Yves and Piper, who'd both overheard the exchange, looked at me dubiously. True—it'd been dark pretty much the whole time, but I still felt his cryptic hint might apply.

Quaid gestured to a row of symbols ranging from skulls to a gas mask to the biohazard triple scythe.

"'Dark' would seem to be an understatement," he said. "I don't see us waltzing in with a flashlight, finding the source code gift wrapped in the center of the room, and *boom*—planet saved."

Piper said, for maybe the tenth time, "Hell no. I'm going home."

I asked Yves what he knew about a hyper-gravity chamber.

"Only rumors. The scientists believed they might constrain these microscopic black holes, bend them to their whims." The old man shivered. "I assumed it was mere folly."

Bullets began zinging behind us. Suddenly, a fine limestone spray was everywhere.

I met Durwood's steel-gray eyes. He was holding a grenade.

"This stops *now*," I said. "The evil. Here and now."

He looked at me, looked at the grenade. Then he pulled its pin and rolled it toward our pursuers.

I yanked open the opaque glass door and everyone spilled into the chamber.

Behind us, the grenade detonated. The beginning of the explosion was bright in my ears, then the door closed and there was nothing—no sound, no light, no more wet humidity. A total, unrelenting void.

All directional sense deserted me. I raised my shoe to stride and had no clue when, or if, it would find solid ground. (When it did, the surface was gravely and porous.) The sensory block was just as oppressive. I heard the start of murmurs around me—quickly swallowed— and whooshing that made me think of a roomful of washing machines on *Delicate*.

I saw fleeting eddies of light, such transitory flashes that I wondered if they only existed in my mind.

Yves Pomeroy hissed from somewhere, "Do not leave the gravel!"

Imagining Fabienne Rivard and Blake Leathersby hot on our trail, I kept moving. My heart thumped, my thoughts blared, my eyes groped around for cues. It felt like falling forward through a cave.

After several crunching footfalls, my foot landed quietly—on a smooth surface. I had barely registered this as trouble when an organ-rattling force jerked me rightward.

Both legs flew out from underneath, my torso suddenly parallel to the floor. Next, I felt Durwood's rough hand around my wrist.

"What *was* that?" I said.

The disembodied voice of Yves Pomeroy: "The scientists wanted to limit their effects to light—perhaps they have not fully succeeded. Hence the gravel."

"What happens if...if matter gets sucked into one of the mini-black-holes, if something like a body..."

I trailed off, leaving a chasm of silence.

The Frenchman said, "It ceases to exist."

Those washing machines seemed to whoosh louder.

My children were never going to see me again. *How do you hold a funeral for a body that "ceases to exist"?*

Durwood asked something, quickly lost, about how they were supposed to find the way out.

"This will be *très difficile*," came Yves's voice. "One must catch outside light in the instant before the gravity fields seize it."

We wandered through blackness for a full minute, poised, ready to lurch after any speck of light. Several false alarms were shouted and taken back.

When Piper's shoulder brushed mine, I jumped half out of my skin.

Short pops and bangs started from one end of the chamber. I couldn't tell whether ahead or behind, left or right.

Durwood said, "I jammed the door to keep 'em out. No telling how long it holds."

My breaths shortened. My concentration started to fray. How long had we been here, five minutes? Ten?

Twenty?

"I saw it!" called a voice I thought was Quaid's.

"A blip, a flash—something! To the left, about the level of my chest."

Durwood grumbled. He seemed annoyed by his partner, who'd already reported four similar sightings. "We need a whole door. Not a flash."

"Yeah, a door—it must've been a door!" Quaid said. "I only glimpsed it, but I gotta believe if we—"

"Believe. You done enough believing for us all."

We'd loosely joined hands to stay together, and now I felt Durwood's tighten.

Quaid said, "I'm about done with your negativity, Wood. You know, it is possible for a non-jarhead civilian to make a useful observa—"

"Both of you, *stop*!" Yves said. "One cannot find our location by sight here, but it remains quite possible by sound."

Durwood and Quaid gave up their bickering, and we all held our breath. In the opposite direction from where Quaid had indicated, a walkie-talkie sounded, followed by a squeak that might've been body armor creasing.

Fingers closed around my wrist. We began moving again, all of us, toward Quaid's flash. I walked in a crouch and with my free hand spread in front of me to detect any nearby surfaces.

A gunshot *cracked*. We moved faster and lower and yanked each other's wrists. Another *crack*. Then a third.

As my feet scurried to keep pace, it felt like the air did figure eights around my head. *Could these mini-blackholes bend a bullet's path?*

I squashed my nose into somebody's back. We stopped.

Durwood whispered, "This the spot, 'bout here?"

Quaid answered, "Sss-sure."

There was the sound of knuckles tapping a surface.

"No door yet," Durwood reported.

"Might've been a couple feet left," Quaid said. "I think we drifted some."

A sharp intake of breath came from Durwood. Before he could probe further, a drumroll of *plings* sprayed the wall overhead.

We scrambled away to the right, coordinating with pokes and jerks and shoves.

Then a knob twisted.

"Yahtzee!" Quaid called, attracting fresh fire.

But a rectangle of light had appeared. I dove for it. We all did—

rolling, twisting, desperate. I landed in a heap with Yves and Piper. The door sucked shut behind us, and we could see again.

We were in yet another limestone hall. It was enough to give a person déjà vu—except this stretch felt different. The others had been narrowing steadily, if irregularly. This hall shrank precipitously. Only a single crawling figure would be able to fit through. It felt like the end of an excavation, like we were encased in rock.

Like one last pocket of wickedness.

We crawled twenty yards like soldiers through a trench, emerging in a broader space where everyone could fit shoulder to shoulder.

There was another door.

With another sign: *LE GRAND COFFRE-FORT. UNE PERSONNE SEULEMENT.*

Accompanying the words were stick-figure depictions of a heart-beat monitor, temperature gauge, and pressure-sensitive floor.

Yves wasn't speaking up, so I translated for the group.

"The Great Safe," I said, the words hoarse from my dust-coated throat. "One person only."

Quaid and Durwood stood on either side of me. I could sense their dread. Quaid squinted at the dire warnings as though puzzling out how to squeeze the abilities of two people into one body. Durwood shifted his jaw, no doubt ready to volunteer.

But it couldn't be him. I knew this. We all did.

It had to be Piper.

CHAPTER SEVENTY-ONE

The cowboy acted like he wanted to be the one, but Molly was going to ask Piper. Piper could tell. Whenever Molly had a hard question to ask, she did this thing where she hugged her elbows and winced—like she wanted to take back the question before she'd even asked it.

Molly was wincing now.

Piper said, "I'll go."

It wasn't that she needed to be a hero or show off her hacking chops. She just wanted control.

When she and Marcus had gotten back to their mom's place after busting out of Windhorne, he'd said, *You got 'em back, sis. You did, the cheats and then some. But don't let that end sneak up on you.*

He'd talked about his mistakes at Harvest Earth. Going along with Sampson, not imagining how the end would go.

You need control, he'd said. *If you don't have it yet, you better get it.*

Now Piper looked at the Great Safe. She didn't know which way this ending would tip, but she wanted control. The more the better.

The cowboy and the aging playboy looked at the danger signs, then at each other.

Playboy Quaid said, "I like her odds better than ours."

The cowboy didn't trust Piper, she knew. She was a lawbreaker. Durwood probably didn't trust people he saw jaywalking.

But he did step aside.

Piper twisted a pressurized hatch and entered.

The Great Safe was cold every way a place could be cold. The chamber unfurled from its door like some nautilus or cornucopia, growing, sprawling, with little split-off areas full of weird gadgets or diagrams.

The walls were limestone like the rest of the bowels, but the floor was slick, translucent with green-gold circuits humming below the surface and pulsing orange coils weaved throughout. Some kind of supercooling.

Piper walked four steps inside and just stared.

One split-off area had a layer of blue frost covering its walls. Another smelled sharp and wet like worms. A third, a tunnel Piper couldn't see the end of, gave off high-intensity vibrations that Piper experienced as the first tremors of an earthquake in her own heart.

She lost herself for a second. Then she swept all the Dr. Evil jazz from her mind and looked for a computer.

The moment she wanted it, there it was. Floating in midair: a screen, a souped-up rig, a pair of long gloves that must've been part of a virtual-reality interface. Right in front of Piper's face.

They're in my brain. The room reads brain waves.

A message flashed across the phantom screen: *POUR VOUS CONNECTER, PLACEZ N'IMPORTE QUELLE PEAU* CONTRE LA SURFACE.

Next, a pad appeared showing a stick-figure diagram of a person placing their finger, tongue, or kneecap against it.

A biometric reader. She'd heard of sensors that sloughed off cells to compare against a DNA database.

Man. You'd think piranha-infested waters, Frankenstein plants, nanoblades, and baby black holes would be enough security.

The reader glowed impatiently. How long before it timed out? Before it decided you weren't authorized and...what, shot acid rain in your face? Started an avalanche?

Piper slicked her fingers over her palms, trying to figure how to beat the security. Short the circuit? Some admin override?

Looking at her own busy hands, she got an idea.

Fingernails!

Outside the oubliette, she'd gripped Leathersby's arm with her left hand, hadn't she? Now she scraped underneath the nails of that hand, gathering all the skin cells into a nasty little ball and smearing it across the reader.

In a blip, Blake Leathersby's cocky face appeared on-screen.

ACCESS CONFIRMED.

The long gloves floated forward invitingly. Piper slipped her arms inside.

Quickly she was navigating Rivard's master directories, swiping and tapping and thumb-twitching, cruising through every project the French conglomerate had cooking.

She found designs for an antimatter-fueled spaceship. For invisibility wands. One wild diagram was labeled: *Beyond Airborne: The Awesome Potential of Radio-Viral Pathogen Transmission.*

There was enough here to keep you up worrying for the rest of your life, but Piper couldn't sweat it now. She needed the kernel source code.

She waded through servers and files and directories and subdirectories.

Suddenly, the screen flashed red. The text turned white.

ALERTE! ATTAQUE ENTRANTE, 500 KILOMÈTRES.

A radar map of Northern Europe popped up. Roche Rivard was the black star in the middle. A blinking airplane symbol was approaching steadily. It had another symbol moving with it, just above. The nuclear icon.

That couldn't be good.

Piper dismissed the alert and kept looking for the source code. She found a bunch of directories for Yves Pomeroy's Enterprise Software group. One had a folder called *CyberParle*, which she remembered Molly talking about after that secret trip where she posed as a Silicon Valley executive.

Piper drilled deeper into this folder. The file names were getting weird, full of letter-number juxtaposes and nonsense punctuation. Piper started clicking the bigger ones and spot-checking their contents, seeing if any looked familiar, if any resembled that beast she'd been mangling data with for the last eighteen months.

Then, wham.

The file name was total gobbledygook: *!?ePP3;Q__&7T*. But this was it. Piper followed the logic, squinting at the code, nodding along, unconsciously rubbing her fingers in their gloves.

The algorithm slipped in, corrupted the data, and slipped out— covering its tracks as it backpedaled.

The kernel.

Slim, simple, efficient. A deadly-gorgeous piece of programming.

Piper took her Bluetooth key chain drive from her pocket. The Rivard mainframe immediately connected and made it available to receive files on-screen.

Piper swiped *!?ePP3;Q__&7T* onto the drive, pocketed it, and backed her hands out of the gloves. Another *ALERTE!* flashed to the screen, but Piper didn't read it. She whirled to go, and the computer vanished.

She took a last look back over her shoulder at the devil's workshop of goodies. Then she gripped the hatch of the pressurized door with both hands and heaved clockwise.

The first face Piper saw, standing outside in the limestone hall, was the cowboy's. It looked sorry.

The second was Blake Leathersby's. He was poking his gun into Durwood's back.

"Didj'a bring me a present?" The English jerk pointed to the drive in Piper's hand. "That was kind of you, lass. I knew we'd end up friends."

CHAPTER SEVENTY-TWO

Quaid was separated from the others, made to stand apart while Leathersby bullied Durwood with his Webley top-break and Thérèse Laurent zip-tied the wrists of Pomeroy, Piper, and Molly. Fabienne presided over all with a slim handgun whose laser sight traipsed from one captive to the next.

Sue-Ann lay on her side, out. She'd suffered another kick from Leathersby and had fallen against the canvas bag the mercenary had ripped off Durwood's shoulder and tossed aside.

Quaid was the only one not restrained or incapacitated. He'd been allowed to remain unbound, loose between the two groups.

Why?

Fabienne took the key-chain drive from Leathersby, who'd taken it from Piper.

"It was misguided to keep the source code intact—even if only here, in the Great Safe." She turned to Thérèse Laurent. "See to it every copy, anywhere in the world, is destroyed."

The blond nodded, finishing Molly's wrists with a hard cinch.

Piper said, "It's not reversible anyway. I looked. Any data that's diseased is gonna stay diseased. One-way street."

Fabienne considered the hacker for a long moment.

"You lie," the heiress said. "Perhaps only you in the world could craft the antidote—but craft it you could. We will not take the chance in any case."

She instructed Leathersby and Laurent to corral the others into a small area with an overhang. Durwood had to crouch to fit— Leathersby helped him along with a shove. Durwood accepted the shove, but when the Brit reared back to kick Sue-Ann again, he clipped the man's heel and sent him sprawling.

Leathersby got to his feet. "*I'm through being messed with!*" He raised the Webley. "Too many bloody years chasing you around the goat pen, Jones. It's time you met your maker."

Durwood was on his knees. "If that's His plan, okay. I'm ready. Maybelle's waiting."

As Leathersby smirked and tried to think up a comeback, Quaid wondered again why he remained free. He'd learned in many years dealing with the Rivards—as both a client and adversary—that nothing was ever accidental.

Now Fabienne did clarify. "Mr. Rafferty, you have a choice to make. Your skills would be of use to me. Your diplomacy and contacts among the American elites. There is still water to be carried, establishing the new world order. Should you submit to me, fully and without reservation, you may be allowed to carry some."

She licked her crimson lips.

Piper said, "Why can he switch? I got skills too—you just said."

Fabienne shook her head languidly. "You are not the child who joined the Blind Mice. You have changed—and not in a manner that suits the goals of myself and Rivard LLC."

She approached Quaid with swerving steps and laid the tip of one finger on his pants.

"Mr. Rafferty is a man," she said. "Men do not change. He has always had a, eh, how would one say in English? A 'moral flexibility.' I know his character. I have worked with him—more than Mr. Oak Jones is aware."

Her voice was thick with gloating, with power, with lust. Quaid felt it in the pit of his stomach. A wedge had torn away from Fabienne's dress, exposing her leg to the hollow of her pelvic bone.

"Besides," she continued, dragging her finger up Quaid's torso and face, through his wavy hair. "Davos deserves an encore."

Molly's eyes stormed over.

Fabienne batted her eyelashes. "It's true we've had longer encounters. Bucharest, where we discovered our mutual affinity for that too-often-neglected part of the body..."

As she continued in this lewd vein, her finger found its way back down to Quaid's belt.

To clear his mind, Quaid looked to Durwood and tried focusing on tactics. *What's our play? How do we wriggle out of this?*

A new alarm had joined the one that'd been bleating for the last half hour. Deeper pitched and—incredibly—even louder.

He said, "Is that something you need to investigate, all these alarms? It sounds like you've got half the German Luftwaffe incoming."

Fabienne gave a bored sneer. "It is just American Dynamics. Jim Steed and his conquest fantasies."

"Fantasy or no," Quaid said, "there wouldn't happen to be some ultra-, mega-reinforced doomsday bunker we could shelter in, would there?"

He tried inching away, but Fabienne tugged him back by a belt loop.

"Roche Rivard is impenetrable," she said. "Steed's hapless pilots will be lucky to strafe us with a single round."

Maybe so, Quaid thought, but what if that round found the inner shaft?

Molly spoke out, "What happened to you? I suppose Henri wasn't around, but your mother—or the nannies who raised you, whoever—must've made some tragic mistakes."

Quaid thought he detected an angry twitch in Fabienne's mouth, but in a second, it was gone.

"That's right, everything must trace back to childhood. To one's parents. Even for you"—Fabienne gestured with her gun—"parenting has enlarged your breasts, *oui*? Perhaps this is why Mr. Rafferty returns to you occasionally when he cannot find a more exciting option?"

Molly's eyes stormed again, lightning in the whites now.

"I am only twenty-four, of course," Fabienne said, "but I have heard childbirth enlarges other parts too. It loosens and stretches—"

"That's enough," Quaid said.

Fabienne turned back to him and said, quietly, so no others could hear, "*Is it?*"

Then did a thing with her hand that nearly blew Quaid's mind.

She kept whispering, "*Dying here is pointless. Even if your ultimate goal is to defeat my agenda, isn't living the better choice? Join me now. Accept the opportunity. The future may hold anything, it may hold nothing. Only by living can you know.*"

Quaid had a knack himself for parroting another's thoughts back to them persuasively—now Fabienne was doing the same to him.

What benefit *was* there in going down with the ship? If their entire squad suddenly ceased to exist, what chance did the world have?

Piper Jackson wouldn't be around to engineer a data antidote, but if he—Quaid—knew of the source code's existence, he could keep hope alive. He could stick close to Fabienne and win her trust. Tease out the company's darkest secrets. Bide his time.

After much thought, Quaid said, "I'll do it, I'll join you. On one condition."

Fabienne froze her hand in place.

He said, "Keep them alive. You spent a fortune building that oubliette—so use it. Put 'em in the deepest, darkest cell. Throw away the key if you like."

The heiress turned and considered her captives. Blake Leathersby growled impatiently.

"*Non,*" Fabienne decided. "I do not believe you can reach your full potential with Rivard so long as Mr. Oak Jones lives. Or Ms. McGill, who is such a pathetic figure and magnet for your sympathies. They must die."

As Fabienne leaned her exposed thigh into Quaid's zipper, a fight raged inside him—in his mind, in his body. Everywhere.

He groped for a way to split the difference, drawing on his adroit politician's logic. Could he accept Fabienne's offer, then intervene before the killings? Doubtful. What if he offered to commit the killings himself to prove his fealty, then didn't follow through?

Possible. But very long odds.

As he was considering, debating if this line of reasoning was clever or cowardly, Sue-Ann roused. The geriatric dog struggled up, seemingly on a single paw, managing to get her belly off the floor before collapsing back down.

She kept fighting. Her milky eyes found Quaid's and held them. With the cataracts, it was hard to say for sure, but he would've sworn he saw judgment there.

He would've sworn he saw contempt.

CHAPTER SEVENTY-THREE

Durwood gave a short whistle. Sue-Ann's ears twitched, and she turned to find him—too fast, crumpling. But she didn't fall. She recovered and looked to him for a command.

Durwood squinted and performed a half twist of his right ring finger. He barely got the command right, consumed by fury. Fury at Leathersby, fury at Rivard. And fury at his partner.

It hadn't surprised him to learn Quaid took a roll in the hay with Fabienne Rivard. He'd been close-lipped about that night in Davos afterward, and closed wasn't typical for Quaid Raffery's lips.

No—what stuck in Durwood's craw was that bit about his working with Fabienne "more than Mr. Oak Jones is aware." (The French-woman's accent made his own name sound like some fancy appetizer.)

This comment called everything into question. Had Quaid been playing both sides on that space-laser gig? She'd mentioned Bucharest, so Durwood figured the cryptocurrency mission hadn't been square either.

What about this, the Anarchy? Had Quaid been involved in the early phases? Awful suspicious how well the kernel zapped govern-ment data in the States. Quaid's Rolodex was thick as flies on a dog's back—had he used it to help Fabienne spread her evil software?

He could've even been working to keep the Blind Mice on the loose. Molly's first night, at Blackstone's mansion—it had been Quaid's dalliance with the mayor that kept Durwood from intervening. Durwood might've stopped this whole mess before it started.

The heiress was wrapped halfway around him now, waiting for Quaid to say whether he'd join up.

Quaid looked over her jet-black hair to Durwood. His blue eyes looked watery. Probably from the limestone dust.

"I won't do it," he said. "If you're killing them, go ahead and kill me too."

Leathersby smiled his oaf's smile, started fondling the Webley.

Fabienne spoke right at the side of Quaid's neck, "As you wish."

Then she drove her knee into his giblets.

Quaid doubled over and moaned. Fabienne, waiting for the purple to pass from his face, told him to join his friends under the overhang.

Durwood watched Sue-Ann out the corner of his eye.

The coonhound approached his canvas bag. She moved gingerly in a way that attracted no attention. She nosed around some and pulled out a black rectangular device with her teeth.

All eyes were on Quaid. Sue-Ann kept to the shadows, never giving the hostiles line of sight. She carried the device loose, which was a good thing. Blueticks are known for their soft mouths, and Sue's was soft as any.

It was taking Quaid a while to get to the overhang. Leathersby helped him along with a roundhouse kick.

"Move along, tosser," the mercenary said. "Ain't got all day."

Quaid staggered along. "What's funny is I like the English. I wish I could've debated in the House of Commons instead of slogging through our political muck. The English are clever. They're kind, mostly, and they don't suffer phonies. They're like Americans if you skimmed off the best ten percent of us and left out the jerks. Maybe that's what you are, Blake. Maybe you're that ninety-percent-jerk contingent boiled into one bloated, ignorant, petty..."

He was stalling. Durwood whispered to the others, *"Plug your ears."*

Finally, Sue-Ann, her breaths rattling, reached the overhang and presented Durwood with the rectangular device.

Leathersby was busy taunting Quaid. Durwood held one thumb firmly in his left ear. Knowing he would need the other hand to activate the device, he chipped limestone from the wall and jammed a jagged piece in his right ear.

The piece was too large. He turned it around until he found a smaller side, then he wedged it in. A trickle of blood started down his cheek. He pushed until the rock point touched his eardrum inside.

He took a last look around. Besides Quaid, who was still baiting Leathersby, the others had done as he'd said and plugged their ears.

This wouldn't go well for Quaid. In a black part of his mind, Durwood thought this was his partner's penance.

The device's lone button sat flush on its casing. The button and casing were both slick with Sue's slobber. Durwood poised a finger over the button. His scalp felt tense, like he was pulling on a rubber swim cap.

He pressed the button.

The world got loud.

CHAPTER SEVENTY-FOUR

G *ooooOOOOOOMMMMmmm.*
At first, I thought it was another alarm, something worse than *alarme primaire*—something to do with the American Dynamics attack.

The noise, even with three fingertips pressed in each of my ears, was exquisite. Noise beyond noise, a relentless, invisible intensity from all sides. I once had a ten-quart pressure cooker blow on me, and the sensations before that—in the moment before my cilantro-lime black beans sprayed the ceiling—were kind of similar: tetchy, charged.

Quaid and everybody from Rivard's side were sprawled out holding their heads. Durwood jumped into action, dragging Quaid by the arm and Sue-Ann—who'd been flattened by the sonic disturbance—by the foreleg.

Bumping along the limestone, Quaid cried out in agony. Durwood pantomimed for him to plug his ears, but Quaid didn't open his eyes to see.

Yves, Piper, and I staggered away from the device, which lay on the floor vibrating, still blaring its awful sounds.

Durwood dropped Quaid and Sue-Ann safely apart from Rivard, then he rifled through the canvas bag for two grenades. He yanked both pins and tossed them sidearm into the overhang. Then he kicked that noise box—whatever it was—in after them.

The explosion raised the pressure in my head unbearably—then, suddenly, it was over. The quiet was disorienting.

"There!" Durwood said, rushing into the fresh gap in the limestone. "The supply tunnels!"

While Rivard writhed among the rubble, Piper and I scrambled forward to look over Durwood's shoulder. The explosion had blasted an exit straight down: an eight-foot drop to tracks of some kind. Steel rails glinted in the dark.

Durwood said, "They'll take us right into gay Paris. Let's roll."

He lent his arm to each of us in turn, lowering everyone into the tunnel until they were close enough to drop.

I landed crookedly on one of the rails, twisting my ankle. Yves Pomeroy came next, in a heap. I thought he'd been knocked unconscious until he popped up in a panther's stance and cried, "*Paris, ma chérie, je viens!*"

Once Piper made it, the three of us supported Quaid—still incoherent and crunching his eyes—and Sue-Ann's inert form as Durwood eased them down to us. The dog hadn't moved a muscle on her own. If she was breathing, I couldn't tell.

Finally, Durwood descended himself. He looked left up the tunnel, then right. Both directions were dark.

He looked again using night-vision goggles from the canvas bag. After adjusting a dial on the nose piece (these were from Yakov, no ordinary night-vision goggles), he pointed.

"The box cart," he said, dropping the goggles. "Hang tight—it's close."

He ran off. Minutes later, a chugging began from that direction. I squinted to see. A ramshackle cart puttered into view, clanking, clanging. Durwood stood in the back working what must've been a steering stick.

The cart croaked to a stop. We helped Durwood off-load unneeded guns and ammo, then all pitched in loading Quaid and Sue-Ann inside. Yves and Piper crammed in with them while I sat up on the cart's front edge—the only remaining seat with Durwood manning his steering stick in back.

He yanked a cord, and we lurched forward.

I don't know how fast the box cart actually went, but it felt like 150 miles per hour on the New Jersey Turnpike as we veered and zoomed and tipped, the wind whipping my hair. Pebbles glanced off my teeth. I lost a shoe over the side.

The air got hot and cold and hot again for no apparent reason. The tunnel's lighting was spotty—sometimes, I saw dips and curves coming; others, we hit blind and my stomach bottomed out in total darkness.

The motor sounded like a sick lawn mower, but Durwood pushed it for more. I felt something on my bare foot and looked down—Yves was hanging on to my ankle like a subway strap.

After five wild minutes, the cart's wheels—which hadn't exactly been riding smooth to that point—started to wobble badly. A *tink* sounded in the undercarriage, then grinding. It smelled like toast turning black.

Durwood threw his whole body against the stick, slowing us. The cart's rear end raised up like a cat's when it gets scared. I hung on with all ten fingers, sure the cart was about to tip over and crush me.

But it didn't. We stopped. Yves and Piper slammed to the front of the cart.

Everyone tumbled out—even Quaid, who could move again but seemed incapable of removing his right hand from the side of his head.

His left hand, though, found mine. The warmth in our joined fingers was like some clammy perfection in the chaos.

Durwood said, "We walk from here."

I looked into the blankness ahead. "How much farther is it to Paris?"

Durwood said he didn't know.

I swiveled back the way we'd come. "And how often do trains come?"

"Often," Durwood said.

Those of us who could, jogged. The rest walked. Durwood loaded

Sue-Ann into the canvas bag and carried it over his shoulder. I thought I heard him sniff away a sob.

Five minutes passed. Muscles ached everywhere, from my skin to my bones, and judging from the others' groans, I figured their conditions were no better.

It reminded me of hiking the Billy Goat Trail in Maryland with my kids and second husband. The guidebook had beguiled me with descriptions of "7.8 miles of fun rock-hopping and spectacular views of the Potomac," but instead I got sandal blisters, whining, and under-his-breath comments about the golf tournament my soon-to-be-ex could have been watching on TV.

A pinprick of light appeared up ahead. My pulse raced. Could that be an opening?

Paris?

When I traced the light to its source, though, I realized it was coming from behind—from a circle of pale light in the middle of the tunnel.

And the circle was growing.

And now I heard a motor's snarl.

"Dang," Durwood said.

He ran ahead to scout for a turnout, a utility ladder up, anything.

"No luck," he said. "We're just gonna have to make ourselves skinny."

We edged away from the track until our backs and heels were flush to the limestone. I felt moisture on my bare shoulders, seeping into my pants.

My toes weren't four feet from the rail.

I asked, "How wide are the trains that pass here?"

"Most are supply trains," Durwood said, "packed to the gills. It's gonna be a squeeze."

I sucked in my stomach, gulping, pressing my fingers flat into the rock behind.

The oncoming train's headlight grew brighter and bigger. Heat rippled toward us.

Several hundred yards up the track, a teeth-rattling *crunch* sounded. Soon we all saw the box cart, splintered and disintegrating, being pushed toward us by a needle-nose train. The box cart was lifted completely off the tracks, tumbling up the train's nose, screeching, sparking, ejecting debris to either side.

Is the train slowing down? Will it stop?

As the train-and-box-cart jumble got closer, though, I realized it was moving too fast. It wouldn't stop in time—no chance. I pinned myself freshly against the limestone and prayed.

The box cart kept riding up the train's windshield. I didn't see a conductor inside—it must've been driverless. The box cart's screech became deafening. It was scraping the roof of the tunnel. The train kept barreling ahead, its momentum forcing the box cart higher still, harder into the roof, the flying-apart mass compressing and grating and fighting against the ceiling.

I closed my eyes. Every protrusion of my body—my chin, my throat, my kneecaps—felt giant.

Steam and debris hit my skin first, then a blast of new, cold air. Splinters fell into my hair. Charred chunks of wood glanced off my face.

In a flash, hot steel consumed the tunnel in front of me. My nose whiplashed with the passing train's wind. My eyelashes felt like they would shear off.

I stayed against the wall. I expected the train to whoosh right by, but it slowed instead—the box cart's friction against the roof was too great. The screeching sound turned into tearing and gouging. The dust was noxious.

In another fifty yards, the rambling wreck stopped.

The supply train derailed, toppling sideways. The box cart had cleaved a groove in the tunnel's ceiling, which accounted for that new air. The train's cars—full of dark clumps that could've been coal, or some exotic hazardous material—made a ragged staircase up to the surface.

Sunlight beamed through plumes of limestone dust, choked and filtered but insistent. We peeled ourselves carefully off the wall.

Quaid's tanned face was caked with dirt. "Where on God's green earth are we?"

The question, Quaid's first words, put a smile on Durwood's face.

He was walking toward the light with his canvas bag. "We musta cleared the Boulogne Woods. If not farther."

I was running now, forgetting the pain in my ankle. Yves Pomeroy hustled along beside me, grinning—minus a few teeth. Piper had an egg-size lump on her cheek.

Now that I was climbing over them, the supply train's cars smelled of decay—manure or compost. I stepped quickly up the smoking metal, unsure if the Rivard cargo could explode—and not eager to find out.

I cleared a hunk of split-apart concrete at last and was aboveground.

In Paris.

"The Seine, *ah oui!*" Yves said, his nose lifted savoringly. "I could live one thousand years without her scent and know it still."

Indeed, we had emerged on the banks of the legendary river. Instead of chic joggers or wines being uncorked on picnic blankets, though, we were surrounded by ripped tents, campfires, and open trash pits. A woman nursed an infant. Two men flipped cards onto an overturned drum.

It said something about the times that the faces looking up from these various pursuits were only curious—not shocked, not terrified— at the group of half-naked people climbing out of the earth.

I stretched my arms high overhead and breathed. To the west, the direction of Roche Rivard, a column of black smoke poured heavenward.

I said, "Do you think the attack on the shaft, the American Dynamics thing, took out...?"

"Wouldn't count on it," Durwood said.

He was kneeling over his bag, lifting out Sue-Ann. The ex-marine held the back of his hand against the dog's neck, feeling for a pulse.

Some street kids approached to investigate. Their faces were smudged and bodies gaunt—they looked like they'd escaped a war zone like we had.

One pointed at the nose-eyes-whiskers tattoo on Piper's wrist.

"The Blind Mice!" said the kid, who I pegged as around twelve years old. That can be a hard age to tell with.

He looked into Piper's face. *"C'est Piper Jackson, le pirate informatique! Mon Dieu!"*

More kids rushed over, swarming and making a fuss over Piper. As she waved them off—*nah, nah, not her, go mob somebody else*—I noticed something in her back pocket.

A key-chain drive.

CHAPTER SEVENTY-FIVE

Ten Months Later

Sergio Diaz, smiling, poured a pair of drinks at his mahogany sideboard. Three of the four walls in the mayor's office had been repaired—the last just needed some light plaster work—and the portrait of Don Juan again hung over the fireplace. Outside, New York City hummed with the sound of jackhammers, hydraulic lifts, and shouting construction workers.

Quaid accepted his drink, a prairie fire prepared with Cholula hot sauce. "Good to be back in the old digs?"

Sergio nodded. "Yes, quite. We're still finding raccoon nests, and occasionally I do catch a whiff of burned tire. But these are trifles."

"*Rifles?*" Quaid said.

"No, trifles—I said the raccoons and smell of tires were trifles."

Nearly a year since escaping Roche Rivard, Quaid still hadn't fully recovered his hearing. Durwood figured it would come back eventually—he had a call in to Yakov asking what specific mechanisms the sonic weapon employed. The arms dealer hadn't called back, still sore over being strong-armed in a New Jersey storage shed.

"Right," Quaid said now. "I suppose you've got time to fumigate, don't you?"

The mayor smiled again. He looked good, notwithstanding the

gray streaks in his formerly jet-black hair. Only last week, he'd been reelected to another four-year term. While mayors of most US cities had gotten hammered in the first post-Anarchy elections for capitulating to Forceworthy and other private muscle companies, Sergio had been lauded for holding out—for trying to govern humanely.

"The sideboard came through well," Quaid observed. "I'm amazed looters didn't take it."

Sergio ran his hand over a carved hydra. "Perhaps the piece benefited from supernatural protections."

The old friends considered this over a swig.

Quaid drank his in one, finishing with throat and eyes stinging. "Or from weighing half a ton and nobody being able to budge it."

He poured himself another and joined Sergio at the window.

Six busy months after Data Rejuvenation Day, the Manhattan skyline was beginning to shed its blight. Holes had been patched in skyscrapers. The orange-black haze, whose onset climate researchers had never precisely understood, had lifted.

The journey back from the Anarchy's abyss hadn't been easy—though the technology piece had come together quickly. Once Piper downloaded the kernel source code off the key-chain drive she'd stolen (back) from Blake Leathersby, it took her less than an hour to write an antidote patch and post it to every public server and message board around. She then tweeted from the josiahTheAvenger account that the Blind Mice had "accomplished their goal of bringing the high low and the low high" and were gifting the world back its data.

Few trusted this. Corporations took it for another prank. Cities feared it could further damage their systems. Rivard LLC propagated rumors that the patch actually contained advanced AI laying the groundwork for the enslavement of humans by sentient machines.

Eventually, the success of American Dynamics and New York City in restoring their data convinced others to try the antidote. Gleeful pictures of bank statements and accurate property records began appearing on social media. The process was hampered by hoaxes, opportunists, and cover-up murders, by doubt and guilt and pessimism.

None of these, finally, were enough to stop people from coming together again. From trusting each other.

The Anarchy already showed signs of becoming instant nostalgia. Hawkers sold buttons with the silhouette of Josiah—missing but presumed lurking somewhere—superimposed over the nose-eyes-whiskers symbol. People wore shirts that said, *I Survived the Anarchy and All I Got Was This Lousy Mass-Manufactured T-Shirt.*

There were fireworks displays, protest marches, news stories about first speeding tickets or Little League practices. CNN was promoting a two-hour special, *Descent into Madness: How Eighteen Months Changed a Species.*

Now Sergio said, "Today, I thought of you. I hired an intern."

"You say it's almost winter?"

"Intern—I hired an *intern*, a woman. Made me think of you."

Quaid crimped his brow. "I'm not sure I like where you're headed with this."

"No, no, nothing like that," the mayor said. "Well, only a little. Her name is Imogen, she's a socialite. Knows all five boroughs intimately. She will file a report each night to me personally, naming the choicest parties in the city."

"Wow," Quaid said. "This dark interlude hasn't changed your MO much, has it?"

Sergio glanced dubiously at Quaid's tumbler.

"Her report lands on my desk at eight thirty p.m.," he said. "Can I expect you then?"

Quaid crossed one loafer behind the opposite calf. "I actually have someplace to be tonight."

"You do? Maybe we're heading to the same spot. Imogen said in her interview she favored club music, electronica type. Apparently, the scene has shifted toward—"

"I doubt that," Quaid said. "The spot I'm headed to is more known for its, uh, beef stroganoff."

Sergio puzzled over this, then he began to laugh lustily. "McGill? Three weeks you've been away, and you are spending your first night back in Morristown, New Jersey?"

Quaid kneaded the side of his neck. "So it appears."

Like the rest of civilization, Quaid Rafferty and Molly McGill had emerged from the Anarchy by fits and starts. They'd spent a solid week together after the escape, tending the other's physical and emotional wounds. Fabienne Rivard's revelation about Davos had shaken Molly's faith in Quaid, but he worked to restore it. They laid in bed for hours, her strawberry-blond hair across his chest. They held hands wherever they went.

It felt natural as sunrise to Quaid, and he'd been prepared to call it happiness.

In time, though, logistics reared its ugly head. Molly said she needed time and space to focus on her children, and Quaid, too, had to get his affairs in order at Caesars Palace—which had reserved his former room but was requiring all guests to validate their identities and charge card information.

Las Vegas, of course, is no friend of commitment. Quaid got reacquainted with the swim-up blackjack tables. He and Molly talked on the phone, but phone wasn't his best mode of communication. Without close interpersonal contact—the nudges and eye talk, sympathetic tilts of the head—he struggled to engage.

Molly got annoyed. He got annoyed back. They would take a break, then Quaid would fly east and they'd be on for ten torrid days, then off, then on again.

To clear his mind, to regain perspective, Quaid tried focusing on work—on growing the Third Chance brand in the wake of their success foiling the Anarchy.

A handful of sidehustle jobs fell into his lap, gigs too small to require a female accomplice or too morally ambiguous to lure Durwood. Jim Steed had mop-up work related to AmDye's scrapped experimental weapons program. The Turks had a long enemies list. Earth First! demanded that the plunder of coral mineral deposits be stopped.

He did these dutifully, splitting the proceeds between rent, bar bills, and donations to progressive charities working to piece their missions back together.

Still, nothing captured his imagination. Nothing got his toes tapping. The big fish of the trouble-making world seemed to be lying low, sleeping off their hangovers.

Maybe it was a sign. Maybe it was Fate nudging Quaid toward a more settled life. Toward McGill.

"You must be careful, friend," Sergio said. "Does this engagement with Miss McGill tonight include dinner?"

"I said I'd swing by around five, five thirty," Quaid said.

Sergio smacked his own forehead. "That's the dinner hour!"

"I suppose it is."

"Last we spoke, you wanted to minimize your obligations. Now you'll eat dinner with the woman...perhaps tomorrow you'll eat dinner together again." The mayor's eyes bulged. "At some point, social conventions will kick in. Obligations."

Quaid looked down at his empty tumbler. The Cholula had left red specks around the rim. "I understand."

"This dinner is not good." Sergio shook his head, gazing out over the skyline. "This is dangerous territory you're approaching."

These words, helped by the hastily dispatched prairie fires, sloshed through Quaid's brain.

Dangerous.

Dinner was dangerous again.

CHAPTER SEVENTY-SIX
West Virginia

Durwood drank coffee on the screen porch. The morning fog was low. He couldn't see the sorghum fields or the river that formed his border with Crole's property. The Appalachians soared in the distance, though, clear as if He'd sketched them onto nature's canvas at first light.

Sue-Ann lay slumped against the boot mat, tired from her walk. Her eyes were closed.

Durwood set down his mug and leaned down. He poised his hands apart.

"C'on, girl!"

He clapped as he said this.

Sue didn't budge.

Durwood sucked his lips into his mouth. He didn't blame himself for deploying the weapon that had caused Sue's deafness. He blamed himself for bringing her in the box cart in the first place. He'd known it was a mistake. Known it right when it happened, giving in to that whimper in Paris.

How she was now, Sue couldn't be loose on the farm. There were too many predators about. The vet, Mae Spuckleseed up in Cumberland, said Durwood might see results massaging linseed oil through the dog's ear canals nightly.

So he had.

A handful of times this month, she'd seemed to turn at some noise. But when Durwood called her, or whistled, or clapped sharply as he'd just done, she showed no response.

She'd put on weight, all this lazing around inside. She was not herself. Squirrels skittered up to the window and twitched their cheeks at Sue. Her head wouldn't leave the floor.

Durwood wouldn't allow her to continue like this. Much longer, and he would take her out back of the barn with the M9 and perform a mercy.

Now Durwood turned on the shortwave radio. American Forces Network scratched forth from its speaker. He pulled off his boots and sat to listen.

"We have instituted reforms, significant reforms," said a voice that turned *i* into *ee*. "Multiple layers of safeguards are in place. The sort of deceptions one saw before are no longer possible at Rivard LLC."

The United Nations panel, on its third day of questioning, asked Miss Rivard if she had identified the employees responsible for unleashing the kernel.

"*Absolument*," Fabienne said. "A rogue faction in our Plovdiv office propagated the malware, a core group of eighteen engineers. Regrettably, all eighteen died before they could be held to account. We believe they had a suicide pact."

The shortwave was silent for several moments.

The heiress's voice resumed, "Perhaps we erred by placing too much trust in a part of the world which does not share the core values of La France. We believed, naively, that bedrock Rivard principles of honor and integrity could overcome a local culture of corruption. Alas."

Durwood's jaw worked in place.

The woman belonged in jail. Every dandy European on the panel knew it, but it wouldn't happen. There would be a settlement. The deal's outlines had already leaked to the press. The fine would be a record, in the neighborhood of two trillion dollars. Half of it, Durwood figured, the politicians would waste on bloated social programs and lining their own pockets.

He listened to another hour. He thought Yves Pomeroy might get a chance to speak. Yves had been reinstated as Enterprise Software's vice president, and Henri Rivard, shaved and spiffed up in a Gucci suit, had returned as his daughter's "senior strategic adviser."

Durwood and Quaid had asked Yves whether it was wise—rejoining the very organization that'd locked him up, shot at him, sicced piranhas and mini-black-holes on him.

"Of course it is!" Yves had said. "With Henri aboard, Rivard can do anything. We will rebuild the world: bigger, better, fairer!"

Yves never did talk. Some Belgian diplomat started in on needing larger investment in regulatory bodies, creating greater transparency, establishing compliance officers at "every business of consequence, in every country of the world." In other words, more money for him and his pals.

Durwood switched off the radio. It wasn't quite eight, the time he was meeting Crole, but he got out his bait caster and tackle box anyhow.

He whistled from the porch steps.

Sue-Ann didn't budge.

He poked her with the end of his rod. Her milky eyes opened, and seeing Durwood with fishing gear, she got up. It took her a five count to fall in beside him. He held them up applying linseed to her ear canals—a double dose—then walked to the river.

The property looked respectable again. Durwood had beaten back the johnsongrass and the critters—chucks, voles, possums—who'd flourished in his absence. He had fixed the split rail and re-sided the barn, this time with cedar. (All that vinyl Horkencoocher over at Ace Hardware had talked him into had been stolen in the Anarchy.)

There were still problems. The winter wheat was coming in thin, more dirt than green. Especially that north forty.

As Durwood surveyed the acreage, tackle box rattling, he imagined how Blake Leathersby might attack. Would he set up in a berm and try his luck with a rifle? Or sneak in under cover of night, seeking a hand-to-hand fight?

Durwood doubted either would come to pass. On pride alone, Leathersby wasn't likely to set foot in West Virginia.

Anyhow, rumor was he was busy leading Fabienne's shadow war against American Dynamics. AmDye never did get its nuke through Roche Rivard's defenses that day, but the heiress punished the attempt, destroying thirty-odd factories in retaliation for "the naked aggression of Jim Steed, a dangerous man who deserves humane treatment for his mental wounds."

Durwood and Sue-Ann reached the fishing hole, a craggy bank along the river's south edge. There were similar clearings all along here, but you couldn't miss theirs for the jug of moonshine Crole left next to his favored rock.

Sue sniffed the jug.

"*Ahhck*," Durwood said. "You don't want any of that, girl." Crole made two kinds, one with Jolly Ranchers, the other with jalapeños and rhubarb.

The dog shrank back, agreed, and fell asleep on the bank.

Durwood fished while he waited for Crole. He got no bites, even on the stink bait he'd mixed up the other day with past-date Velveeta.

He sat in the quiet, in the peace of simple pursuit. There were complex things in his life. His remaining son—who'd forsworn the upbringing Durwood and Maybelle had given him years ago—had lost his Wall Street job and run out of cash. Quaid Rafferty had grand plans to expand Third Chance Enterprises. Website, business cards. Turn them into a regular Fortune 500 outfit.

Durwood didn't know what to think. He missed the clarity of his Anarchy patrols—if not the headaches. The injustices had been out in plain sight, like haystacks ready for bailing. He knew injustice still lived. He had an idea kicking around his head, a way to seek out wrongs and address them.

Didn't Quaid have his sidehustles? Maybe Durwood would start his own thing too.

The faint crunch of grass sounded to his right. Durwood ignored it, feeling a tug on his line. Maybe a channel cat finally. Crole didn't need some big welcome anyhow. Durwood had seen his rot-toothed face every day for months.

Then, to Durwood's left, a different noise. The sound of scrabbling paws.

The bait caster flew out of Durwood's hands.

He glanced over in time to see Sue-Ann, responding to the crunch, rise and trot up the shoreline to greet Crole.

"How 'bout that?" his neighbor said, scratching the dog's armpit. "Somebody took a dip in the fountain of youth."

CHAPTER SEVENTY-SEVEN
New Jersey

I checked the time on the microwave, ignoring my Frizz City hair in the door's reflection. Zach had to be at Morristown High in twenty-five minutes, and Karen needed to be standing at her bus stop basically now.

"What's the story with these algebra worksheets?" I asked, picking a stapled packet off the couch.

"All me." Zach grabbed the packet from my hand in stride and stuffed it into his backpack. "Finished last night, I was just looking for it."

I snatched my keys from the magnetic hallway organizer and started for the door. I had one hand on the knob when I noticed Karen's new jacket on the coatrack—the one we'd just picked out together at the outlets.

"Honey, your coat," I said. "You'll need it for morning recess."

I almost added, *And at the bus stop*, but at this point, I didn't think there'd be a wait. In fact, she might have to chase it down the block.

Karen, falling in next to her brother at the door, asked, "Is it okay if I just wear this again?"

She had on the canary-yellow sweater that'd been her favorite before the Anarchy. It had a grape-juice stain in front, and she'd outgrown the sleeves, which showed the nubs of her wrists.

"You don't want to wear your new one, the purple? With the cute fringe on the collar?"

She shook her head no, staring at the floor. There was a whole dynamic to unpack here about routine and security and object transference, but this wasn't the time for shoehorning my psychology training into a wardrobe issue.

"Sure," I said. "It's perfectly okay to wear the yellow sweater."

With that, we zoomed out the door. I'd packed Karen a PB&J before she woke; Zach was buying hot from the cafeteria; and both kids had filled and remembered their water bottles.

While Zach folded his five-nine-and-bigger-everyday frame into the passenger seat of the Prius, I hustled Karen to the corner. The school bus eased to a stop just as we reached the curb. The driver smiled, unfolding the accordion doors and pretended to doff his hat, chauffeur style.

There was more of this now, camaraderie, the savoring of pleasantries. Parents are a beaten-down subspecies of man, but it felt like we were all fresher post-Anarchy. There was a communal feeling that, yeah, it was a grind, but remember how much *worse* it used to be— when every public diaper-changing station had been stripped bare and driving meant surrendering your family's lives to the whims of fate?

I ran Zach over to Morristown High next. He was adjusting well there. He liked his American history teacher, a woman he described as "crazy loud" who wore skirts with sneakers and apparently turned everything they'd learned in middle school on its head.

Naturally, he thought he deserved more freedom.

"Do we hafta have a sitter today?" he asked now as we approached the high school.

"You most certainly do," I said.

"But that's lame! Why can't Reggie take me home? Reggie could totally—"

"Reggie is sixteen years old. I don't care what the state of New Jersey says about learners' permits and what age kids are allowed to drive to school. You will *not* ride in a car driven by Reggie."

Zach rolled his eyes but didn't pursue the argument.

His resistance had limits now. We'd had a blow-out confrontation after Paris about the drug use Quaid had observed while I was in the oubliette. I expected him to deny it or swear up and down the stuff belonged to his friends, but he didn't. He accepted my consequences without complaint.

I wanted to believe this new Zach was the result of personal growth, that he'd acquired a greater appreciation for rules and their importance in the wake of society's breakdown. I worried, though, that he'd simply been spooked hearing the details of my captivity, that he understood more fully that his mother was a real person who could be hurt. Who would die one day. Which was an awful lesson for a teenager to learn, almost awful enough for me to want the old Zach back.

Almost.

He hopped out at the school's circle drive. Pulling away, I called Piper to confirm she was available this afternoon.

"Yup, I'm there," she said. "You got stroganoff leftovers?"

"Not a ton," I said, "but the kids didn't love it, so whatever's there is yours."

"Their loss."

Piper had been babysitting for me while she decided what to do for a career. All the Big Tech firms had offered her positions after the crush of publicity she'd received for curing the data loss, but she didn't relish working for a faceless corporation. Public advocacy was another possibility, but she hadn't exactly excelled so far as a talking head. She'd scoffed at Oprah's oversimplified explanation of the Anarchy, then she'd told the House Ways and Means Committee, "None of y'all understand what I'm saying, so can we just bag it?" She had refused during her testimony to say a word against Josiah, who'd become a co-scapegoat with Rivard LLC in the American press. Commentators attributed her loyalty to Stockholm syndrome.

The Blind Mouse making the biggest waves, in fact, was Hatch. He'd signed on for a reality TV show—*Hatching Insanity*—and was spearheading a resurgence of the Libertarian Party. People say he'll run for president.

Back home, I parked in the driveway and dragged the freshly emptied recycling bin around the side of the house. Then I took a moment tidying up inside. Even on good mornings, the kids left behind a minor hurricane on their way out the door. Now I refolded a tried-on-and-discarded shirt (Karen), containerized a half-eaten bagel (Zach), and dealt with a sugar bowl spill (could've been either, or the cat).

The place was nearly presentable when I heard a pair of shuffling footsteps upstairs.

Then I heard a second pair.

"What'n blazes are you doing here, louse?" Granny's voice rang out.

I didn't hear the response.

Granny went on, "You say *I* saw *you* last night? I didn't see you! That's bunk."

As Quaid and Granny reached the midpoint of the stairs, I began picking up Quaid's words.

"You did, Eunice. We ate dinner together—and tasty it was. Beef stroganoff," he said. "You complained Moll didn't make any Pillsbury Grands, if I recall."

"Oh, that's right! Well, why *wouldn't* you serve rolls with dinner?"

Quaid, from a lower step, talked over his shoulder. "Like Moll explained, the dish already comes with a starch. The noodles. Seems unnecessary to add bread."

"But Grands are *delicious*." Granny came into view, her face shaking with indignation. "And eight fresh tubes sitting in the fridge. Shop-All just had 'em on sale..."

As the argument continued, Granny showed no signs of remembering her initial objection to Quaid's presence. Quaid took the last two steps in a hop, kissed my cheek, and poured himself coffee. Granny sat at her traditional spot at the head of the table. I brought her orange juice and half a grapefruit.

I gestured at the sport coat Quaid was wearing. "Leaving already?"

"And miss all this stimulating conversation?" he said. "I wouldn't dream of it."

From behind, he wrapped an arm around my waist and kissed me again—only this one was no peck, more of a something-starter. I felt warm shoots up my neck and my middle going wavy.

"You just missed the kids," I said. "Five minutes earlier, and you could've helped me get them out the door."

"I did help," Quaid said. "I stayed far, far away."

I laughed and faced him. I wasn't sure whose feet were moving, but the space between us closed, our bodies finding the other's hollows.

Granny took her grapefruit to eat in front of the TV.

We enjoyed each other's heat for a long while.

"Well," Quaid said.

I exhaled. "Well."

"I had a text come in overnight from Tokyo," he said. "The Hazisaki Brothers, the ones with labs in the Mariana Trench? They're seeing irregularities and might require our services."

"*Our* services?" I said. "That must mean I'm a full-fledged member of Third Chance Enterprises."

Quaid took a step back and pretended to size me up. "Credit where credit's due, McGill. You proved yourself on this Mice job. You did. It just might be time to put your name on the business cards."

"You have business cards?"

"They're in the works. I'm talking to graphic designers."

"That's exciting," I said. "Does Durwood approve of these cards?"

"I don't care if he does or doesn't." Quaid leaned his face close to mine. "Let's not sour the mood with thoughts of that unimaginative curmudgeon."

As his hands roamed lower on my back, mine rose higher on his shoulder blades. I could smell his shaving cream and taste sweet excitement on his breath.

"I'll have to give some thought to those cards," I said. "McGill Investigators is picking up new cases every day. It's going to be tough squeezing a Tokyo trip into my schedule."

"But you speak Japanese."

"I do."

"We need you."

"So do my clients here."

Quaid turned his face askew. "You'd give up the chance to be at the vanguard of deep-sea exploration, adventure of a lifetime, so you can stake out cheating husbands?"

"I've had much more interesting cases than infidelity."

"Such as?"

I closed my eyes and didn't answer. I felt Quaid's heart beat faster through the fabric of our shirts.

He continued, "It isn't a steady gig, you know. We'd only be getting Third Chance Enterprises together, all three principals, when the world was in mortal jeopardy."

My eyes stayed closed, and I felt a dreamy, careless expression taking over my face. My lips only parted for an instant before Quaid's were hungrily upon them. We kissed and kissed and kissed.

When my eyes finally opened, he was still waiting for an answer.

And I was still not giving one.

"Also I was, uh," he began, looking at his loafers. "I was thinking of giving up the room at Caesars."

This unexpected disclosure pierced my quiet game. "Really, why? Are you moving to a different resort?"

"No, not to a resort." He looked up from his shoes and took my hands, as though preparing to make some proposal. "I thought I'd try my luck out East. Back this way."

I probed his blue eyes for sincerity.

"But what'll happen to all those blackjack dealers who 'depend on your magnanimous tips'?" I asked, quoting from our last breakup.

Quaid spluttered indeterminately.

"And let's not forget Crystal from the club." I took half a step back. "The poor thing who can't find a thing to do with her Ohio State marketing degree besides exotic dancing?"

"I—er, a lot of this was said tongue in cheek," Quaid tried. "In my line of work, to be fair, it's often necessary to meet with oligarchs—and oligarchs conduct a lot of business in the presence of strippers. Those aren't my morals, that's just how the game is played."

"Sure," I said casually. "Sometimes I have to play along too. In *my* line of work, it's usually younger guys with amazing hair..."

His jaw dropped and a hand went to his own wavy locks at the reference to Garrison, who I actually had seen a few times on a purely professional basis. He was helping me update McGillInvestigators.com to take credit cards.

"I need to find out what that kid uses for conditioner," Quaid said. "Wonder if I could lure Durwood up here, have him tail the kid's mommy to the grocery store and see what brand—"

I stopped his moving lips with another kiss. Leading with my chest, I pushed him back toward the stairs. Buttons popped loose in my shirt. Half Quaid's belt jangled against his hip. Morning sun poured through the bay window.

My head was bobbing weightlessly—a quick, happy balloon. None of today's troubles mattered. Whether I stuck with McGill Investigators or chased Quaid's big scores, whether the blinds were dusty, whether Zach's obedience was temporary or Karen ever wore the purple jacket from the outlets: none of this upset me.

Because I could handle it all.

"*Molly!*"

Granny's cry from the living room interrupted my moment.

I squeezed my eyes hard. "Yes?"

"The cable went out again," she called. "I lost my judge show—she was about to hand down the verdict!"

As I pulled away from Quaid to go quench Granny's thirst for schadenfreudal justice, I caught him glancing at the front door.

"Is there someplace you need to be?" I asked him.

He grinned and set his feet underneath.

"There are always places I need to be," he said. "But I'll wait today. I'll wait till you're ready to come along."

I raised my eyebrows. "It could be a while, fair warning. Usually, she's just hit the *Input Source* button on the remote, but these problems have a way of snowballing."

"I know how that goes," Quaid said, fixing a blond curlicue at his temple. "But just the same, I'll wait. That's a promise."

And so I headed for the living room feeling confident—reasonably confident—he wouldn't vanish into thin air.

Keep reading for a sneak peek at book two
in the Third Chance Enterprises saga,
featuring Durwood Oak Jones:

DEAR DURWOOD

DEAR DURWOOD

Sneak Peek

Dear Mr. Oak Jones:

I am Carol Bridges, mayor of Chickasaw, Texas. We are located in the western part of the state, Big Bend Country if you know it. I thank you in advance for considering my injustice.

Chickasaw is the home of Hogan Consolidated, a family-run manufacturer of industrial parts. Hogan employs 70 percent of able-bodied adults in Chickasaw, and its philanthropy has sustained the town for ninety years. It's due to the Hogan family we have an arts center and a turf field for youth football.

Recently, East Coast lawyers and investment bankers have taken aim at the company. Multimillion-dollar claims have been filed, accusing Hogan of putting out defective parts. It's rumored the company will be acquired or liquidated outright. Massive layoffs are feared.

My constituents work hard, Mr. Jones. They have mortgages and children to feed. I have tried to find answers about the Hogan family's intentions, to see whether I or the town can do anything to influence the course of events. Jay Hogan, the current CEO, does not return my phone calls—and is seen dining at sushi restaurants in El Paso (eighty-five miles away) more often than in Chickasaw. I have gotten the runaround from our state and federal representatives. I believe it's their fundraising season.

As mayor, I have a duty to explore every possible solution to the challenges we face. I do not read *Soldier of Fortune* regularly, but my deputy police chief showed me your ad soliciting "injustices in need of attention." I feel certain injustice is being done to Chickasaw, though I can't as yet name its perpetrator and exact nature.

Alonso (our deputy chief) knows you by reputation, and assures me these details won't trouble you.

Thanks sincerely for your time,
    Carol Bridges
    Mayor of Chickasaw, Texas

CHAPTER ONE

Sneak Peek

D urwood got to the Chickasaw letter halfway through the sorghum field. He was flipping through the stack from the mailbox, passing between sweet-smelling stalks. Leaves brushed his blue jeans. Dust coated his boots. He scanned for clumps of johnsongrass as he read, picking what he saw. The first five letters he'd tucked into his back pocket.

The Chickasaw letter he considered longer. Steel-colored eyes moved left to right. He forgot about the johnsongrass. An ugliness started in his gut.

Lawyers.

He put the letter in his front pocket, then read the rest of the stack. The magazine forwarded him a bundle every month. In September, he'd only gotten three. At Christmastime, it seemed like he got thirty or forty. Folks felt cheated around the holidays.

Today, he read about two brothers who didn't steal a car. About a principal who got fired for being too aggressive fighting drugs in his school. About a bum call in the Oregon State Little League championship twenty years ago. About a furnace warranty that wasn't worth the paper it was printed on.

Durwood chuckled at the Oregon letter. This one had been writing in for years. Maybe he figured Durwood didn't read them, figured some screener only put a couple through each go-round and one of these days his would sneak through.

But Durwood did read them. Every last one.

He put the letter about the principal in his front pocket with the Chickasaw letter.

Off his right side, Sue-Ann whimpered. Durwood turned to find the bluetick coonhound pointing the south fence line.

"I see," Durwood said of the white-tailed doe nosing around the spruces. "Left my gun back at the house, though."

Sue-Ann kept her point. Her bad hip quivered from the effort. Old as she was, she still got fired up about game.

Durwood released her with a gesture. "What do you say to some bluegill tonight instead? See what Crole's up to."

Durwood called Crole from the house. Crole, his fishing buddy who lived on the adjacent sixty acres, said he was good for a dozen casts. They agreed to meet at the river dividing their properties. Durwood had a shorter walk and used the extra time to clean his M9 semiautomatic.

Leaving, he noticed the red maple that shaded the house was leafing out slow. He examined the trunk and found a pattern of fine holes encircling the bark.

That yellow-bellied sapsucker.

Durwood wondered if the holes were related to the tree's poor vigor.

Out by the river, Crole limped up with his jug of moonshine, vile stuff he made from Jolly Ranchers.

They fished.

Sue-Ann lay in the mud, snoring, her stiff coat bristling against Durwood's boot. The afternoon stretched out, a dozen casts becoming two dozen. Then three. In the distance, the hazy West Virginia sky rolled through the Smokies. Mosquitoes weren't too bad, just a nip here and there at the collar.

Durwood thought about Chickasaw, Texas. He thought about East Coast lawyers. About the hardworking men and women who'd elected Carol Bridges to be mayor and stick up for them.

He thought about that CEO picking up raw fish with chopsticks in El Paso.

He thought, too, about the principal who'd been fired for doing right.

Crole said, "Got some letters today?"

Durwood said he had.

Crole grinned, showing his top teeth—just two, both nearly black. "Still running that ad in *Soldier of Fortune*?"

Durwood lowered the brim of his hat against the sun. "Don't cost much."

"They give a military discount?"

Durwood raised a shoulder. He'd been discharged from the marines a decade ago. He didn't accept handouts for his service.

Crole nodded to the bulge in his pocket—the letters. "Anything interesting?"

"Sure," Durwood said. "Plenty."

They fished into twilight. Durwood caught just five bluegills. Crole, twenty years his senior and luckier with fish, reeled in a dozen, plus a decent-size channel cat despite using the wrong bait. The men strung their catches on a chain. The chain rippled in the cool, clear water.

The Chickasaw job appealed to Durwood. The opportunity to fight crooked lawyers, to do something about these Wall Street outfits that made their buck slicing up American companies, putting craftsmen out of work until every last doodad was made in some knockoff plant in China.

Still, Durwood had trouble imagining the case. What would he do, flip through documents? Sit across a folding table from men in suits and ask questions?

Then he thought about the principal. About those gangs the letter had mentioned, how you could look out the windows of the dang school and see drug dealers on street corners. Intimidators. Armed thugs.

Durwood had an easy time imagining that case.

The sky had just gotten its first purple tinge when Durwood lost his bait a third time running.

"These fish." He held his empty hook out of the water, shaking his head.

Crole said, "There's catfish down there older than you."

"Smarter too," Durwood said.

Still, the five bluegills would be enough for him and Sue-Ann. Durwood unclipped the fishes' cheeks from the chain and dropped them in a bucket.

Back at the house, Durwood spotted the yellow-bellied sapsucker climbing the red maple. Not only was he pecking the tree, the ornery creature kept pulling twigs from the gray squirrels' nest, the one they'd built with care and sheltered in the last four winters.

"Git down!" Durwood called.

The sapsucker zipped away to other antics.

Inside, Durwood scaled and beheaded the bluegills. Then he fried them in grease and cornmeal. Sue-Ann ate only half a fish.

Durwood moved the crispy tail under her nose. "Another bite?"

The dog sneezed, rattly in her chest.

Durwood rinsed his dishes and switched on a desktop computer. He looked up Chickasaw. There was plenty of information online. Population, land area. Nearly every mention of the town made reference to Hogan Consolidated. It looked like Hogan Consolidated *was* Chickasaw, Texas, and vice versa.

On the official municipal website, he found a picture of Carol Bridges. She wore a hard hat, smiling among construction workers.

Handsome woman. Warm, lively eyes.

Next, Durwood looked up the fired principal. The man lived and worked in Upstate New York. For a few weeks, his case had been all over the local news there. A city councilman believed he'd been railroaded. Nineteen years, he'd served the school district without prior incident. The only blemish Durwood found was a college DUI.

Durwood hadn't started with computers until his thirties. His calloused fingers regularly struck the keys wrong, but he managed. This one he'd gotten from the Walmart in Barboursville, forty-nine bucks on Black Friday. It had its uses. A tool like any other.

"Well?" he said aloud, even though Sue was out on the porch. "Looks like a toss-up."

Durwood changed computer windows to look again at Carol Bridges. Then changed back to the principal.

At the bottom of the news story about the principal, he noticed a bubble with *47 comments* inside. He knew people who spouted off online were unreliable and often foolish. He clicked anyway.

Good riddance, got what he deserved!

TOTAL RACIST WINDBAG, glad they fired him.

Durwood read all forty-seven comments. Some defended the man, but most were negative.

It was impossible to know how much was legitimate. Durwood left judging to Him, and Him alone.

But Durwood did know that the petitioner, the one who'd written the letter to *Soldier of Fortune*, was the principal himself. Not some third party. Not an objective observer.

What had seemed like a case of obvious bureaucratic overreach suddenly looked less obvious.

Now Sue-Ann loped in from the porch. Appalachian air followed her inside, nice as perfume. Sue settled at Durwood's feet, wheezing, rheumy eyes aimed up at her master.

He said, "What do you say, girl. Up for seeing the Lone Star State?"

The dog sat up straight, responding to the action in his voice. The effort made her mew. That hip.

Durwood laid his thumb down the ridge of the dog's skull. He felt pained himself, thinking of documents, folding tables, and men in suits.

F BOND, JEFF 8/20
Anarchy of the mice /

CPSIA information can be obtained
at www.ICGtesting.com
Printed in the USA
LVHW040848160820
663317LV00003B/433